After The Deluge

"Earth provides enough to satisfy every man's needs, but not every man's greed."

– Mahatma Gandhi

After The Deluge

A novel by
Pratibha Ray

Translated from Odia by
Prafulla Kumar Mohanty

BLACK EAGLE BOOKS
2021

BLACK EAGLE BOOKS

USA address:
7464 Wisdom Lane
Dublin, OH 43016

India address:
E/312, Trident Galaxy, Kalinga Nagar,
Bhubaneswar-751003, Odisha, India

E-mail: info@blackeaglebooks.org
Website: www.blackeaglebooks.org

First Published in Odia 2004
by Adya Prakashani, Bhubaneswar-5

First International Edition Published by
BLACK EAGLE BOOKS, 2021

AFTER THE DELUGE
A novel by **Pratibha Ray**

Translated by
Prafulla Kumar Mohanty

Cover & Interior Design: **Narottam Behera, Adya Prakashani**

ISBN- 978-1-64560-203-3 (Paperback)
Library of Congress Control Number: 2021943420

Printed in the United States of America

DEDICATION

Each loss of life that day was a heroic tale of honor. Although they were all vanquished by death, to call their bold encounters with death defeats would be an insult to their glorious fights. Those who perished or survived fighting the 1999 killer cyclone, those who were martyred in the *Kargil war*, and those who wore the laurels of victory, this book, *After the Deluge*, is dedicated to them, respecting their resolute and stubborn will to conquer.

ACKNOWLEDGMENT

It was 29th October 1999. The killer cyclone had struck and its landfall point was between Erasama and Balikuda in Jagatsinghpur district, southwest of Paradip port. It devastated half of Odisha state but the eye of the cyclone hit Erasama. The tide surged high and the sea(Bay of Bengal) crashedinto the coastal villages and completely wiped away the villages. At that time my husband, Akshaya Chandra Ray was Chief Engineer, Department of Water Resources, Government of Odisha. The cyclone-affected districts were under his jurisdiction. He returned from the area after four days of inspection of the enormous devastation and urged me to visit the area for a first-hand experience of the destruction and trauma. Initially I was reluctant to come face to face with the agonizing situation I had already seen on television. But he insisted, coaxing the writer in me to venture into the midst of the homeless victims. He made the arrangements for my stay in the lone Inspection Bungalow that had survived the fury of the cyclone. I finally visited the area and was stuck there for indefinite number of days. I still remember distinctly how I had to walk among the cadavers strewn all over the area and was engulfed in the misery all around. I arranged some relief by personal efforts and got busy counselling the destitute women, men and children. My son-in-law Lalit Das, IPS was the Superintendent of Police of that district then. He helped me distribute relief by providing armed police as the hungry villagers had turned into angry mobs. These visits caused the germination of the idea in my mind for writing about the sorrow and misery of the innocent humans. The theme and all my characters arose from the devastated soil. I remember with fondness my husband's vision in pushing me to visit the area and am thankful for that. My affectionate thanks to my son-in-law Lalit for taking care of everything and ensuring my safety at all times. I saw the deluge through the eyes of the unfortunate as well as the fortunate survivors. As their companion, I heard the heart-wrenching narrations of loss and trauma. Even today, I salute their patience in the face of acute pain and their friendly behaviour which emboldened me to write a novel on this difficult theme. This is the only novel in Odia on the gruesome drama of nature, the killer cyclone. The novel took four years to be completed and was published in Odia in 2004.

I would like to thank Professor Prafulla Kumar Mohanty for his sincere efforts and perseverance in translating the book into English. "After the Deluge" was possible only because of his patience, hard work and moreover love for the novel.

I would also like to thank the Director, Black Eagles Books, Satya Pattanaik for publishing this book in English on a global platform. His valuable support, constructive ideas and suggestions during the course of our work together has been a great help.

My sincere thanks to the editor of the book, Ginny Glass for her appreciation of the novel, focus and dedication in timely completion of the process. I also thank Ashita Mohapatra, my daughter-in-law for reading the book and sharing valuable observations during my stay in Canada with them. Finally I thank Professor Adyasha Das, my daughter for re-reading the book several times and giving the final touch. The creative talent of Shri Narottam Behera, the artist of the cover design is praise-worthy. I thank Ashok Parida, Black Eagles Books, for his assistance in the layout of the book.

I pray that the story told here never befalls innocent humans in future again.

- **Pratibha Ray**

ENDLESS SORROW

Foreword by the author

The devastating cyclone of October 29, 1999, turned into a deluge and destroyed countless lives in the coastal belt of Odisha. Abandoning a once-replete world into the care of an empty horizon, the sea receded, and the deluge fell silent. But half of those who loved life and had battled with the fury of the cyclone never returned. Those who returned could not regain even traces of their homes, hearths, families, or wealth. They are still struggling against the hostile aftermath of the deluge in their devastated villages. Like their own blood, each battle with death and fight for life was not only a hair-raising experience, but also unique to the individual. They fall short of words to describe their own agony. Even after merging with their souls, imbibing their experiences, and absorbing their anguish, one cannot muster adequate words to convey their sorrow. Where is the power in mere mortals to describe creation and destruction?

The 1999 cyclone wiped out this author's village area, the walls where images of goddess Durga were drawn to protect the newborn in swaddling clothes, the homestead, the school where she had started her first lessons writing Brahma,

Vishnu, Maheswar, and the thousand memories of her childhood and adolescence. It also swept up many soulful dear ones from known and unknown villages. From that pain and compassion, was born this novel, *After the Deluge*.

But even after writing this novel, the pain did not end. While searching for the heart of the author's own village, there emerged from somewhere a few intimate and intense characters who this author had never met there. Maybe she'd met them in some coastal villages before, during, or after the deluge, in this or in a previous birth, in dreams or imagination. All these characters were born in the pages of her novel.

Overriding her thoughts, they twisted and turned her, made events happen. In the course of the narrative, wherever they wished, they went in different directions, forsaking everything. What they are doing now, whether they are happy or sad, whether the wasted villages have raised their heads, whether the decay and loss caused by the cyclone have been indemnified-there is no news. Trying to soothe the chaos caused by "fate" by letter, word, or language, pain is not redeemed; this they already know. Therefore, why should they respond to the author's call?

The addresses of their whereabouts are also lost forever. Yes, one may meet others exactly like them in those villages, because the contorted confusions of man's agony and the colors of mourning over the dearly departed are the same everywhere in the world.

It's said that, except dates and years, everything else in history is false. In a novel, except the dates and years, all other things are true. But although *After the Deluge* is a novel, here the dates and years are true, and the other things are not lies. On the soil of truth, there is the intricate play of imagination. While being cocooned within the framework of a regional natural calamity, this tale lends itself to any place facing a devastating disaster.

The faces of time and society are reflected in the mirror of literature. If, in the pages of this novel, someone's face is seen, then it may be presumed that literature has not faltered on the path of literary responsibility.

After the Deluge is the song of man's never-ending sorrow, the burden of which rings with the tune of man's indomitable will to live. But even after completing this novel, this author is plagued with waves of endless sorrow.

Pratibha Ray
1/21/2004

"Akhyaika"
27, Gajapati Nagar,
Bhubaneswar-751015
Odisha, India
E-mail: pratibha_ray@yahoo.com

Translator's Note

Pratibha Ray's novel, *After the Deluge*, celebrates the primordial relationship between the earth and human beings. The focus in this novel is on the regenerative energy of the earth, which, despite the evils of human molestation and natural calamities, reemerges out of the nadir of devastation to hold in display all her beauty, grace, harmony, and equipoise–including the self-immersed humans who constantly try to build a civilization contrary to her nature.

The novel is centered around the 1999 super cyclone that almost broke the backbone of Odisha, especially the areas of Erasama, Jagatsinghpur, and Paradip–in fact, the entire coastal belt of Odisha, from Balasore to Gopalpur. The cyclone and its description perhaps foretold the tsunami waves that uprooted the life, culture, and means of living of the people of Tamil Nadu, Andhra in India and almost lopped off the citadels of human power in Sri Lanka, Malaysia, Indonesia, and other parts.

The turbulent energy of nature's fury in the 2004 tsunami and the 1999 Odisha super cyclone shattered people's confidence. But humanity goes on. Life goes on. Pratibha's *After the Deluge*, published a few days before the tsunami in 2004, reveals how nature's vengeful counterforce is a reminder to man to change his self-seeking power-play in order to accommodate the harmonious and benevolent creativity of nature. To dominate the earth is man's self-stultifying heroism, which is denied by nature time and again. Moving through the lessons of Atlantis, Harappa, Aztec, and Greco-Roman ruins in history, man learns not and sees not the superstring equilibrium of the forces of nature.

The super-cyclone and tsunami are the latest lessons to man, and it's doubtful whether human pride would ever admit what Hamlet said, "There are more things in heaven and earth, Horatio, than are dreamt of in your philosophy." Pratibha Ray, in her creative fictionalization of the super cyclone, seems to have learned the lesson of nature and history. She envisions a new globalized reality where the earth is one village–Basumatipur–a harmonized mind of a rich variety of all valuables, and the humans are of one family of nature.

The novel *After the Deluge*, elaborately establishes in the opening chapters the geographical, anthropological, and cultural setting of Erasama, which came under the eye of the super cyclone, and traces the changing contours of civilization that man built up over the long centuries. The profession-based castes, the gradual politicization of institutions manipulating economic and social life, the rigid superstitious beliefs built into priest-craft and its impact on life, the cultural confrontations in castes and religions, and the exploitation of nature and her innate ways have been depicted with a naturalistic and realistic narrative full of village lore, rural vocabulary, and vivid imagery.

The locales of the novel are the Abhayapur and Bandar villages in Erasama Gram Panchayat, with all the rivers and sea in lurid colors. The families, homes, village roads, festivals, conflicts, both internal and external, fishing activities, innocence, and evil have been described with an all-seeing eye, allowing freedom of identity to places, people, and postures. The slow spread of education and the vast sway of politics on the gullible people, the influx of refugees from Bangladesh and Pakistan, the bilingual, multi-religious cultures slowly creating rifts and bipolarity, the mobility of the society gaining pace, and also the politicization of issues and themes rising to break the brittle unity of the rooted, earthy culture have been described as if the rural area grows in its own stream.

The authorial voice does not assume omniscient powers in the narration of events. But a gradual shift of balance from the moral to the manipulative–and a growing domination of the politics of evil–make the innocence of the villagers guilt-ridden and pejorative to such a measure that both nature and man are betrayed by their own naturalness. Divisiveness, possessiveness, and infected would clash into a clamorous pitch, drowning in its crescendo all normal and natural articulation. The village and the people get divided into victims and victimizers without any awareness of the basic causes. Moral and social confusions spurred on by political motivations shake the moral fiber of the society.

And then comes the super cyclone, as if nature lost all patience at the immorality of man and capsized the edifice of human pride. The description of the cyclone is photographic, imagistic, and to the present-day viewers of tsunami devastation, provides a parallel in authentic language. I shall do well to quote two short passages to illustrate my point. The description is soul chilling. The images stick in the mind of the reader like the dark glue of death, scaling off all rational thought.

The village was drowning, drowning. One was climbing up a tree, another the thatched roof. Women, men, old emaciated people, snakes, frogs, all became at one go tree-climbers, ocean swimmers. The water level rose above the priest's cowshed.

Bharjan was not aware that he had climbed up a palm tree. On his shoulders were sitting his two little sons, clasping Bharjan's matted hair. What was that tied around Bharjan's neck–a pestle stone or what? What was that again in such a calamity? In the evening, out of curiosity, Panchu Gosain's eight-year-old son had come to see the children of the Mallick household. Seeing the water level rise, Bharjan himself went up on the roof, hanging the boy on his back. He lifted up the children onto the roof. When he saw the roof undulating before the water level rose, he put his children on his shoulders and, clasping a palm tree, climbed up.

Before his eyes he saw cows, men, and other small creatures being swept off into the maws of the sea. His wife and six other children were carried away by the flood into the mouth of the Jatadhari estuary. The known and unknown human faces were swallowed up by the roaring rush of the fearful waves. Bearing the weight of three children, Bharjan was going up the tree, jumping up toward the sky in concert with the swelling waters of the sea. Now the water has touched the top of the tree. How could such strength come to the weak arms of Bharjan Malik? From where did the weak legs of Bharjan muster such force?

***

Does the dawn come like this? The chirping of birds was not heard; the "God-save-us" prayer of the cocks and hens was silenced. The playful prattle of the children in the villages was gone. The farmer's farm song, following the yoked bullocks, was not heard. The bells around the bullocks were silent. The tender calf's restless hungry call was not heard. The tinkling of anklets of the village belles and daughters-in-law was not heard at the river *ghats*. The temple bells and the "Allahu Akbar" of the mosques were not heard. The sonorous whisper of the breeze was gone in the absence of bamboo bushes; nor was floating in the morning air the fragrance of the champak and jasmine. In fact, there was no proper earth: from where would come trees, plants, birds, animals, and men. Many cyclones had come in the past. Trees were uprooted. But the bamboo and cane bushes had stood stubbornly in defiance. This deluge was such that in that part of the world all vegetation–bamboo, cane, screw pine shrubs, and forests were wiped out. Treeless, bird less, lifeless was the flowerless world in ninety percent of the villages in the district of Jagatsinghpur.

That day, not a slice of live earth was available for the morning to place her sacred foot on. A stunned, awestruck morning was standing hapless on thousands of cadavers. Cyclones blow away roofs from the walls, but this 1999 cyclone blew villages and settlements from the solid earth. All villages set up along the life-giving sea had vanished. Even the slender plants of Dhobei and Jatadhari forests had surrendered to the deluge. Except the trunks of coconut trees, the other dismembered heaps of fallen trees were beyond identification. The bloated corpses on the sea had become strangers; the entire world was beyond recognition for the few survivors here and there. After a day and a half, the salty waves had retraced their guilt-ridden steps from the dead bosom of the villages.

After the floodwater receded, wherever one looked he saw only cadavers, the festering bodies of dead birds, and isolated, helpless, barren buildings standing among the eye-piercing sight of uprooted and rotten trees. In this atmosphere of chaos and ruin were wailing a few ill-starred, yet lucky, human survivors, who had lost their relatives, dwellings, cattle, golden harvest, and one lifetime. Such description makes the human being not only humble, but also hapless, listless, and small. The images do not inspire horror or panic but illustrate how man is a plaything for nature. One is reminded of Shakespeare.

As flies to wanton boys are we to the gods.
They kill us for their sport.

-*King Lear*

The cyclone is nature's moral fury to subdue man's passions to an order of humility. And nature thus reminds the humans that reality is not the handiwork of man. It is nature-that is, the earth, that creates form and meaning for her own moksh.

In *After the Deluge* there is no conventional plot or a plot-making hero. In the first few chapters, although the storyline grows around Udhab, the authorial intention is not to weave a plot around him. Here people of all hues–Udhab, Gandhi Das, Mantri, Bikram, Girima, and even the so–called choric characters-comprise humanity. The locale also is enlarged by references and thematic interfaces to include Kargil, Bangladesh, and, in fact, the entire world. The titular as well as the dramatic hero of this novel is the earth herself, which is in a trance for a new creation. The earth absorbs, reflects, holds, sustains, and even destroys man's glory, pride, and tyranny. Pratibha Ray, in the first page of the novel has made this clear.

But when man transgresses all limits, torturing the earth, the earth's tolerance also reaches the limit.

She turns and changes sides with indifference, and the human edifice of pride crumbles like ninepins. This is what makes *After the Deluge* the thematic, dramatic, and titular hero of this novel. The earth is in a creative trance. If she destroys in intolerance of human tyranny, she regenerates life into a new order. In the novel, after the devastation, the earth again resumes creation. The momentary suspension of creativity is a break in the trance to teach errant humans to come to their moral sense and reorganize life and civilization in tune with nature's harmony. Ray shows that the process of creation, destruction, and regeneration is the perpetual property of this earth that unites diversities, harmonizes disparate elements, and integrates all formal manifestation of life with creative inclusiveness.

Bikram and Girima—one who has seen the inhumanity of man in the Kargil heights, man's gory exploits to win inches of the earth; and the other, a survivor of the earth's wrath, an unattached destitute without name, family-clan relations, or possessions— these two come together after having learned their lessons from man–made war and nature's war against human depravity. They build anew a new order of life that this regenerative earth ordains.

All of the destitute now comprises one family, the earth's own family, the generative earth's human face reflecting her divinity. As the new leaves grow in the slush of rotten flesh, so does grow a new order of humanity where castes, religions, languages, and color differences merge in a true human fraternity. The individuated name of the village changes into the name of the earth–Basumati. This Basumati is not a lump of earth, but a mass of divine, creative energy, a multisensory superstring, synthesizing and orchestrating the entire universe.

The novel creates the poetry of the earth in the language of the fisher folk of Erasama. The unsophisticated and colloquial vocabulary is woven into a new paradigm of life where the rivers, trees, fish, nets, rituals, and pain, hunger, horror, and helplessness intone the native language of the earth.

After the Deluge is, perhaps, the greatest earth novel written in any language in the world. While translating it, I had the creative surges of the earth leading me to a trance of revelation. I hope the readers would discover the creative energy in their personal worlds after reading this work.

Prafulla Kumar Mohanty
Chitrakavya,
365 / 2787, Sishu Vihar
Bhubaneswar-751 024

India

Pakistan

Jammu and Kashmir
Kargil

China

Arabian Sea

Bangladesh

Odisha

Jagatsinghpur
Erasama

1999 Odisha
Super Cyclone
affected Erasama

Bay of Bengal

Letter from the Editor

In the closing of Pratibha Ray's After the Deluge, one of the characters imparts, "The seminal thing is to search. Has anyone lived in this world without searching for things?" This piece of reflection echoes strongly throughout the book, and applies to so many more of the book's elements than just the search for survivors after the horrific regional calamity depicted in the tale.

Despite the many tragedies that happen throughout the book, when the storm recedes, a hopeful balance is struck between mourning for what has been lost and looking toward–and being resolved to search for–a brighter possible future.

As I was editing this English translation of After the Deluge, I definitely felt the impact of the universal themes of human searching and suffering, and the author did a remarkable job of making the characters jump off the page. There is a depth of emotion that is felt for the characters in a way that transcends any cultural differences. I hope that you, the reader, will feel the same profound connection.

Though there can be challenges in translating any manuscript from one language to another, with careful consideration of meaning and utilizing notes between the author and editor to help achieve the original intent, I believe that this translation has really captured the author's very powerful original story.

I truly hope that you are transported by the pages of this book, and that the journey through tragedy within it leaves you with the lesson that we can triumph over anything, as long as our spirits are still willing to search for a better tomorrow.

Best,
Ginny Glass (Editor)

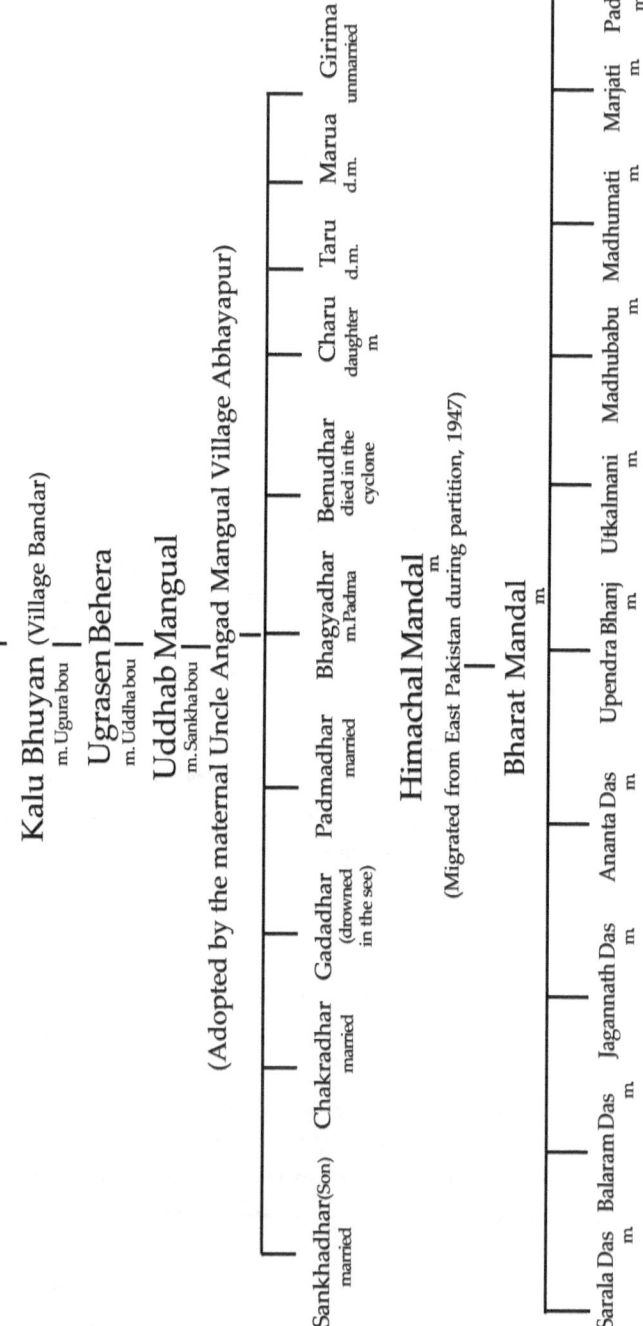

Dasha Raja

(Mythological Ancestor)

Kalu Bhuyan (Village Bandar)
m. Ugura bou

Ugrasen Behera
m. Uddha bou

Uddhab Mangual
m. Sankha bou

(Adopted by the maternal Uncle Angad Mangual Village Abhayapur)

Sankhadhar (Son)
married

Chakradhar
married

Gadadhar
(drowned in the see)

Padmadhar
married

Bhagyadhar
m. Padma

Benudhar
died in the cyclone

Charu
daughter
m

Taru
d.m.

Marua
d.m.

Girima
unmarried

Himachal Mandal
m

(Migrated from East Pakistan during partition, 1947)

Bharat Mandal
m

Sarala Das
m

Balaram Das
m

Jagannath Das
m

Ananta Das
m

Upendra Bhanj
m

Utkalmani
m

Madhubabu
m

Madhumati
m

Marjati
m

Padma
m

ONE

B andara–the last village in the world. As you walk straight east, there's absolutely nothing else, let alone a village. A few miles away flows the ancient dame, Mahanadi's daughter, river Devi. And beyond that, it's all sea, swallowing the vast sky and the unbroken line of the horizon. On the horizon are not seen trees and fronds, villages, or houses, only the sun, moon, stars, clouds, lightning, and cyclones. Can any village or settlement survive where there are no trees, no fish, no earth? Without a pinch of soil beneath the feet, can humans survive seeking the shelter of the sky? Could the sky be as tolerant as the earth? The sky kicks everything to the netherworld, but the earth opens her lap. This is the code of the sky and the earth.

Humans need the earth, both for life and death. For this, human being depends on the earth. Whatever spread of earth he or she possesses, human kind's desire for fertile soil is never satiated, and from the earth, humanity gets food, raiment, and a roof over its head. It's only because human being has a right over the earth that she tolerates, tongue-tied, all the shenanigans of people.

Does the mother ever dry her breast because the sucking baby bites her nipples? Does she throw away her babe because of pain? Yes, at times when it's too unbearable, she presses the naughty milking baby's cheeks with her fingertips and says, "Oh what a life-sucking child!" But that much makes the little one cry, tears and saliva become one. But when humanity transgresses all limits, torturing the earth, the earth's tolerance also reaches the limit. A little frown of the earth blows away–like mustard seeds-all the achievements of humankind in this vast world.

Human being does not see the frontiers of its greed, but everyone sees the borders of humankind's tyranny. Spurred on by that greed, people set up village upon village, bulldozing the hills and mountains of earth and invading natural habitats. Speak of Bandar, Abhayapur, or any other village in the nearby area, and these are all human being's handicraft and an illustration of humankind's oppression of the earth.

Who set up this last village of the world? Perhaps this might have been answered by one of the eyewitnesses among the forefathers now in the other world, had one been living now. But who mounted the first mound of earth in the world? Who set up the first village? When and where? Udhab cannot answer this, nor can anyone else.

How can anyone answer?

Earth first or human being first? If the earth preceded humankind, then people can never write the complete history of the earth. Whatever human being writes would be half, incomplete. Yet the earth has been writing its own history in its own language on trees and bushes, on the river, sea, sky, and air. But who listens? And who understands?

Udhab's father, Ugrasen, in his limited knowledge, says, "It's not necessary to learn the alphabet to know the history of the earth." If humankind can understand the language of trees and bushes, gauge the hunger of birds and weird spirits, study the pulse of the sea and river, test the arrogance of the sky, and penetrate the breath of air, then humanity wins. You may call such a person unlettered, but why call him or her an idiot?

Ugrasen Behera asked everyone, all his life, "Do you know your earth? Have you read the language of trees and bushes? Ever heard, straining your ears for hours, what song the wind sings? What does the rain speak, what message brings the cloud?"

Who cares to answer such mad questions? Maybe the answer can be found in the roaring tides of the undulating Bay of Bengal.

Have the fisher folk and netting fishermen ever strained their ears to hear what the Bay of Bengal and Devi river, to the east of Bandar village, converse about, merging their faces since times immemorial? Had they strained their ears, they would have heard how the Bay of Bengal goes on narrating the history of Bandar village, how river Devi goes on singing the ballad of Bandar's life story. Despite having ears, the busy people have no time to hear this. All villages, like Bandar village, have a long, glorious history. But this history cannot be written by ignoring the sea. Ultimately, where's the history of the Odia without the sea?

Turning the pages of Bandar's history, Udhab's memory, first of all, recalls the story of his father, Ugrasen Behera. He remembers his mother too. Also, he remembers the daily spat between husband and wife, centering on the family pride of Udhab's father. Again, he remembers the peacemaker of the husband-wife tiffs, the all-knowing "master" of those times, Sahani Sir, who was the teacher of the unlettered and wise. Sahani Sir was the trusted one for everyone, a last resort during a mental crisis.

Udhab's father, Ugrasen Behera,had a rash temper. He claimed his hotheaded nature was a family trait of fisher kings. His bad temper had earned Ugra Behera a lot of enemies in the family—and countless foes. But Ugrasen used to say, "Some other fisherman may fear his enemies. Why should Ugrasen, of royal lineage, fear? Does a king retreat from royal expeditions for fear of enemies?"

Ugra Behera's wife, although an overbearing, nagging woman when it involved her husband, was sweet natured like rice-flour cake to all others, amicable like yam, and cool like dewy *khirsa*–a simple dish made of rice, sugar, and milk. She was a pleasant woman. As raucous as she was inside the house, she was innocent, agreeable, and soft outside.

Udhab's mother always cautioned his father, "Why are you creating enemies for nothing? What do you think you are that everyone would be afraid of you? Why should everyone take your word as gospel?"

Urgasen Behera had no less bluster than many others, but he'd submit to the mothering of his wife. In his veins flowed the royal blood of the Odia fisher king, Kalu Bhuyan. How many generations before was Kalu Bhuyan? Ugra Behera could have found out had he calculated with a piece of chalk. But for that, he would have to beg for Sahani Sir's intelligence, meeting him during his leisure hours; hence, he had not probed his family lineage due to sheer negligence. When is there free time for such things in the life of a fisherman?

Ugrasen vowed occasionally that he'd go to Sir and learn about the history of the fisher–folk. Isn't it the first proof of manliness to seal not only the mouth of your brethren but also of your foul–mouthed wife?

In the nearby villages, he who was known as Sir was actually named Basudev Sahani, a khadi-donning Gandhian teacher from Osakana village. On weekends and during winter and summer vacations, he used to propagate the history of the Odias, moving from village to village. Sir's was a large, joint family. No one in that area had such a large, joint family. His was a princely salary of five rupees those days. But Sir spent his entire salary on his family members. He used to buy rolls of cloth at a time and make dresses for all the children of the large family. In his house were more than thirty children. When they came out in their new dresses, well, it was an army in uniform! Sir used to say, "Yes, I'm making an army. A war is ahead. These people would fight. We need hosts of armies to chase away the British government beyond the seas."

Ugrasen Behera had heard from his grandfather that they were the descendants of the fisher king Kalu Bhuyan of Tamralipta country. But where that Tamralipta country was and how the

Utkal fishermen went there and became kings, well, that history the fisher clan of this village didn't know—nor did Ugrasen's father have any memory of it. Therefore, Ugrasen often said to his wife, "Hey, you! What does your father think of me? Do you think I am a mere shrimp–dressing fisherman? I'm a royal fisherman. Since your sister-in-law is barren, why should I send one of my sons for adoption to his uncle's house? It's futile to entice a royal fisher with house plots and mango trees to give away his son in adoption."

Ugrasen's wife would laugh boisterously as she listened to him. She would say, "Is there a country called Tamralipata anywhere? And there was some king named Kalu Bhuyan? Where did the country go, and where's the throne? At last, the royal duty of the kings has been reduced to going fishing with nets. And the boat's the throne!"

Ugrasen wasn't able to counter such piercing words. What reply could he give? It had never been heard that there was a fort called Tamralipta in the vicinity of Bisunpur fort, Paradeep fort, or Kujang fort! How could Ugrasen convince such a disgruntled woman?

Udhab was recollecting his past childhood as if it had happened yesterday. That day, Ugrasen was also arguing with his wife regarding his clan and lineage. At the same moment was heard the voice of Sir outside.

"Ugrasen, are you there?"

Only Sir calls Ugrasen by his name. All others of the village called him Ugra fisherman.

"Sir, I bow down to you," said Ugrasen, and went out to the road and fell flat at his feet. Biting her tongue and pulling her sari over her face, Ugransen's wife stepped aside.

Sir said, "I heard everything, Ugrasen. Your wife says the correct thing. It won't do if you simply say that you belong to a royal dynasty. If you mention the name of Kalu Bhuyan, but don't explain properly the history of Kalinga fishermen, how can the woman understand? Don't underestimate women. Until they're rightly convinced, they won't be swayed by mere words. Do you know yourself where Tamralipta was and how Kalu Bhuyan became king there?"

Shaking his head, Ugrasen said, "I'm illiterate, Sir, a poor fisherman. When the dawn comes, we go to the river and sea and make both ends meet by killing fish. How do I know history? And what value in knowing it?"

Sir was going to sit, dusting the front veranda. Ugrasen's wife, pulling her sari above her nose, brought an old mat and spread it on the veranda.

Sir said, "You, too, can sit here, my child. Don't underestimate the fishing community because it catches fish at the break of day. The fisher folk are patriotic. If you do not know the history of your clan, everyone would suppress you. If you think lowly of yourself, the rapacious kings, zamindars, and moneylenders would crush you."

Ugrasen sat on the other side of the veranda, facing Sir. Seeing Sir there, a few others also gathered around. As the weather was somewhat cloudy, and as they scented a storm in the chilly east wind, the fish folk that day had not ventured out to the river and sea.

Seeing Sir on Ugra's veranda, they sauntered in one by one and waited to know why Sir had pitched his tent at Ugra's door. Like fishes float together in troubled waters, the others followed one after the other. Seeing a small gathering, a larger crowd automatically collected in front of Ugra's house.

Sir would take a meeting and would open up the mythic chapter of the unseen and unknown fourteen generations. Everyone had their scripture, containing sacred Hindu text-this no one disbelieved. Therefore, in late afternoon in the Bandarai Goddess temple, a vibrant gathering buzzed on. Basu Sir sat at a place like the polestar. Close to him, the eager listeners of a few villages of the area sat in a semicircle like the constellation, the Great Bear. In front was the clamorous Devi river. On the other side of that was the fathomless sea. Everyone's eyes and ears were alert. Sir's ringing voice pushed through his pearly white teeth, negotiating the waves of the Devi, touching the bosom of the sea.

"In the days of yore, the merchants of Kalinga were carrying on business, crossing the seven seas and thirteen rivers in far-flung countries. Could anyone make a safe journey on the river without the help of the fishing community? The prosperity that had come to Kalinga through external trade was possible only because of the navigational skills of the fisher folk. The fisher folk were not only able boatmen but also were a brave, bold, naval force. They were also facing the daring challenges of the sea pirates on the ships and boats."

Sir resumed, "At that time the Odia empire was spread from river Ganga to river Godavari, and Midnapur was a part of Utkal. Tamralipta was a famous port city of the Kalinga empire of Midnapur. Since ancient times, much before Ashoka conquered Kalinga, the Mayurdhwaja dynasty of Utkal's Mayurbhanj kingdom ruled over Tamralipta. Through this Tamralipta port, the merchants of Utkal brought much wealth, trading in faraway countries. Tamralipta was also known as Tamluk fort. Immediately after the age of Buddha, who knows by whose curse, the Mayurdhwaj dynasty disintegrated. At that time, fisherman Kalu Bhuyan went from the Utkal coast to Tamralipta and occupied the throne. He was the first fisher king of Tamralipta. He took four hundred fishermen families from Utkal and settled them there.

"These families grew in the course of time and reached eight thousand. Time rolled on. The fate of Odias capsized. The last independent king of Odisha, Mukunda Deb, was defeated in the Gohiratikiri war of 1568 and died. There set the sun of Odisha's independence. Thereafter, Afgans, Moghuls, and Marathas ruled Odisha for about three hundred years."

"Now in the hands of the race coming from across the seas, the Englishmen, the royal scepters of not only Odisha, but also the whole of India, rested. Exhorted and looted by the same rulers, the backbone of the freedom-conscious, heroic Odia race was splintered. The large Odia empire dissipated into smaller territories and got annexed to Bengal, Bihar, Central provinces, Madras, and Telengana. The Tamralipta fort city was separated from Odisha and was tagged on to Bengal. The Odias there gradually started speaking Bengali.

"Like this, the once spread out, large Utkal empire from Ganga to Godavari was fragmented. During this period of political turmoil, the royal descendants of Kalu Bhuyan came back homeward and settled along the coastal areas of Odisha. Maybe one of those families was that of Ugrasen's father."

"Well, Ugrasen, if your grandpa left Tamralipta when your father was just five, then according to his age, this must have been of that period–"

Ugrasen replied, "Right, Sir. Maybe seventy or eighty years."

Sir said, "Not only your grandfather. Many proud Odia fishermen families came back to Utkal and settled along the coastal areas." Sir arose, sighing heavily.

Ugrasen Behera bowed to him and said, "You've saved my prestige, Sir. Whoever else admits it or not, Udhab's mother would admit this time that I'm a royal descendant of King Kalu Bhuyan. Ugrasen isn't a man who'd send his younger son Udhab for adoption, eyeing for a patch of land from my father-in-law, leaving the ancestral homestead."

But the villagers did not accept easily. It's true that those who had seen Ugra and his father–Kalia fishermen–had heard from their mothers about their royal origin. But where was the proof? Who cared for tall claims? He, who at every night's end came out with them to fish in the river and sea in a boat, even if he was of royal descent, had once been the subject of the king of Harispur. After the Sunset Law, he became the subject of Zamindar Laha. Who cared or was afraid of him simply because one of his ancestors was a king?

The lifelong enemy of Ugra, a fisherman named Haria, said, "Yes, we admit that one Utkal fisherman, Kalu Bhuyan, became the king of Tamralipta. Also, we admit now that Tamralipta is in Bengal, separated from Odisha. This fact Sir has read from a printed book. How can a printed book be false? But Sir has never said that you are a descendant of Kalu Bhuyan, nor is it there in printed letters. That you claim yourself. Can you show the proof?"

Ugra said, with blazing eyes, "The proof is my father. His

name was Kalu. He was Kalu Sen. You idiots of this village made Kalu into Kalia. If the name of the first king of our dynasty hadn't been Kalu Bhuyan, why then was my father named Kalu? Isn't it reasonable to believe that my grandfather Bhimasen, to perpetuate the glory of his family pride, gave that ancestral name to his son?"

Haria guffawed loudly and said, "You've the brain of a king of fools. Look at his logic! In that case, that credible Muslim, Kalu Mian, is also a descendant of King Kalu Bhuyan, is he not? Here comes Ugrasen from Tamralipta–fisherman of royal lineage!"

Another group that wasn't opposed to anyone but derived pleasure when someone was snubbed started laughing at Haria's logic. In a moment, Haria and Ugrasen would have come to blows.

Two hefty young fishermen, with their yoke-like grips, immobilized the two from both sides. But Haria was incorrigible. In a mocking tone, he asked, "Well, do you have any more proof?"

"Yes, there is. Our relations and friends are still there in Midnapur. All registered documents of their homestead and land are in the Odia language. That means they're Odia fishermen and descendants of Kalu Bhuyan, and it also establishes that Midnapur was an integral part of Odisha."

Haria retorted, "Many relatives of people of this area are in Midnapur. Are all of them descendants of Kalu Bhuyan? Moreover, Maharaja Ugrasen, your title should have been Bhuyan. Why has it been Behera? Please explain this much to our villagers."

Ugresen said, "You've reminded me of the main fact. Thank you. In the documents of our ancestors, the Bhuyan title was written for a long time. Even now, some old documents are available with me. The messengers of Harispur Zamindar one day mockingly called my grandfather Bhuan-Bhuan, which means wildcat-and angered my grandfather to such an extent that he said, 'I'm no more Bhuyan. From this day, I'm Behera.' When he transferred his property to his son, he registered their names with the Behera title. Would you like to see?"

Rushing inside the house, he took out the old documents from an old weather-beaten box. But who would read them?

"Leave it alone. What's the gain from bluffs? All fishermen, young and old, are illiterate. How can anyone know whether in the documents there is Bhuyan or Bhuan?" Haria, therefore, declared that he would never accept Ugrathe fisherman as Ugrasen, fisher king.

Encouraged by this little clue of his family pride, Ugra was not subdued easily. The next morning, holding the hand of Haria, he dragged him up to Sir. A group of fishermen like a line of black ants followed behind the two to watch the fun. Would the surname Bhuyan emerge from the documents, and would Ugra fisherman be transformed into a royal descendant? To become a peon of the Zamindar or a Zamindar is something. But straight from a king to a subject?

To resolve the present squabble between Haria and Ugra, Sir scrutinized the papers with utmost calm. In no time-from an old, half–torn piece of paper-came out a name: Jalandhar Bhuyan. Not only the title, but also the name was regal. Which fisherman from this area had a name like Jalandhar? In other words, that Ugrasen was of the royal clan of Kalu Bhuyan, there was no doubt at all. The face of intolerant Haria looked pale like a discarded banana peel.

Ugra the fisherman–alias royal descendant Ugrasen fisher king–bowed to Sir with comparatively less reverence, and he returned homeward with pride, tucking the documents under his arm. In the eye of Haria, a cruel glare appeared. No, he'd never admit Ugra as higher than himself. He'd destroy the pride of Ugra.

Sir hadn't expected such a negative result. Had he divided into king and subjects the fishermen living and dying together under the oppressive rule of Laha Zamindar while creating self-confidence in Ugra? This was now a crisis. If the fisherfolk weren't united, they would be tortured and oppressed more than in the past by the Zamindar, clerks, peons, and moneylenders.

Haria was evil minded. Ugrasen was aggressive and defiant. There had been no previous enmity between them. Today's event had embittered more than sweetened the relationship between them. But Sir hadn't told a lie, nor had he read wrongly. How could he have shirked from speaking the truth?

Sir called Haria and said, "Listen, Hari. At the end of the month, in the yard of goddess Bandarai, I would speak on the past glory of the fisherman community. Ugrasen might be the descendant of fisher king Kalu Bhuyan, but the entire fisherman race is in the lineage of the best fisherman king, Dasa. King Kalu was also of the dynasty of King Dasa. Therefore, from one viewpoint, although the entire fisher folk of the coastal areas of Utkal are not direct descendants of King Kalu, as Kalu Bhuyan was in the lineage of the Dasa king, by distant connections, all fishermen are related to each other. Moreover, those who are descendants of Dasa king, why do they need the identity of King Kalu?"

"Who again is this Dasa king, Sir?" Haria asked with hope in his eyes.

Sir said, "Haven't you read the *Kaibarta Purana*? You must have at least heard of it, even if you haven't read it. The genesis and the glory of the fisher race are written there. How can you know if you do not read? Call a meeting of the village on the last day of the month in the yard of goddess Bandarai. In front of the goddess of the village, if you all gather before nightfall, the *Kaibarta Purana* would be read out. How can you know about the pride and glory of your clan and race if you don't read the Purana? Where is Ram without the Ramayana? Where is Krishna without the Bhagabat? Similarly, where is the existence of the fisher folk without the *Kaibarta Puran*?"

Sir started the history of the fishermen singing a verse beyond comprehension from Puranas of Fisher folk.

"Maybe not from the creation of the sea, but since the making of boats, the Odia merchant had earned a name for himself in sea trade. Including the island clusters of Java, Sumatra, Bali, Borneo, and Malay, and even on the golden island Pegu, the Odia merchant has spread his commerce and business.

"In the golden lands of Cambodia and Burma, the Odia merchants ruled as kings. Not only that, but also the enterprising traders of Kalinga crossing the Pacific Ocean had commercial ventures in China and Japan. This was about the eastern seas. In the West, mastering the Arabian seas, the Kalinga merchants were the monopolists; their commercial crafts had reached even Madagascar in the continent of Africa. About twelve to fifteen hundred years ago, between the Tamraparni islands and Kalinga, there was elephant trade along the sea route. Tamraparni later was named Lanka, where King Dasa of the fisher clan ruled for ages, taking the steeds and chargers from the Vindhya mountain areas.

"The black elephants of Lanka Island were famous all over the world. The Lanka elephants were massive, like Ravana and Kumbhakarna, and very strong. The Kalinga kings, therefore, were buying elephants from Lanka and selling them to the north Indian kings, thereby making elephantine profits. The relationship between Lanka and Kalinga had started back in the first year of the reign of the Dasa king.

"Along the Utkal coast, there were many seaports at that time. Most famous among them were Masalipattanam, Konark, Dantapur, Charitra, Tamralipta, Adjeeta, Kalingapattan, Chilika, Puri, Subarnarekha, Hijli, and also Marichpur and Harishpur fort. The seaport, however, is not seen in the Bandara village today. The lighthouse is not there either. It has long since collapsed due to corrosive, salty winds.

"Through this port, the external trade of Utkal was carried on for hundreds of years. Washing the image of Bandarai Goddess with milk, the prosperous forefathers of the trader community of Utkal were spreading their fleets–the handmade Kalinga boats in the Bay of Bengal. Those days, the silk clothes of Haripur and other parts of Odisha were famous in India and abroad as Kalinga clothes. They were so popular in Lanka and the golden islands that the Tamils of Lanka thought of Kalinga clothes as the only textile. Eventually, in Tamil dictionaries, the word *Kalinga* was known as *clothes*."

Listening to these words from Sir's mouth, all were dumbfounded.

TWO

Those days, the Utkal diamonds were famous all over the world. About two thousand years ago, Utkal diamonds were sold in Rome at fancy prices. Among the Indian traders who settled abroad as merchants and spread the culture and civilization of India, the Odias were the vanguards. The cargo ships of Utkal churned the Arabian Sea and Indian Ocean. The traders of Utkal were rich owners of boats and ships, but it wasn't possible for them to build seaworthy ships without the help of the navigators and able builders of the fisher folk. The sea trade was unthinkable without their cooperation.

"Fleets of warships and gunboats from Utkal were commissioned to protect the trading ships in the Indian Ocean. The ancestors of the fisher folk were boat builders, navigators, and also protectors of cargo vessels. They visited foreign countries to build boats and to hoist the flag of Utkal's honor. Therefore, you should all be proud of your dynastic aristocracy."

Sir looked at the faces of the entire group to confirm whether they were proud of their ancestors, listening to the fame and glory of the Utkal traders. Like the indifferent faces of small and big fish, all those faces looked alike. But by that time, Haria was about to lose his patience.

Where had the primal fisher king, Dasa, and his

glory gone? What more could be had from Utkal's sea trade, skins and shells? In the sea trade, the efficient fishermen were boat builders, navigators, and protectors, true, but their destiny-makers were the traders and merchants. Calling the fisherman royal or protector did not make him the owner; he remained the tenant. Calling the fisherman a navigator did not make him a merchant; he remained a mere boatman. Haria, therefore, demanded that Sir speak about Dasaking, leaving aside trade.

Sir had invited, by special messenger, sage Nabaghan Das, a Vaishnab fisherman of the Balipatna village, which was situated on the banks of river Devi. Nabaghan Das was an expert in reciting the *Kaibarta Purana*. He was a man who had killed, in his youth, legions of fish and crab, but after accepting Vaishnavism, he never allowed onion, garlic, or even bottle gourd and Indian spinach on his plate, never mind about non-vegetarian food!

After becoming a Vaishnab, he changed his name from Nabaghan Majhi to Nabaghan Das. But whatever you do, your caste sticks to your body like fish scales until death. If you remove the scales from fish by force, fish remains fish, never a vegetable. Cooking fish and offering it to a goddess doesn't take away its non-vegetarian character. Otherwise, why do the village people call those who turn into vaishnabs fisherman *Vaishnab, Karan Vaishnab, and cattleman Vaishnab*? Karan Vaishnabs did not even marry into Mohanty families.

Ahead of Borikina, toward the left, a small village across the canal could be seen. Its name was Naradia. Those days, in Naradia, there lived a Karan Vaishnab–Balakrishna Das. In his way of life, he was a serious Vaishnab. But only he, rising above the caste differences, ate food cooked by the Dalits. Being in close company with Adhikary Balakrishna Gosain and christened by him, Nabaghan Majhi became a Vaishnab. Balakrishna Gosain, before he whispered the transformative mantra in his ears, had taught him the alphabets, taught him the *Puranas* and *Bhagabat*. Reading the *Kaibarta Purana*, Nabaghan was wallowing in the past glory of his own caste.

Getting the message from Sir, Nabaghan Das arrived at the

yard of Bandarai with the *Kaibarta Purana* under his arm. After partaking prasad, the children had already made for their homes in the thickening darkness. The fisher children are not afraid of the sea; they fear the fearful silence of darkness. They don't fear the sharks and crocodiles; they fear ghosts, goblins, gnomes, and witches. This is because, in course of time, they learn the tricks and arts of saving themselves from the sharks and crocodiles, but all their lives they never learn the art of escaping from the nocturnal netherworld creatures. Their parents, grandparents, and fourteen previous generations didn't know how, either. Only the witch doctors, who are seldom born in the villages, know how.

Witch doctors aren't found in all villages. One is found in around ten or fifteen villages. Where are the witch doctors in proportion to the large number of gnomes and witches? As one rice pot satisfies the hunger of ten bellies, one witch doctor controls the mischief of the ghosts and evil agents of ten villages. Since women are the playthings of the ghosts and witches, they're victimized more. Thank God! Otherwise, how could men go to the fields, river, and sea riding on them? The ghosts rarely possess males. It's true that the ghosts had never possessed Nabaghan Das, but once or twice, they had beckoned him for fishing.

When one is ghost possessed, the impossible is achieved. Who, in this world, is not possessed by ghosts? One who's not possessed by ghosts is incompetent and always depends on the help of others. At times, Nabaghan was flooding the eggplant fields, crane lifting water from tanks and ponds, making them stone dry, in the company of a ghost. But after Nabaghan Majhi became Nabaghan Das, accepting the order, the ghosts stayed away from him.

People said, "Another ghost has now possessed this Naba Majhi."

Nabaghan Das hears this and speaks to himself. "Yes, this is the Vaishnab ghost, and the sublime one. Once this ghost

[1]This is a mixture of honey, ghee, milk, curds and jaggery called (five) ambrosial mixture.

possesses you, it never leaves-because no divine ghost-buster has been born in the entire universe to exorcise the Vaishnab ghost."

At Sir's instance, Vaishnab Nabaghan Das opened the palm-leaf book, Kaibarta Purana, which was covered in a seven-layered dirty cloth. Touching his head with the book, he bowed to the book god, the lord of letters. The illiterate fisher folk also bowed to the book god. Nabaghan started reading the text. Nabaghan's voice, although heavy like sugar candy, was sweet like Panchamrita.

The text was used to sober up even the narcotics users. But the hardened ganja addicts weren't sobered up–rather, they were pepped up. The recitation was more intoxicating for them. Bowing to Achyutananda's Kaibarta Gita, Nabaghan, in his sweet bass voice, started his discourse and began from the birth of the Dasa king, in the second canto.

Nabaghan Dasa tried to explain to the fisher folk that even though they are called lowly rural fishermen, they had actually originated from the dirt of the Lord's ears. During the deluge, the creator of the universe–God himself–had slept on the banyan leaf. Mighty waves of the flood had undulated the leaf. The Lord's yogic sleep had been disturbed.

God actually does not sleep. If he really slept, who would manage the universe during that time? The Lord, therefore, has a yogic siesta, alert and conscious. Unseeing, he sees everything. God envisioned that, seeing the deluge, the creatures were stunned, lifeless, and frozen. Who would then stop the deluge? Who would still the banyan leaf and restore its balanced state? Leaving everything to God does not mean sitting like a helpless leper. Who's the man who would be the savior boatman?

The fisherman race had not been born at that time. The Lord took a bit of sandal paste dirt from his earlobes and made a male figure out of it. He then infused life into it. From the Lord's dark-hue-adorned dirt was born a dark, strong, bold, powerful, and truthful male. He was Dasa Kaibarta.

That man sat on his knees at the feet of the Lord. With folded hands he asked, "Who am I, Lord? What's the purpose of my life? What duty do I have to serve in this human birth? Command. I'll obey at the risk of my life. I'll consider myself fulfilled if this trivial life's service is needed in achieving something great."

The Lord ran his loving hands over the head of that man and said, "You'll be known as Kaibarta, as you've sprung from the base of the ear. As you originate from the dirt of the ear, you'll be the steward and navigator at the time of deluge. You'll still the undulating banyan leaf. You'll serve mankind. I, therefore, give you the name Dasa, the servitor. He who serves for the good of the world as a servitor of gods and men is a real king. In the end, you'll be king and become famous as the Dasa king."

Hearing such words from the Lord's mouth, that massive man, holding an oar in his hand, stilled the banyan leaf. But he was so immersed in the Lord's grace that he was oblivious of the external world. Taking this opportunity, a big shark-like fish swallowed the Dasa king. Seeing that, God tore apart the belly of Raghab, the fish, and rescued the Dasa king. The Dasa king was in such a divine trance that he didn't know that the fish had swallowed him and that God had rescued him.

The Lord said to Dasa Kaibarta, "The fish that swallowed you is your foe. You'll kill him in every birth, be it so. Your family, clan, friends and kin, killing this creature would make their living."

Listening to the *Kaibarta Gita*, the fisher folk were transformed into the proud lineage of the Dasa king. But fisherman Haria was not satisfied. Yes, it was believable that Dasa Kaibarta was born out of the ear dirt of the Lord, but when had Dasa Kaibarta become the king, and how? It wouldn't do if the fisherman was elevated to the stature of Kaibarta. Only if he was royal Kaibarta, a real match with the Kalu Bhuyan descendant, would royalty-claiming Ugrasen be tolerable. Otherwise, Ugra's pride would be limitless.

Hari asked in an agitated manner, "Respected Nabaghan Dase, keeping aside devotion and service, why don't you speak on how the servitor of gods and men, Dasa Kaibarta, became a king? Where was his kingdom? Who made him king?"

Sir laughed and said, "Have patience, Haribandhu! It won't do if proof is available of royal descent. One must work like a king. Why do you want to tie the royal turban before Nabaghan Dase even finishes reading the *Kaibarta Gita*? Listen with patience to what the text says."

All, including Haria, sat patiently.

Clarifying Haria's doubts, Vaishnab Nabaghan said, "My dear brother, please listen. God is so pleased with the devotion and service of Dasa that God made the stem of the leaf into a strong and powerful horse. Summoning Viswakarma, the divine builder, he built a beautiful boat through him. He commanded Dasa king, 'Listen, Dasa. The horse from today would be your carrier. It would remain as the chief deity of the Kaibarta clan and would be worshipped on every full moon day of *Chaitra*. Taking Basuli with you, go to the Sinhala Island, and row the boat. As the present king of Sinhala is childless, the royal elephant is moving through the kingdom with a golden pitcher full of holy water. As no royal person is available there, the elephant does not pour the holy water on anyone's head. You go there. The elephant would anoint your head with the holy water. You'll be king of the Sinhala Island.'

"Dasa Kaibarta, obeying the command of the Lord, went to Sinhala, and the elephant poured the water from the gold pot on his head. Dasa Kaibarta became the king of Sinhala. The Lord again said to Dasa Kaibarta, 'Do not consider the Sinhala island small or insignificant. The horn of the fish-form of the Lord later became the Sinhala island. The vast ocean surrounds the island. On its west is Karnat, on the south is Hengulat, and on the east the Jambu island. The merchants of Utkal would move to all these islands. Living in Sinhala, you'll hold high the flag of Utkal's fame; propagate the greatness of Utkal.'"

Ugrasen asked, "The Dasa king lived in Sinhala and married some Sinhalese woman and ruled over the island. How did we Odia fishermen become his descendants?"

"You've asked a key question, Urgrasen. Listen to me, then, and not my words. The great saint Achyut has composed it in the

Kaibarta Gita. Known by different names, the Mahanadi river, with its many tributaries, has crisscrossed Utkal. Never think of the Mahanadi as an ordinary river. Mahanadi is the pre-eminent queen of a king in the lineage of Vishnu. You have seen the form, shape, and flow of Mahanadi as a river. If you now listen to the description of the grace and beauty of the female form of Mahanadi, you'll surely lose your senses." Nabaghan Dase started reciting the beauty of Mahanadi as a woman.

After reciting, Nabaghan Dase smiled at the stupefied male fishermen. He said, "In the river form of Mahandi, you, too, see the style and beauty of poetic description. Therefore, you are lost in the mystic charm of the river for ages. From the female form of Mahandi's womb, impregnated by the semen of a Vishnu dynasty king, a daughter was born, named Girima. That daughter became the chief queen of the Dasa king. Their two sons were Hirarnab and Nilarnab, respectively. Girima, in turn, gave birth to ninety-nine sons. Thus spread the Dasa dynasty, the fisher clan, in the areas enriched by the tributaries of Mahanadi. The same Dasa king in the treta yug also became a Ram devotee. This is not the story of the Dasa king's life and lineage; this is also the genealogy of the Kaibarta clan."

After that, Vaishnab Nabaghan tied the palm–leaf *Kaibarta Gita* and touched his head with it. Listening to the glory of the fisher clan, the fisher folk returned after bowing to Mother Bandarai. When Nabaghan Dase was tying the cords on the text, Ugrasen asked, "If all are descendants of the Dasa king, why are there these upper and lower caste differences among the fisher folk? Every fisherman is of the same royal caste-why is this difference, Dase?"

Sir answered this question. He said, "Illusions; all these are illusions of the human mind. Caste is born out of profession. There is no high-low. Man has created this high and low. You are all born out of the ear-dirt of the Lord, and the caste differences arise because of different professions. If you resolve your differences and join the Gandhi movement, then the British and the king-zamindar groups cannot escape from you. You are a patriotic race. Forsaking mutual bickering, I believe you'll all join the Gandhi movement. But now it is night already. Another day I would recite the Gandhi Puran."

Listening to the Kaibarta Gita, Haria no longer carried any grudge against Ugrasen, and Ugrasen, too, had overcome his arrogance. One day the fisherman was king; today he is subject. The entire fisher clan rode the same boat at the mercy of the river and sea. Why then the difference between king and subject?

River and sea, sea and river–the difference is between vastness and smallness; so is the difference between the seine and the trammel nets. But for Udhab, both Bandar and Abhayapur were equally exciting and soulful, with their village roads, dusty games, *hututu* game, and many other pranks of childhood.

When his mother was alive, Udhab enjoyed visiting his uncle's house with his mother, returning when he missed his friends and their childhood games on the village roads. This journey to and fro was as enjoyable for Udhab as going from mother's lap to his aunt's lap. When mother would be free from her worldly chores and Udhab would have his school vacations, going to the uncle's house was a sweet experience, like the taste of freshwater fish. As long as he stayed in his uncle's house, so long as mother was in her parent's house, he never, ever thought of returning home.

He used to pray to God for his mother to stay longer in uncle's house. He was friendly with his younger uncle, Meghanad. On certain days, his younger uncle would venture into mid-sea with five-year-old Udhab on a small pedal boat. Udhab was afraid, seeing the demonic tongue-like waves of the sea. But underlying that fear was the adventurous aristocracy of the fisher folk.

His mother would stand still in thigh-deep water on the shore with her eyes fixed on the path of their return, like the wooden statue of Basuli, a mythical horse worshipped by the fisher folk. In her eyes one could read sincere prayer and endless love for Udhab. Uncle Megha, seeing the wooden frame of mother from a distance, would reach the shore, and, holding the frail hand of lean Udhab, throw him onto the wet sand like throwing a dead fish by the tail.

He would say, "Take your son and pamper him as much as you like. Keep him as an effeminate, fit-for-nothing fellow. Only, for you, my sister, Udhab would grow up to be an useless fellow, neither fit for the field nor for the net, neither for the tree nor for fish. Well, tell me, sister! For a fisher boy, the sea is the school, the boat his slate, his chalk is his oars, and the alphabets are fish, crab, and turtle. When would he learn all these?"

At that time, looking down, Udhab would see the wet sand, and looking up, he'd see his mother' swet eyes. Clutching the sari of mother, Udhab's world was from the pedal of the pounder to the hearth, from cow dung to fish. But Uncle Megha's pedal boat and the eye-defying, oar-mocking vast, deep sea was larger than Udhab's small world, more pleasant than the village play fields.

After mother left for the other world, the husking pedal, hearth, fish, and dry fish courtyard did not please Udhab anymore. The uncle's house beckoned him; to forget "Mother is no more," the only medicine was Uncle Megha, Meghanad Mangual. In his glazed, dark, large, round, full-blown face, the eyes were big and circular. In his curly hair, the sheen of Karanja oil, the comb of sunlight glowed brightly. Uncle Megha was the most desirable young man of the village. Udhab, it seemed, looked like his son.

Many unmarried fisher belle were worshipping Lord Shiva and praying to marry Uncle Megha. Megha, however, was choosy and a crafty taster. From where would a princess be selected by grandfather? After the astrologers, soothsayers, and ayurvedic doctors declared the elder aunty barren, it was prudent to be more careful in selecting a bride for Megha. Grandfather, therefore, was vetting possible brides for Megha one after another.

Like the stars fading one after another at dawn and the unfading sun smiling in the sky, Uncle Megha was wandering like a bachelor ghost while girls appeared one after another and faded before the proposal advanced. Not even one bride matched Uncle Megha's brideless zodiac sign. Thereafter, instead of searching for a bride, Grandfather searched for a strong astrologer who would, by his knowledge and trick, match the horoscopes of the groom and bride and finalize the marriage, blowing the conch shell of

Uncle Megha's endless future, dispelling the evil forces. Such astrologers were available, but the propitious time for marriage hadn't arrived!

That day, Urgasen had just returned from the sea. News came that his younger brother-in-law had been lost at sea. After three days, his dead body was found on the sandy shore, five miles away. Sensing an approaching storm that day, many stalwart fishermen returned from mid-sea. But look at the audacity of Meghanad!

He said, "Is the sea the king? Everyone must stand before him with folded hands? As long as the arms are strong, and the oar is in hand, swimmer Meghanad doesn't care for these half-blowing small storms, nor does he care for the threats of the sea."

Thereafter, he didn't return. Meghanad had done this multiple times. He'd vanish into the sea, but he'd return after three or four days. Once, he'd returned after a month and had unpacked many an exciting story–half true and half concocted. Not to simply brag, but to create a buzz in the village. Let the timid young people be excited if they so pleased. Many a romantic fisher hero would emerge from among them. If the fisher boy is afraid of water, business would die. This was the basis for Meghanad's bravado.

The meaning of finding the corpse of the younger son, Meghanad, was that even if his elder son, Angad, was alive, Nakul Mangual's clan perished. If Angad was childless, in spite of Nakul's five daughters having twenty sons, his family name would end. It's said, "Son's son, grandson, lights the wicks in heaven." Now, it was out of the question. But there was a way out.

It was considered that if Angad adopted his sister's son, Udhab, his clan would be saved. Nakul's son would have been born of the womb of his wife Angad's born of his sister–not entirely a far-off stranger. If not the whole blood, at least half of Nakul Mangual's clan blood was flowing in the body of the sister's son. Moreover, Udhab's appearance was so very similar to that of Meghanad that he looked like a small Meghanad.

Getting the news of his brother-in-law's death, Ugrasen

went with his son to his father-in-law's house. In the same year, two thunder strikes fell on the old couple. There, in Bandar village, Ugrasen's wife died of childbirth the same year. Here, a hefty youth like Meghanad was gone in the sea. Perhaps they'd fallen prey to someone's evil eye. Nakul had hoped that whoever had been fated to be Meghanad's wife would give him five sons-five Pandavas!

Humanity does not have the strength to escape divine retribution. But humankind has the strength to tolerate divine punishment. By being able to do so, God shows that he has given people the strength to defy thunderbolts. Angad's old parents were bedridden for about a month. Again, they arose from the bed, ate rice, and yearned for fish and curry with rice. Of course, all this with a broken back and hollow chest, as if someone had taken out the liver from within. Only a hollow human frame remained. Even after Udhab came to his uncle's house as an adopted son, those two humans remained as two empty cases. After that, the old man lost his speech. He became dumb with sorrow and passed away in no time.

Six-year-old Udhab at first pined for Uncle Megha, but he couldn't understand the intricate sorrow of his uncle's death. For few days, he searched for the uncle, but gradually forgot easily. The elder aunt lavished on him the care of a mother. Feeding him fish rice baked on cow-dung cake fire, she taught him. "Dear Udha! Instead of calling me aunt, call me mother now. Call elder uncle father. Do you understand? You are our only son. I would give you whatever you ask for. Who else is there to share with you? Goddess Basuli has closed all paths."

When Ugrasen prepared to return home after offering his condolences, Udhab's elder uncle's wife opened up her mind. "Long I have wished to take Udhab to my lap. But two things blocked the way. Your wife, my sister-in-law, would not have allowed Udhab to go. Udhab was the apple of her eye as the youngest child. The other was that it was naturally expected that Megha would marry and have children. All would not have been ill-fated and barren like me." The elder uncle's wife sobbed, covering her face. Ugrasen too cried.

All said and done, how much sorrow a worldly man has! Pain at losing one's wife, pain on the death of the younger brother-in-law, the barrenness of the elder brother-in-law's wife, leaving Udhab for all time to come, all of these are heartbreaking. But Ugrasen was thinking–a male heart absorbs mountains of sorrow. Life is a solid mountain of all kinds of sorrow! At the sorrow of his brother-in-law's wife, from the agonized Ugrasen's mouth slipped, in a liberal voice, the boon, "So be it."

Ugrasen said, "Listen, no point languishing in agony. From today, Udhab is your son. Let the motherless child get from his uncle's wife all the love and care of a mother. That's his fate. Mine too. How can I give him mother's love taking him on my lap? Even if the deluge comes, and as long as the river and sea exist, can the fisherman wrap his limbs around his son and sit at home?"

Before returning, the father cried a lot, clasping Udhab to his chest. He said while leaving, "Stay with uncle's wife. I'll come again. You'll study in a good school. With uncle and his wife, you'll enjoy love. You'll want for nothing. During festivals at Bandarai and Marichei, I'll come and take you. My life, my wealth, my dear, never be sad. You are, here, the only darling–the apple of all eyes."

After that day, Udhab became the darling–not only in the uncle's house, but also of Abhayapur. In the record books of Abhayapur, his name was entered–*Udhab Mangual. Father, Angad Mangual. Po, Abhayapur. Panchayat, Ambiki. Block, Erasama. Dist, Cuttack.*

One day, news arrived that Udhab's father has married again. And with that, Udhab's umbilical cord with Bandar village was finally severed. What Udhab understood who knows, but the boy cried like mad, hiding his face in his new mother's breast, wailing, "Mother! Mother!"

The new mother's chest swelled with pride as the boy addressed her as "Mother." Kissing him wildly, Malati said, "My darling, my life, my necklace, my moon! Don't cry. I'm here. Why bother? Now I'm your mother."

Udhab ran his hands over her body, smelling her sari for mother's fragrance. But, disappointed again, he pined for mother. The little boy deliriously thought about why mothers, after releasing their babes from their wombs, again clasp them to their hearts? Why do they die untimely and give death pangs to their children? The life breath escapes the earthly body of the mother, but the children do not easily free themselves from her memories. Still lodged in the heart of his dead mother, Udhab became the adopted son of Uncle Angad.

When Uncle's wife kissed him, clasping him in her lap, and asked him to call her mother, Udhab's innocent mind became overeager to test the mother's love in her breast. Really, could he forget his mother's loss by calling his uncle's wife mother? However Udhab tried to forget his own mother, looking at the ample breasts of his uncle's wife in full concentration, his mother entered his mind all the more. He remembered the love of his mother's heart, her warm breasts, and the oozing honeyed ambrosia of her breasts till he was five years old.

Malati went on kissing the tear-streaked face of Udhab. Her face slowly seemed as mother's face to Udhab. He felt as if he was enjoying the love of his mother. The new mother gradually replaced the old. He asked the new mother, removing her sari away from her chest naughtily, "New mother, would you give me a feed? My mother used to pound the paddy while feeding me. Would you feed me like that too? If your breasts feed me, I'll call you mother. Otherwise, I'll tell you no." Udhab pulled her sari from her chest.

Malati, reacting to the guileless fawning of innocent Udhab, suddenly slapped him sharply. She tore him away from her and threw him aside. Turning away her face contemptuously, she said, "Fie! Ill-bred brat! Go. Go away from my presence. Spoiled old child. Fie, fie! This fellow would save the clan? No need to hear mother from you. I am barren, barren, barren. Go! Get out."

Beaten thus by his aunt, six-year-old Udhab didn't lose consciousness. Rather, he grew up instantly. His innocence was gone. He didn't wail because he was hit. He was stunned. He felt as if he'd committed a sin. It wasn't easy for him to stay at Uncle's house. But there was no way to return to his father at Bandar village. In Bandar village, he had father's new wife, worse than his aunt.

Adjusting her sari on her chest, Malati went out, stamping her feet. She called the uncle. "Hey, do you hear? Would you come here for a while? I tell you: take this brat to the school. When he grows up, he should go with you to the sea. If he stays at home lingering around me, this fellow would be completely spoiled. He won't save the clan, rather drown it. If he isn't harnessed right from now, he'll outgrow the dark lascivious Krishna. Ha! Fie! Fie!"

Many things are lost and forgotten too, but not mother, nor father, neither the birth soil, nor the forsaken village. Udhab remembers the unforgettable memory of his childhood. He remembers his mother's bright loving face with a golden stud on her nose. Before the sun rises, before the rooster crows, before Udhab wakes up to the tinkling of the mother's anklets on the pedal of the pounder, his sleep fades away like darkness at dawn. By the time Udhab turns and touches the mattress, searching for the warmth of mother's lap, a sweet, warm scent already floats in the air from the freshly pounded rice flakes. With sleep-laden eyes, Udhab reaches the pounding hut, crossing the inner yard. Rubbing his eyes, he wails aloud, "Mother, why did you leave me alone?"

Half of the fishermen's street wakes up listening to the first rooster, another half at the sound of the pounder. Still others wake up listening to the wailing sound of Udhab. Mother's feet pause on the pedal. Lifting her son to her left waist and wiping his eyes, she again places her feet on the pedal. Putting her right hand in the noose of the rope hanging from the hut's roof and holding her son on her left hip, she goes on pounding–*dhap, dhap, dhap*–as if possessed. Changing the son from one arm to the other, mother changes her foot from the right to the left and goes on pounding till the house and the yards become brighter with sunlight.

In the arms of mother, Udhab feels like playing monkey games on tree branches. Clasping mother's neck with both arms, Udhab waits for one auspicious moment. Mother not only changes her legs by turn, but also changes her hands to hold the hanging rope. In the process, mother's cotton sari, wet with sweat, slides to one side, and Udhab gets a glimpse of the ambrosia pitcher from the churned sea. Conscious of that, mother tactfully goes on changing her hands from left to right, and Udhab looks on with acute concentration.

With the teething rows of his mouth, he suckles the dusky ambrosia pitchers without hesitation, drinks with un brushed mouth the ambrosia to his heart's content, until mother reproaches him sweetly, "You life-sucking brat! How hard you bite. When would you quit this habit?" But he goes on suckling her breasts. That was the diet to keep him energetic the whole day. Un brushed breakfast.

Mother too knew what the first meal of Udhab was. But when did she have the time to enjoy the warmth of the unmade bed and breastfeed her son, letting him seat on her lap? For that, mother too wanted Udhab to take his feed to his heart's content during the paddy-pounding routine, before the chores of the day started. It was fun for Udhab to hang like a bird on mother's chest, moving from left arm to the right, and suckling her while she changed by turn her legs and hands.

After drinking milk to his satisfaction, Udhab got down, leaving his mother's chest. He sat at a distance from the pounder's head. In rhythm with the rise and fall of the piston, he raised and lowered his eyes just as the kitten raised and lowered her eyes from his father's mouth and the fish plate when his father ate water rice and fish fry. Udhab bided his time like a wild cat; when would his aluminum plate be filled with the freshly pounded flakes–warm, sweet and flat like the brown scales of the rohu fish?

Udhab bought a small bowl and, after blowing away the dusty husk, his aunt put a palm full of rice flakes in the bowl. Udhab's mother asked, "Would you like to take jaggery, my darling? Dearest, just one more round, and it'll be over. Just eat slowly, my little pigeon. The moment I get off the pounder, I'll give you jaggery from the pot."

Udhab threw the flakes one by one into his mouth, expecting a thumb measure of jaggery from mother. Looking at mother's legs, his eyes swam up to her face. He looked from the face to the thighs, thighs to the waist, waist to the ample bosom, bosom to the locket on the neck, locket to mother's dusky, tattooed nose tip, and then, the eyes moved up to mother's pan-stained, love-soaked, full lower lip and its silent swell of filial affection. He studied the nose ring, like the back of a flat-bellied, small fish, the small mango-bud-like nose pin, the full, smooth cheeks like cereal cake, her sharply small eyes like the *mahurali* fish, eyebrows like the fading second day moon.

There was the vermillion mark between the brows like the rising sun, and just beneath the vermillion mark a tattooed clove. At the top, like the receding waves of the sea, she had deep-blue, wavy, coiffure hair. Finally, like the winking, thin, red belly of a burst watermelon on the thin parting line of mother's wavy hair, there was a line of liquid vermillion; Udhab's charmed eyes would be fixed there. He'd stare at mother's earrings, pendants, at her armlets. On the full, symmetrical wrists, there were silver bracelets, silver bangles studded with balls like banyan fruits. All combined, mother looked like a goddess.

Soon, unexpectedly, mother turned into a goddess. She didn't speak anymore, didn't respond to calls. Mother was no more seen in flesh and blood, but remained only a memory. He could only convey his grief by closing his eyes and calling out to his mother, just as people spoke of their pain and misery at the Mother Ganga temple or Mother Sarala temple.

After mother's death, father became old suddenly, and Udhab, too, suddenly lost his innocence and grew up in a trice in his uncle's house. He was no more a child. He could not meet the eyes of his uncle's wife, his new mother. He never stared at any other woman's full bosom. And he never called his uncle's wife mother as long as she lived. Uncle's wife remained as his aunt, but he called his uncle father. Uncle loved Udhab more than his own father had.

One day, Uncle took him to the school. He said, "Teacher, sir, this brat is now under your care. He has forgotten whatever he has learned. Let him start from the alphabet again. At home, he's becoming naughty. Once he attains the age of going to the sea and river, I'll withdraw him from school. If he doesn't stand behind me, who would manage such a big family?"

The day Udhab sat on the school veranda of Abhayapur, he knew that his name was now finally deleted from the history of Bandar village; his shadow had finally receded from Devi river. The number of times he used to come to uncle's house when he was at Bandar village, now he didn't go to Bandar that many times. He became the hope of the Mangual clan of Abhayapur. He had no time to move like a free bird. He was caged.

THREE

Eastward, the sea is one step away; from the north and south, with outstretched hands, Mahanadi and her daughter River Devi embrace between the two streams with languid rhythms of hope and despair, washing their nightwear in the sea, sealing the hopes and aspirations of generations of family lineage and pride, cleaning the unborn future in river water. There are a few villages, which get embraced in a golden hue twelve months a year, in that rural area, which is known as Erasama, of Jagatsinghpur district.

The east coast Cuttack district of yore is now divided into four districts; one of the pieces is Jagatsinghpur, whose name was once the Haridrabasana (yellow-robed maid). The deity Somanath was worshipped on the banks of River Alaka, the daughter of Kathjodi; and Lord Jagannath worshipped at Nezigarh, in the arati music of these temples. The "yellow-robed" in popular form had become for the ease of the common man, Hariharpur. Lured by the culture and prosperity of this area and charmed by the riches, business, and the art of textiles, the British merchants had setup their first commercial center at Hariharpur and changed its name to Jagatsinghpur.

In the eyes of the British, this area was royal, cultured, prosperous, and therefore, the lion of the world-Jagatsinghpur. These coastal two-crop villages, whether in rain or drought, in all seasons, all the twelve months of the year round, sway under bumper crops both autumnal and summer. This is why people call this area the rice bowl of Odisha. Moreover, the people of this area are educated and intelligent, famous in India and abroad. It is the birthplace of the father of Odia literature, Sarala Das. This is the cradle of the Bhagabat-Gaddi and Odia poetry. A chunk of the same fertile soil of Jagatsinghpur is Erasama. The Mahanadi and its branch Kathajodi skirt around the Cuttack city. The same rivers branch off, stretching out like a hand holding the offering plate, the spread-out villages of Ersama at the estuary. But who named the Kathjodi flowing from Cuttack Devi? In this region, it's not known. Udhab believed that Kathjodi had been named Devi because the fisher community worshipped the river as a goddess.

Mahanadi, Kathjodi, Devi, Alaka, Hansua, Saonlia; whatever name you speak, the river is the mother and the sea the father. Within the love ambit of father and mother, the Jagatsinghpur district, Erasama block, and the Ambiki panchayat, a very small coastal village is Abhayapur, sitting in the embrace of nine rivers. In the Erasama block, many a low-lying village washes its feet in the sea. It's difficult to guess whether the sea originates from the villages or the other way around.

In the beginning, however, so many of the small villages touching, scuffling, and claiming equality with the sea didn't exist. Between the sea and the village, in the hinterland, was a saline forest of date palms, tamarisks, and other such wild trees. Guarding the Jatadhari estuary, the Jatadhari and Dhobai jungles were the trusted watchmen between the sea and the villages. The two jungles were watching the villages lest they disturbed the sea, and also the sea, lest she threatened the villages.

In the hide-and-seek game between the sea and villages, the jungles were a blindfold on the sea. The sea would stretch her hands but wouldn't touch the villages. Piercing the blindfold, the wild sea would return, wetting the villages. Ah! What romance there was those days in that touch-and-go game with the sea!

As the forefathers of Udhab had been to Tamralipta and

had returned from Tamralipta to Bandar again, likewise the upstream waves return to the bosom of the sea; Udhab, too, hurled out from Bandar village to save the clan of his uncle's family, and is old by now in Abhayapur. The romance of the two-way traffic of life is ceaseless. Like breaking waves in the sea, Udhab Mangual, experiencing the sun and shower of life from one village to another, is advancing in years, breaking the tides of life.

Devi river of Bandar and Hansua of Abhayapur-both rivers for him are the sacred Mahanadi. During childhood, Udhab loved more the saline jungle stretched over miles along the shoreline. His playmates were the birds and animals of the jungle. The day Udhab's father, Ugrasen Behera, got the news of Megha uncle's death and took him along the river route on a boat to his uncle's house, Udhab did not know then that destiny had tied him to Abhayapur for good.

In Bandar, the child Udhab had been afraid of the roar of the sea, but growing up and later into youth in Uncle's village, he grew fearless and became rather fearsome himself. Udhab practiced all the difficult techniques to tame the sea. In Bandar, Udhab was a six-year-old, beloved child, a mother's darling, and the hope of the family. In Abhayapur, within the discipline and rigorous principles of the Gita and Bhagabat, the crane-like, lean, timid Udhab grew up into a strong, formidable, fearless young man. Now he was old, but ten young men were no match for him. Who would say that Udhab was now four short of three scores and ten!

If Sankha's mother died today, young women would be too willing to marry him. When someone jests fully comments like that, Udhab says bashfully, like a child, "Ok! Let go of that joke. If you really wish me well, then find a suitable match for my Benudhar. Yes, after him is my beloved daughter, Girima. Who knows my granddaughter Devi is destined for what kind of groom! I can't believe that things would fall into place. Nowadays, youth are all hollow. Like the ghost-eaten coconuts, smooth on the outside, but hollow inside.

"Now colleges are in every village. Once they step into the

college, they're neither for the net nor for the farm. Unemployed, fit for nothing. Irresponsible, truant, haughty, and temperamental. But why blame the children? What do parents feed and teach them? The ministers and teachers are all after money. Choose the business where there's more money; let the family business go to hell! Elders are also chanting the mantra to the children."

This may not have been true for others, but for Udhab it was a fact that nowadays in the village no one had a husk pounder, not even a pounding hut. In every village, instead, there was the annoying noise of the huller. People were madly attracted to nylon shirts, ribbons, and saris. Now they were running after nylon rice flakes, nylon rice and grams.

The machine scraped the rice and flakes to such an extent that only the kernel remained. The outer, richer layer was scraped off with the husk and went into the belly of cattle. The cattle grew strong; the humans grew spineless. Why blame the children?

It seemed pounded rice and rice flakes did not go down the throats of people. They used to eat it, so why not now? What's to blame, the throats or food? The machines scraped off the skin of green and black grams to such an extent that it was difficult to distinguish one from the other. Moreover, to the rural people, pounded rice and flakes stink more. If you moved around ten villages, you'd not get a quarter kilo of pounded rice or flakes, even if you were ready to pay a hundred bucks. For the cattle, the husk was sweet. For men, the machine-pounded rice tastes like husk, but they had no choice in the matter.

But Udhab had not given up the pounder, nor had he given up the pounded rice and flakes. Where was the taste of pounded rice and flakes in the machine-polished rice? Was it only taste? There was also strength. Red rice flakes, black molasses, the thick, reddish mounds of curd , saffron cheese, grated coconut like white flower petals, the ripe bananas , what satisfaction! Was it there in purees, jalebi, vada, or stale bread?

On certain days, Udhab ate, instead of rice, a bowl of rice flakes. When the mouth and throat were sweetened, he bit a raw chilli with salt and swallowed with it a handful of rice flakes.

Thereafter, only sweet sleep, sweet snores, and sweet, sleepy babbles. Sankha's mother said, "Those days, a sweet scent spread from Udhab's breath as he yawned, snored, and sneezed. All Udhab's children are fond of red rice flakes and bananas. Because of that, each one is a bow-wielding, fighting, fit soldier, and above that, a real fisherman. The children of the rest of the village are hollow, empty, and fit for nothing. They're not to blame. The nylon rice and rice flakes are the guilty party."

One day, while feeding rice flakes to Udhab, his mother had real labor pain. When she put the last bite in his mouth hastily, he bit her hand. She said, "Ah! this brat would be the death of me." She rose up, clutching her stomach. With that pain, she passed away eventually. At that time, it was Udhab's firm belief that he'd eaten his mother.

A friend of his said that it seemed there was poison in the teeth of children. Udhab's dental poison flowing in his mother's body had killed the babe in her womb. Unable to give birth to the dead babe, his mother had died. Even today, at this old age, a feeling of guilt twists his guts. Had he not bitten his mother, who knows? Perhaps his mother would still be living. If his mother's mother, the old Bela grandmother, lived up to fourscore and upward, why would his mother not have lived up to eighty? In his memory, certainly, his mother lived, reigning forever in rice, curry, cakes, and rice flake balls. Mother always served steaming heaps of hot, reddish rice in a large, brass plate to father. With it, half a bowl of vegetables and drumstick leaves cooked with white-gram lentils, fish curry, or baked, dry fish.

Even today, his mouth salivated when he remembered. Of course, in Udhab's house, the same fare was served to this day. The same reddish rice, lentils, fish curry, and baked, dry fish. But there the aroma of his mother's hand was missing. The taste was different. Udhab's wife, the mother of his ten children, Sankha's mother, is a competent cook. She was from a well-ordained family and an expert in running a household. But the aroma of her hands was different. Her cooking was of a different taste. Mother was mother. Wife was wife.

Women were a strange breed. The same woman; one character as mother, another as wife. His wife's face became so different when she bore his children that he could not believe that both were the same woman. But mother and wife rang the same one note; that was to subjugate the male, to drag the male by putting pincers on the nose. Adult son or aged husband, both before the woman were mice. When this happened, the home was heaven. Otherwise, a battlefield. However, it must be admitted that the homemaking skill of woman was often perceived by the world as home breaking-often homes break too.

For a mere human like Udhab Mangual, a small village like Abhayapur was a vast world. However reckless one was, where would man go, leaving this world? After coming to Abhayapur as an adopted son, Udhab had never desired to go anywhere. He had loved Abhayapur-its soil, air, and water, joy and sorrow, happiness and misery-so very deeply that he had nourished a hope to be cremated in the village crematorium. If he died falling on the way somewhere, his dead body would certainly reject any other burning ghat.

From Bandar village too, the thread of his relationship had not snapped. How could he sever his blood relationship from father, brother, sister, friends, the village, Devi river, Sankhua estuary, mother Bandarai and Marichai? Spreading its branches to the sky, could the tree ever sever its relationship with the earth? After merging into the sea, could the river forget its love for the hills? Similarly, Udhab's ties with Bandar village had not weakened after the death of his father.

A village that was eternally threatened by the sea had been ironically christened as Abhayapur-the fearless village. The roar of the sea could be heard in the village. When fish jumped out of the water, their form and scale was clearly visible from the village road.

Perhaps a mother someday must have said to her frightened child, "Why fear? Why be scared? The four-armed god is there for all snares."

The reassuring words from a mother's mouth must have entered the kernel of the timid village, and its name must have become Abhayapur. Once, this village was a part of Ambiki. Although the big villages have been broken into smaller ones, the rivers, streams, canals, swamps, and sea have joined these villages edge to edge like a marriage knot; but have also divided them. Almost sixty tidal streams branching off the Mahanadi were the rice pots of this area.

The fishermen of Abhayapur-and also the non-fishing communities-depended on these rivers, streams, and sea. Abhayapur, so to speak, was a pure fisherman village. Yet if you took into account Abhayapur, Pakistanpara, Labanipur, Kunjabedi, Phiringipara, Japanagari, Nagarighat, Chandanpur, Kiada, Shovanpur, and others in this area, thirty-six communities lived together. Many communities, including backward ones, lived together harmoniously, protecting their own traditions and respecting other's traditions. But the fishermen were the majority. Therefore, in these villages the fishermen were the village leaders.

The motto of these coastal villages was unity, like the sands on the shore; humble, simple, and loving villages. The villagers lived together in familial harmony, celebrating and suffering joys and sorrows, deaths and funerals, marriages and festivals, echoing mutual life rhythm. If mustard seeds were roasted in one house, the fragrance reached other houses. If a death occurred in one house, the hearths in the other houses remained cold. If the birth cry of a baby was heard in a house, in the other houses, drumsticks and yard eggplants-stipulated food for the new mother were collected by the villagers.

Fishermen, non-fishermen, rich, and poor had almost the same pattern of houses. All houses were of earth and wattle, with thatched roofs. Felling the nearby jungle trees, commissioning from the village carpenter simple, one-piece doors that opened and closed on one side, they lived secluded lives, far away from the city and market, living and dying behind the one-sided doors. Not counting the chief minister, not even a minister had stepped into these villages.

Almost everyone with joint families had courtyard houses.

Udhab's house was not big, not small, but of a moderate size-two big blocks on two sides, separated by a courtyard. The house had a two-way entry. Those who came from the road entered the front block, and those coming from the rear entered and went out through the rear block. Behind the rear block was the pounding hut on one side, and on the other, the kitchen. The open hall on the front side ought to have been a cowshed, but the fishermen being fond of fish, not farming, cattle were scarcely found. Udhab, therefore, had occupied that hall. Udhab had only a couple of cattle. Adjacent to the pounding hut, Udhab had made a cowshed facing the rear.

Out of Udhab's four daughters, three-Charu, Taru, and Marua-were married, but they were often in their father's house with their children. Udhab had given his daughters in marriage in the nearby villages. The third son-in-law did not, but the other two accompanied Udhab for fishing. The third son-in-law's house was in Sendhakud village, near Paradip port. He worked in the Oswal Company.

Udhab's house was always crowded with daughters, sons-in-law, and grandchildren. Out of his sons, Sankhadhar, Gadadhar, Chakradhar, Padmadhar, Bhagyadhar, and Benudhar, four had been married already. Their wives were good housewives and never went to their parent's house. Starting from making dry fish with their mother-in-law, to selling it in the nearby fair, they were constantly busy with household chores. A host of grandchildren gathered when the daughters visited during festive occasions. When the guest grandchildren and the children of Udhab's sons came out to the courtyard together, the big and small ran riot in the junk-filled courtyard, much like the big and small fish that thrash about panic-stricken in the slushy waters of the common village tank on days of community fishing.

Udhab had no time to enjoy filial joy, taking on his lap the grandchildren, nor did his wife, Sankha's mother. While Udhab was immersed in fishing activities, Sankha's mother was engrossed with dry-fish preparation. Yet despite limited resources in the large family, there was no dearth of love and affection. When did a working person have time to worry over wants? Even when one found time, would the life-sucking children allow you to listen to your own thoughts? From dawn to dusk, there was chaos and commotion like when the rat snake (Zamenis Mucosus) entered the crow's nest.

The same courtyard one day was lying empty in eerie silence. Living in the house were Udhab's maternal grandfather, Nakul, Grandma Bela, younger Grandma, younger Grandpa, Uncle Angad, and his barren wife. The four brothers had separated after Grandpa Nakul had died young. The children of the diseased youngest grandpa had died very young too.

The courtyard was full of playful children today only because Udhab had been adopted to save the clan. This was said by Udhab's grandma, old Bela. From her toothless mouth, pan-spit flew in scarlet affection. Udhab's grandpa, old Nakul Mangual, was almost blind, but his ears were sharp until his death. He was a child with children, and would have lived to a hundred years, but succumbed to the shock of Uncle Megha's death and passed away. Grandma Bela too would have lived to be a hundred. After Grandpa's death, she, too, closed her eyes without cause. Now, in Udhab's house, two aged men were sitting, hands and legs folded. They were Udhab's younger grandpa and his uncle, Angad, whom he called father. Of course, in a working man's house, especially in the fisherman community, there was nothing like old age.

Whether three scores or three score and ten or fifteen, if he was able to go for fishing, fight the unrelenting sea, fight the storms with fists and arms, and fish hilsa, then no one had the audacity to call him old. There was nothing like old age. Look at Udhab! He was three scores and six, yet what cruel, ear-pricking words did Shankha's mother not speak to him! She spoke such things that even the saintliest person would react. But she never said old because Udhab never sat, tired and worn out, at any time. He had not betrayed symptoms of old age. In the fishing team, even today, Udhab was the vanguard. Even today, he could make a pedal boat if he got a friend to work with. Alone, he could venture into sea. Alone, he could tame a sea storm.

Compared to his skill of negotiating the river, sea, and storm, the youth of the five neighboring villages paled into insignificance. Udhab, therefore, was not old. Udhab's uncle and grandfather had long said, with folded hands before the panchayat, that they were now incapable of going to the sea and river with the fishing teams. They had become old; therefore, they were exempted from group fishing. The sixteen-member group sat and considered the matter; declared the two persons of Udhab's house as "in-house old."

From that day, Udhab became the master of his house. These two old men did not get any share from the common catch, nor did they pay subscriptions for the village needs. Their days were spent idly, eating and playing with the grandchildren and great-grandchildren. It was no small matter to feed two in-house old men whose income was zero but not serve a morselless in their meals. Of course, Udhab had no regrets.

If the stomach were to shrink when busy hands slump, many old people would not be tortured to death by hunger. Udhab, being a religious, person fed two in capable men and two old women, his younger grandma, and his uncle's wife. Everyone did not do that. This was a selfish world.

Udhab's two younger sons, despite being of age, never went fishing with the fishermen teams. One's mind was in the theater; the other's was in the army. Well! Was there any less theater or war than in the village? These people lived by fighting hunger, disease, storm, flood, drought, and small and big cyclones every year. What was the need of a battlefield and an external enemy! And the village becomes a theater, with black marketers and villains on the center stage. The competitive farce of the politicians was going on here; what was the need of joining a theater or war party?

The day they were fourteen, Udhab Mangual had presented them before the Panchayat. The fishing teams of the village had gathered there, and Udhab, according to his capacity, had distributed ghee cakes and sweetened fried paddy to the villagers. When the "son's-dedication-to-the-village" ritual was over, the sons of Udhab were counted among the capable fishermen in Abhayapur.

As responsible members of the village, they were registered in the fishing groups. Now, paying subscriptions for feasts and festivals of the village was mandatory for them. Only when one attained the age of fourteen would he be counted as a pledged member of the village brotherhood. But it was not an automatic fact. If he couldn't catch fish, control the boat, net, and navigate river and sea, he was fit for nothing. Even after they ate the ghee cakes and sweetened, fried paddy, the villagers never accepted them as responsible humans and head-sold brothers, nor did they admit them to the fishing groups.

Udhab had not made all his sons familiar with the alphabet, but had taught them to recognize the river and sea fish, one by one. He had taught them the nature and behavior of all types of fish, their moods and patterns of movement according to weather and season, the scales of fish, tails, wings, eyes, the style of swimming, the reactions to danger, form, color, nature and character. Such was the depth of knowledge and skills imparted, that his sons sang out the names, forms, complexions, and characteristics of the fish without looking at the sea or river, similar to a good priest who recites the lines from the Gita and Bhagabat without looking at the texts.

Udhab wonders how, when he is not able to remember the names of ten to fifteen grandchildren, how his sons sing out about sixty names of different fish and describe their form and character! Of course, the names of the fish are always at the tip of the tongue of Udhab. He may confuse the names of his grandchildren, but never the names of the fish. If a fisher boy forgets the names of fish, then even if he recites the names of gods, his fate would be sealed. It is impossible for him to return from the sea with boatloads of fish. The fish would go its own way, the net in another. Recognizing the fish, season wise, reading their nature and character, and weaving nets accordingly, Udhab had established himself as a master. If net traps are not fish-specific, the father and son would be awake the whole night, but the net would be empty-not a fish inside.

But how can man devise as many different traps as there are fishes? Can man match God's creative mystery? Of course, many kinds of fish are caught in the nets, but many more escape through the squares of the trap nets. It's more difficult to tame the smaller fish than the bigger ones. The immediate proof is the two younger sons of Udhab-Bhagyadhar and Benudhar. With them, the youngest daughter, Girima. The four elder sons are true disciples of the father; the three elder daughters are the mother's pupils. But as the two younger sons outwit the father, the youngest daughter also rides over the mother. Ah, simply a virago!

Of course, in this, Udhab's complicity is more. Why did Udhab, instead of familiarizing them with fish and dry fish, take his two younger sons and youngest daughter to school to study alphabets? However cunning and alert the fish may be, it is difficult to escape the expert hands of a genuine fisherman. The fisher folk are famous as Kaibarta, as none escapes them but letters, alphabets! What to speak of the fishermen? Even now the human race has not escaped the grip of letters. Man does not tame the letters. The letters tame men.

Learning a few letters brings about a change in man's behavior, dress, conversation, and even the heart. But a little learning is always dangerous. As Bhagyadhar says, "He would hold the flute and harmonium, not the oar." Benua is adamant that he would not fight the stormy sea, but Pakistan in the war. Udhab knows a bit about war, but the new generation? What do they know about the sea or war? They know only hard cash and revelry. And for that, leaving the family business, one has joined the theater, and another, business.

Joining the war, of course, is serving the country. There is fame. Udhab's father-in-law's village Chandanpur's Paika boy, Bikram Balabantray, has gone to the army. Paika is a warrior caste in Odisha. The boy has gone not for money, but for the country, because he is from the family of warriors. In his blood flows the tradition of war. But the fisherman boy, Benudhar Mangual, what is he? What is his family background?

Girima, being a woman, talks like a man. She argues with

her father, "If the fisherwomen, daughters, and daughters-in-law go out and bargain with the businessmen in the village fair, why should they not hold the oars?" In truth, the fishermen catch fish, but the fisherwomen recognize the fish more. Getting the extra fish from the fish warehouse, the fishermen hand it over to the women. Isolating the different kinds of fish, the women only make dry fish. Because of the culinary skill of the women, they know more about the taste of the rohu head or hilsa tail than the eating mouths of the men folk.

What does the fisherman know as to how much salt is required for what kind of fish in making dry fish? The fisherman is haughty and wild; the fisherwoman is calm and quiet. The matter is not ended by catching fish. The real work is to store the carefully isolated fish, to cook according to the type of the fish, and to serve in style. Spices are needed for fish, true, but all kinds of fish do not match all spices. All fish do not taste the same. Moreover, all varieties of fish are not good for health all the time. The fisherwoman knows from experience which fish would suit the body in what season.

The youngest daughter, Girima, knows the varieties of fish, but does not know how to cook. She has no interest in cooking. She is fond of catching fish. She is ever ready to fight, tying the edge of her sari on her waist, to catch fish and fight with the sea and river. How could Udhab convince her that it is taboo for women to go into the sea or river in the dharma boat? Or that the scriptures have forbidden women to catch fish with a throw net? But does the wild Girima care for the orthodox rules?

Breaking his reverie, somebody calls Udhab in a commanding tone, "Father, would you go for fishing today? I would definitely go to the sea today with you. I have a great urge. What crime have I committed being a woman? In the bygone days, the girls of this village never went to the school to study, but now they are all studying in schools. Then why should I be kept away from the sea simply because women previously never went to the sea? Your grandmother, Bela, the old woman, it seems she was going to the sea and river. She was rowing the boat occasionally. She used to escape to her father's house. You have told me all this. Am I inferior to her?"

Udhab looked back. In front of him was standing Mahanadi's daughter, Girima.

She was dusky like the soft, smooth sea moss; the spring touched a soft glow of the new leaves of youth on her well-formed, rotund body, sacred like a blossoming flower. She had wavy, dark hair, thick and flowing, and a cheerful moon face. Matching the face, a pair of floating, wide eyes like sailboats in a river. She was always humming like a black bee. She had eloquent and curious eyes, shadowed by beautiful, thick, arched brows; lips shaped like cashew nuts; slightly dimpled cheeks as if they'd been fondly pressed by loving fingertips.

A swimming laugh deepened the cheeks like ripples in river water. She had a dazzling stud on the shapely nose, a neem wattle in the ear, a silver ball and bead chain threaded on a black lace tape around the neck. A carefree, hurriedly done bun hung below the nape, two strands of defiant hair hovering around the face. The sweet, sixteen-year-old fisherwoman standing before Udhab was clad in a reddish-black, stripe-bordered cotton, handloom sari.

She who wanted to challenge the sea was not an ordinary fisherwoman. She was Karubaki, the daughter of Kalinga, who had fought the mighty Ashoka and had become the youngest queen of the transformed Ashoka after the Kalinga war. Seeing her bravery, spirit, and beauty, it seems, Ashoka had attacked Kalinga. This was that fisherwoman Karubaki. The difference was in the era. Girima was the modern-day Karubaki.

Charu, Taru, and Marua had not stepped into any school. They were all married and had been packed off to their in-laws' homes before they turned fifteen. Now they were experienced housewives with their world of fish and children. Their manners were like Sankha's mother; at times, the voices of the three sisters sounded like the sharp, penetrative tone of their mother.

Previously, the wave of education had not entered the fisherman's street. But by the time Bhagu was born, the fisher children had already started going to school. A higher primary school had already been established in the village. Holding slates in hand, brothers and sisters went to school.

When Girima was admitted in the school, Drona Sir, sitting firm like the old banyan tree at the edge of the village, had asked, "What is the good name of the girl, Mangual? What's in the name of a girl? That name also fades when she goes to her in-law's house. Somebody's daughter-in-law, someone's wife, someone's mother; that's all for a female. That is enough! The name given by the father is only for two and half days, like the warbles of a cuckoo in spring."

Udhab, defiantly, had answered, "The names of my three daughters are Charu, Taru, and Marua. This child was born in the year when a severe flood came to Mahanadi. I, therefore, kept her name Girima, Mahanadi's daughter."

Four female children, born for other homes, burdens on the head of the father.

The teacher thought for a while and said, "The name does not match with the names of her elder sisters. Call her Karu for Karukala. How do you like it? A good name for the girl has occurred to me. Hey, Udhab!"

Udhab had frowned and said, "Kala? Dark! My daughter is dusky. If you admit her as Karukala, whoever hears would think that she is dark."

The teacher smiled and said, "The name of our state is Utkal, as it is the land of excellence in arts, that means kala-"

Not allowing the teacher to complete his sentence, Udhab interjected, "Write whatever you like, but don't write kala. After all, she is a girl. Why should you make my dusky daughter dark?"

The teacher looked at Udhab's face with disdain and said,"You have selected this name from Kaibarta Puran. Mahanadi's daughter, Girima. Alright, then. You call her by that name at home. But her good name I select from the history of Kalinga. Karubaki. You and I remain firm in our own ways. You don't know about Karubaki. She was the Kaibarta princess of Kalinga. Kalinga princess, Magadh Queen!"

Beauty is not a special trait of a princess. But a flawless

beauty like Karubaki's was one in a million. It's not a big deal to be beautiful-one in a million. Karubaki, over and above her beauty, was a heroic woman, too. She was an expert in boat rowing and horse riding.

Only for that, the fame of Karubaki's beauty and brains had reached the ears of Magadh emperor, Ashoka. Ashoka had failed earlier in conquering the invincible Kalinga empire. It was Karubaki's beauty that had regenerated the hope of acquiring Kalinga in the heart of Ashoka. By showing him a portrait drawn by a top artist of Kalinga, Ashoka's minister Upagupta had inspired in the king the indomitable desire to win the Kaibarta princess, Karubaki.

More than the ambition of conquering a kingdom, to gain a princess has always been a stronger desire in all men. The manin this case was the all-conquering emperor Ashoka, and the princess was the celestial glowing beauty, heroic and bold Karubaki. But the easy way of winning Karubaki was blocked the day the Kalinga prince accepted the hand of Karubaki as his queen. Ashoka was saddened receiving the news of Karubaki's marriage. But would it ever be possible for Ashoka to deviate from his aim, laden with sorrow?

The determination to have Karubaki was transformed into the resolve of conquering Kalinga by hook or by crook. With a large army, Ashoka attacked Kalinga suddenly. The heroic warriors of Kalinga bravely countered Ashoka's advances. A hundred thousand Kalinga soldiers courted death instead of fleeing the battlefield. Thousands of Kalinga soldiers were wounded, and thousands of soldiers were taken as prisoners of war.

After the defeat of the king and prince of Kalinga, brave Karubaki herself confronted the invincible conqueror Ashoka in the battlefield. Ashoka was charmed by the beauty and battle skills of Karubaki; was amazed at her bravery. Finally, with her depleted army and dwindling resources, Karubaki was defeated by the mighty Ashoka in a last-ditch battle. In the midst of the heart-rending wails of orphaned children, widows of brave soldiers, and hapless, destitute mothers, the freshly widowed Karubaki took her final farewell from her motherland. She scorned her own matchless beauty, which was the cause of immense loss of life and misery. What's the value of such beauty?

FOUR

Beauty has great power. Beauty can transform violence into nonviolence, war to peace, and hate to love. In the midst of generals like Nyagrodh and Upagupta, Karubaki declared boldly, "I would never accept the cruel, bloodthirsty wild Ashoka as my husband. If I have to lose my life for that, what fear? How is my life qualitatively superior to the lakhs of valuable lives of Kalinga?

She hadn't an iota of fear for death after having seen the death of so many of her dear ones. Therefore, she would let Ashoka kill her himself and make his hand bloody-the hand that stretched, begging for her love. The blood of the people of Kalinga and her own blood were one and the same. She was not averse to washing the feet of Ashoka with her blood.

If this human massacre was for this flesh-and-blood frame of Karubaki, could Ashoka fly his flag of victory on the inert, earthly form of Karubaki? Let Ashoka ask the god in his conscience.

The anguished, repentant, pitiful Ashoka, moved by the horrendous sight of war-torn bodies festering in the battlefield, asked, "What can Ashoka do to gain the love of Karubaki?"

"Shun violence. If he does not accept the path of swadharma, I cannot marry the wild Ashoka."

"This wild Ashoka, guided by love and nonviolence, would be changed into religious and pious Ashoka, oh divine one!" said Ashoka. Karubaki alone was the inspiration behind Ashoka's journey from violence to nonviolence, war to peace, hate to love. After Ashoka was transformed from the wild to the religious Ashoka by accepting Buddhism at the inspiration of the Kalinga Kaibarta princess, Karubaki, she held his hand as his bride. Karubaki was Ashoka's second queen. Drona Sir sang the Karubaki episode out emotionally.

Udhab had considered for some time registering his daughter's name as Karubaki Dei in the school. But wherefrom would he get a suitable groom for his daughter in this area? If Girima became Karubaki, she could not be a fish-netting fisherman's wife. For her, a Kalinga-son was required, one who, in mind and intelligence, ought to be a prince-or else a religious, transformed, Ashoka-like groom. That meant Karu would remain as the first unmarried woman of this area.

Sankha's mother was repeatedly telling him, "This knot I tie at my sari edge! The boldness with which you want your daughter to learn two letters! You'll see. She would not care for any fisher boy. She would remain unmarried. Yes, that's certain. Where would you find for her a heroic fisher prince?"

Udhab mumbled, "Everything is in the hands of the Almighty. Udhab fisherman is not doing anything, O' Sankha's mother! He is only the medium; nowhere is seen his handiwork. That unseen hand manipulates things and makes us dance to its tune."

But why should Udhab dance to the tune of the teacher's will? The name that Udhab had selected meticulously was in no way bad. A fisherwoman meant a lover of river and sea. Mahanadi's daughter Girima was, after all, a fisherwoman.

Udhab spoke out firmly. "Sir, the name which the astrologer has given, after considering the stars in her horoscope, it is not to be changed. What would her father get if the poor fisher girl is made the namesake of the Kaibarta princess Karubaki? My daughter has been born on the banks of Mahandi's branch, Hansua. I named her Girima for that reason. You may change her name, but you cannot change her horoscope, her fate. I say again that, for princess Karubaki, the Kalinga war was fought. Lakhs of Kalinga soldiers died. The waters of river Daya turned black with the tear-washed kohl of destitute women. The Kalinga kingdom lost its sheen, however beautiful, intelligent, and heroic the princess might have been. But you tell me, how many inauspicious things happened to the kingdom only for her? Why should you, therefore, write such a name?' Let my daughter's name remain Girima, Mahanadi's daughter, a genuine fisherwoman name. Let the daughter of a fisherman remain a fisherwoman. Moreover, the kings are no more. What's the fun of carrying the name of a princess?"

Dawn was breaking.

At the soft touch of the dawn breeze, from the sweaty forehead of the darkened sky, the stars had faded one by one. Washing her sleepy face in the light drizzle of a passing cloud, the morning star was rising faintly like the flickering flame of a lamp, empty of oil, showing the path to the sea through the wild Ketaki bushes to the group of fishermen straight from their beds, walking with acute concentration on the pathway in the visible darkness.

This fisherman group which moves toward the sea before break of dawn, before the morning star fades, as if possessed by ghosts in cloudy weather, looks alike externally. It appears that the fishermen live the same kind of life. But, no, their happiness may rhyme with each other's, but their sorrow is highly arrhythmic. Their happiness is comprised of a roof over the head, rice for the stomach, curry, spinach, and sweets for the mouth. But their pain, misery, and agony are not seen from outside.

Sorrow is such a submerged, quiet Satan, that it shows only a thread. The major part sucks in the blood, flesh, liver, and age unseen, relentlessly. And what's the gain in displaying sorrow? Sorrow would remain in its own place. Only aahs and oohs, sympathy, and kindness-which do not mitigate sorrow, but rather enhance the pain-suppress man all the more.

Like the little-seen joys of humans, the houses look alike from outside. Inside, there are a million problems, a billion tensions, but who keeps any note of it? Like politicians, the houses look innocuous from the outside. To the eyes, selfless and open, but beyond the eyes, selfish fences, borders, and boundaries. No house has a boundary. Looking from outside, there is unbroken friendship, God-promised vowed soul mates. But in the backyard, there are thorny wattles and canker growth, enclosures of small and big backyards, all separate, one from the other.

As a god or goddess's temple is needed in a village, so is a burning ground. No entry to a temple is tenable-not so to a burning ground. The lowly houses, spaced like garbage dumps at the edge of the village, grow in fateful clusters due to casteism.

A man from another village knows that these are the dwellings of the untouchables, even if no one tells him. Even today, they have their dwellings at a distant site from the village. Of course, people today do not call them untouchables. They are called Dalit. Naming the fisherman as Kaibarta is the same as calling the untouchables Dalits. Same meaning, same fate.

Although it is illegal to do so, the Dalits are forbidden to enter the temples in the villages. They live their whole life paying their devotion and salutations from outside. But none has the power to forbid them the cremation ground. Would it be possible to keep the corpse in the house? Yet, untouchable corpses are burnt in a distant spot. If the smoke of a Dalit corpse mingles with that of a high-caste body, the high priests of the society have warned the people for ages that a race of bastards would be born.

The Dalit group of the villages are loyal to the high-caste people. In life and death, they move on the other side of the no entry zone. The village people, out of kindness, have set apart an area in a corner of the burning ground for the Dalit bodies. The Brahmin, Karan, and Khandayat burning areas are easily spotted because a few memorial temples raise their heads here and there. In the midst of half-burnt logs, broken pitchers, and other remnants of cremation, these memorials look like angelic messengers among the messengers of the god of death, Yama; like the light of hope in the darkness of despair, like immortality in the land of death. Often, the Dalits bow to these memorials of the high-caste people while passing that way. The knee-high whitewashed memorials look like the village deities, powerful even in death.

Udhab knows that the aquatic creatures have different castes, forms, and shapes, but land-born bipeds are of one caste. Touchable or untouchable, this is a man-made cover under which man's joy, sorrow, hunger, anger; cruelty, fear, and love are all of the same hue. Brahmin tears are salty, and cobbler's tears saltless; there is no such thing.

The fisherman has understood this much, hence, he is a fisherman. In his auspicious boat, there is no caste-religion divide. If the boat does not capsize when a Brahmin rides, and sinks when a scavenger sits, then it would be certain that the boat became inauspicious because a scavenger sat; the boat was damned by sin and sank.

Last year, a group of Brahmins, with their families, went to see the Jagar mela at Dhabaleswar Shiva temple across the river. The Brahmin-loaded boat upturned in the river. Ten to twelve priests drowned to death. How could that happen? The boats following, with loads of mixed, low-caste people crossed the river safely. The devotees, after worshipping Shiva, returned by dusk. From that day, Udhab's belief has firmed up that casteism is the creation of man, not of god.

When rhyming with the neck bells of the home returning herd of cattle, the playful summer breeze forcefully blowing through the narrow spaces between coconut tree branches, sings heartwarming songs, does not it touch everyone, irrespective of caste? The temple arati cymbals and the hourly calls of the jackal- are not they heard by everyone without any discrimination? When Kundala Gosain recites the Bhagabat in his undulating voice, does everyone not hear it? Even in the Pakistani Muslim Golmasta's ears, the temple bells ring the same tune. It means men are equal.

The murky darkness has not yet receded from the thick, green caves of leaves on the bakula tree in the temple complex, nor has sleep gone from the eyes of the fisher boys. Yet they are walking behind Udhab Mangual. He is their navigator. In the small, thatched Goddess Basuli's temple of fisher caste, he is the priest. Bowing to the deities with un brushed mouths and unwashed bodies, the fishermen group is briskly walking toward the riverbank, wading through the Ketaki bush lane. Fish are not trapped in the nets if weather, moment, and chance do not combine auspiciously. Besides, the river and sea belong to all. He who goes first may catch the first batch of fish. Who would forbid them?

There is a special reason why the group is in such a hurry. Before nightfall, on the platform at the head of the village, a meeting of the sixteen brothers-gram panchayat-is scheduled. There is a big decision to make. The problem is complex. Therefore, in consideration of this, sixteen brothers would meet with the fishermen. There would be present Dronabira Sir of Kunjabedi village and from the Pakistan pada of Abhayapur, Sheikh Ghulam Mustafa alias Golmasta. Also present would be Kundala Panda of Bandana village, Gandhi Das of Sovanpur, the Chairman of Ambiki Panchayat, the sarpanch, and many others.

This area is such that on one side it holds tight to the river and on the other side the sea. Here the Brahmins, there the Muslims. While the Hindus offer sirni (a mixture of milk, ghee, honey, bananas, etc.) to the Pir, Golmasta becomes the master of ceremonies during the Durga puja, Astaprahari, Bhagabat valedictory, and other festive occasions.

Sir says pre-independent India was divided into two parts when the country achieved freedom from British rule. But if undivided India can be seen anywhere, it is in these small village clusters called Abhayapur in the Ambiki Panchayat of Erasama block, in the district of Jagatsinghpur.

There are several such India in the villages of this area because Indians, Pakistanis, and Bangladeshis live here together in peace, harmony, and joy.Like the five fingers of a hand, these villages are separate from each other, but there is no wall or partition dividing them. In the joy and sorrow of the villages, the Odia, Bengali, Hindu, and Muslims of Bangladesh and Pakistapara united like a closed fist.

They all enjoy their festivals, faiths, songs, and dances

individually, like open fingers-in their own customs, free and joyous. If Hindus and Muslims fight in the rest of the world, in Abhayapur or Ambiki Panchayat there is no sign of acrimony. Therefore, for ages they have lived here together without fear or uncertainty. Had there been the fear of violence or riots, the name of the village would have been Bhayapur, not Abhayapur.

Recounting the endless glory of God, Udhab bowed, and, taking long strides, threw back his old age and crossed the young group. Filtered through the Mango and Punang trees of the Bhuasuni ghat, the smiling face of the newborn sun was seen. Observing the youthful spirit of the old man, the young sun was laughing mirthfully.

Golmasta and some other Muslim families had taken the sea route to the Erasama area when the Hindu-Muslim riot happened in the wake of India's partition. How old had Golmasta been at that time? Twenty or twenty-five, maybe! This area was a rainforest then, a palm, date palm, kewra, and ketaki entangled jungle. During the day, the rabbits, wolves, deer, wild hens, and even the jackal moved openly. In such situations, men do not wait for permission to fell forest trees, raise farmland, and build houses. Humans, therefore, destroyed nature. Following nature's course, the human population grew. Now, there were two hundred Muslim houses. But Golmasta says with pride that they are registered refugees; therefore, they have rights on this soil. Even if they live in Pakistanpara, they are genuine Indians.

Udhab's thoughts have stuck on his old boat. A fisherman's real pride is his boat. His boat is over twenty years old. Back when Udhab's uncle's hair was graying, Udhab and his uncle, Angad Mangual, had built the boat together, toiling hard for a month. The old man had tested the boat's sea-worthiness for a month. The boat was strong, since their own hands had built it. It would have cost about ninety rupees (including the cost of wood) even at that time, had they made it paying wages to carpenters.

The carpenter would have taken a pair of dhotis over and above free food for a month. From where would Udhab have gotten so much money? Besides, Udhab stood on the inherited traditions of

Bandar village. His father and grandfather were experts in building a variety of boats. He's heard and seen how boats are built.

While growing up, he went often to Abhayapur from Bandar and learned the art of boat building. Udhab is the most efficient boat builder of the village. The carpenters of this village often take tips from him. But none of his sons have inherited his expertise in boat building. They are not to blame; it is Udhab's fault. If the father does not lead the way, what can the son do?

The boat and the two rafts made by Udhab were so strong that the sons never had a chance to make boats. If one boat follows a school of hilsa, then not one but a dozen netters, oarsmen, and catchers are required. Udhab himself, his four sons, and a few others of the village venture out together for community fishing in the hilsa season, so there's no need for another boat.

Moreover, wood for boat-making is not available as easily as before. Felling the coastal jungles, one could forcibly occupy acres and acres of land illegally. Udhab's heart sinks when he sees the occasional hapless trees standing alone. Even if he feels the need for a new boat, his hand goes numb when he thinks about cutting a live tree. Therefore, ages have passed with him simply repairing his one boat.

But this year, he must make a new boat. His time has passed well under the grace of mother Basuli, but how would his sons' time pass smoothly? He is, therefore, planning to make a new boat before his strength ebbs. He is only waiting for Manguli Pundit to suggest an auspicious time. He would also teach his sons the art of boat-making, taking this opportunity.

Rumors are afloat that somewhere a sinister war is about to begin. Let the war start if it must, but let not Benua join the army. Who knows where-or how-Bikram Balabantray is? Wherever he is, let him fight. Let him not come to the village, but let him not come in a plane decked with flowers. Udhab knows this much; that those who earn salary joining the army would travel normally in the general compartments of trains.

Even if a telegram is sent that someone's mother is dying, they never get enough money to travel by airplane. One or two of them, of course, have come by plane covered with flowers-but not alive. Only when they die at the battlefront do the low-paid employees of the army get a chance to fly by plane for free.

Man's real form is seen when danger befalls him. The people of Ambiki Panchayat know, more or less, that Udhab Mangual's moral conscience and spiritual mind are modeled on the influence of the Bhagabat. He is a selfless, patriotic, philanthropic, and honest fisherman. But, sometimes, Udhab encounters the self-centered man from within, and he shrinks before himself.

Once, the fishermen of this region were adventurous sailors. They were saving the sea traders from the pirates; protecting the forts from external aggression. During war, the fishermen were the military power of the kings. The ancestors of Udhab, the Bandar fisherman, had once saved the British merchants from Portuguese pirates.

Only because of the ancestors of Udhab had the Englishmen entered Odisha, set up commercial centers, and ultimately ruled Odisha. Otherwise, at the hands of the Portuguese pirates that day, eight Englishmen would have earned their watery grave. Because of this daredevilry and the ruthless temper of the fishermen community, they gained the patronage of the royal powers of Kujanga.

They received the authorization to fish in the rivers and streams and maintain their families. The Shendha kings had their sway over the land, but the fisher folk were the kings of the entire watery kingdom. The fishermen were living like royalty. There were enough fish in the rivers. Catching fish and making a living from it was a traditional profession of the fishermen, and a monopolistic right.

The kings were not tyrannical toward the fishermen. Because of this, the fishermen were loyal to the kings. The fishermen, however, were gifting loads of fish to the kings on festive occasions like Sunia, Dasahara, and marriage ceremonies. Therein lay the pride and prestige of the fishermen. The kings reciprocated with due respect. In an atmosphere of ruler-subject goodwill and amity, the life of the fisherman was tension free.

After the British took over the reins of administration, the kings lost their power and authority. The kings became subjects of the British. The property of the kings came under the control of the British government. A small portion of their property was left with them for their sustenance, yet the income on such property was taxed. The kings became taxpayers.

Udhab has not witnessed this, but he had heard that the king of Kujanga, the Shendha king, Chakradhwaja, was a proud freethinker. He did not pay his tax in due time, and, joining hands with the king of Khurda, had declared war on the British. It had only been one year since the British had taken over Odisha. Chakrddhwaj's reign had not completed even the first year. Considering the defiance of the young king as insubordination, the British had arrested Chakradhwaja and the king of Khurda and had put them in prison in the Barabati Fort of Cuttack.

The group of fishermen, listening to Udhab's story, followed him briskly, like the cart behind the yoked bullocks. The past that was rising in Udhab Mangual's memory was indicative of the heroics of the fishermen. To ease the strain of walking, Udhab sang in a mirthful voice in satire of the British.

After India became free because of the Abolition of Zamindari Act in 1952, the fishermen lost their rights to the forests and forest products. The free wood they were getting to make boats during the time of the kings and Zamindars was also denied to them. Some people, of course, were making boats stealing wood from the forests. They argued that, if anyone could clear the jungles to make arable land and make enclosures for prawn-fishing, thereby becoming rich, then why should the fishermen be honest and be poor? What justice was this?

Udhab knows that such arguments are made alluding to Bharat Mandal, Bhairab Majhi, Ranabir Maiti, Ajoy Mana, and other Bangladeshi refugees, as well as the Brahmins, Karans, and Khandayats who fell the jungle trees to make agricultural land and prawn farms and get currency notes and voting rights. But why blame the refugees alone? Who is a saint in any of this?

[2] Sagara was a mythical king whose thousand children created the seven seas.

Bhairab Majhiis highly criticized, yet who in this area has not eaten in his house? Who has not begged him for help in difficulties? He is not only counted as a rich man, but also as a honorable man. Even then, the jealousy of people is unrelenting. But Majhi does not care a bit for such things.

Udhab gets along well with Majhi, but with Bharat Mandal, he has intimacy. Udhab knows that Mandal's refugee life is not a straight river. There are many bends and turns, many ghats, several gorges and recesses-exactly like Udhab's meandering life.

FIVE

One of the beautiful branches of river Padma is Madhumati. Like the sub branches growing out of the branches of trees, Madhumati too has divided herself into three separate streams: Harinaghati, Bangara, and Marjati. Within the encirclement of many big ones, small rivers and sub-rivers are precariously stuck in many poor miserable east Bengal villages, like flies fluttering in spider webs. Whether a Pakistani or a Bangladeshi village, they were originally rooted in India.

In a remote village, nurtured by the loving care of the tangled rivers and streams of Khulna district of what was then East Pakistan, Bharat Mandal was born. His father's name was Himachal Mandal. Bharat Mandal had named his seven sons Sarala Das Mandal, Jagannath Das Mandal, Ananta Das Mandal, Upendra Bhanja Mandal, Utkalmani Mandal, and Madhubabu Mandal. His three daughters had been named Madhumati, Marjati, and Padma. With sons, sons-in-law, daughters-in-law, and grandchildren, Bharat Mandal's family is large and wide like the sea.

In this area, so to speak, every family is of the Sagara dynasty. This region, for Bharat Mandal, is not the miserable, small, riverine village almost stifled by the embrace of Madhumati and Marjati in his erstwhile Khulna in Bangladesh. That village-where he was born-now appears remote and uncertain. It's not merely beyond a country, but beyond this birth.

It has been two scores and ten years from 1949 to 1999 since leaving Khulna, his country and village. Bharat Mandal, too, has advanced from adolescence to old age. How soon man's youth, spirit, dreams, and age fade away as you look ahead! Where do they come from, and where do they go? Had he known the place, Bharat Mandal would have snatched back, by hook or crook, his youthful body, golden days, and the unarticulated dreams of his heart!

When Bharat Mandal was just eighteen, he was shouting, "Bharat Mata Ki Jai," and, "Gandhiji Zindabad," joining the Gandhi-led freedom movement. His bosom friend, Hyder Ali, had joined his voice with Bharat Mandal's. Hindus and Muslims, in one voice, were shouting, "Bharat Mata Ki Jai" and "Mahatma Gandhi Zindabad."

But once the cause to which they had dedicated their souls and shouted slogans was successful, suddenly-and for no apparent reason-even the word Bharat became taboo in their village. The voice of Hyder Ali had a strange transformation as well. Bharat Mandal was not able to comprehend anything.

East Bengal, Padma, Madhumati, Harinaghati, the Marjati Rivers, none had moved an inch from their original places. How then could they be separated from motherland Bharat-India? Moreover, how could his village get connected with Pakistan, sixteen hundred kilometers away? What was this Pakistan? Where had it been until now?

Bharat Mandal was bewildered seeing all the inexplicable changes. Because of long-held habit, from his lips used to slip, "Bharat MataKi Jai," and, "Mahatma Gandhi Ki Jai." His father and grandfather warned him, "Hereafter, say 'Pakistan Ki Jai.' India is the enemy country."

"Enemy country! Motherland India?" Bharat had asked.

"Yes. Where does the enemy live? The enemy is in the mother's womb. Although India and Pakistan have the same umbilical cord, now they have snapped into two. Now there is a border dividing the territories of India and Pakistan. Earlier, Bengal was split, causing a political divide. But between East Bengal and

West Bengal, the cultural ties are intact. After independence, East Bengal was included in Pakistan, but that relation, too, snapped. Division, division, and division was the fate of patriotic Bengalis."

That day, as a result of the division of the country, Bharat Mandal was among the stateless, homeless, oppressed seeking for shelter with his father, Himachal Mandal, uncles Shankar and Nepal Mandal, his mother, aunt, and sisters. His grandpa, Kasinath, and grandma, however, continued to live in the Pakistani village, embracing the torture of the new masters, as they could not forego the attachment to their place of birth. Himachal Mandal would have stayed on his native soil had he not been compelled by their tormentors to change his sons name-Bharat-to something unconnected with India. When his family was tortured, Himachal left his home and birth place which was no more India with his entire family for good.

In the beginning, these ill-fated and homeless people were not called refugees. They were called migrants. It was hoped that they would return to their homes and country once the situation improved. But they never thought of returning; they remained as refugees in different states of India.

Although it was a problem to settle so many refugees permanently, the hospitable Indian government made arrangements to settle the refugees on humanitarian grounds. As per the policy of central government, different states took up the responsibility of settling the refugees. The government of Odisha, at that time, had settled about twenty-five thousand refugees. Himachal Mandal, at first, had lived in the refugee camps of West Bengal. The West Bengal government, in the first phase, had sheltered one million refugees. Each family was given some monetary help with the agreement that the refugees would pay back the amount in twenty years.

Himachal Mandal and his twenty-year-old son were recruited as "donkey men" in the Hooghly harbor. They were working day and night, carrying heavy weight on their backs. The British, for this reason, designated that post as Donkey man.

Like Himachal and Bharat Mandal, Dhanu Mandal of Barisal

district and many other refugees like him were eking out a living as donkey men. It was immaterial whether they understood the meaning of donkey. They had no hesitation in identifying themselves as donkey men.

A few landless Odias were also working there as donkey men. One of the Odias understood the meaning of donkey. If a coolie is called a coolie, he may not mind. But a load-carrying man would definitely mind if he is called a donkey. When the Odias visited their villages they never spoke about their positions to their wives as it was embarrassing for them.

Had some woman, while washing her bangles with the soap brought by her husband, bragged that her husband was working as a donkey man in Calcutta, then the school children would have chided her in the open market as "donkey, donkey!" Who knows; the elders might have alienated them and asked them to do penance!

But whatever the designation, at least they were getting regular salary every month. The poor people were managing their homes; is it absolutely necessary for a poor man to have prestige and designation? After some time, it was heard that a kindly port officer was thinking in terms of changing the word donkey. But the Odias and East Bengal refugees had never thought of appealing to change the insulting designation because they knew that whatever slipped from the mouths of the Englishmen was of scriptural authority in India.

One day, however, the port officer proposed to change the designation into something respectable. But the experienced trade union leaders opposed his efforts to change the term.

They asked, "Since long we have been maintaining our living by this donkey man post, what is the necessity of changing the designation now? Would there be any monetary gain for the donkeys? If there is no monetary gain, why should we give up this dear donkey designation? If you decide to change, let there be a hike in our salaries. If this kind officer does not have any ulterior motive, why does he try to create an identity crisis by changing this age-old designation?"

This caused waves in the minds of the labor leaders. This

donkey man had come as a brainwave in the white minds of the British, since the time they'd used men as donkeys at Calcutta Port. That was not insulting; rather, that was the correct identifying adjective for the tireless, un-protesting donkey's-burden-bearing men. The only creature that bears heavy burdens silently, even when the back breaks, is the donkey. A small creature, but how tolerant, powerful, and how selfless and docile! None have seen its raised ears shaking in protest.

Therefore, when the Englishmen gave names like donkey or monkey to Indians, the poor natives, without understanding the meaning, swelled with pride at being addressed as such in English. The British officers gave titles like writer and babu to the clerks. The Secretariat of the Ministers and bureaucrats even today is called the Writer's Building at Calcutta. Even today, the Odias, Bengalis, and other Indians feel honored when addressed as babu.

Why then wouldn't the donkeys have felt honored as donkey men? Whatever the meaning, since the Englishmen had created such posts, and as the words were English, the donkeys thought any attempt at changing those names was insulting. Maybe the Bengali port officer had some hidden political motive. Many doubted that the officer might gain something by this donkey abolition act. Otherwise, whose heart would bleed whether these poor people were donkeys or monkeys or even gutter insects? Yes, crocodile tears are shed by many a leader and officer. Hence, if the kindly officer was to gain something, why not raise the salaries of the donkey men?

When the authorities declared that no extra allowance or salary hike be given to change the donkey designation, the situation took the form of an agitation. The donkeys were divided into two groups-supporting or opposing the change-and clashes began.

It was demanded that the officer, from whose fertile mind the donkey abolition thought had originated, must be punished. When the situation was out of control, the apprehensive Odia leaders and Himachal Mandal, Bharat Mandal, and Dhanu Mandal of Barisal, forsaking the allurement of the donkey designation and the job, thought of going elsewhere.

At that time, because of problems of space regarding the settlement of one million refugees in West Bengal, it was decided to shift some refugees to other areas. Considering the Andaman suitable for the living of the farmers and fishermen refugees from East Bengal, about two thousand refugees were sent to the Andaman despite their protests. In that list were the families of Himachal Mandal and Dhanu Mandal of Barisal.

In the Andaman, paddy and fish were available. The Bengalis had no dearth of their favorite food. But there was no Bengali culture. The Bengalis are not only cultured, they are intensely proud of their culture. The Bengali's pride for language and national pride is incomparable.

Himachal Mandal was a great lover of his culture. Determined not to go to Andaman, he took the sea route overnight to coastal Odisha with Bharat Mandal and the entire family. Clearing the jungle on the hinterland between the river-entangled Erasama and the Bay of Bengal, he developed for himself a house plot and some arable land in Abhayapur.

Himachal Mandal learned from the Odias that Bengalis from West Bengal had been living in the Erasama, Jagatsinghpur, and Kujanga areas for some time. Bengali administration had started in these areas since the promulgation of the Sunset Law by the British. Nobel Laureate Rabindranath Tagore's elder brother had purchased the Pandua estate in Erasama at that time. The poet had spent quite some time in the Pandua mansion, charmed by the natural beauty of Erasama.

For Bengalis like Himachal Mandal coming from the land of river Padma, there was no fear or concern for the sea, rivers, storms, floods, or cyclones. Therefore, Himachal Mandal and his family slept peacefully while the roar of the sea threatened the earthen walls and thatched roofs. They had experienced far more sinister threats in East Bengal from rivers and seas. They did not have an iota of fear. Cyclones, floods and, sea storms were as mundane as a throat-clearing cough, which they used to ward off with a snap of finger.

During their one-year sojourn in the refugee camps, of all

the relationships which the family of Himachal Mandal had with the other families, the twenty-year-old Bharat Mandal's relationship with the sixteen-year-old daughter of Dhanu Mandal, Belarani, was deeper, a bit special. They never spoke to each other; only their eyes spoke and exchanged undefinable feelings. How does the heart hear the language of the eye? What strange antics of the maker!

In the painful days of refugee life, in the days of the despair of having lost everything, in the uncertainty of what lay ahead, many young men and women united their hearts without words. No promises were made either. It created a feeling of getting back everything, in spite of having lost everything, and it was flowing in their veins unconsciously. It was not the time to propose or speak of feelings, nor was it the time to take adventurous steps to realize youthful dreams.

That time would have come. The opportunity would have come. The dreams could have been realized, had the families of Himachal Mandal and Dhanu Mandal been settled at one place. But when Bharat knew that Dhanu Mandal was being transported to the Andaman, he told his father, "I think we, too, could go to the Andaman with the family of Dhanu Uncle. The government has prepared the list of names. It wouldn't be proper if we refuse."

Himachal was in deep distress. Going to Odisha and living there illegally-with difficulty-was not a small dilemma or conflict of will and fate. Even then, his young son, instead of endorsing his father's views, was entertaining thoughts of moving to Andaman. Himachal had thrown his tantrums.

"You want to go to the Andaman? Go, be gone! Live there like an animal eating and drinking. There you would not live like a Bengali, but a prisoner. Andaman is not the place for a refugee. Go, go! Get lost."

Bharat Mandal understood. He did not think of Andaman any more, but could not wipe Bela from his memory. Belarani was at her own place; life flew on its own course. It was nothing new. Since the beginning of creation, poetry books have not been able to record the love at first sight of all Bharats and Belaranis.

Such things ring and hum in the mind and soul until one dies and mingles in the dust.

Bharat consoled himself, "Who knows how true or false is the language of the eyes?" He hasn't heard Belarani's mind, her feelings and thoughts. Maybe it had been one-sided. He'd been stretching his hands to pluck the sky flowers, maybe. "Well, let it go."

But Belarani's mind became clear when she said with tears in her eyes to her mother in the refugee camp, "Talk to father. We'll not go to the Andaman. There, Bengalis don't survive. We'll go to Odisha. Odisha, they say, is very beautiful, like the twin sister of Bengal. Cooking and food habits are almost same. Language sounds similar. Himachal Uncle is going to Odisha. Let's join them."

Before mother could speak, Bela's father, Dhanu Mandal, screamed, "Am I a criminal or a thief? Illegally, would I go? Stealthily fell the jungles, illegally, and take up farm land without rights on another's soil? Live my entire life illegally? My children, clan, and my own people would live like unlawful inhabitants? We are going legally as registered refugees to the Andaman with our heads held high.

"Let there be no Bengalis in the Andaman. I bet that if one Bengali family is banished into an African jungle, roots and shoots of the Bengali race would go very deep. The African jungle would become a Bengali forest. The tigers and bears of the jungle would begin to roar in Bengali language. Because the Bengali knows how to keep alive his language and culture."

But Dhanu could not gauge his daughter's mind. Belarani looked at her father with tearful eyes. She had no answer. His daughter's sorrow certainly pained him inside. But he said in a gruff manner, "Why did the ghost of Odisha possess your mind? What for? What's there? The same poverty, flood, and drought, cyclone, storm, epidemics, illiteracy as in East Bengal."

Bela went out crying. Wiping her tears, she packed her things to fold the tent. Tying up her raw dreams and hiding the untraceable part of her heart, she locked her heart and threw away the keys, putting up a brave front.

Bharat realized everything. Bharat's sister, Rupa, was a friend of Bela. Retelling the entire thing before brother Bharat, she cried again. Bharat cried too; not in the eyes, but in the heart. Blood rises into the eyes of those who cry in the heart. Rupa knew that.

Trying to console her brother, she said, "Bela told me to tell you this much-what is not possible in this birth may be fruitful in the next birth. Man is never born to be a refugee for seven births."

By then, Belarani and her parents had already been ready to be transported to the Andaman. At the time of parting, the two fathers embraced each other. The two friends and the two mothers clasped and wished each other good luck. But the lovers never had that good fortune. The distance between Erasama and the Andaman, like a landless flood, transgressed both shores. This side, the Bay of Bengal, and on the other side the Bay of Bengal; who knows how many births separate them?

Now the face of Belarani has faded away in cataracted memory. Belarani's tearful, dreamy, lovelorn doe eyes swim in the waters of the river Hansua even today. Everywhere the eyes can see from Abhayapur, there is only water, water, and Belarani's eyes.

Memory is never worn out, never gets old, and never dies. The memory of river Padma and Bela's memory are fresh, beautiful, and intense. There is no hope to realize the dream, only a painful, sacred joy in yearning. Its name is love. Yes, love.

But it cannot be said that Bharat's life was unfulfilled because Bela could not be his wife. That he loves his wife less, even he himself or none has guts to claim. Yet it cannot be said that his life was full in all respects. There is space for many more stars than are shining in the sky, but can we say that the sky is not full?

Life is like the sky, never full, never empty. Now calm, now stormy, now bright with the sun, now cloudy. At times the full moon, at times the crescent, and at times the new moon, but now pitch dark. But fully or partially, who is not in love with life?

Bharat Mandal thinks, at times, let not my children suffer my untold unfulfillment. But how innocent man really is! Are his children beyond this world? How can there be no unfulfilled desire in their lives? He has never kept his children half-fed, but where is that parental authority on his children's dream that he would say, "Alright! Be satisfied with this."

No, the mind is never content. Was it ever content in his grandfather's time, and would it ever be content in the times of the grandchildren and great-grandchildren?

Such thoughts, at times, console Bharat Mandal. For that, Udhab is such a good friend of his. Walking toward the river and sea, many times Bharat has spoken of Belarani to Udhab. Whenever Belarani occurs in conversation, Bharat gets transformed into a twenty-year-old youth. That day, the fish-laden boat sways to the brink of sinking.

The long morning walk is over. Udhab is listening to the story of Belarani with the sea in front of him. He battles with the sea to eke out a living. The long walk ends, but the story does not end. Memory lingers. Life is unfulfilled like this. Sighing deeply, Udhab makes himself light hearted. Now, rest of the life is to guide the boat with strong hands; whatever remains of it. Who knows the fate of a released boat?

Spreading heady romance, Chaitra, the honeyed month of spring ended soon. It gave pleasure, also pain, pleasure for the simple reason that this year the Chaitra festivities ended with pomp and ceremony; pain for the basic fact that the traditional horse dance, which had been celebrated since the days of the Dasa kings, was not held during the festival. Horse dancing and the horse fair disappeared from this region long ago. The lads of modern times do not appreciate such dances anymore.

The horse dance, it seems, identifies the fisherman as fisherman. Oh, dear! If people recognize the fisherman as fisherman, what is your objection? If the horse dance is stopped, would people recognize the fisherman as Brahmin, Karan, or Khandayat? Caste is the scale of the human body. If you remove the scales, new scales would grow. When the snake abandons its scales, it regenerates. The snake remains a snake. It does not become a tiger. Whatever business one does, his caste is never lost.

The adage that business is awkward for the lower caste is outdated. Udhab Mangual, Bharat Mandal, and Bhairab Majhi of this region are engaged in fish trade not because they are fishermen; even the Brahmin, Kundala Panda, Khandayat Kapil Pradhan, Sarapanch Kumpani Soin, Chairman Tahali Mohanty, farmer Banchu Tarai, Oilman Mathuri Sahu, the cobbler Dhobei Behera, the Khaddar clad, non-Khaddar clad ministers, past ministers, and the homeless and door less all-all are in the fish trade. No need to ask about their caste or gotra because all are fishermen by profession.

Udhab, Bharat Mandal, and Bhairab Majhi, who for generations have been fishermen, are poor. But the Brahmin, Karan, Khandayat, and social workers of the higher caste are now rich fishermen traders. Therefore, in the Kujanga and Erasama areas, there are two classes-rich fishermen and poor fishermen; the trammel netters and the seine netters. Those who have no prawn enclosures are not counted as human beings.

The throw net fishermen are poor. Carrying the nets of their forefathers and their fishing boats, they catch fish from the river and sea, risking their lives. In the fish dumps, they lie in wait, watching the throw nets, braving sun and storms. Selling their catch dirt cheap to the rich traders, they barely make both ends meet in their large, needy families.

The high-caste, rich traders filter money from the sea with their trawlers. Now they have prawn enclosures, as they lost money on the trawlers. In this area of intertwined rivers and streams, wherever one looks, big and small prawn enclosures meet the eye. The rich have big, lake like enclosures, and the poor have small, pond like enclosures.

Prawn culture in this region is a sort of aristocracy. Earlier people asked, in order to assess the aristocracy and status of others, "How many acres of land do you have? How many pairs of bullocks? How many coconut trees? How many harvest dumps? How many fishing boats?" Now they ask, "How many prawn enclosures do you have? How large are those? "If you are not owners of prawn enclosures, then you are small-fish-selling, poor fishermen, fit for pity.

For money, Brahmins have even opened shoe stores. But they are not cobblers. They are still Brahmins. Why, then, are the fishermen averse to the horse dance? Would the fisherman ever become a Brahmin, forsaking the horse dance?

When the titillating spring breeze touches the veins and sinews of trees and leaves, Udhab Mangual becomes morose and gloomy. The East Bengal refugees in transit-the fishing friend Bharat Mandal, the permanent resident of Nagaritutha, West Bengal, Bengali Bhairab Majhi, the Pakistani Muslim, permanent resident of Pakistanpara in Abhayapur, Golmasta, alias Sheik Ghulam Mustafa, also become true and faithful partners of Udhab's gloom. They are each other's friends in joy and sorrow.

There was a time when Bharat Mandal, Bhairab Majhi, and Golmasta, frenzied, were participating in the spring festival, enjoying soulfully the horse dance of the Odia fishermen.

Every year, when the full moon day drew near, Udhab used to go down memory lane, watching the half-smiling spring waves of river Hansua. He is a boatman. He used to be proud of his Kaibarta caste when the spring horse came dancing to his door; proud of being a descendant of the Dasa dynasty. The spring horse is not a mere bamboo horse mask dance. That horse has a soul and heritage value.

The spring horse is the deity of his fate, the family goddess, Laxmi. The refined rice, the nylon rice flake eating-modern youth do not understand that. The youth today are not ashamed of dancing half-naked in films or operas, but are ashamed of the horse dance, the ritual dance of their forefathers for the appeasement of their family deity.

Bhairab Majhi's younger son, Kartika, has now joined the Ma Sarala opera group of Basu Rath of Jagatsinghpur. Bharat Mandal had had an eye on the boy to have him as his son-in-law for his darling youngest daughter, Padma. Kartika had flunked his bachelor's degree and gotten frustrated searching for jobs. He was not interested in fishing or farming. He was educated, why should he do the work of the illiterate? However his father tried to convince him, he refused to be convinced.

"Oh, you mad fellow. Even the graduates, the master's degree holders and engineers from Brahmin, Karan, and Khandayat families are now earning thousands doing prawn farms. What is the shame in the fish business?"

He dared his father, "Give me one hundred thousand rupees. I will begin a large prawn culture, buy a motorcycle. I would do fish business in style. Can you give it to me?

"No, that's not in our fate. We are fishermen by caste. The rivers and streams are ours. We would catch fish wearing loin cloths, risking our lives, eating half a bellyful, backs naked. Is this the aristocracy of the fishermen clan?"

In the end, Kartika, denouncing fishing and defying his father, joined an opera party. He brought shame to the name of his father. As the other five sons were illiterate, they joined their father in farming and fishing and lived like the other fishermen.

In Padmapur, Harishpur, and other villages, there was a Bengali concentration from West Bengal. Majhi brought five daughters-in-law from these villages. See whether this lad gets a dancing girl from somewhere! Bhairab Majhi does not count him as his son. He is too big for his boots.

Despite this, Bharat Mandal still has hope. He would be happy if his Padma got an educated fisherman. Padma is so beautiful, exactly like the river Padma. Elder to her are two more daughters, Madhumati and Marjati. Although nineteen and twenty, they are a thread less than Padma in all respects.

Bharat has given Odia names to his sons only because Odisha is their destiny. His sons are pure Odias. That's good. When in Rome, do as the Romans do, but daughters are for other homes.

Who knows whether they are destined to marry in some families in the west? The question of East Bengal does not arise anymore. Even after Bangladesh became independent of Pakistan, the Muslim torture of Hindus did not end. Every day, refugee groups cross the border and migrate to India. The leaders of this region settle them illegally only for their votes. Entering their names in the voter list, handing over chits to them, and winning the election are all that matters. Their work is over.

Alas, the poor Bengalis are neither here nor there. No one counts them as people of this region. The leaders use them as medium for votes and exploit them, but never make any legal arrangement to count them as citizens of this land. Here they are the eyesores of the locals, hated by the environmentalists. In this region, the refugees are a helpless lot.

Bharat Mandal had made up his mind to give his elder daughter in marriage to Midinapur Bengali families and wished to give his darling youngest Padma to Bhairab Majhi's house to keep her nearer to him. But the lad kept moving with the theater party from Calcutta to Midinapur, and to Surat in Gujarat. What did fate have in store for the girl?

Udhab Mangual has given his word that he would mediate, and in the coming December, he would get Padma married to Bhairab Majhi's son. If he arranged some money, he could finalize the marriage. Let the son-in-law buy a motorcycle. If he wants to construct a prawn enclosure, let him. But let him raise a home with Padma, forsaking the theater group, and live near him.

It seems Udhab's younger middle son, Bhagyadhar, and Bhairab's youngest son, Kartik, were college mates. Kartik flunked out, and Bhagyadhar passed. Bikram Balabantaray of Chandanpur was also their classmate in the same college. The three were close friends.

Kartik and Bhagyadhar, during their childhood, sang in tandem the ascending and descending order, along with dancing the horse dance in such a manner that ghosts and vampires would listen with rapt attention. Even if alerted by apprehensions, the birds used to forget flying, the vampires forgot to suck blood. So melodious were their voices, even sweeter than sugar. But Udhab did not allow Bhagyadhar to join the theater group. The opera owners were worse than old bullock traders. Blood sucking misers. They would make you work like donkeys, but salary? Better not ask for one.

In the circus, the animals eat well. Otherwise, they won't dance, and would simply sleep and not obey orders. But the party men of operas eat filth, yet dance better than tigers or bears. Their situation is worse than the circus animal's. What pleasure does the lad derive from drama? God alone knows!

In the modern theater parties, there are raw pleasures because young girls now have joined the operas. No longer do the boys, painted as young women, attract the attention of the viewers. Bubbly young lasses are performing risqué dances to wild rhythms. With them, the lads must be romancing. Well, let them do whatever they please, but let them not burn. Let them not tarnish the name of the families. Let them return home and settle down in life with a homely woman from a good household.

The male is like a brass pot. When hot, it would darken, but when it cools down and is washed, it again dazzles. The female is an earthen pot. Once it is used, it is gone; unwanted and sinful. Yet none have seen the sons of Bhairab Majhi going astray. Kartik Majhi must not be flirting with the theater girls like the others. This was crystal clear to Udhab Mangual.

Sitting on the village altar, enjoying the playful spring breeze, Udhab's mind was wandering between the sky and the netherworld. The rise and fall of the music of the horse dance of those times was ringing in his ears. Udhab Mangual hummed the riding and alighting songs himself, waiting for the others to come. The meeting would begin when all would gather.

Everyone says that the boatman was born from the earlobes of Vishnu
Since the Dasa kings, they have played their glories under the sun
Before that, I ask, about the deluge of the Brahma
I'll speak of how the divine fisherman was born.
From the humming, he moved to singing the descending order,
When the deluge came, there were none in the world
The water flooded twenty-four netherworlds
While the formless one was in the sun

Udhab had closed his eyes in a trance. His ears opened. He heard the mixed rhythms of the drum, timbrel, and the mahuri. The Raut and his wife were dancing to the rhythms of the horse dance. Udhab was watching in his imagination, on the screen of his closed eyelids. With them were dancing the drummers and the fan bearers. The spectators, too, were dancing uninhibitedly. Moving from door to door, the horse dancers had now started the appealing song for tips in front of Mangual's house.

> *Changing the clothes into headgear,*
> *The poor implore your grace.*
> *Don't be angry*
> *The world would see your eternal fame*
> *But if we return empty from your doors*
> *Who would be blamed for that?*

Then piled up were coins, rice, and sarees, in jingling sequence on the edge of Udhab's reverie. Flapping its wings, a bird flew away from the branch overhead, toward an unknown destination. Udhab was jolted back into his present reality. A long sigh was released and followed the bird.

From a distance was seen Gandhi Das of Sobhanpur, a Sarvodaya leader, walking with firm, quick steps on the pathway across a field. Gandhi Das, who had never seen Mahatma Gandhi, resembled Gandhiji, although a good measure short of the Mahatma's stature.

SIX

Gandhi Das was not Gandhi by surname. Gandhi was the name given by his father. The bloody history behind this naming had once stunned with sorrow not only this region of India but also the entire world. Even today, the old freedom fighters drown in sorrow when they see Gandhi Das, remembering that heartrending incident.

Gandhi Das's father, Subala Das, was a true Gandhian freedom fighter. During Gandhiji's visit to Odisha, he had marched with Gandhi. That was in 1930. The British government had banned making salt on the seacoasts of Odisha. Law was promulgated that the rich and poor of this country must use only the high-priced English salt imported from England.

The fire of protest burned throughout India. Gandhi gave a call to defy the British law and make salt. The Mahatma's call spread like wildfire from the Arabian Sea to the coastline of the Bay of Bengal. The patriotic Indians were in a state of frenzy. Gandhi marched to Dandi on the Arabian coast to make salt. Thousands of men and women joined him on that historic march to Dandi.

At that selfsame time, the salt making agitation was aflame in the coastal villages of the Erasama block, in Siha, Sunabedi, Hiradiha, Panchapalli, Goda, Harishpur, Chatua, Sobhanpur, Abhayapur, and many other villages. Among the leaders of that agitation was Subala Das of the coastal village Sobhanpur.

The men were bringing salty soil from the salt tracts of the sea, and the womenfolk were pouring water in pots with the soil. Heating the pot over a fire, they collected the residue after the water evaporated. For the poor, making raw salt was routine, like picking grains from harvested fields, like collecting cow dung from roads and pathways, like collecting twigs and wattle from arbors and forests, like plucking bitter greens from pond banks. That was a living for the poor. It was not possible for them to buy salt for their use.

The Satyagrahis walked up to Cuttack with a fistful of this raw salt in paper packets. Distributing pinches of salt in the city streets, they appealed to the people to keep the salt agitation alive. The patriotic people of Cuttack, accepting the Gandhi salt from them with enthusiasm, donated money generously. This monetary help was a morale booster to keep the agitation going.

Subala Das was the leader in distributing this Gandhi salt. The people of Cuttack were worried the day they did not get the Gandhi salt. "Alas! Today we couldn't get Gandhi salt. Has Dase been captured by the British government? Has the agitation failed?" Thus, were they apprehensive.

One day, a group of agitationists under the leadership of Dase put the salt packets for fomentation in a bag and went in a procession to Cuttack, shouting, "Victory be to Mahatma Gandhi," and, "Victory be to Mother India!" From the Siha salt fields to Erasama, the entire route was crowded by people.

At that time, magistrate Sadhab Mishra alighted from his horse, facing the procession. He ordered, "Stop the slogans. Throw away the salt packets."

Dasa was young, about seventeen or eighteen. He replied tauntingly, "We are carrying these salt packets only for you. The other day, while escaping from the Satyagrahis, you fell down from the horse. You were bruised and bleeding. The strain and pain must not be gone from your body. Now your horse, too, would kick you for joining the agitationists. For that, you may need a lot of salt packets.

"Brother Sadhab! You are a Brahmin! If you foment your

back with British salt, would not your sacred thread be polluted? Only for you we are moving with local salt!"

Sadhab magistrate had nursed a long-held grudge against Subala Das. Moreover, he was a loyal officer of the British government. How could he swallow this insult? He ordered for baton attack on the agitationists. The cruel sticks fell on the Gandhi followers mercilessly. For dear life, the innocent people who had joined the procession ran away helter-skelter. Only a few tough satyagrahis remained. Their heads were injured, their hands and legs were mutilated. But Subala Das did not give up the salt bag.

Victory be to Mother India and Victory be to Mahatma Gandhi slogans went up in the air. The police were tired of beating the hapless people. The blood of the Satyagrahis reddened the soil of Erasama. Subala Das lost one of his legs. Since that day, he is as famous as Subala, the cripple.

But Subala Das did not withdraw from the freedom struggle. Between 1930 and 1942, Subala Das was jailed seven times. His firstborn was Gandhi Das, born at midnight on January 30, 1948. By dawn on January 31, listening to the cry of the newborn, the people could know that, after twelve years of barrenness, Subala Das's wife had given birth to a male child. But instead of dancing in joy, Subala Das was wailing like a child.

"What's the matter? What's the matter? Did Subala Das's wife die after childbirth?"

Dronabira Sir, present there, replied, "Had that happened, no such deluge would have come. Many a woman dies in the labor room. Nothing new. Alas! The father of the nation, Mahatma Gandhi, has been shot dead by a scoundrel." What to speak of consoling Subala? Sir himself started wailing and crying!

Controlling his tears, Subala Das clenched his fists and said, "An Odia gardener, it seems, pounced on the murderer. The assassin has been captured. Had I been there, I would have finished him instantly."

"Are you so weak?" asked Drona Sir. "Subala Das, how do you speak such things? You are Gandhi's disciple! Did Gandhi ever say that violence is the answer to violence? Before falling down from gunshots, Gandhi said, 'Hey, Ram! Pardon the assassin.' Listen, Dase, Gandhi is not dead. Gandhi never dies.

"Is Gandhi a mere mortal like you and me that he would die by bullets? Gandhi has been born in your house. Now, in every house, hundreds of Gandhis would be born. You now cannot stop the birth of Gandhi. One Gandhi would be killed, even two-but then? Ha ha! Gandhi is immortal. Victory be to Gandhi." Drona Sir laughed madly, and then cried like a child.

On the twenty-first day of the baby, there was no worship of Lord Satyanarayana. Gandhiji was worshipped. On Gandhi's photo, garlands were offered, along with incense, lamps, and flowers. At the moment of the naming ceremony, Subala Das declared, "Write in the horoscope of the child-Subala Das's son, Gandhi Das."

None in this region had such a name, even now. Gandhi Das had not seen Gandhi, only heard about him. Since childhood, he had heard about Gandhi from his father in such a manner that it was more vivid than seeing him in person. While at school, he had won a prize by drawing a perfect picture of Gandhi. As he came of age, he modeled himself on Gandhi-not in appearance, but by observing the principles of Gandhi to justify his name.

All revolutionary steps in this region, like the entry of the lower caste people into the temples, widow's remarriage, anti-dowry and anti-liquor movements, women's education, and social work have been taken up at Gandhi Das's initiative. He has a few paternal acres. He makes both ends meet with difficulty. After the death of Subala Das, Gandhi Das is a leading personality of this area. He has also fought for the rights of the fishermen and agitated against the exploitation of the fish traders. He is known as Ambiki Gandhi in this area.

Gandhi Das is a short-statured man, brown-complexioned, and much shorter than Gandhiji. But his facial features resemble Gandhi's. Knowing that he was born on the night of Gandhi's martyrdom, the people of this area feel that maybe he is Gandhi's reincarnation on Erasama soil. Therefore, in their eyes, Gandhi Das's face, eyes, and forehead appear to have a touch of Gandhiji.

A khadi chadar on his bare body, a dhoti not touching even his knees, a pair of slippers on his feet, a staff in his hand, and his back erect-but his head was not bald like Gandhiji's. To make it look bald, he always had his head clean-shaven. From a distance, it looks like a shining, baldhead.

None know whether his eyesight is weak, but he always wears the round Gandhi glasses. Winter, summer, spring, rain; always the same dress, the same appearance. While walking, he takes such strides and walks so fast that it looks as if a miniature Gandhi is on his Dandi march, as if the salt agitation is not over and man's freedom struggle is on.

Sour lemons do not grow on the mango tree. Even all mangoes of one tree are not equally luscious and sweet. Sudam Swain and Subala Das are brothers of the same womb, yet the elder brother, Sudam, is bitter and sour while Subala is juicy and sweet. It's also not strange that the two brothers are diametrically opposed to each other. One who has heard of Ravana and Bibhisana, why should Sudam and Subala amaze him?

Yet the elder brother, by his worldly-wise ways, had appeased goddess of wealth Laxmi. While Subala Das was a Gandhian activist, Sudam was a peon of a British-loyalist zamindar. During the British Raj, under the protective umbrella of the zamindar, he was leading a happy life. Therefore, he was a supporter of the British and an unabashed yes-man of the zamindar. Gandhi was the bone of contention between the brothers. Later, the Sarvodaya leader Binoba stood as a wall between them.

Exploiting the opportunity of Subala's Gandhian ways and simplicity, Sudam Swain had captured the paternal property. His first son was born toward the extreme end of the British Raj in India. Some loyalists in those days named sons after the British gods, as Saheb, Collector, Magistrate, etc. Sudam knew that the East India Company was the muscle power of the English rulers. Therefore, he decided to name his son as India Swain. But someone with knowledge of English advised him that India meant Bharat.

They said, "If you name your son Bharat, it would be

construed that you are a patriotic Indian. In other words, you're an admirer of Gandhi. You may incur the wrath of the British. You may consider choosing another name."

Sudam did not have to go far to select a name for his son. Cancelling India, he wrote in the horoscope of his son, Company Swain. Later, in the mouths of the unlettered villagers, Company Swain became Kumpani Soin. But Kundala Panda, with his evil mind, called him Kumpi. In truth, Kumpani Soin was really a stingy fellow.

After the abolition of the zamindars and the feudal system and the death of his father, Kumapani Soin earned notoriety for swindling the property of the poor by the business of money lending. For this reason, his relationship with his cousin, Gandhi Das was the same as the one between a snake and mongoose. With the promise of the lion's share for being elder to him, Kumapani forcibly occupied eighty percent of the joint property.

Gandhi Das used to say, "You take the entire property, but don't raise ridges on the land. Don't raise walls dividing the front door. The souls of our ancestors, living and dead, in the joint family would be pained. They would not accept our offered water. Especially my father's soul would be tormented."

But Kumpani Soin, in sheer defiance of Gandhi Das's words, raised a wall in the middle of the house, fenced the backyard, and ridged the land.

Gandhi Das felt humiliated. Not because Kumpani Soin had grabbed a major share of the property, but because walls were raised, dividing the doors, the kitchen, and the yards.

In the Kaliyug, everyone is a Dhritarashtra. But that Kumpani Soin was worse than Dhritarashtra was clear to many from certain deeds since he'd become the sarpanch of the village. Living up to their father's name, his two sons, fronting fake companies, were exploiting many a half-educated unemployed youth of the nearby villages.

After becoming the sarpanch, Kumpani Soin had no want of money. Added to that, his title and power had made him a notorious nuisance. For that reason, Gandhi Das was wary of acknowledging Kumpani Soin as his brother. But he was never found wanting in respecting his brother, compromising his own culture and values.

Although Kumpani Soin was the sarpanch, he never enjoyed the love and respect of the people of the area, as Gandhi Das did. The real reason for Kumpani Soin's anger was there, something for which Gandhi Das had no counter. The antidote was with the people of the region.

If Gandhi Das contested in the election, no one doubted that he would become at the least a minister, not to mention a sarpanch. But Gandhi Das had no greed for power, no desire for minister ship. Because he not only knew, but had openly said, that in order to survive as a minister one has to sacrifice principles, ideals, and even character. There is heaven-and-hell difference between ministers of those days and ministers of today. Let anyone claim that there is a minister now like Lal Bahadur Shastri!

Gandhi Das was walking purposefully across paddy fields, taking long strides with his short legs toward the village-end platform at the foot of the banyan tree. No meeting would begin until Gandhi Das arrived. Although Gandhi Das was not a fisherman by caste, he was the leader of the Fishermen Development Committee. Many an educated person appreciated his intelligence and judgement, despite his lack of proper education.

As people believe that Udhab Mangual is holding forth the prow of the boat of dharma, so do they have faith in the sense of justice and impartiality of Gandhi Das? In Gandhi Das's court, irrespective of caste, creed, or religion, his balance of justice does not tilt even a thread. Small farmers, Banchu Tarai, Mangulu Biswal, Bhairab Majhi, Bharat Mandal, Udhab Mangual, and even the Brahmin priest Kundala Panda and people of the adjoining village-including the village chiefs-have great respect for Gandhi Das of Sobhanpur. Dronabir Sir, who is respected as a true teacher in the Kujanga-Erasama region, also praises the judgement of Gandhi Das.

Like two rolling lines of water from the ridges of either side, Bharat Mandal and Banchu Tarai joined in the steps of

Gandhi Das. Gandhi Das was younger than them, but they respected his superior wisdom and knowledge. Leaving high school in the last year, Gandhi Das had joined the Bhoodan movement, a movement of land donation to the landless people at the call of his father. But his knowledge and sense of judgement was much higher than that of the modern college graduates and master's students.

He was not in favor of the village youth getting university degrees by cheating in the examinations, only to aggravate the unemployment problem of the country. Therefore, when his own elder son failed his bachelor's degree twice, Gandhi Das thundered, "Pack up your books and attend to farming!"

Bhudan, too, despite being inspired by his father and grandfather's ideas, could not clear his bachelor's. For a few days, obeying his father's command, he worked in the fields and could understand the plight of the small farmers. He also failed in his dream of making megaprojects for the improvement of the area. Failing in all efforts he soon became mature, and, in the company of other college dropouts, he became a rebel. He not only blamed his father, "Ambiki Gandhi" Gandhi Das, but also his grandfather, "Erasama Gandhi" Subala Das, and even the father of the nation, Mahatma Gandhi. He never liked even his name given by his grandpa, Subala Das.

Bhudan became Bhuda. The children distorted it further; Bhunda, Bhunda-Buddhu-that is, fool! Parents often stamp their ideals and dreams into the names of their children. At that time, they never bother to think that when the children grow up and develop their own sense of right and wrong, they may not be prepared to pay the price of their parent's dreams. Bhudan had many grudges against his father and grandfather.

So much land was given to the low-caste family, but what happened then? Dina Bhoi became too big for his boots; now he is a farmer! Why should he work on Gandhi Das's land and farm as a daily wage earner? Nowadays, farmhands are not available. Now whatever land he's saved from the Bhoodan sacrifice depends on the mercy of the sharecroppers.

Gandhi Das's share of paddy does not suffice for a year, and his own income is not even a penny. All his life he did moral politics but never gained anything. His income, however, was the respect, love, and honor of the people. But that does not feed him, nor does his family outgrow their wants.

After leaving college, Bhudan shouted at his father, "Give me money! I'll go in for prawn culture. Very lucrative business. Very soon, our condition would change. If Kumpani uncle's son makes enclosure after enclosure, why shouldn't we do it?"

Gandhi Das is stubborn; he may break but would not bend. He replied to his son, "Being my son, if you do prawn culture that is outside my ideals. In this area, the mangrove forests are gone because of the illegal prawn farming done by opportunists. The environment is polluted and endangered. I'm fighting for protection of the environment. Going from village to village, I am consolidating public opinion against illegal prawn culture. Yet, being my son, you-"

"It's then my misfortune to be your son. Would my future always be limited because I was born of an ideal man like you? Tell me then, what shall I do? Where is land that I would be a farmer and feed myself? What have you kept for me, being my father? What is your savings?"

"My savings are my honesty, ideals, and popularity. You also do such work, and you would be distinguished among a million. Pure social service is now rare. Behind all work there is self-interest," Gandhi Das replied.

The son said, "Then I would form an NGO. I know this much- if genuine social workers like you form NGOs, money would flow from country and abroad. So much money would come that we would ride cars and construct our own building. There wouldn't be any fear of the annually recurring storms, hurricanes, and cyclones. I would work with heart and soul for the NGO. You would be the director, and we would hire a few young men and women, the educated unemployed of this area. Even if their salary would be low, they won't hesitate to work for their living. Many nongovernment service organizations have turned into profitable business organizations. I am keeping proper information about these NGOs. Do you agree it would be successful?"

Gandhi Das was speechless for a while. All his ideals and family pride failed him. He had no words to argue with his son, no advice for him. He finally said, "Do whatever pleases you. I have no knowledge about these things." He walked, a relieved man, to the meeting place. There was a spring in his step.

SEVEN

The month of May was full of potential for change in the year 1999.

"War has started in Kargil, and no one is bothered about it! There our children are being shot dead and what are you people doing? Dying to eat fish and rice! Stopping your work for a day! You never think about why the war is on, what to do to end the war. Our children would not die untimely deaths by bullets. They would live a full life eating fish and rice and then die naturally." Kundala Panda announced the news of war in his own style.

"Why did the war start? Hey, why? From where did this Kargil devil come? Our children have no concern with that!"

The fisher folk, looking with flickering, innocent eyes, discussed among themselves. "They fight everyday with the sea, river, with cyclone, storm, and floods, with hunger and pain, for two square meals. War is their fate. To survive, so many battles have to be fought. He, who doesn't fight, doesn't survive.

"But this warwhich has started always recurs, and it is not for life, but for death. In such wars, the enemy alone does not die. Both sides perish. Destruction is the outcome of war. When the time of death and destruction comes, war becomes inevitable. But why this meaningless war?"

On the glistening, fatty, round O of Kundala Panda's

face were fixed fifty pairs of eyes. Perhaps Kundala Panda was ill at ease. He has heard that war has started in Kargil. But what is Kargil, and where and why this war? He has no idea about the details. What's the point of knowing?

To avoid embarrassment about the self-raised issue, Panda said, "Wars happen. Since the beginning of creation, wars have occurred. Was there not a god and demon war? Was there no Ram-Ravana war? War between Bali and Sugriba? And the great Mahabharat war? Somewhere in the world there is always a war, big or small.

"Between men, some skirmish or war goes on over land, territory, or woman. They also fight for their gods and faiths. Don't, therefore, ask *why* there is a war. In the past ages, Satya, Dwapara and Treta, too, there were wars. How can there be no war in Kaliyug?

"In the past, wars were fought to establish faith and religion, for the destruction of evil. Nowadays, wars are not fought for faith or values. Wars are fought for non-values, for greed, and because of the lust for violence. The worst time of Kali, the worst time of Kali! Listen to me. Let's have a Yajna to stop the war. The war would stop. Our children would survive. All of us can belch, eating rice and fish."

All Kundala Panda's justifications aim at the yajna, a ritual of fire. It closes with a feast of rice and fish. Except for the last five days of Kartika (Panchuka), Panda eats fish all year. Of course, death or obsequies in the family make him live without fish— although with much difficulty. Therefore, his real name might be Balu Panda or Nalu Panda or Manu or Dhanu Panda. Seeing his round, fatty, rice-and-fish eating belly and mocking him for his earrings, people called him Kundala Panda, which later was shortened to Kunde, respectfully.

The name given by his father was thus lost, and he was known as Kundala Panda. Now, if you ask, no one can say the real name of Kunde. He is from Bandara village. Some say Bangladeshi, some others say he's a Midinapur Bengali. But Kundala Panda swears by his sacred thread that he is pure Odia. As there are a large number of Midinapur Bengali families in his village, people assume that he is a Bengali. But whether Telugu, Odia, or Bengali, the Brahmins are a separate caste.

One can be a priest only if he recites Sanskrit shlokas; can dispel calamities by conducting prayers and sacrifices in the villages. Therefore, no one bows down before him thinking of him as Bengali or Odia. Everyone bows to him because he is a Brahmin. Even Sheik Ghulam Mustafa of Pakistanpara bows to him.

Golmasta is not inferior to Panda in any way. As Panda knows all the Hindu scriptures by heart, Golmasta too has the Koran at the tip of his tongue. He offers the milk, honey, and cheese delicacies to the old Pir, sings *Allah ho Akbar* at dawn. He enjoys respect not only as the mullah of the Muslim community, but even the respect of the Hindus. He always raises his hands to say salaam to Kundala Panda, but no one has ever heard Kundala Panda say, "Salam Miyan" to Golmasta.

This is a sample of Kundala Panda's long-inherited classical wisdom that, "The Brahmin is the highest. All others are inferior." Irrespective of caste, creed, or color, all are inferior to the Brahmin. Therefore, when Kundala Panda sees Golmasta, he blesses him, saying, "Let all sins be purged, all diseases be cured. May you live long."

With a broad smile, caressing his green beard, Golmasta receives the blessings of Kunde. Many people think that Panda's pigtail and Golmasta's beard match royally. On the western hemisphere of Kunde's rotund bald head hangs a pigtail. At the end of the tail, there is a knot like a cobra head. While he walks, swaying his big, fat belly over the earth, the tip of the pigtail sways in tandem. The knot opens up because of Panda's heavy tread, and the strands of hair fly freely in air in the careless style of unkept promises.

That day, disturbing the fisher folk meeting, Kundala Panda had announced the news of the Kargil war. When this matter arose, Gandhi Das became still like an anthill. As if watching the war, his dull eyes had widened, gazing out to the Kargil battlefield. He knew that the amicable relationship between the Hindus and

Muslims of this area or the peace resolution of Abhayapur could not stop the Kargil war.

Most village groups like these would meet and discuss the irrelevance of war, ethics, and moral values. War created a sensation in this docile, rural life. In the evenings, returning from the fair, inauspicious afternoons, on the hoary platforms at the foot of ancient banyan treesat the edge of the village, many an account of hearsay loss and death and many concocted stories became acceptable facts.

He who suffers the *loss* of war, whose son would be martyred in the war, maimed for life, or captured by the Pakistan army, his agony is his own. However, everyone would suffer the *consequences* of war. As the people of this region suffer the consequences of depletion of the mangrove forest, likewise everyone in the country would suffer in the Kargil war. But the parents of the youngmen of this region who are fighting the Kargil war, they would never sleep at night. If they sleep, they would have nightmares. Is the result of Gandhiji's non-violent freedom struggle this eternal Indo-Pak war?

With the news of the Kargil war, Udhab Mangual's singing of the horse dance song quieted spontaneously. He was dumfounded. Like the faded face of the moon in the womb of murky clouds, the face of his daughter, Girima, automatically floated before his eyes.

"Why? Why?" Udhab asked himself and slapped his own cheeks. "You idiot Uddhaba! Do you think you are omniscient? How can you gauge your daughter's mind, you foolish fisherman? What relation does your daughter have with Bikram Balabantaray, that hearing about Kargil war; you thought your daughter would swoon? Moreover, have you ever seen in this universe a match between the son of a Paika-traditional warrior caste family and a fisherman's daughter?"

Although he wiped from his mind the gloom of his daughter, he was sad that Bikram Balbantaray was in the army. Simply because Bikram is from a Paika family that does not mean that he means nothing to Udhab. He is the friend of Bhagyadhar, his son, and so, too, is he a son of this region. What's the difference between Udhab's son and Bikram? If he is fighting the Kargil devil, well, then it's a calamity.

For the safety of Bikram, Udhab vowed to offer prayers at the feet of the crisis-dispeller Mahabir Hanuman, and was amazed at his own reaction. A father of ten children, he has never vowed to offer prayers for the wellbeing of any of his own children. All those things are the duty of the womenfolk. But why is his mind and soul agitated for Bikram? Udhab's Bhagabat-nurtured mind answered, "The universal soul does not distinguish between yours and others. No man should have such distinction in his mind."

Small men have lofty dreams. Oh, war is on in Kargil. It was as if lightning had fallen on Udhab's head. A moment ago, he was thinking aloud, "This year, the pregnant land would burst out in good harvest. Fish would breed in the river enough for all. Let it be. May the year pass well, may men live in joy, feasting and merrymaking with family and friends.

"Let men live like true humans. Man cannot be an emperor, never a god. It's not easy to become great, but man can be a human being. If man cannot live like a human being, what's the need for temples and mosques on earth? Why murder and crime, mutual cracking of heads? Let's send Gandhi Das to Delhi. Let the country listen to our voice!"

Speaking in a singsong manner without pause, Udhab waited for a roar of approval from his listeners. With unblinking eyes, the small farmer, Banchu Tarai, was looking blank. One cannot decipher anything from such a dumb face.

"Yes or no?" asked Udhab. "What do you say, Tarai? Let man live like human beings!"

"Who denies? But the war?" Tarai gave a worried reply.

"Yes, it was heard that war would start in Kargil. It has started, in fact," Udhab Mangual announced the news again sorrowfully. "What can man do? How can man live like man? Speak!"

Golmasta sighed heavily in support of Udhab. His sigh

scared off a bird sitting on a branch above his head, and a brittle, dry leaf fell down straight on his nose.

Udhab once more looked at the villagers gathered there for the meeting, rolling his head like a wheel cracker. None of these have any worry over Kargil. Paddy, betel leaves, fish, salt, and the coming election; everyone is immersed in these four or five things, these being the regular business of this area.

The election comes, once in a while, to the villages like an unscheduled festival, like an unasked-for blessing of God. Many unemployed youths get excited and convince themselves that they are not unemployed for a few days. Some cash comes to hand. If a smelly, deformed fruit grows on a barren tree that is also counted a fruit-bearing tree.But is that the whole meaning of life? Only food, clothes and self-interest? Udhab's head was spinning with worries over war.

Immediately after hearing the news of the Kargil war, Gandhi Das proposed, "Let the community meeting be suspended today. A fierce battle is on.What's the point in the meeting? And listen to Mangual's words! What would I accomplish going to Delhi? Do you think I am the real Mahatma Gandhi?"

"If the meeting is suspended, would the war stop? Wars go on for years. Boys are martyred. But which work of which political leader stops? Children's marriage, business and commerce, construction of big buildings; which stops or halts?" some young man said.

Looking at Gandhi Das's face to give solace to his own disturbed mind, Udhab asked again, raising his voice, "I say that war has started in Kargil! No one seems to be worried! Does anyone hear me or not?"

"The war has started! Our children there are dying, eating Pathan bullets. And you brats are playing here? And you mock me?"

Hearing, "Pathan bullets" from Udhab's mouth, Golmasta reacted sharply, as if hit by a projectile from a catapult.He protested, "ByAllah! Never speak like that, Mundial brother. 'Pathan bullets' is highly unjust. Why Pathan bullets? Oh, Allah!

Our children there are dying eating *Pakistani* bullets. What's the mistake of the Pathan?

"We've lived here for so many years, ever since India became independent. We've left our birthland and homes and have come here.Here we created a homeland for our children. By the grace of Allah, disregarding communal riots, has there ever been an argument between Hindus and Muslims here?

"Remember, Mundial brother, Golmasta was not born yesterday.Why should I tell lies? You are an elderly person. If you shout the Pathan (Muslim) name, if our children get charged up, don't you think there would be a new riot here? Who would rescue us then? Speak! Who'll control it then?"

Udhab was not sorry that a wrong word had slipped off his tongue. He knew that he meant the Pakistani *Pathan*, not of this country. But from this started Golmasta's bickering with Mangual.

"Do you understand, Mundial (Chief of the village) brother, that my roots are deeper in this village than yours? By the time you came here as an adopted son, I was already here. What do you say, Tarai brother? What's the fault of Pathan?"

Gandhi Das and Dhadia shouted, waving their hands, "Stop it, I say! Stop these inauspicious things. None should raise Hindu, Muslim, or Christian issues here. We are worried about our children. Many from these are as have gone to the army. Should we not worry for them?"

"Yes, that's our worry. But what about the country? Our children have gone to war from all over the country. Since independence, wars have been going on, and our children die from their bullets. Some die, some return. Yah Allah, may you give sound sense to our enemies!"

Sheik Golmasta knelt down to pray to Allah. When he prays, does he remember only Allah? Does he not see, with closed eyes, Lord Jagannath? Does he not see the other deities? Does he not see Udhab Mangual, Bharat Mandal, Bhairab Majhi, Gandhi Das, and his other friends of the village? Does he not see the trees, rivers, and streams of his village; the sea and the welfare of the people, even the graves and the village cremation ground?

Does Golmasta have fewer worries? First, his family problems.His middle son, Sheik Salbeg Miyan, is a hawker. Aluminum utensils, toys, Bombay sweets, chicken, goats, eggs; whenever something catches his fancy, he moves from village to village carrying a load.

On village fair days, he runs to the fair, at times buying fish from the netters, and sells in villages. At other times, he does leather business as well. On occasion, he becomes a mobile stationery shop. He tends his small farm too. He has a large family compared to his income.

Golmasta has nine children alive, four dead.His fourth son, Sheik Salbeg Rahman, has five children; four girls, one boy, all alive.Allah willing, four more sons may come.But it's hard to maintain.The childbearing mother's labor pain is less painful than the pain of feeding the children.Children grow up fast. Their bellies grow bigger. Neither business nor income grows in proportion because when you grow in years, income falls.

But Golmasta does not care for that, nor Salbeg. Salbeg's daughters are very good girls. The son is a spoiled brat.Has got a physique, anyone would say—not Salbeg's, but the son of Jehangir or Shahjahan.He is just touching twenty, but he needs a lover. He's an ill-bred fellow, which is no harm if you're looking for lass in the Muslim settlements. But his eyes roam around all lasses of this area. He whistles at some and offers Kolkata perfume to others, which he's stolen from his father's mobile shop. He calls some girls *surmawalli* and others *dilwalli*. In every meeting of the village, complaints are made against him.

But his two younger sisters, Masuma and Gulrukh, are refined and gentle. They have close friendships with every girl of the village. But their friendship is deeper with Udhab Bhaiya's daughter, Girima, the betel man's daughter, Ketaki, and Bharat Mandal's daughter, Padma. Only because of the innocence of Masuma and Gulrukh is Salbeg's wayward son Alwar's misdemeanor pardoned.But it is not proper for Alwar to converse

---

[3]Both the Malika and the Jayee Choutisa predict doom. The rural people of the coastal districts respect these books as gospel.

with Kundala Panda's granddaughter, Ganga, on her way back from school. Ganga is not a bad girl, nor is she innocent. She mixes freely with Banchu Tarai's eldest son, Bipin, as with Alwar. Nowadays, even the girls don't differentiate between caste and faith; why punish the boys only?

Golmasta gets confused. If a Hindu boy and a Muslim boy develop a friendship, nothing wrong. But a Hindu boy and a Muslim girl! Absolutely bad.Before a sense of right and wrong enters the innocent minds, the elders put sin in their minds and defame them, dragging mercilessly in the open streets in such a way that the young lovers either are forced to commit blasphemy or compelled to commit suicide.Nowadays in the villages, the rate of suicide has increased, with the boys and girls ingesting poison together only because of the old notorious people like Narku Routray, Tahali Mohanty, Kumpani Soin, and Dhadi Barik.

Once, Tahali Mohanty was a loafer, but now his stars are on the ascendant. Being the Chairman of the Panchayat means the grandfather of the king of Shenda dynasty! The Shenda king was at least concerned about the misery of his subjects. But this one is not a king. He merely plays the king.

In the past, people used to neutralize dangers by worshipping *babas*. Nowadays, there are female saints called *mata*. The matas, too, have spread their influence in the towns and villages. A mata comes to these areas once in a while.A visible goddess, she responds to your call. Her name is Praneswari Devi. Whenever the mata comes and she holds her durbar in Tahali Mohanty's house. Prayers, scripture readings, and offerings are held on a large scale. People even whisper that animal sacrifices are made. If the election is near, a yajna is also held. Wads of money come and are spent.

People believe that because of the influence of the mata, Tahali Mohanty's greedy belly, like a deep, flowing river, has met the sea underground. How else could the chairman, who can eat a whole chicken, have cheeks so hollow? People even say that sucking the juice not only makes juicy things stone dry, but also hollows the soft, flabby cheeks. Above the butterfly moustache of

Tahali Mohanty, the bulbous nose is slightly sunken near the eyes.As a result, at the meeting point of the eyebrows there is no nose, just flatness.

Tahali Mohanty inherited a dilapidated thatched house from back in his grandfather's times.Now he has a mansion. No dearth of wealth, cattle, farm land, or prosperity.But he has vigilant eyes on his boys and girls. The three daughters tarnished the reputation of the family. He had to spend a fortune to get them married to good boys of good families.

Tahali Mohanty's mood was off as today's meeting went awry for no reason. While returning home, Tahali expressed his dissatisfaction. "If a war started in Kargil, how does it affect that Gandhi Das? If Gandhi Das goes dumb, as if he's holding the country on his head, how does it matter to the villagers? Why was the scheduled meeting not held? Who spread the news of Kargil war here?"

"Who else? Kundala Panda. He is the source of all mischief. He is planning to perform a yajna! Do you understand?" said Sarapanch Kumpani Soin.

"Then let the yajna be held in advance from our side with Praneswari Devi as the chief priest. Two elections are coming up. Go and give advance money to Praneswari Devi. If some other party books her in advance, then Paraneswari would slip out of our hands, and our lives, too, would go. A difficult time is waiting ahead. Do you follow me, Dhadi?" Tahali Mohanty said.

"Yes, Sir I know. I have told you everything beforehand. But don't increase your stress by putting our party and their party in your head. Lately you have developed diabetes, and many more diseases are reported these days. Why are you afraid of changing parties? Today you are a Hindu, tomorrow a Muslim, and the day after a Christian. If changing religion is so easy, what is the difficulty in changing parties? Whichever party has the wave in its favor that is our party. Why should we have distinctions like yours, his, and theirs as the self-centered people do?" Dhadi Barik consoled Tahali Mohanty.

Approving ward member Dhadi Mohanty's words by clapping his hands, Tahali Mohanty tried to smile in style, trying to cover his deformed teeth. "I'm also saying that. Why the distinction between your son and my son, between your wife and my wife? I have no distinction between mine and thine, O' Dhadi."

Dhadi Barik was grim at Mohanty's bawdy words. Changing the topic, he said, "That Gandhi Das's son, Bhudan, and that Muslim girl, Masuma, must be taught a lesson. I have seen with my own eyes, Sir. On the full moon day at the Ketaki grove, Masuma held tight the hand of Bhudan — and both were enjoying a hearty laugh. Have the lads and lasses of this village lost caste, religion, shame, fear, and family culture?

"Gandhi Das has formed an all-religion committee only to take credit to see that Hindu-Muslim enmity does not grow. But does it mean that Gandhi Das and Golmasta's son, Salbeg, would be in-laws? Does Gandhi Das think that he has really become Gandhiji? Did Mahatma Gandhi have a Muslim daughter-in-law?"

"If he thinks that he has become Gandhiji then he would die, certainly die. In my Panchayat, such bawdiness would not be tolerated. Would there be no caste or religion? All would be one! Gandhiji died, and this Gandhi Das too would die," Tahali Mohanty said, taking a deep breath. Kumpani Soin supported silently.

Dhadi Barik said in serious tone, "The last days of Kaliyug have arrived, sir. Whether it comes to other regions or not, it has arrived here. The *malika*[3] prophecy would come true, no further delay." Dhadi Barik turned toward his home, walking on the ridges. In the middle of the paddy fields, a snake was violently struggling, half swallowing a toad.

"Oh, hell! Times are bad." So saying, Dhadi traversed the ridgeway by taking large strides.

Gandhi Das was an unelected leader of this region, and the Kargil war provided an issue to demonstrate his leadership. Having meetings in villages, he preached patriotism, fearlessness, and the virtues of martyrdom. In the meantime, inspired by Gandhi Das's exhortations, a few unemployed young men were eager to join the army. Even the young fishermen were planning to register their names in the army, forgetting their love for sea and river as well as the fishing trade.

"If Gandhi Das is such a great patriot, why doesn't he send his son, Bhudan, to the war? What leadership at the cost of other's children!" Tahali Mohanty was spewing venom before Narku Routray against Gandhi Das.

From the dais of the general meetings, Tahali Mohanty often castigated Gandhi Das more than others. But Gandhi Das never cared for such criticism. He doesn't play politics. He has no lust for power or position. Therefore, criticism, condemnation, or canards don't affect him. But Tahali Mohanty could not comprehend why Udhab Mangual became such a patriot after the Kargil war started.

Every evening Udhab Mangual sits before the television in the village club and says, "Boys! Open the newspaper. Let's have an idea about the state of Kargil war." The boys laugh boisterously. They understand that by *newspaper*, Udhab indicates the news program on TV.

Udhab used to go to the *Bhagabatgadi* in the evenings. He used to warn his sons, Bhagyadhar and Benudhar, not to watch TV, as it spoils one's character. Now he does not sleep without watching news on TV. He reads the newspaper every day. At times, he asks, "Any news about Chandanpur's Biku Balbantaray today?"

One day, Tahaili Mohanty's son, Sakula Mohanty, not only saddened but also agitated Udhab by saying, "Bikram's news would come on TV only when he dies in the war. His photographs would also be shown. Such Odia Kargil heroes' pictures have already been shown."

Udhab was sad at first. In the next moment, he was agitated, and said, "Do you not have love or compassion for anyone? Don't you have humanitarian values? Bikram is of this region, and he was playing, dancing, and studying with you people. Our Bhagyadhar, Bhudan, Bikram, and you, may not be brothers from the same womb, but are from the same villages. How could such dreadful words come out of your mouth?" Udhab's throat was dry.

Dronabir Sir came in. Since the beginning of the Kargil war, Sir, too, comes to the clubhouse to watch news. Hearing everything, he consoled Udhab. "Hey, Udha! Does hot water burn a house? Nothing untoward would happen to Bikram. His father consulted an astrologer. In Bikram's horoscope, there is honor and glory now. The war is coming to an end. India's victory in this war is certain. The villain of the Kargil war, Pakistan, has been condemned all over the world."

Udhab asked in confidence, "Sir, are you speaking the truth? I don't know who or what this Kargil is, and I don't know why our children are getting killed. I only know that Bikram is fighting there for the country. When would the war be over? Would India win?" Udhab asked like an innocent child.

Sir said, "India has almost won. It's a matter of a few more days."

"Oh, God, you do everything. There is no other way without you." Wishing Bikram's welfare, Udhab prayed with folded hands.

"Oh! Whoever is martyred is someone or other's son. A man is martyred, and it means lightning strikes the head of a father," said Golmasta.

Golmasta knows what it means to lose a son. Golmasta's eldest son, Salbeg, was working in a confectionary owned by a Muslim in Hyderabad. The Hindus were not only buying sweets from a Muslim's shop, but also offering them to their deities. But when riots broke out, some of the same Hindus went mad and killed the two sons of the man and also Lalbeg.

Lalbeg had gone for work, defying everyone's advice. He was sending money, too, but whoever knew that an innocent man would be a victim of mad rioters? Since that day, Golmasta fears the city, fears to utter even the name of Lalbeg. He thinks there is no safer place for Muslims than Abhayapur. Udhab, too, has the heart of a father. The sorrow of losing a son has also penetrated his heart.

From behind a strand of loose clouds, the second-day new moon, like a big-eyed fish, was trying to assure the world of moonlight. From the other side, dark clouds akin to menacing whales devoured the white clouds—big fisheating small fish.

Bhairav Majhi said, sighing, "The big fish eating the small fish is not true only in the water. On land and in the sky, was there lack of space to steer clear and move forward? See? Like a car riding over a cycle, the murky cloud patch has ridden without reason over the moon and has darkened all quarters."

Sighing heavily, Bharat Mandal said, "What else would happen in the future? Running from police station to the courtrooms and losing all, this would be our future. Tell me, brother, who has not done prawn culture in this region? Did our Sarala Das commit a murder by making one? I had managed to stop him before now. This time I did not. To speak the truth, I, too, became greedy.

"Sarala Das was working enthusiastically. He was getting quite a bit of money. Why Narku Routray couldn't stand this? On his complaint that my son has done it illegally, the police have arrested my son. Would such a thing have happened without Narku Routray's mischief? The prawn enclosure, it seems, would be taken over by government. Everyone has prawn enclosures. What crime have we committed? Kindly speak, Gandhi sir!"

While sipping tea noisily from a glass at Mathuri's teashop, Gandhi Das said, "You have not committed any crime alone, Mandal. Everyone is making illegal prawn enclosures. So did you. But had you done this in a legal manner, the police could not have done anything to you. That is the difference.

"As per the Supreme Court's ruling, the enclosure should be at least three kilometers away from the sea. Why did you encroach into the sea? If everyone does it, our village would be lost in the maws of the sea in a trice. "While thinking about personal gain, should you not think about your village? If the village is swept off by the sea, would you not float somewhere helplessly?"

Gandhi Das fights for everyone, but he is nobody's man on matters of principle. If he finds fault with anyone, he would say it to his face. He would not even spare his son, forbidding Bhudan from having an enclosure.

Mandal did not like Gandhi Das's words. He said, "Dase, sir, from experience I know that even if there is no want of food for the prawns inside the enclosures, at the slightest opportunity, the strong prawns not only attack the soft ones, but also swallow them. We poor people are the weak prawns. The politicians and the rich owners are the strong prawns.

"Adjacent to Tahali Mohanty's enclosure, my son, Sarala Das, has enclosed a plot of lowland and had started culturing prawns. Tahali Mohanty's farm is on two acres of land, two kilometers from the sea, and is a large one. He has become a big shot by doing prawn culture. Narku Routray, an ex-minister's son, is a partner in that business. How could that be legal and my son's farm illegal?

"The truth is the sub-inspector of the police station wanted a share of tiger prawns. Whatever my son gave, he was not satisfied with that.Should Sarala give up the enclosure then?" asked Bharat Mandal.

Gandhi Das said, "Better to give it up. The NGO that our Bhudan is setting up, its main aim is to oppose all illegal prawn enclosures and to protect the interest of the small fishermen as well as protect the environment. You would see, if you respect law, that our Bhudan would point the law courts to Tahali Mohanty and Narku Routray." Finishing his tea, Gandhi Das arose.

EIGHT

If the river is life, the sea is the fate of the fishermen. This coastal, estuary-facing river has neither control over herself nor any on the sea. Oared by the south wind and the loving enticement of the full-moon night, the spring tide rises in youthful ecstasy from the heart of the sea. The saline waves enter the bosom of the river until the river's heart is sweetened in the rainy season. This is life.

If the sea waves carrying hordes of fish never rise to the bosom of the rivers, season after season, how could the fisherman survive? If the river is his rice broth, the sea is his rice pot. But Bharat Mandal does not go for fishing now. That business is now taken over by the sons. Bharat Mandal, forsaking the fishing net, has now been rowing boats for ten years and ferries the passengers to and fro on river Hansua.

It is better if the hands move as long as the belly needs food. Otherwise, human life is so very miserable. How long can an idle man be tolerated, even if he is your father? Of course, in this respect, a hundred salutations to Udhab Mangual. He's fed the younger grandfather, younger grandmother, uncle, aunt, four old men and women-lord knows for how many years!

Udhab has passed his prime, but his strength has not ebbed. Bharat Mandal, however, has lost both age and strength. There are reasons for that. Bharat Mandal has withdrawn from the world since his youth, thinking of himself as a refugee. That refugee stamp has remained into his old age. This unwanted feeling has slowly killed Bharat Mandal's spirit. All his life, Bharat Mandal's father and grandfather were boatmen of river Padma. Although his sons now have become fishermen, he wishes one of them to be a boatman. Otherwise, how would people of this region cross the river? How would they go to Cuttack, Bhubaneswar, Jagatsinghpur, Kolkata, and Midinapur?

Abhayapur village is a lone, imprisoned island in the network of rivers on all sides. During the rainy season, these small fisherman villages get cut off from the world. A river in front, a river behind and ahead the yawning, twelve-month estuary, Jatadhari. During floods, there is no rowing of boats for fear of accidents. The people are imprisoned in the village.

Every election, promises are made by the political parties.

"There would be a bridge on Hansua."

"People would walk on the bridge."

"Buses would take up the route."

Bharat Mandal would cease to be important. His income would stop. But Bharat Mandal's never bothered about that. He knows that, during his lifetime, no bridge would be constructed. It's all an election stunt. He has seen many elections. Coming up ahead is the parliamentary election, to be followed by an election for the assembly.

Election promises are beginning to be heard that two bridges would be constructed on Hansua. The people of Abhayapur are as ecstatic hearing the election promises as they are savoring the experience of real theater by watching bioscopes. Candidates prove, time and again, that these simpletons easily trust self-centered, corrupt liars. They cast their votes in their favor, get cheated, and never protest.

Mantri Mallick is not really amantri, a minister; the name given by his mother was Mantri. He is a Dalit by caste. Therefore, his surname is Mallick, and his full name Mantri Mallick. There is a whole story as to why Mantri's mother did not name him Raja - King. The whole village Abhayapur knows it, and it has now become a legend.

Mantri Mallick's grandfather, Bhikari Mallick, was a watchman of this area. All night he used to patrol, beating his baton on the ground. He reported births and deaths of the area to the police station. He was an honest and faithful watchman. The salary he was drawing from the panchayat is not worthy of mention. Except for the title of "watchman," it was in no way an attractive job.

Everyone was his master, as he was a Dalit. Bhikari Mallick was a good-natured human being and had high self-esteem, but he was short-tempered. As he was of a low caste, whenever his self-respect was violated, he took it out by physically abusing his wife and children-thereby compensating for his impotence at not taking his anger out on the offenders.

After calming down, he used to slap his cheeks for his folly, cuddle his children, and comfort his wife in the style of a husband. With fond anger, he used to say, "Why are you wasting your invaluable tears? After me, you may have to cry a lot. Where would you borrow tears from then? We have got such a hateful life that no one would loan us a death, let alone other things. Like gathering twigs, firewood, cow dung, and paddy, we have to gather our death."

As a matter of fact, his wife, the mother of seven children, Bharjan's mother, does not find time even to cry alone after her husband's illogical torture. While doing the painful chores, she used to wipe her flowing tears. When does a poor mother get to indulge in sulking when she has to ensure her children are fed and looked after, along with myriad of other tasks? To add to that, the eldest son, Bharjan, is cleft-lipped over and above his defiance. He is strong and hefty like his father, true, but since he was the only son among six daughters, he has become lazy through overindulgence. After him were born six demonesses from her cursed womb. They would ruin the homes they go to after marriage.

Lest the deformed child thinks himself incompetent and ill-fated, his mother fondly called him Bharjan, meaning competent. Because of his don't-give-a-damn nature, he could not get a watchman's job after the death of his father. He became a farmhand in Tahali Mohanty's house. Half the days he does not turn up for work out of anger and frustration.

The wife's belly waits for the income of her husband but does not wait to be a mother. Bharjan's wife delivers a child every year, and, with her emaciated body, she sweeps the house of her master, washes the cowshed, and lifts filth. Before and after childbirth, when she fails to go to the master's house, the master does not lose anything; she loses. She works as a daily wager, not on annual contract. Therefore, if work stops, wages stop.

As the life of Bharjan's mother was miserable, Mantri's mother's life was no less miserable. Mantri's mother consoles herself. Well, would everyday be the same?

Her eldest son-she insisted on naming him Mantri-would go to school, would become a babu. If he does not read well, at least he would become a minister. Then she would take out all her anger on her husband. With that determination, she named her son Mantri.

That year, her master, Tahali Mohanty, had become a minister. The post of a minister was much superior to that of a modern king. The kings now have neither kingdom nor any royal powers. The kings now are like dead snakes. People do not step on them, but fearlessly jump over them.

The family members of the king of Dhobei Garh are now coolies. If people require day laborers, they go straight to him and ask, "Your Highness! Would the Prince go for a job today? Not a very strenuous job, but women's work. The labor is just weeding the field farm land and plantation work."

While addressing day laborers as "Your Highness" or "Prince" is still in use in this region, the royalty and other shenanigans have disappeared. This address is like putting salt into wounds for the fit-for-nothing royal unemployed.

The title of a minister nowadays is respectable, desirable, and also lucrative in all respects. Therefore, Mallick's wife had given the name Mantri and not Raja. Bharjan also wanted his son to get some education. At least let the stigma of ignoramus be wiped off.

Whether he passes or fails the matriculation examination, it would not be difficult to get a government job on reservation quota for Dalits. Thereafter, if he becomes a minister, much better.

Gandhi Das was inspiring the Dalits of the region to study in the schools. Government help was also expected. Only a handful of low-caste people, however, were going to schools. But at the insistence of his wife, Bharjan was chasing Mantri to the school. If one son gets educated, the sin of illiteracy may be atoned in the clan. If one boy is properly settled, the rest could be taken care of. But instead of being a well-settled man, Mantri became a cremation ground dweller.

Mantri Mallick remembers everything vividly since the age of five. Like tattoos on a woman's body, his memory of pain, loss, hunger, humiliation, and struggle for survival was indelible. Scratching old wounds, the pinpricks of sorrow pierce the heart. The scars of childhood do not fade easily.

Like lines of cars, jeeps, and men following a minister, behind Mantri was a line of undesirable siblings. All in all, ten brothers and sisters. Two had died at birth. For them, maybe the mother grieved; the father perhaps less, but that scar was not there on the eldest Mantri and the other children. Before they came of age they had fallen from their anemic mother like frostbitten, raw mangoes; weak and hungry since birth.

Mantri was ten or twelve when two of his siblings had died, and he had taken it as a blessing. It would have been better if two or three more down the line had slipped off. They would have only claimed their share of rice, water, and gruel, like enemies. Observing his father's and uncle's day-to-day life, it was clearly visible to Mantri what joy and happiness the seven landless, poverty-stricken, low-caste untouchables would enjoy.

Mantri never gets time to think about others. Since early childhood, he has suffered hunger, pain, physical and mental agony. Like breathing, hunger is the proof of being alive for all the Dalit children of his street. Mantri was always hungry. Only death relieves the hunger of the poor. Father's earnings, minus his bidi (local, cheap cigarettes) and tobacco, were like a drop in the sea.

Mantri's mother sweeps the front yard of Tahali Mohanty's house. But twelve months a year, in her womb, there was hunger along with a would-be born-at times, a stillborn, at times, another hungry mouth. She was always groaning or moaning in pain of the body or mind. Despite that, she still worked in her master's house. Whatever she got, she put in the mouths of the children.

In Mantri's house, the day hot rice is served on aluminum plates with salt or tamarind is a feast. Mantri's mother cooks very tasty rice. Otherwise, not only in Mantri's home but in all homes in the slum, it is watered rice or broth of boiled rice. As soon as the rice starts boiling, Mantri's mother pours half a bowl of water into it. At night, she prepares ragi grain gruel and mixes it with watered rice. By sunrise, balls of ragi gruel float in the pot like filth in floodwater.

Even that much is not given to the children in the morning. She keeps it till midday, when hunger is at its hottest. In the morning, the children get a plateful of black tea. The father gets a bowlful. With that, a handful of puffed rice. They do not get even a spoonful of jaggery every day. On certain days, even this much is not available, and the hot belly is to be chilled by river water.

At midday, if the children get an occasional piece of baked, dried fish, it becomes a nuptial feast. Or else salt, raw chili and tamarind paste. The children don't relish chili, and even if the tamarind paste is not tasty, the ragi-rice does not get stuck at the throat. Whatever is placed on the tongue, the hook of hunger drags it into the belly tank like the fishhook dragging the fish.

Because of this hunger, Mantri developed a bad habit in childhood. Many children of their street had the same habit. When hungry, the hapless, naked children of the street, hiding their shame by wearing a loincloth, sucked their fingers to kill hunger, however unsuccessfully. But as Mantri Mallik was the firstborn son among seven sisters, his growth from the nascent stage to youth was as much delayed as his freedom from the nasty habit of finger-sucking.

His mother, however, gave birth to sons on her ninth and tenth pregnancies, but Mantri was ceaselessly sucking his thumb even then, like his younger brothers and sisters sucking the dry breasts of his mother, one after another. On the mother's children-dedicated, liberal breasts, the last two children were hanging, looking like two goat cubs, sticking to their mother's breastbone, skin glued together. Had the mothers of poor children, like cows, goats, dogs, and pigs, had eight or ten nipples instead of two, how would God have been poorer?

In Mantri Mallik's house, there was an old cow. Her history, like Mantri's life, was miserable. When she was diseased, lest she should die at the tether and thereby earn for the master the sin of cows laughter, the master freed her to move anywhere. The cow was gasping near the cremation ground. Out of kindness, Bharjan Mallik served the cow with some food and herbs, and the animal gradually got well and started moving.

When Bharjan informed the master, the master, in a charitable disposition, said, "The thrown spit is never swallowed back, Bharjan. It's not right to bring home the cow that was left at the crematory. It may be a bad omen. You have saved the old cow by serving her. You take her. If you feed her, maybe she would give birth to one or two more. Let your children get a few drops of milk. How badly you torture human children."

Not out of greed, but thanks to the charity of the master, Bharjan brought the cow home to look after her. He built a shed close to the wall of the house and thatched it with coconut branches and leaves. He fed her grass and husk. When this cow came to his house, not only did his prestige grow on his street, but also the hopes of his children grew.

"If the cow delivers a calf, they would drink milk, have curd, cheese, and ghee."

Like stars blooming in an empty sky, all of a sudden in the imagination of the poor children, hopes of milk, ghee, and butter blossomed. In fact, one day, the cow started lowing so wildly that they were all restless. Mantri's mother said, "Do something! God willing, the cow may deliver."

Roping the cow, Bharjan dragged the lowing creature and tied it to a tree at a place frequented by wandering bulls. The children of the street, old men, and women gathered around the cow. Mantri was curious about everything. His curiosity was not limited to the earth's boundary. Often, he wished to fly away to the kingdom of the sky on the back of a vulture or eagle and examine how big the wicks in the stars were, and how much kerosene in them that they never fade out. Who lowers the flame in the morning, and who raises it in the evening?

He thought that the moon was the petromax light in a rich man's house in the sky village. Stars were the dim lamps in poor homes. Such absurd curiosity was in Mantri's innocent imagination. Hence, Mantri, too, ran after the cow. In the street, the people were saying, "If the cow is impregnated fruitfully, Bharjan's fate would change."

Mantri's curiosity was not in the cow, but in the fruit. Trees bore fruit, but how could a cow bear fruit?

Seeing Mantri run behind the cow, his father shouted at him, "Where are you going, you notorious fellow? You have flunked school today. Wait! I would skin your back."

Fearing his father, Mantri went to school. In the evening Bharjan returned with the cow as if he has conquered a fort. He declared in a loud voice, "The cow is in the family way. Take care of her." This was meant for his wife.

That day, Mantri's father was so happy that Mantri was confused. He asked mother, "Mother, our cow is fruited, or father?"

Biting her tongue, his mother said, "Quiet, quiet! If father hears, he would beat you. Hey, you naughty boy! Do men get pregnant? Go, go, go away from here. Children should not bother about these things. Count the days until our cow would give birth to a calf. Milk and curd would overflow our pots. If God is merciful and kind, you too would taste it."

Mantri forgot about the cow's fruition. He remembered only milk and curd pots. He dreamed at night of a newborn brown calf frolicking in their front yard. On its head was a milky moon sign. Again, he dreamed that he was drinking breathlessly the foamy milk, burying his head in the pot. Oh! Milk is sweeter than jaggery and honey!

One morning when he got up, he saw a real female calf jumping in front of their house. Everyone was saying that luck had dawned on their house. For seven days, the children ate cheese with great joy. Thereafter, the children's joy was eclipsed. The milkman came every day, and the milk was taken away. The children did not know how much money he gave father at the end of the month, but their bellies were hit.

Mantri's mother was irritated, as she had to save food for the cow from the meager provision of the children. Husk, too, was being purchased for the cow. Mantri's mother was almost on a starvation diet. For women in poor households, starvation was a routine thing. In difficult times, even more.

Mantri asked his mother, "Why does father feed so much to the cow?"

"The cow would not yield milk if she does not eat. Milk is in the mouth of the milking cow."

Interrupting her, Mantri said, "Then, if you eat more, you would have more milk. After the little ones are satisfied, we, too, could suck. How is it that father does not understand this? You speak to father. Else, let me speak. He must give you more food to eat."

Mantri's mother sighed and said, "In a poor family, the cow eats more than the housewife. Better cared for. This is the fate of women. The cowherd's cows eat better than their wives. The cow's belly never shrinks in hunger."

Mantri goes to the lower primary school without food. He goes out of fear of his father. By dawn, there is no rice flake or puffed rice for the children in a large family. Mantri's breakfast is a little gruel or raw tea with a few grains of puffed rice, or a small bowl of rice broth. Mantri had imagined that, when the cow would be milked, he would drink milk and go to school and study with concentration. But since Ghana Behera has milked the cow dry, Mantri is totally frustrated and is certain that he would not succeed at school.

There were two teachers in the lower primary school of the village, senior teacher and junior teacher. Both were of the upper caste. The school was a twig and wattle thatched hall and a narrow veranda. The veranda was so narrow that even two rows of students could never sit comfortably. Inside the hall, the upper-caste students read, sitting on mats. Dalits were forbidden to sit with them, for it would be blasphemous to put the upper caste and Dalits together. The teachers, too, would lose their caste if they came in close contact with them.

Therefore, about eight to ten Dalit students used to read sitting on the narrow veranda, with their backs to the road and faces toward the wall of the hall. On their backs the sunrays beat down, rains blew, and frosty winter struck the bones. Seasons with a liberal temper pour whatever they can on the backs of the poor, low-caste children.

Trying to withstand the onslaught of the seasons with grit and determination, their alphabets go awry.The teachers' anger rises.But they cannot beat them with hand or stick, lest the sanctity of their caste be defiled. Therefore, in a basket, they keep pieces of wood, small twigs, broken bricks, and pebbles, and when the need for spanking the Dalits arises, they throw one or two pieces at them.

Mantri was not pained by the beatings, but by the insult meted out to them. Mantri used to think, Is the caste of the upper-caste people so superficial that it goes if they touch anybody? Whereas those who are sidetracked as low-caste people, is their caste so deep that, even after death, their ashes never lose the caste mark, and the crematory waits for them at a distance because their ashes are low-caste ashes?

Mantri remembers the events of the endless revolt on his last day at school. It was the rainy season. The river's belly was swollen to the bursting point. The bellies of the tanks and ponds were full, but the bellies of the Dalit children were empty, without two morsels of food in the morning and evening.

More than stray dogs, the poor people are hungry. What the dog eats, man cannot eat. They are looked upon as worse than dogs for their untouchable caste. That is the poor man's helplessness.

Mantri was remembering the events of that day. On a rainy day, wet all over, they were sitting, hungry and sick; Mantri Mallik, Neta Nayak, Bideishi Behera, Saheb Bhoi, Collecter Kandi, and Barrister Mallik, all Dalit students. There was hunger in their bellies, the lashing rain on their backs. The letters on the slates were being washed away by the rain.Over and above this, the teacher was throwing the missile pieces from the basket at them, saying, "Why are you eating away the letters?"

Mantri protested in hunger and anger, "Why should we sit on the veranda, beaten by sun and rain?"

The senior teacher said in a harsh voice, "Go and ask your father."

The junior teacher said, "Because the country got freedom, you dare to come up to the school veranda. That's enough. Don't think you would be master by writing, Mallik. This is what happens when the ants climb up the lamp stand."

The other children laughed derisively. Although Mantri could not understand the full meaning of the teacher's words, he felt insulted. His innocent mind could understand that coming to the school meant to recognize yourself as a low-caste human; to know that you were born for humiliation, for exploitation, and to suffer from low self-esteem, social masochism, and finally, to blame fate and destiny; to be insulted without cause and to be victimized by your teachers' wrath.

Gall rose to the head of Mantri. He held the hands of Neta Nayak and Bideshi Behera and rose in a huff. Entering the hall, he gave a bold call to the other Dalit children, "Come all! The letters are washed off the slates by this lashing rain, and you get beaten unnecessarily. Come, we would sit in this hall and read. The teacher's dog is sleeping in this hall, fearing the rain. Why should we sit outside?"

Mantri's mind was simmering in revolt against father, mother, neighbors, people of the village, teacher, god, Yama, the god of death, and all others. But he could never give voice to his futile revolt. When hunger and insult rose to his head, he ignored the fear of the teacher, of father, and voiced his protest.

The teachers and the upper-caste students reacted violently and pounced on the Dalits. The teachers could not control their ire, knowing full well that they had to bathe in this rainy weather if they touched the Dalit boys. Outnumbered and beaten by the upper-caste group, the Dalit boys ran, here and there, for dear life, and in that downpour disappeared beyond the school gates.

The father of the ringleader, Mantri Mallik, was summoned to the school. It was declared that the name of Mantri would be struck off the register. Bharjan was ordered to pay for the purification yajna and the cleaning of the school to get back the sanctity of the temple of learning. The poor fellow, not thinking about arranging money to pay and atone for his son's "sins," ran out to search for his clan-tarnishing son.

Mantri, by that time, had taken shelter under the banyan tree near the crematory, wet from head to toe. At that time, the fire of a freshly-burned corpse was dying in the rain. At the foot of the banyan tree, half a pot of rice offered to the dead person was kept. Mantri thought, "Such rich men are there in the village that, even at the time of death, they leave so much extra rice in the pot for the dead!"

His mind became restless. His hunger was in high flames to see so much unclaimed rice. Sacrificing his sense of right and wrong to the flame of hunger in his belly, Mantri sat at the rice pot and ate like a glutton. The pot, with some rice left in it, he hid in the kewra bush nearby, to eat again when he would be hungry.

Poor fellow! In no time, wet and exhausted, he fell asleep on the half-wet earth under the tree. That day, Bharjan, holding a stick and a straw rope in his hands, was tired from searching for his son in the entire village. Had he found him, he would have tied him to the school pole and beaten him black and blue in the presence of the teacher. And he would have tearfully requested that the teacher not strike Mantri's name from the school.

But Mantri was not found. He also did not come back home in the night. Mantri's parents thought he might have gone to his uncle's house out of fright, crossing the river. The boy was friends with the boatman, Bharat. Many a time Mantri had gone to uncle's house ferried by Bharat. Therefore, there was no cause for worry.

Mantri woke up when the crematory sunlight, sawed off by the sharp edges of the datepalm branches, fell on his face. Since he had slept peacefully without encountering any ghost, goblin, witch, or gnome in the crematorium, his fear about burning ghats disappeared from that moment. In the kewra bushes, the pot was there, but there was no rice. Although he could not know whether evil spirits or a dog ate the rice, he was grateful to the agents of evil that they ate the rice and not him. He was resentful of the dog because he had licked out everything from the pot.

Mantri returned home and was beaten by the father, but did not reveal where he had stayed the night and what he had eaten. It was assumed that, out of fear and hunger, the helpless boy must have slept on someone's veranda or under some shelter or even on the village platform. But since that day, Mantri's studies were sealed off. Mantri escaped the fear of studies and the blows of the teachers, but could not escape the anger of his father.

Bharjan always ground his teeth in seething anger at Mantri's dismissal from school and asked him to earn his keep by working as a laborer somewhere. Mantri, thereafter, went to work in the master's house whenever his mother felt weak or ill. The rest of the time he spent in the crematory. It became a luxury for him to eat the rice offered to the dead in the cremation ground. Whenever he heard chants accompanying the dead or the drums beatenat the edge of the village for a dead married woman, like a dog following the smell of a feast, he followed the rows of people carrying the deathpot of rice. That day was his feast day.

Mantri adapted the cremation ground as his survival arena. Those days, the crematory was the safest place for Mantri. Neither Father nor the villagers could see him there. Who has any work in the crematory, if no death occurs in a family? Who goes for a daily stroll in the cremation ground like going to the fair or farm land?

Onreaching the lonely cremation ground, Mantri feels as if he is the king of the crematory. He now has no fear of the burning ghat. When a body burns, the unpleasant smell of the dead flesh floats down his street. If the funeral fire burns, in the kerosene-scarce murky village evening, it serves as the sacred evening lamp.

All dead bodies are taken to the cremation ground by the route near his street, accompanied by the chanting for the dead. The cremation ground is rather dry and clean compared to the Dalit streets. Once the body is burned,no trace of the dead man remains; whereas in the Dalit streets, all the year round, death calls from someone or the other's house because of hunger, disease, sorrow, or old age. Therefore, Mantri feared the nights in his own house, but not the cremation ground. For others, the pond of another village and the cremation ground of one's own village are fearful, but for Mantri there was no fear.

Shining like the tilak on the forehead of the Dalit street, and the pride of Mantri's family, the cow not only reached menopause, but also became sick. Bharjan was not only troubled by expenses, but also earned the sin of cow slaughter. One night, the old cow died on the halter. The poor world of Mantri was struck by lightning. Wearing a straw rope around his neck and holding grass between his teeth like a dumb cow, Bharjan moved all around the village, begging for alms by making gestures, to atone for the sin

Mantri was surprised by all he saw. The cow was sick and old. All cows are tethered, and so she, too, was roped to the peg, and in that state she died. How did his father become a sinner? And how was it such a sin that, however great or established you were, you must beg for alms to atone for it? A lot was spent on atonement of the sin of a cow dying on the tether in their house.

Hearing the news, Kundala Panda came striding in up to the riverbank. He took the calf to his house. It was not necessary to seek the permission of the tearful Bharjan. Only as he left with the calf did he say in a liberal voice, "Do you understand? You are unlucky in everything. The goat is cumbersome for a gardener, and business is cumbersome for the low-caste people. How can a Dalit understand the glory of a cow? How can an untouchable understand cow service and cow business? This calf also would betray you unreasonably. Why invite another cow-slaughter sin?

"And, moreover, you do not have the means to feed the calf to grow into motherhood, she might die. Why should you suffer for nothing? If you keep this in your house, you will definitely invite ill-fate. I clearly see this. Additionally, the calf is not legally yours, as you had not purchased the cow by paying money. Therefore, donate this animal to a Brahmin with a rupee or eight annas as sacrificial fee. And to expiate the sin of cow slaughter, everyday send a big bag of grass to my house. All your sins would be neutralized."

Bharjan kept a rupee at the feet of the Brahmin. His wife and children fell flat at his feet, but the rogue Mantri stood defiant at a distance. His crimson eyes alternated between resting kindly on the calf and wildly on the face of Kundala Panda.

While savoring a sense of relief that all malefic effects were gone after gifting away the calf, Mantri committed an unheardof, unatonable crime. During the rains, the romantic scene of crows and vultures enjoying the weather with closed eyes, sitting side by side on the branches of the massive, hoary banyan tree standing proud at the edge of the cremation ground, was deeply exciting for Mantri. From his childhood days, he could climb trees, beating a monkey, and swim in the river, trouncing the pride of water snakes.

Therefore, if it rained heavily while he was exploring in the cremation grounds, he used to climb up the tree and sit among the leaves, challenged by the clouds and winds. He used to spend so many hours in the tree that it was difficult to search for him. One day during the rains, Mantri was enjoying sitting on the crowded branches of a big mango tree on the other side of the road near the crematory. It was midday. Dark clouds loomed large in the sky, darkening the earth.

Kundala Panda was returning from the Erasama market, crossing the river, and walking with long strides. His batua (a bag with material for preparing betel) was under his armpit, and a packet was hanging from his shoulders. Heavy drops of rain started lashing all of a sudden, and, sensing that the sweets, puris, and other delicacies hanging from his shoulder being spoiled by the rains were fit enough for offering the gnomes and ghosts, Panda sat at the foot of the same mango tree.

That mango tree, in fact, was the preferred shelter for all

tired passersby. Taking out the packet, Panda examined whether the goodies were wet. He rested, content, waiting for the gushing winds to blow off the clouds.Mantri had dozed off on the tree branch, as he had eaten heavily at the eleventh day obsequies in a family in Jagannathpur. How could Mantri know that Kundala Panda was having his siesta at the foot of the tree? His mind was in the realm of clouds and wind. There was no indication of Kunde's presence under the tree.

Mantri suddenly felt the urge to defecate. How could he come down in the rain to go to the fields when the urge was urgent? Mischievous Mantri's habit was to find a neat place to relieve himself. Mantri's belly was rumbling. Poor fellow couldn't find time to climb down the tree. On the bifurcated branches of a thick bough, he sat, keeping his legs on the small branches as do the children of rich families in their toilets. Hanging on to another heavy branch above, he finished his work. He felt relieved. When the priest declared that his father was free from the sin of cowslaughter, he must not have felt so relieved.

He suddenly heard a loud wail, and, deciphering the sound, Mantri's liver shook in fear. It was no ghost or goblin, no unredeemed soul. The most respected person of this region, Kundala Panda, was dancing wildly, screaming expletives. Even Mahadev might not have danced that wild tandav so wrathfully at the burning of chaste Parvati in the sacrificial fire. Panda was not in a condition to be calmed. On the plaited hair on the crown of Panda, the hellish crime of the bastard Dalit boy Mantri Mallick was sitting gracefully like a mound of sandal paste. Panda was not able to remove it nor touch it.

Panda was vomiting the free, sumptuous lunch without retaining a bit in his stomach. Dancing wildly, Panda was cursing the past, present, and future of the condemned soul. Mantri could not muster courage to come down and brave the screams of Panda. But in spite of fear and worry, the boy Mantri had mirthful laughter bubbling up to the brim. By that time, some villagers had already gathered there. Kundala Panda ran mad to the banks of Hansua river in that state of sickness and vomiting.

People thought, not tolerating the insult of having Dalit excreta on his head, he might have preferred drowning in the river to showing his face again in the village. Hearing the news, the important persons of the village, Gandhi Das, Bharat Mandal, Udhab Mangual, Golmasta, Tahali Mohanty, Kumpani Soin, and Dhadi Barik had all gathered there in the meantime.

Gandhi Das said, "Many things done by children are based on reason. The Dalits, hated as untouchables, have been carrying on their heads the excreta of the upper-caste people for the past hundreds of years. They might not be averse because of long years of habit, but certainly there is revolt. Mantri is a different kind of boy, a rebel. I know his nature.

"It cannot be said that this is not the work of that subconscious rebellion. Rather, I fear that these Kaliyug children would sit every day at high places and defecate on our heads. They would remind the upper-caste people that because of the devil in their heads, a group of people have been treated as untouchables for many centuries. In short, to ease the fatigue of long walks of the villagers, the shades under the trees are no more safe places. What do you all say?"

Many people said in one voice, "Maybe! But what's the way out?"

Gandhi Das replied, "At first, let the anger of the high priest subside. Rescue him out of the river first. Then we would speak about the way."

NINE

For a long time, Panda bathed in the river, keeping his head under water, reciting mantras and cursing the evildoer. Rising up, holding his water-filled pot, he walked with pride toward the gathering.

In a calm voice he said, "He who has the Brahma(God) inside is a Brahmin. Therefore, this low born, short-lived lad has not insulted the Brahmin, but has desecrated the Brahma. The village should disown him. If he goes home, the entire Dalit street must be thrown into the Hansua river. In other words, the conflict between Dalit and the upper caste is inevitable. In this conflict, the Dalits alone would be decimated. This is the truth borne by history. Therefore, let the village banish him. Otherwise, I would reduce to ashes his family and the entire Dalit settlement by the curse of Brahmin."

In the meantime, Bharjan Mallick, like a tail-tucked, cowardly dog, Mantri's mother, and a few elderly Dalits had fallen at the feet of the priest, holding grass in their teeth. Some Dalit elders said, "Oh, you great one. That boy's name is now wiped from our street. If his parents allow him to enter their house, we'll burn the house. At the call of Gandhi Das, Mantri, like a mouse rescued from floods, all wet and miserable, got down from the tree. From the crowd, Gandhi Das dragged the mean fellow, Mantri, and took him to stand before the priest.

He said, "Oh great one, the punishment for such a

low crime should be harsh. You curse this boy and burn him to ashes in the presence of everyone here. Only then would these barbarous fools understand the power of a Brahmin and the consequences of a Brahmin curse. Or else, there won't be any difference between Brahmins and Dalits."

Everyone understood the irony of Gandhi Das. They also understood the helplessness of Panda. Panda said, "The law says that we should punish the enemy by keeping him alive. Once dead, what else is left for vengeance? Only fools kill the enemy. Therefore, let the barbarous, short-lived black sheep live, but let him live all his life hated like the devil. Let him suffer the consequences of his sin, life after life."

Immediately Dhadi Barik, the barber was summoned. In the presence of everyone, Panda shaved his head, sacrificing the carefully maintained hair. At his direction, a few strands of hair were left below the neck. Tying a brahma knot on that, Panda vowed, "No more shall I grow the desecrated hair on my crown."

From that day on, gradually, the crown became bald. But the brahmaknot, like the knot at the edge of women's sarees, was tied and untied. The knot became loose slowly, but his anger did not subside a bit.Then and there, Panda declared, "Under this same inauspicious mango tree, Goddess Kali, the deity of the cremation ground, would be consecrated. She would suck the blood of the sinners. This mango tree, however, shall not be felled. Like a witness to the eternal sin, the tree would warn the future generations of Dalits." He also announced that, by worshipping, Mantri would sanctify the crematory Goddess Kali for the rest of his life.

The proposal was immediately accepted. After that, Gandhi Das declared, "From today on, the open latrine system is banned in all villages."

"From today on, no Dalit would clean the latrines, nor ever carry filth on their heads. By this practice, bitterness for the upper castes is brewing. This has been declared illegal already. If Kundala Panda could clean himself of the excreta of a Dalit boy that fell on his head, why should not we clean our own filth? Be he

Tahali Mohanty or Narkeswar Routray, no one is higher than Kundala Panda. Thus, this rule applies to all."

Kundala Panda had no choice but to agree with the well-argued and articulated proposal of Gandhi Das. Many people felt that two good things had happened simultaneously. At Panda's instruction, on the trunk of the mango tree was scratched, "Here an inauspicious work was performed. Be careful."

No one had any cause for headache over what was written on the trunk of the mango tree. But where would the twelve-year-old Mantri Mallick go? Where would he live? Everyone looked at each other. Bharjan Mallick, opening his cleft lips, tried to make clear what was causing confusion, and announced, "This black sheep of the clan created a scene in the school. That was somehow settled. But what he did today is unpardonable. I swear in the name of the crematory Kali that this rogue is dead to me from today on. His name is wiped from our streets. He has no place in my house. If anyone else gives him shelter in his house, Bharjan Mallick would not be responsible for that. Bharjan's words are the words of a true male, strong like the tusk." The last two sentences were meant for Mantri's mother, whose sobs and tears had soaked her to disintegration.

Mantri's mother struck her head on the ground three, four times. "Oh, my mad darling! Which demon has possessed you? What have you done? How can I sacrifice you while living? Without you, my dead body would go from this house. Oh, my life of life. "She moaned in delirium. She then returned home with unsteady steps. Really, where would Mantri take shelter? He'd been banished by the villagers!

Coming out of the crowd, Golmasta stood before Kundala Panda and fearlessly said, "May Allah do good to everyone. Mantri would live in my house as my son. We Muslims live like a banished lot, away from the village. Would anyone lose anything by this? Let me tell you, it would not happen."

After this, a search was made for Mantri Mallick. Meanwhile, Mantri had disappeared somewhere, sneaking away from the crowd. No trace of him was left anywhere. No one could find him in anyone's veranda or house till midnight.

"Must have gone somewhere out of fear. He would certainly come back. He would not leave the village," Golmasta consoled everyone. People went back to their homes.

The next day, the cowherds saw him sleeping, coiled up in the cement funeral pit in the crematory, which was meant for the upper-caste people. All around him were the broken pots of offerings to the dead, and leftovers.

Since that day, not only his residence changed, but also his name. He was known as the crematory demon. But Kundala Panda, in his original style, screamed Mantri's name and said, "See? Within the night, the brahmacurse has shown results. See? The sinner has turned into a devil. He is not a crematorydemon, but a crematorydevil. Devil!"

Man is saved when death takes him away. He is released from worry and fear. But Mantri thought that, even without death, he had been saved by making the crematory his home. His back was now free from the lashing of sun, rain, cold and the teacher's missiles. He was also free from the beatings of his father, the ill-temper of mother, and the daily quarrels with his brothers and sisters for a fistful of rice, a few grains of cereal, and a spit measure of curry.

He was of no use to anyone except to himself, and there was no scope for anyone's desire or command to be thrust on him. He was free like the ghosts and gnomes of the crematory.In a strange thrill of freedom, his mind flew to the sky from the earth. The urge to play kabaddi and other games was automatically springing from his heart.

Like seeing a miraculous creature, his Dalit friends were amazed whenthey saw him. He did not take much time to understand the reason for their behavior. He was still alive, pulling out the charcoal-mixed skeletal frames of freshly burnt corpses from the funeral pit and sleeping there for warmth! Despite eating the rice offered to the dead, how is it that the ghosts and other preternatural creatures did not suck his blood? Why did they not feast on his bones? How was he alive, encountering the ghosts and witches? This was definitely a miraculous event for the village boys.

Kundala Panda, however, said that Mantri had no control over it. Since he was transformed by his curse, the crematory was his natural habitat, and the ghosts and goblins were his friends. Hence, they did not harm him. Panda was spreading this theory, and the others believed him. Mantri himself was delighted that he had been transformed into the devil by Panda's curse. At least, in the entire village, he was the lone devil who could eat anything he pleased and do anything that took his fancy. He had no ties or restrictions.

The crematory, for Mantri, became a more pleasurable place than it had been earlier. As people fear the water of other areas, the crocodiles and sharks, but not their own rivers and tanks, Mantri similarly had no fear of the crematory of his village. He was not afraid of ghosts or evil spirits. He was afraid, rather, of living men, the village elders, the teachers, the Brahmin priests, the Tahali Mohantys, and the Narku Routrays. But the day he'd been banished by them and become a resident of the crematory, his fear for all those went away. He was fearless, free of ties and relations, a vagabond, crematory devil. The crematory embraced him, alive, and rekindled the shrunken humanity in him, which began rearing its head slowly.

The crematory had always been a mystery box; now it became the gymnasium for his growing years. So many things lay scattered there for the entertainment of children. On one side, a slanting stream of river Hansua, on the other side, a dense, high, wall-like kewra jungle. Adjacent to it, a large, heavy banyan tree with aerial roots. Like the hands of the mighty demon, the aerial roots were clutching the grounds. A short distance away from that aerial-rooted banyan tree, also a shade beyond the crematory, was another half-sized, massive banyan tree, under which pots of rice were offered to the departed souls as a part of their last rites. Under this tree were scattered broken pots and skulls.

---

[4] The Manabodha Chautisa gives a cynical view of life and advocates surrender to God.

Mantri observed with keen interest all the rituals of the funeral ceremony when new bodies came for cremation. Those persons who were famously arrogant in the village, some of them were burnt to ashes before his own eyes. All the lines of pride, arrogance, and cruelty on their faces faded forever. Not only old haggards-at times, children and young ones also came to the crematory.

Mantri, from one perspective, liked the dispassionate embrace of the cremation ground for the rich and poor, upper caste and lower caste, young and old, one and all. For others, the sight of dogs, jackals, crows, and vultures feeding on the corpses might be heartrending, but for Mantri it was natural. His adolescent mind could understand that a dead body is like a lump of earth and does not feel any pain when the jackals and vultures draw the entrails forcibly. He knew that pain was felt by the living.

For everyone whodied of hunger and starvationoutside the crematory, flocks of human vultures and jackals sucked the life out of them, dragging and pulling. Here, the poor men's bodies were simply thrown, wrapped in rags. Then the nuptial feast of the dogs and vultures started. But they shared the cadaver, never monopolized. It never happened in the crematory that one ate his fill and saved the rest in boxes or barns, while ten others cried in hunger.

The principle of the cremation ground was live and let live. The crow, vulture, myna, hornbill, and other families of birds, big and small, were all different in shape, size, and color. Their powers to fly were also varied. But for the crow being servile to the vulture, the myna building a nest for the crow, or the hornbill exploiting the drongo, differences were not seen in the world of birds. Mantri observed this, sitting in the crematory.

Mantri accepted the crematory as a place of pilgrimage, for the caste conflicts in his village as well as in his own Dalit Street were not found in the birds or animals here. And the best thing that pleased Mantri was their songs. The birds, too, must have had their share of sorrows, family problems, and physical ailments. Although they looked similar, their fates must be different from each other's.

But Mantri never heard the birds babbling or moaning in distress. He never saw them cursing their fates, striking their heads against the trees. The birds must have had their needs and faced deprivation in their bankrupt lives. But Mantri never saw one bird snatching food from another's beak or begging at another's feet. How does the bird spend his season of need? How does it manage its lonely old age? Who gives Ganges water in the mouth of a dying bird? Who lights the funeral fire to its face? Who observes the obsequies for the salvation of its soul? Who is a Brahmin or Dalit, Muslim or Christian in their world on wings?

Mantri was amazed, listening to their eternal song, watching their daily business, mental strength, and self-reliance, irrespective of their age. The bird has no temple to threaten the sinner, no police station to lock up the criminal, no doctors or hakims for the treatment of diseases, no minister, MLA, chairman, sarpanch, ward member, village chief, priest, barber, washerman, loan giver, godown, business chief. With none of these, if such a large, winged world has been maintained without a hitch since the beginning of creation, why then so much sin, crime, pain, and disturbance in the human order, which has established so many institutions to maintain the social order? Is man fated not to live in peace and happiness, or is it the consequence of his own deeds?

While observing silently the things around him, in the small head of Mantri, big mountains of questions raise their heads. Sitting on the school veranda and listening to the teachers teaching in the room up to class three, Mantri had learned a few letters. He'd learned writing numbers, the multiplication table, and the spellings of a few combined letters.He'd studied some mathematics, literature, and history. But Mantri had not read on the slate, the literature of life and death. On the open slate of the crematory, in the warm light of the funeral fire, in flaming letters in the midst of beastly sounds, in the inauspicious hooting of the owl, in the sky-kissing smoke of burning corpses, in the futile mourning of relatives, Mantri acquired a real education. Those lessons taught him many things, awakened him to reality, made him an introvert and also an extrovert. The inner world and the outer world opened up before him.

The naughty Mantri became speechless. His mind and body awakened in realization. Not only in light, but also in darkness, many things became visible to him. He conversed with the crematory even in the dead of night. His all-season friend in the crematory was the naked Sadhu. Ghosts and goblins shrunk in fear of Sadhu's massive figure, clothed in red robes. Because of him, Mantri thought, there was no mischief from the ghosts and gnomes in that crematory.

The big vermillion mark on the wide forehead of the Sadhu, like the blood-smeared tongue of Goddess Kali, was awe-inspiring and fearful. The trident in his hand caused fear in the heart, as if piercing the heart through heaven, earth, and the netherworld. But there was no congruence between the appearance of the naked Sadhu and his nature. He was a very patient, loving, and calm person.

When he was a small kid, Mantri had been attracted to the crematory by the Sadhu, as if mesmerized. And he'd watched Sadhu's daily routine. Now he became a disciple of the Sadhu. Near the crematory, Sadhu used to sit all night under the void of the sky, lighting his purgatorial fire. Some devotees of the village gathered there, bowed down to the Sadhu, and, sitting on the platform near the Kali temple, they'd smoke grass and sing prayers to the Sunya (Unseen God), and also sing the Manabodha Chautisa.

Although Mantri had been banished by the village, the villagers had never banished him. Mantri, too, had a soft spot for the village. How could he banish the village from his mind? Can the mother be banished? Can the mother banish her child? If Mantri's mother cooked some delicacies or received some from the master's house, she used to bring those to her son, under wraps.

On the crematory trees, the thrill of spring awoke, flowers bloomed and buds winked. They fruited to the mating song of the birds. It was as if Mantri had been transformed into a tree. Like all other trees, his roots, too, had gone deep into the crematory. His branches were spread against the endless skyon which spring had flapped its wings, and the breeze had played the flute, reclining on the vast trunk of the tree on which the thrush had ululated, enchanting the tender, new leaves of dreams.

Like a dream, Mantri, too, came of age, as did his friends Neta Nayak, Bideshi Behera, Saheb Bhoi, and Collector Kandi. From a scrimpy boy, he grew up to be a hefty young man. Eating the crematory food, he became a taller, larger, and stronger bullish male. But for him, perhaps, a demoness was not born anywhere. Therefore, while his friends became fathers of half a dozen or more children, Mantri was moving carefree as a bachelorghost. As long as the naked Sadhu was there, Mantri served him. After Sadhu went elsewhere, Mantri lit the purgatorial fire at his seat. The same cymbal players were in session, as usual. Mantri, perhaps, was happier than his friends in the respect of prayers and food.

On Mantri's round face were a hillock-like mound of a nose, eyes full of mist like a brimming river in spate, a forehead like a vast grazing ground, peaceful and serene, and luxuriant, shining black hair like a nux vomica bush. He had long hands like the aerial roots of a banyan tree, strong legs like the pillars of palm trees, a broad chest like the platform at the edge of the village, a pointed moustache like date leaves, thick, fleshy lips like rice cakes, and noisy strides like a rogue bull. All these had given him a distinctive identity in about a dozen villages around. Mantri could have become the village chowkidar. But although a crematorydevil, he was more than a chowkidar. Such a bullish young man remaining a bachelor, everybody felt, was a quirk of fate. But Mantri's mother, full of filial love, was dreaming that, like the banyan-peepal match, somewhere a matching girl must have been born for him.

Adjacent to the edge of the crematory, with date branches, Mantri made a shelter for the imaginary daughter-in-law of his mother. As he grew up eating the crematory food, he developed a sense of responsibility for the place. Gradually, he became the watchman of the crematory, its servitor. His thatched shelter was full with the things coming with the dead bodies to the cremation ground, abandoned after cremation. More things were there in his hut than were found in the houses of the people of his street. As he grew up in years, his hut, too, grew in size. It seemed as if a few sharp-edged, leafy branches of date saplings-which had grown on his roof-declared the totalitarian umbrella of Mantri's authority. The umbrella would take on a golden hue when the summer-ripe clusters of dates swelled to sweetness.

Mantri Mullik fenced his house with thorn plants and allergy-causing bushes, and planted musk rose, jasmine, bell champak, and marigold flower saplings. In summer, the jasmines made the crematory and the hut of Mantri fragrant. These flowers did not bloom for gods and goddesses, but for the dead bodies. For those unwanted bodies which were laid on the pyre, Mantri hurriedly made a garland with banana plant threads and put it on the neck of the corpses.

Mantri takes money for other funeral requirements, but never for garlands.

When he sees the naked neck of a corpse, he himself adorns it with a garland. Why should he take money for that? On the other side of the crematory, a Goddess Kali temple was built up as a victory pillar for Mantri's traumatic childhood. If anyone asks flowers for mother Kali, Mantri rudely says no and comments, "Is there a dearth of flowers for the mother? These flower plants are for the dead bodies only. It is unjust to share them with gods and goddesses."

Like a vulture, Mantri lies in wait for the dead bodies. When a body comes, the crematory gets crowded. The village people meet Mantri and talk about their lives. Otherwise, the crematory becomes lonely for Mantri. When a body comes, he feels no joy or pain. Instead, he becomes normal and at ease with himself. As the poor teachers sit alone in the school when students do not come, Mantri similarly gets lonely when a corpse doesn't come in.

Who else knew more than Mantri that human beings never fail to spread imaginary stories about the netherworld? Strange things were rumored about Mantri in the villages-that he not only eats the rice and curry offered to the dead, but also the flesh of half-baked corpses. Sleeping on the half-burned bodies of young women in the funeral pit, he indulges in sexual orgies. It seems he also played and flirted with the filth-eating witches. As a result of such canards spread against him, the crematorydevil sobriquet became permanently stuck on him, and no Mallik family woman was available to induce him to social life. Whoever would gift away a daughter for honeymooning in the crematory, to the crematorydevil?

Mantri had no interest in marriage. If a woman happened to be interested, well, then welcome! If none were available, so be it! What was wrong with that? Unnecessary problems, quarrels, children, worries, wants, struggles, sickness and disease, and finally, what? Death! If the rhythm finally stops with death, then why take so many anxieties on the head? "Oh, the same rigmarole!"

Mantri Mallik was also rumored to be mad and possessed randomly by evil spirits. He could pluck out coconuts without climbing the tree, could cross rivers to and fro without rowing a boat. He could walk on river and sea, could fell a tree without an axe. All good and bad deeds he could accomplish. Who would give his daughter to Mantri? One who chats with dogs, jackals, and vultures, how could he give joy to a wife?

All through his life, none had come to Mantri with a proposal, and none had been offered from his side. He himself was his master. To marry and raise a family had never been his dream. Also, he had never looked lustfully at any woman, single or married. Whenever he looked, in his eyes a love-soaked wick burned for everyone.

Mantri remembered who was cremated in the village crematory on which day, who was just thrown out without a funeral, who died for what reason, whether the death was pleasant or painful, male or female, what was the apparent age of the body, who else had come to the funeral-every detail he remembered. He noted all this down in a torn notebook, in a haphazard way. The next day, crossing the river, he would inform the police. The village panchayat had not permitted Mantri to sell firewood, nor had they permitted him to inform the police.

He was not appointed by anyone to do what he did, and no salary was paid to him for his labor. But they collected details from him. Although the villagers never allowed him to enter their houses, after the harvests, some of them gave him, unasked for, a small measure of rice and lentils. Even that was sufficient for him to give in charity to the poor. Occasionally cooking a big pot of khichidi, he called and fed the naked, half-bellied children, and derived a lot of joy. When bananas ripened in his trees, he allowed the children to feast on them.

Once, however, Mantri cried seeing a body. A female corpse dimly resembled his mother. That woman had hung herself with a rope. Alas! What sorrow weighed heavy on the heart of such a beautiful woman that she took her own half-lived life? She had left behind four children like tender calves. Her fifteen-year-old son had cried and refused to set fire to the face of his dead mother. Enraged, the father had lost his senses and given a nasty blow. The boy had closed his eyes and put the torch as the last rite done by the elder son on the face of his mother, and, leaning on Mantri, he'd cried so bitterly that Mantri, too, had cried with him. Later, it was heard that the husband had tortured her so badly that she could not bear it any longer and had taken her own life.

One night, some people brought the dead body of an unmarried woman to the crematory in the dead of night. At the howling of jackals and dogs, Mantri, with a lantern, opened the door of his hut. By that time, four lads had placed the body in the pit and were about to light the fire. The smell of gasoline had already fouled up the moonlit night. On the road, Narku Routray's jeep was parked.

"Who's there? Who's there?" Shouting, Mantri Mallik, wielding a staff, ran like mad toward the dead body. The four lads dashed off and jumped into the jeep. Mantri chased them, lantern in hand. By the time the jeep moved, Mantri saw the face of the driver. He looked like Tahali Mohanty's son, Sakula.

"Sakula! You can't escape," shouted Mantri Mallik. The jeep disappeared in a wink. Returning to the body, he saw the dogs and jackals were rending the entrails of the corpse. But the face was making the moonlight brighter by its unblemished beauty. Mantri chased away the animals, raising his staff. He tried to recognize the young woman in the light of the lantern. Mantri was sad that, even after death, girls didn't appear dead.

Going nearer, he saw that she was unknown to him. The girl, it seems, had come from some organization in the city at the request of Gandhi Das. She had been motivating a few young women of Abhayapur against dowry. Tahali Mohanty's son Sakula's marriage had been called off by the anti-dowry propaganda of this woman. After negotiations for dowry, the marriage had been finalized with the daughter of some contractor of Manijanga. But the would-be bride had clearly refused to marry that street Romeo, photo-shop-owner lad on grounds of dowry demand. And ever since that day, Sakula's-and Tahali Mohanty's-evil eye was on that girl. But for that, such an inhuman crime?

Mantri guarded the corpse the rest of the night. That night, too, tears came into his eyes. But at dawn, seeing the horrible signs of force on the body of the girl, his eyes became fierce torches. In the first light of dawn he shouted, running on the village road, "Sakula Mohanty and his friends have raped and killed an innocent woman! They were about to burn the body, but escaped, abandoning the body when they encountered me." Mantri spread the horrendous news in a few nearby villages by shouting and screaming. He went to the Erasama police station and made a report with details of the murder. That single event shook the foundations of Abhayapur village. It not only shook the marrow of the village, but also stunned the entire region. Such a heinous, heartrending event was the first of its kind in the area. But what was the result? When the villagers reached the crematory, there was no sign of the dead body. Hansua River's crematory-filth-mixed, foamy waves were flowing fast toward the Jatadhari estuary. A saree stretched, like a bloody snake, from the edge of the crematory to the unused bank of the river.

The accusation of the cranky Mantri Mallik was not accepted. The officer-in-charge of the police station did not conduct an inquiry. Instead, a few villagers helped in the disappearance of the bloodstained saree toward the estuary. A few witnesses testified that Tahali Mohanty's son had been admitted to the Jagatsinghpur hospital for treatment of dysentery and had been there for the last three days. Mantri Mallik was proved to be a liar, a narcotic-madcrack-pot. But where had the girl from the NGO disappeared to? It was a question, but who cared for an answer?

Udhab Mangual said, "In this Kaliyug, the last leg of righteousness of Abhayapur is also broken now. The end of Kaliyug is in sight. The final solution is the deluge. The Kalki incarnation of God would start from this region with the ninety-ninth hand measure of sword. Wait and see whether my words come true."

Golmasta said, "Oh Allah! Where would my son, Mantri, go? Poor fellow! Oh, what wrong did he do to anyone? Alas Allah! A girl like my daughter. Alas, alas!"

Gandhi Das thundered, "Mantri Mallik would not move a thread from his place. If now righteousness in Abhayapur is standing on one leg, that leg is the crematorysaint, Mantri Mallik. The spokesperson of the village panchayat is not that worthless newspaper of Narku Routray's, nor is the ex-minister Routray the conscience of this village. Let there be an emergency meeting of the village assembly. We must save Abhayapur from these vileelements."

Centering around the crematory ban of Mantri Mallik, there was a great uproar in the village assembly. It was stage-managed by a few conscienceless, unemployed, hired goons of Tahali Mohanty and Routray. But all villagers in the assembly had strongly opined in favor of Mantri Mallik's story in the crematory. Everyone had realized that Mantri was the true friend of the crematory. Everyone said that, if Mantri Mallick was guarding the crematory in spite of not getting any salary from the panchayat, the panchayat should not interfere with that. All felt that Mantri had appeared as an angel for the dead bodies and relatives, in the dark wintry and rainy nights.

At the end of the meeting, Mantri Mallik announced, "Hereafter, if anyone tries to cremate an unclaimed corpse in the night, without informing the police, he would not be spared by Mantri Mallik." In fact, after that day, Mantri Mallik did not sleep at night. Tying a turban on his head, holding his staff in hand, and tucking a knife in his waist, Mantri did rounds all through the night in the crematory. And, shaking the innocent night, he shouted, "Beware! Beware! Be careful!" Many passersby, returning late from the fair, even saw him dancing the tandav.

Kundala Panda passed his judgment. "That crematorydevil was half-cracked. Now he is completely mad. Just wait. That mad fellow would be the first sacrifice before mother Kali. Mother Kali would give him the punishment of his sin."

The new-moon-born Ketaki's face looked fresh like the full moon, but everyone knew that she was unlucky. Elderly men said that, God had not fixed a groom for her, as she was born on the new-moon day with anill fate. In this same village, switching the horoscope with the younger sisters, new-moon-born Sebati's marriage was fixed with the Panchapalli Rout family's eldest son. The boy was working in Cuttack. A day before the marriage, the boy was on his way to the village, sitting on the pillion of his friend's motorbike. At Raghunathpur, a truck collided with it, head-on. The boy died on the spot.

The horoscope of Sebati, who'd been born under the new moon, could not remain secret any more. Like a newspaper item, the matter was discussed in every village. What injustice Sebati's father had done by hiding his daughter's horoscope! How could he knowingly try to pass his new-moon-born daughter on to another man's son? Man may hide the palm leaf horoscope, but would God hide the fate written on the forehead? Some people said that the groom's family knew that Sebati had been born under the new moon. Out of greed for the heavy dowry, they'd kept the matter secret in order to take Sebati home as their daughter-in-law.

Marriages could be solemnized hiding the age of the bride, but neither the father nor heavy dowry had the capacity to hide fate. The last word was that, whether knowingly or unknowingly, because the Rout boy had been coming to marry Sebati, he'd met his untimely death. The sorrow which Sebati suffered for not marrying was less than the pain she suffered for being the cause of death of the unknown, unseen Rout's son. Many people said many things to rub salt in the festering wound. The inauspicious night before marriage had no dawn. But Sebati's night of suffering had dawned.

Sebati went to the river to bathe before the break of dawn. Unlike everyone else, she had no fear of the blurred half-darkness, nor did she wait for her friends. Women who went later to bathe in the river saw that she had somehow taken from the house the bridal silk saree, and was hanging from the branch of a punang tree, using the saree as the rope. The body was warm, but there was no life. The women started weeping wildly. That day, Sebati's palanquin would have risen from Abhayapur, but her dead body was lifted. Sebati was to go to her mother-in-law's house; she went to the abode of Yama. People consoled themselves, saying that, "After what happened, there was no thread of difference between living and dying for the new-moon-born Sebati. Whatever Jagannath (God) does is for the good of the people."

TEN

After Sebati, everyone focused on the second newmoon girl. This was Ketaki, the daughter of the betel leaf grower. Who knows under what curse, one after another, girls are born on the newmoon day in this village! If the newmoon girl doesn't marry, it is painful, and if she marries, it is even more painful. Therefore, it's better not to marry. To counteract the curse of single life, it is a sin to be the cause of death of another's son. After eating up another's son, to mess up one's own life is a worse sin.

On which ever branch soul would sit, that branch would break. To whichever well or tank the soul went, it would run stone dry. For seven births, the restless soul woulden circle in the air, hungry and thirsty. No perch would be available to even rest for a while. If, by a quirk of fate, you were born as a new moon girl, then you should know right from birth that, by the destiny-maker's decree, and not by human wishes, one is born on the newmoon day to suffer life as an unmarried woman.

Kundala Panda says that the new-moon-born women, instead of thinking of a groom, should concentrate on God, as per the decree of the scriptures. That decree is not seen in any scripture, but if that rule is transgressed, Sebati-like death would beck on the new-moon-born girls, through wells, tanks, rivers, tree branches, roof beams, pesticides, or poison, in different tunes. The betelleaf grower's daughter, Ketaki, however, is not beckoned by death. But someone calls her from the realm of snakes in the nether world, into the dense entrails of the betel plantations. When night thickens, he comes only for Ketaki.

His name is Nagaraj (the Cobra king).

Since she'd come of age, Ketaki had known that no man had been born for her in the world. If she put the garland of choice on someone's neck clandestinely, the bridal night would come not in this life, but in the next-because a new-moon-born woman is the assassin for a man in a woman's form, a female cobra. But as a concubine, she could bed a luscious lover. The woman, thus born, instead of surrendering herself to God, looks at men lustfully. There is no harm done. Otherwise, there would be unwed pregnancy and the consequent scandal-and worse, banishment from the village. All this, or else the fate of Sebati await.

The loitering lust-partners of such women move like untethered studs. They are not fated to die untimely. Therefore, Ketaki, instead of waiting for a husband or lover, has focused on the betel plantation since her childhood. The betel plantation for her was a world of mystery; the realm of the cobra. She was a female cobra, newmoon born. Therefore, she had an irresistible fascination for the betel plantation.

The family business of Ketaki's father, grandfather, and great-grandfather was the betel plantation. Therefore, since she'd come of age, her soul had been entwined with the betel creepers and the plantation. Ketaki's toothless grandma narrated many stories and legends about the betel creeper. Ketaki had heard from her grandma that the betel creeper had been a proud beauty in Indra's Garden of Eden. King Bani Bastchha Raja, by austere meditation, pleased the king of angels, Indra, and, getting the sapling from Indra's garden, planted it in his own garden.

Ketaki's father Aparti was not as hardworking as Dambaru, his father, but in business sense was steely and crafty. A lot of betel leaves were grown in the father's betel plantations. Apartia was selling those betel harvests in Calcutta. He sold the same leaf under different names, at different prices, depending on size and shape. The big leaves were Jagannath betel. The midsized ones were Odissi betel. The small ones were Rasi. And, again, the importance was in the places and names of villages.

Kujangi leaf, Ambiki leaf, Abhayapur leaf, Shovan, Rai Kishori and so on were made popular by Apartia in the city of Calcutta. Businessmen from Calcutta and Bombay were coming to the villages and buying baskets of betel leaves. Despite the objections of Dambaru that the only son of the house need not go to Calcutta for business, the youthful Apartia never cared for his father's admonitions. He had earned a lot of money in Calcutta, but had spent a large chunk of it in luxury and on high living.

Here, carrying water to irrigate the plantations, Dambaru had developed a hunchback. The tall, five-hand-measure male, by the weight of years and the stress of backbreaking labor, was bent like a bow because of the hunchback. He was carrying a much bigger pitcher of water than the other betel growers to the planted area, drawing water from a well nearby, which he himself had dug out. And he irrigated the plants until he became old, bent, and unfit to carry out the work.

But Dambaru was not unhappy, as he was convinced that, although Aparti was entrapped by the city because of his youth, he would come back to the village to carry on the work in the village after his death. The betel plantation was life for Dambaru, not a mere profession. Dambaru used to say that before men could hear the footsteps of the seasons, the betel creepers heard them, and Dambaru, too, was able to sense the seasonal lushes of the betel creepers.

By touching the raw and ripe leaves, one by one, he was able to read the horoscope of the seasons and was able to predict the summer storms, floods, cyclones in the sea, lightning strikes, the megha malhar(rain song), autumnal love songs, and the ecstasy of the spring breeze. Touching the betel leaves, Dambaru was able to say when the paddy fields would start flowering, whether the mango buds would come sooner or later in a particular year.

He was also able to predict by touching the betel leaves on which current of the river the hilsa season would break and open up the luck of the fisherfolk. He could tell in which month the ragi fields would turn almond-brown in frolicking joy. Such was the love of Dambaru for the betel leaves. Dambaru's predictions were so accurate that paddy growers and fishermen always waited for his words. Without bothering about loss or gain, until his last breath, he raised the creepers up and up, and one day breathed his last within the plantation. One grim noon in April, placing his head on a large coil of leafless creepers, he dedicated his last few gasps to the betel.

Two other names Ketaki had received as ornaments from her childhood were new moon born and female cobra. Ketaki, therefore, believed that, like the betel creeper, her original birth place was the Nagaloka, the world of snakes. Her childhood luxury was to search for the world of snakes in the betel plantation. She was attracted to the betel plantation to unravel this mystery. The key to that mystery was the betel flower, which she wanted to discover. Like the dimiri flower, the betel flower was an impenetrable mystery in her village.

Although many people in their village had betel plantations, none had seen a betel flower, let alone the betel fruit. Ketaki's grandma, however, had a different story to tell. She had heard from Dambaru that because of someone's curse, the male and female betel creepers could not grow tied up together inside the enclosure. Therefore, flowers and fruits would be seen on the creepers, but the betel grower would not thrive, because if flowers and fruits appeared, the betel leaf would not grow in size nor would it be tasty.

Like the babe sucking milk from the mother's breast, the flowers and fruits would suck away the juice from the betel leaves. Not only would the juice dry up, but also the fragrance would die. Because of low yield and small size, the female leaf was less lucrative and hence had no place in the plantation area. In the male creepers, male flowers could bloom, but greedy and selfish betel growers clipped away the flowering branches the way the government and doctors removed the ovaries of women in the name of family planning.

When flowers bloomed in the betel creepers, the size of the male leaves shrank. The harvest dwindled. In other words, for man's selfish interests, the betel creepers sacrificed their flowers and fruits and lived a life of barrenness. The betel creeper was so very self-effacing that, deprived of the pleasure of union, distancing herself from the glory of flowers and fruits and opening up hundreds of leaf buds, she prolonged her clan at the wish of the betel grower.

Ketaki often felt that she was not a woman, but a betel creeper. She would be deprived of the pleasures of union and motherhood by the decree of society. For this reason, she had developed an intense love for the betel creeper. But for some unknown reason, her grandpa always forbade her entry into the plantation enclosures. He used to say, "Inside the enclosure, under the shadow of the creepers, male and female cobras play. The betel leaves enclosures are not to be trusted. Who knows when the cobras would bite? This cannot be ruled out."

But when asked why the cobras were not ever seen by the old Dambaru, the old man, showing his loose teeth, would say, "What juice is left in me that the cobra would bite? The cobra is enamoured by virgin women. You are fated to remain a virgin forever. How can the cobra leave you alone?"

Dambaru's explanation excites Ketaki all the more to explore the world of snakes. Whether the cobra of the cobra world chases her or not, Ketaki stalks the cobra inside the dark world of the betel enclosures, defying the restrictions of her grandfather. But never could Ketaki see the amorous dance of the cobra, nor did she ever see the cobra raising its hood, standing on its tail, and hissing to bite her.

Ketaki's curiosity and obsession for the cobra snaked its way up from childhood to adolescence and youth, rising in a labyrinth from the netherworld to the zenith. In the indomitable desire for locating the cobra, there was no trace of frustration in the new-moon-born Ketaki. She firmly believed that one day or another she would encounter the deep, dark cobra. She had no proof that the cobra of the snake world was chasing her, but the snakes of the society had been chasing her from the day she'd touched adolescence.

Not only Ketaki, but everyone knew that the loafers from her village and other nearby villages were lusting after her. That, however, was not a strange thing. All through the ages, bees gather when flowers bloom. Although born on the new moon day, the maker had given her such lovely form and beauty that evens a passerby would freeze in his tracks to have a glimpse of her. Ketaki's grandmother said that even sages and saints would lose their way to stand awhile at Ketaki's door.

In the way that lonely moments and flower buds weigh heavy on the heart and mind of a virgin, likewise, at midnight, when the night roars its dark desires, many a bud loads the stems of the betel creeper, rising from every joint and knot. At that time, the virgin cobras come from the snake world and enter the plantation enclosure, pluck out every single flower, and decorate their buns, hands, necks, arms, and waists.

The male cobras play the grooms, wearing crowns of betel flowers, and wear garlands of fruits around their necks. They spend the entire night dancing, love-locked in pairs. By sunrise, no flower is seen, nor any cobra. For that reason, the women are forbidden to enter the plantation-the men, too, after nightfall.

But Ketaki flies to the plantation on the wings of her dreams in the night. Transformed into a virgin cobra, she collects the flowers in the folds of her saree and searches for the love dance of the cobras till dawn. And Ketaki's soul grows on a leaf-crowded creeper like a ripe, scented betel leaf. Ketaki's body, however, remains asleep in the lap of her grandmother on the mat. Ketaki's face, like a scented betel leaf, leans on her grandma's chest. Grandma, with her veined hand, sprinkles her love and fondness on the innocent betel-leaf face, and she curses the seven generations of the poison-bearing snakes.

She babbles, "You ordinary serpents, double-faced vagabonds! Who is a cobra amongst you, that you have the power to bite my Ketaki? Only because a cobra male is not yet born in this universe, my ripe-scented, betel-leaf-like Ketaki has come to the world on the new moon day. You would simply burn to ashes if her breath falls on you. Have you assessed her strength? Touching her is a far cry. Let me see how you come near her fiery glow."

The toothless old woman spreads many myths about her granddaughter, and in course of time believes her own myths. It seems that, at night, Ketaki becomes a female cobra. From the mat, she creeps out fast into the betel plantation. There, in that enclosure is her cobra prince, her lover of countless births. Decorated with betel flowers, both dance as a couple all night, and Ketaki returns in her human form to the house in the morning. The cobra prince hides himself in the enclosure, and, at the right time, bites the thieves and dacoits.

The old woman had no choice but to spread such myths. Dambaru slept forever inside the betel creeper enclosure. The only son Aparti died after prolonged suffering from the secret disease he contracted in Calcutta. And daughter-in-law Khulana, too, found her way to the other world from an unknown disease. In the world was left her only hope, the betel enclosure, and the only worry, the growing new-moon-born Ketaki.

The underage grandson-the sickly, fit-for-nothing Ainthu-could not be relied upon, nor could he be neglected. To save the betel plantation from the thieves and to protect her granddaughter Ketaki from the evil eye of the village bums, she was ushering in daily the cobras from the cobra world to the open bazaar of Abhayapur. The old woman's stories were saucy. Some people really believed that, after Dambaru's death, his betel plantation had become the playfield of cobras, and Ketaki was really a poison girl, a female cobra.

After Dambaru's death, Aparti returned to the village and gave charge of the Calcutta business to his brother-in-law. The secret disease, contracted because of Aparti's philandering pleasures, was no more a secret. Back in the village, he was busy managing his disease in secrecy at the expense of the betel enclosure, but it became unmanageable, and everyone got to know about it. Orphaning his family and leaving them in the streets, he escaped the mortal pain within two years of his father's death.

Not only did the sky fall on the head of Ketaki's mother, but also a hill of stigma was pressed on her for the vile disease of her husband. The villagers boycotted their house. After she'd atoned for it, selling away some ornaments, the ban was lifted. She had no worry about Ketaki's marriage. Ketaki was fated to be a spinster. When she thought of setting up her young, incompetent son in a betel shop and looking after the betel plantation herself, another calamity raised its head. Her belly started swelling.

All through the long years of Aparti's Calcutta shenanigans, no male shadow had ever fallen in her courtyard. But after her husband's death, people thought, her real nature was being revealed. The swelling belly of a widow was construed as nothing but a sinful pregnancy.

Ketaki's mother was herself shocked. How could sin enter her belly when she had done nothing? She vowed before her mother-in-law, swearing on the head of her son, that not sin but some disease had entered her belly. If a village medicine man was sent for and medicines were given, she might survive. She did not want to die.

What could the old woman do? In consultation with the elderly women, an abortionist-the illiterate midwife Sodari-was sent for at midnight. In the dark of the night, while trying to torture her to abort the sin in a crude method, the pain-ridden life of the woman slipped through her hands. In the morning, the bloody corpse of Ketaki's mother was taken for cremation. But the matter could not be kept secret. Rumors spread that, while trying to abort her sinful pregnancy, Ketaki's mother had died. Once again, the house of the male-less, unfortunate betel grower family was banned by the villagers.

Pallbearers were not available to take the body. Fie! Who would give shoulder to a sinner's body? Mantri Mallik, with his devilish mind, ran to the Erasama police station, crossing the river. A case of suspicious death was registered. The body of Ketaki's mother was carried to the Erasama hospital for a postmortem. The doctor gave his report.

"The dead body had a tumor in her belly, not a sinful

pregnancy. A sin-free tumor was growing in her innocent stomach."

Had there been a surgery at the right time, the woman could have returned home in a week. A grief-stricken mother, who'd wanted to live to save her two children, had finally been tortured to death at the hands of a foolish midwife. It was murder. Who would make whom responsible? In which village had Sodari not done abortions that, today, police would arrest her as a murderer? Every family's secret she had tucked in her waist. Had she coughed up the secrets she knew, village after village would have floated in the river of sin, widening the estuary. Kundala Panda, Tahali Mohanty, Narkeswar Rautray - none could have escaped.

The unnatural event was suppressed in a natural manner. Many crimes born out of human blindness have become acceptable in society in such a way that those cannot be termed as murder or crime. From the noble desire to make Ketaki's mother free of sin, while aborting, she'd died accidentally. There was no motive for murder, rather a sacred wish to save a woman.

This event made Ketaki and her toothless grandmother eternally grateful to the crematory devil, Mantri Mallik. Ketaki felt no sorrow in remaining unmarried. But the rumors about father's secret disease and mother's questionable pregnancy had completely destroyed her will to live. By providing the inspiration to live, Mantri Mallik made Ketaki eternally grateful to him. In Ketaki's inner eye, the crematory devil Mantri Mallik appeared handsome, like a God-sent angel. After such a long time, Ketaki could understand that, in the cremation ground, there were not only ghosts and witches, but also gods, who, from time to time, appeared in the world. They were forsakers like Mantri Mallik, and they were to bring to light the distinction between sin and merit.

Mantri Mallik, banished from the village, had taken shelter in the crematory. When he became a sturdy young man, a road opened in the fate of the villagers. At first, Mantri Mallik hacked and felled the trees in the nux vomica forest that stood blocking the free passage of the villagers. Mantri Mallik was congratulated on that effort.

Gradually, Mantri Mallik extended the hut he had made for himself. Then he was possessed by the devil. There were two unclaimed and abandoned betel enclosure plots on the sleepy stream near the edge of the crematory. For long years, the two plots stood like two barren, worry-free couples. No one in the village knew who those plots belonged to. But everyone knew that whoever started betel plantations on those plots, he would grow and prosper, but his family and clan would be ruined.

The plots lay un-inherited and barren, and in the hot summer made the eyes of the pallbearers tearful with flying whirlwinds of sand. On those sandy mounds, the ghosts performed their operatic orgies-a myth perpetuated by generation after generation. But that opera one saw alone. No one has ever heard that more than one together saw the opera.

Mantri hoped that he would see the rare opera one day. He was spending sleepless nights watching the mounds. But as he did not see the opera even once in seven or eight years, one morning he declared, "The opera party of the ghosts left for Calcutta and Gujarat for good because the snores of the Abhayapur people disturbed their song and dance. They protested before Mantri Mallik and disappeared." People listened to Mantri in amazement, and some even believed him.

Hearing this, Kundala Panda laughed aloud, and said, "A bluff master! A big tout. The day the Goddess Kali was installed in the crematory Kali temple, the same day, I exorcised them by the power of my incantations from those mounds. I forbid them to disturb the sleep of the mother with their opera dance and music at midnight. Those ghosts have now taken shelter in the trees of our village, and they have forgotten their dance and song by obeying the incantatory orders.

"After all, they are ghosts of this village! When they obeyed me alive, how can they disobey me dead? Like our villagers, the ghosts, too, are loyal to divinity. And this brat, this crematory devil, he says they left for opera programs in Calcutta, Gujarat, and Bihar! Tell lies if you wish, but tell lies so that people can believe you. To tell lies, you don't need just a tongue, but a mind too. The devil's brain is a void."

That was it. Mantri Mallikclimbed up the mounds and danced and capered like a ghost. Kicking the mound, he screamed, "Wait, wait! I'll hack and dig and mingle you with the soil. If you remain, the ghosts may start their club again one day."

Disturbing the stupor of the sleepy river, Mantri Mallik began digging the mounds, alone. Carrying the soil on his head, he put it on the single-lane pedestrian path. How many months he took to do it, he never kept track. A wide, rough road was opened up to the ferry ghat. With the soil from two mounds, the Westside road became wider than the eastside one and solid too. With so many votes, what the MLAs and ministers had never done, Mantri Mallik demonstrated by doing.

As the road opened, more than half the village people used the road up to the ghat. It was no more a lonely road. People made it throb with life. Gradually, four or five shops were opened on the roadside. The shop that did good business among those that sprang up was named Best Betel Shop, but people called it Ketaki's Pan Shop. The tin nameplate bore coal tar letters and hung in front of the wooden cabin. Below the name, another line was written in clear character-cash today, credit tomorrow.

The old grandma lovingly called Ketaki Delicious Betel. The village lads, chewing Ketaki flower scented betel with catechu, spit blood-red juice, and thereby made the road in front of the betel shop an abstract artwork. Showing their stained teeth like shameless brats, they'd say, "Not only delicious betel, you toothless old woman. Your virgin granddaughter is a *ripe betel-leaf.*"

ELEVEN

In fact, Ketaki's betel-leaf face, not only in shape but also in quality, appeared turmeric bright, as if someone had well-oiled the turmeric-knotted, medium-sized, delicious betel leaf to mature in the sun. The broad forehead was in contrast, etched sharp at the chin, highlighting the soft, clean, glowing face. Straight as the central vein of the betel leaf, her parting of hair had lengthened up to the crown in the middle of deep, dark, bushy hair, piercing the chests of lustful village Romeos.

A careless bun, like a closed, round wallet, touches the nape. Like the betel stem, her soft, slender neck looks fragile. A black lace circles her fair neck like a thread packing a measure of betel leaves, as if it sits there wooingly. At the center of the lace, a clip of gold nose ornament of cardamom design, a tip of a pendant. Like a clove tucked to a limeless betel leaf, a gold fly of Gujarat design is stuck to her thin, curvy nose, as if in perpetual relationship, life after life, to entice the village lads.

When she smiles, from her pomegranate-seed-like rows of teeth ooze drops of sweet juice, into the beholder's chest, heart, and soul. What's the need for the fiery new-moon-born to smile, showing her dainty teeth? What if the village lads are lustful, shameless, and bawdy? Again, in the flower-petal eyes of the luscious lass are catechu-colored, lustrous irises, and in them, well-formed and deep pupils, like grains of cardamom.

Who knows which divine architect divined her! The new moon born is so stately that she walks like an empress. Never does she look with love or lust at anyone, nor does she even look kindly at anyone. It is as if she is not here on earth. Her sight is in the snakeworld, her mind in the realm of Indra. Her face is attractive, but her figure is more exciting. Smooth like the betel creeper, slim, and curvaceous, as if it begged to be entwined with anyone by a mere touch. The well-formed hands hang careless, like the raw branches slipped off from the bamboo frame of the betel enclosure. If you walk by her side, the reins of the mind get stretched to hold the two creeper branches, to safe-keep them in your arms and neck, to clasp the nubile lass to your heart.

The walk of the lass appears as if she is sleepwalking, or a creeper is rising slowly on the frame. The lads not only chew the betel she makes, but also grind their teeth in bloody anger. It is natural. The lass has been endowed with that kind of form and beauty, but she would be wife to none, so she is common property. Everyone should enjoy her. But why so chaste and unreachable? For whom? For what?

When the lass, sitting on her knees, breaks betel nuts or makes betel, she looks like a coiled serpent with raised hood, half human, half cobra, the princess from the snake world. The black-and-red lined, Maniabandhi saree makes her complexion all the more glowing. She tucks the saree edge so tightly at her waist that she really looks like a female cobra below the waist and a woman above. As she suppresses the thrill of the snakecharmer's tunes, the lads feel their hearts cut out. But they dare not play the nageswari (snake charmer's instrument).

Ketaki's bun, in the entire village, was distinctive; so distinctive that, in a crowd of women, if the bun was sighted from behind, it was recognized that the face on the other side was that of Ketaki's. Not only in this village, but in the nearby villages too. No other lass tucked in a creeper or two of betel every day, like flowers in her bun. From a knot of that creeper, a half-ripe leaf also stood, like a hooded cobra. And rhyming with the ramp, the walk of Ketaki undulated, threatening to bite the lascivious onlookers.

Once, the luscious beauty had tied her bun with a green serpent, pulling it out of the betel enclosure along with her usual betel leaf. The head of the snake was trying to free itself, struggling on her forehead. Somebody shouted, "Snake! Snake!" Ketaki opened her bun in a flash, and the snake jumped onto her shoulders, slithered its way between her breasts, and left, touching her feet. When the snake left her, many people had seen with their own eyes that it was transformed into a snakewoman.

Ketaki was not aware or perturbed about anything. Her soul, it seems, had gone out with the cobrawoman that day. The Ketaki that remained, one who prepared betel, did the household chores, played and moved with other village belles, sang in different village festivals for girls, that was simply the soulless body of Ketaki. So to speak, the woman had no soul; only a body—an attractive body.

In the beginning, Ketaki did not sit in the betel shop to sell betel. Staying at home, she arranged all the ingredients for betel. Her brother Ainthu soldbetel at the shop. With the already crushed betel nuts, cardamom, cloves, ketaki catechu, ajwain, zafran, and so on, she sometimes added scented tobacco and made varieties of betel for the rich consumers. For the poor people, she made thick-leaved betel with powdered or rough-leaved tobacco. The business was good. But as the unemployed youth, corrupt politicians, bribe-takers, and well-dressed babus flattered the boy Ainthu, he started selling betel on credit, and was never paid. So Ketaki decided to sell betel in the shop herself.

When her grandma forbade her, she replied, "Do you think, if I veil myself and sit at homeas a good girl, somebody would come wearing the ritual marriage crown to marry me? Why then ruin the business for nothing? Everyone cheats Ainthu-not because he is a kid, but because he is gullible and somewhat foolish. Let me see who would cheat me. I would drink his blood! "She sat in the shop, and the same day under the Mahata Betel Shop sign, she wrote-cash today, credit tomorrow.

From the day Ketaki sat in the shop, the fame of the shop spread in the nearby villages. Ketaki was giving ingredients, assessing the paying capacity of the customers. She made betel according to the taste of the customer-at times diamond-shaped, at times water chestnut-shaped. Before her shop, all ages crowded for betel. But it was difficult to take a betel on the promise of future payment.

When the shameless lads said, showing their brazen teeth, "Today credit, tomorrow cash. Would you give a betel, Ketaki?"

Ketaki was not to be cowed down. She retorted, "Earn a hundred to take betel nuts and a thousand for betel. How much do you earn, ye betel eater? Betel is not a cheap thing. Betel greedy, wallet empty!"

Ketaki and Girima were not of the same age. Ketaki was older by four or five years. But they were bosom friends; one would sacrifice their life for the other. What lesson Girima taught to Ketaki, no one knew. But Ketaki taught Girima the art of singing farewell sobbing songs, those sung by brides at the time of marriage and subsequent parting from their parental home.

Girima told her, "You are fated to be unmarried, so why do you know these songs by heart? Had you remembered your class lessons, you would have topped."

Ketaki said with a smile, "Do all the flowers that bloom bear fruit? For that, do they not blossom? Do they not exude fragrance? Can all the stars that twinkle in the sky be moons or the polestar? Yet, little or more, do they not give light? Look here. Listen to me. It's true that I can't marry. But the day you leave for your in-law's house, should I not hold you and cry heart-wrenchingly? I teach this parting song to many a girl of this village. I'm their teacher. Do you understand, my dear? You have passed the primary school. I haven't gone beyond the lower primary. But can you ever say that I'm not your teacher?"

Girima embraces Ketaki and says, "Divine injustice or human heartlessness? What relation is there between the newmoon day and widow or non-widow? Had we been of the same caste, I would have compelled father to get you married to my brother Bhagyadhar, and taken you home as my brother's wife. But my Bhagya brother is an expert player. Had he not married Padma, it seems, he would have renounced the world and become a Sadhu. He would have moved like Mantri Mallik and lived as the crematorydevil. Oh, what love!"

Ketaki, looking into Girima's eyes, asks, "Do you think your brother alone loved? Does this sister have no love for anyone? Don't try to fool me. Friend, how many hurdles have been devised by male dominated society? Caste, horoscope, dowry, high, low. By setting up shop at the head of the crematory, I know these are all lies.More than what God decrees for man, man himself creates more pain for himself.

"To speak the truth, when I think of you, my heart sinks. Why are you plucking the stars, my friend? You would not suffer alone. Even Uncle would be scandalized. Take my advice and marry Kartika; fish, tanks, coconut trees, acres of land, rice, paddy, no want in any respect. Over and above that, there's ready cash from the theater party."

"Don't utter his name. He is an opera after player. I would rather remain unmarried like you. I would set up a dry fish shop next to your betel shop. At the very least, Kundala Panda would buy dried fish on his way back from the Kali temple."

"Yes, on credit. And this month's credit would roll on to the next month. He would pay you back by giving you the sacred water of the goddess. He is the only man who takes betel on credit that rolls on year after year. Well, a Brahmin priest. If not in this life, maybe in my next birth I would get the reward of merit. Maybe I would be born on a fullmoon day, and this unmarried state would be redeemed."

Ketaki sighs-half in jest, half in earnest.

"Nonsense! You'll see. One day, a handsome prince would come and spirit you away.The beauty that you are, my friend!"

"Yes, my prince would come from the world of snakes. He has written a missive on betel leaf. I live because I read it everyday."

From close quarters was heard, "Be careful! Are you two friends conspiring against me?" Beating his staff on the ground, Mantri Mallik advanced like a whirlwind. The friends tried to suppress their laughter. On the surface, no one appeared to be inferior to the other in faking beautifully, feigning ignorance despite knowing all.

There are temples without icons, but there are no villages without unemployed youth. Therefore, whenever you see a row of shops, there you would see a group of unemployed youth lazing around whether they buy anything or not. Before the shops, they moved in clusters like humming flies on open sweet stalls. However much you ward them off, the shameless groups hum around everywhere. Even if Ketaki does not give free betels to them, they unabashedly loiter in groups in front of Ketaki's betel shop, speaking toothy, bawdy inanities.

The other day, when Tahali Mohanty's son Sakula Mohanty asked for betel on credit, Ketaki rashly said, "There it is written. No credit. Aren't you able to read?"

Sakula pleaded with a rural song,
Oh, my ripe betel leaf
You've made my heart beep
I'd hoped for you
As the cuckoo cheats the crow
You've cheated me too!

Another chimed in, "Oh, my life's life! Give me a betel, save my life. You are my nectar. I'm your bee!" The others laughed like horses and made obscene gestures.

However strong Ketaki appeared on the surface, she was feminine within. Her face reddened like ketaki catechu. Even tears came to her eyes unconsciously. As she was born to suffer her fate as an unmarried woman until she grew old and died, she had to hear such obscene comments. The thought that she has none to fall back upon made her all the more miserable. She had no elder brother. The younger brother was neither fish nor fowl. Who else would match words with these political goons, these horse-faced grass addicts?

Although Mantri Mallik was the crematorydevil, Ketaki counted him as a man. She trusted him, reposed faith in him. Had she not reposed trust in him, perhaps, as a woman, she wouldn't have dared to have a betel shop at the edge of the village. Mantri Mallik's hut, in this area, was like a charmed talisman for her. Ketaki had faith that Mantri's hut could imprison ghosts, thieves, and goons. She could run her shop without danger until her old age and death. And if her brother Ainthu married and settled down, what other worry would she have?

As long as Ketaki's shop remained open, Mantri's eyes, too, remained open and alert. He had taken upon himself the responsibility to keep an eye on Ketaki's shop. This was not unknown to Ketaki. Therefore, fearlessly she defied the goons and maintained her cash today, credit tomorrow principle.

That day, the unmannerly talk and the teasing songs of the lads set his blood on fire. His strong bones started to crackle like the bones of a burning corpse. He jumped like Hanuman from his veranda, and, advancing toward the lads, pounced on them as a vulture on chicks. He gave a few blows to their noses, faces, chests and bellies. In a trice, a few other unemployed and wayward young lads gathered and attacked Mantri like biting dogs.

Mantri fought like the hero Abhimanyu, encircled by the lads. The lads ran helter-skelter for dear life, as they had no weapons.If they'd had weapons, the crematorydevil would have slept forever in the crematory. Ketaki was lucky that they'd been unarmed. As a result, Mantri survived.And Ketaki too!

Mantri Mallik dusted himself, wiped off the blood from his nose and lips, and stood in front of Ketaki's shop in his usual careless pose. With some authority, he said, "Give me a betel. No, not on credit, on cash today terms. Well, sister! Why do you confront those ruffians? Would I be here forever to protect you?"

Ketaki wanted to fall at his feet to express her gratitude, but she couldn't because Mantri was a Dalit. The village people would banish her.She wanted to wipe off the blood from his nose and lips and redden her saree edge. She couldn't do that either. Fie! People would not leave her alive. In other words, even if she wanted, she couldn't express her gratitude to Mantri.

She could not give him a betel for free, for Mantri Mallik

was stubborn and proud. He never took anything free, nor on credit. His own income was enough for his lone belly. His sources of income were also different. He had not sold his head to anyone, nor did he take orders from anyone. If anyone was in need of help, he helped them unconditionally. He was satisfied with whatever one gave. It meant that everyone owed him a debt.

The pallbearers often took things from him on a loan basis. These things were never returned, and the debt accumulated. Who in this village was not in his debt? Ketaki was the biggest debtor. And she would die a debtor. She could never repay Mantri Mallik.

She therefore proffered a carefully made betel to him, and, with tears welling up in her eyes, said, suppressing her sobs, "Do you know what you were to me in some previous birth?'

"Don't you know what I was? Well, I know," said Mantri, easing his breath.

Ketaki asked, "What were you? How could you know when I don't know?"

"As I live in the crematory, I develop friendships with ghosts and witches. From them, I know about past lives."

"Then tell me! What were you to me?"

"Me? I was your debtor. Not in one life, but in seven lives. Do you follow?"

Wishing to say something, he swallowed half his words and spoke that much more bluntly. In a distant bare branch of a cotton tree, a group of vultures was sitting in deep concentration, perhaps smelling the stink of a corpse in the air. Truth was that the death chant was drawing near like the sad breeze over the grass flowers. Alas, somebody was gone! Who? Mantri Mallik ran swiftly toward his hut. Whoever it was, for him there was more urgent work.

Who doesn't die, being human? But death is never lucky. To die with your red vermillion mark on the forehead, however, is great luck. That luck is not for all women. No one has foreknowledge of it. But Ketaki knew she did not have that luck. She would live and die unmarried.

As she is a new moon born, lads burn midnight oil around her. But one of them-

who knows from which village-lights a lamp, standing apart. At times, he comes and goes along that road, takes a betel, pays for it, casts a meaningful glance at Ketaki, and goes on his way. Somehow or other, Ketaki's steel mind melts, stirs, and, like the two-tiered waves, becomes sweet and salty. What's the point, if the sweetness does not form into a grain, if there is no chance of it to reach the heart from the mouth? But if that young man does not come for a few days, the heart gets knotted in another way. She, however, had no chance of knowing whether that boy had the same knotted feeling. Who would she ask? It would be scandalous.

After that man's arrival, one day, suddenly, a marriage proposal came for Ketaki. The matter made small progress, and it broke apart as suddenly as it had come. The reason was an unsigned letter. It seems the groom's family was agreeable despite her new moon birth. They had no objection even to her betel shop. But the letter was about Ketaki's affair with a boy who took betel from her shop, made eye contact with her, and many other concocted things. Such a letter was potent enough to break Ketaki's marriage proposal.

Ketaki was not unhappy. She was secretly happy that, if the rumor that she'd had an affair with a boy had come out openly, then the young man must know about it. If he did not know, he would know now. If Ketaki was not fated to be a married woman, why then she should invite sorrow? At least, if feelings were communicated with that unknown passerby, and Ketaki's life was colored like catechu-smeared betel leaf, she did not need a marriage. That marriage does not always give happiness, but instead gives pain, Ketaki had understood from her mother's married life. But who was that young man?

The crematory devil Mantri Mallik was not unhappy at the failure of Ketaki's marriage proposal, which broke like a pitcher falling from a rope shelf. When Ketaki's betel shop was open, the entire crematory was fragrant with the scent of Ketaki flowers. If it was closed, then there was only pyre smoke, charcoal, and the pungent smell of burning corpses! Besides, who would have treated an unhappy-since-birth lass like a sweet flower? In fact, how many women live like flowers in their mother-in-law's houses?

Ketaki should not be too eager to marry. If she marries, then that fortunate man must have a large heart and be one who would raise Ketaki from the earth and make her the jasmine of the sky, as Mantri would have done with any girl he would have married. In the dream sky of Mantri, many girls, rising from sorrow and slush, bloomed like sky jasmines.

In his dreams, Mantri released even female ghosts in the midst of the stars and became the Polestar himself. But after the passerby eyeing Ketaki, the goons making fun of her, and especially after his row with the political lads, in Mantri's dream world, unknown flowers did not bloom anymore. Even when Mantri sits in the yoga posture with eyes closed, only one flower blooms before him-that is Ketaki!

Had there not been in the world the distinction between caste, creed, rich, poor, high, and low, Ketaki would not have remained unmarried because of her new moon birth. He would have dared the universe. Such thoughts do not play in his mind because of any evil desires for Ketaki. Ketaki's body does not entice him. Ketaki as a whole human being makes Mantri fragrant. But when such thoughts come to his mind, he slaps his cheeks hard. At times standing, at times while meditating, Mantri Mallik slaps himself. He controls his mind.

"Die, you crematorydevil! Is this the meaning of keeping watch on a helpless girl of your village? Can't you think of her as your sister?" Had she been calling him brother, perhaps such indecent thoughts would not have made his mind dusty like a whirlwind. But as he was of a low caste, he could not be anything else except Ketaki's bodyguard or security man. This he reminds himself by slapping his cheeks.

As the marriageable age of Ketaki recedes, Mantri controls his mind all the more stringently. Many girls remained unmarried because of non-availability of proper grooms, but they did not marry whoever came their way. Mantri was worse than the whoever. Therefore, Mantri would rather die than think of such things.

TWELVE

Three autumns, one after another, have flown before the eyes like illusions. Bhairab Majhi has not honored his vow, which was taken three years ago. Sitting at this place, three years ago, like the trinity, the three fishermen had vowed thrice. Today, too, the three of them were sitting at the same place—Udhab Mangual, Bharat Mandal, and Bhairab Majhi.

It's man's device to call the three gods marijuana addicts and offer grass to them, and, having long drags of the prasad, to get stoned. In the name of the deity, the narcotics turn into prasad. But that day, without smoking grass, the threesome was sitting wordless with eyes closed. None could have the courage to walk in the village now with their heads held high. The three family leaders were searching for an escape route from the situation.

It was decided that Bharat Mandal would have Bhairab Majhi's educated son Kartik, whether he be a theater man or businessman, as his son-in-law. He couldn't send his daughter to Midinapur or Bangladesh. He would keep her before his eyes. Therefore, he requested that Udhab Mangual negotiate for a matching son-in-law for his Padma.

As a matter of fact, all three were fishermen by caste. One was Odia, the other a Midinapur Bengali, and the third a Bangladeshi Bengali fisherman. But all of them were now residents of Odisha. Udhab had argued. Why couldn't Bangladeshi Bengalis have marriage relationships with Midinapur Bengalis? Had Udhab been a Bengali, he would gladly have agreed to his son Bhagyadhar's marriage with Padma.

In this area, Odia-Bengali marriages had become acceptable. But Udhab's homemaker was very stubborn, very conservative. She wouldn't have allowed it to happen. Therefore, mediating between Bharat and Bhairab, he had almost finalized the marriage between Kartik Majhi and Padma. There was another reason to mediate in this marriage.

Padma's bosom friend, his daughter Girima, had suggested many times, "Instead of giving Padma in marriage to Kartik, why does Bharat uncle search for a son-in-law in so many places? Would he ever get a better son-in-law than Kartik in some other village?"

Udhab had asked, "Has Padma spoken about it to you? Does she want that? Should I give this proposal to Bharat Mandal?"

"How could Padma speak openly? Is it necessary to speak it out? I'm her friend. I know her mind. When Kartik and my brother Bhagya sing together the horse dance song, how could Padma distinguish from the well-mingled melody that Kartik's voice is sweet, sonorous, and emotion-laden? Speak, Father! Answer. Is it not clear from this who she is fond of?"

This much from his daughter had assured him that it would not be a bad idea to finalize Padma's marriage with Kartik. At this proposal, there was no objection from Bharat Mandal's side. Objection came from Bhairab Majhi. Bhairab Majhi was opposed to a WestBengal and EastBengal marriage. But through Udhab's mediation, he was not only willing to arrange the marriage, but also addressed Bharat Mandal, before the sealing of the proposal, as *samudi* (bride's father). As Padma and Girima are soul-mates, for Udhab, Padma was more than a daughter. Udhab, too, called Bhairab his *samudi*.

But Bhairab's son Kartik dealt a sudden blow. He cross-examined his father in a letter as to why the marriage was finalized without his consent. Again, he raised the issue of how the consent of the person who would marry was not considered. Everyone was shocked. In this region, especially in the fishermen families, it was not deemed necessary to obtain permission of the boy and girl for finalizing a marriage. The question that was raised by Kartik had definitely been influenced by some drama dialogue. Only in the theater could such shameless questions be hurled in the face of the father.

He had quoted a dialogue from a play in the form of a proposal to his father. "If you want me to marry then search for an educated girl like Udhab uncle's daughter Girima. Don't tie an unlettered fisherwoman like Padma around my neck. One who cannot understand the dialogue of a drama cannot understand the dialogue of real life."

Everyone's head was lowered in shame. To convince Kartik was beyond the ken of Bhairab. But the three friends, the trinity, did not blame each other. They did not even blame Kartik. Maybe it was a quirk of fate, maybe Basu Rath's theater party was to blame, or maybe the Kaliyug was to blame for such aberrations! The trio made a mutual compromise between them.

In this regard, Bhairab Majhi had shrunk with a feeling of guilt, and Bharat Mandal, blaming his destiny, was numb with sorrow. After the engagement, the marriage broke down. Now, to get a daughter married would be a tough ask. He could have searched for a son-in-law from Jambu, Bangladeshi, or Malkangiri refugees. Like all other girls, Padma, too, would have gone far away, out of his sight. Mandal drowned in such thoughts.

Resolving all conflicts, Udhab declared that day, "If Bharat Mandal has no objection, and I'll take Padma as my daughter-in-law for Bhagyadhar. Sankha's mother would object to having a Bengali daughter-in-law, I know. But I would solve that problem. If my proposal is appreciated, let the marriage be on the next auspicious date. Fixing the date of marriage and delaying it, such obstacles come. What do you say?"

Breaking the rhythm of the conversation with a bang, Bhairab Majhi said, "I tried my best to convince him. Being a father, I held the boy's hands and appealed to him. Ok, let it go. If the boy does not one day arrive with a nautch girl, I would consider myself fortunate. Therefore, the first duty of all the three of us is to get him married to an educated fisherwoman, to find a son-in-law of Bharat Mandal's choice for his Padma, and to get done with the marriage in haste. All other work can wait."

"Brother Udhab! It is great of you to propose Padma for Bhagyadhar. There is no difference if Padma becomes your daughter-in-law or Brother Bhairab's. Actually, if she becomes your daughter-in-law, her refugee status would be negated. Her roots would go deeper into Odisha soil. She would be an Odia. Her children would be born Odia. It'll be good for everyone. But to speak honestly, I have no strength in my heart to learn another lesson. Whatever collegiate education Kartik has acquired, Bhagyadhar is a decimal point less.

"Who can assure me that Bhagyadhar would not reject this proposal, calling my daughter an unlettered fool? Do you thinkthere is more to learn, brother? Although he has failed in the end, your son Bhagyadhar is an educated fisherman. He has walked on the college soil. First of all, ask him about this. Otherwise, I would be embarrassed once again,"Bharat Mandal said, apprehensively.

Udhab replied firmly, "Bhagyadhar is naughty, true, but he would not disobey his father. He was adamant to join the theater party, provoked by Kartik. I flatly denied. Did he not stay back honorably? He was not going to fish, as I was not compelling him. If he holds another's hand, he would go for fishing, handle the net, row the boat, and would do everything. He is a hardy fellow. If you have no objection—"

Bharat interrupted in a choked voice, "If Padma goes to your house, and there is no greater good fortune than that."

Bhairab Majhi folded his hands and said, "I am asking for Girima from Brother Udhab. It is rumored that Girima is arrogant. Ok. How better is my Kartika? Notorious as an actor. And what he has been doing, only a girl like Girima can bring him round from. What do you say?", Bhairab looked at both friends at one glance.

Udhab said in a serious tone, "The proposal is not bad. Better to give your daughter into a known family. Mine would be a Bengali daughter-in-law and a Bengali son-in-law. But think again. Girima is a pure Odia. In her body is flowing the blood of queen Karubaki and grandma Bela. If she goes to your house, she would not keep you as Bengali. She would make her in-laws and husband such Odias that you would forget your mother tongue, brother! Think over this again. Moreover, without Kartika's consent, who are we to finalize his marriage? He is the boy who has once betrayed."

Bhairab Majhi humbly said, "You be assured, brother! Kartika always praised Girima. He always says, 'If you be a girl, be like Girima.' In fact, it is necessary, in the modern times, to call the bluff of drama sahibs. To bring them to their senses—men like Tahali Mohanty, his son Sakula, and other wayward youth—it is better if girls like Girima are born in every village. The innocent crybabies are fit for nothing."

Udhab was delighted and laughingly said, "It's good, brother. We are saved from a great worry. Wherefrom would I have gotten an educated groom? Moreover, who would have taken as daughter-in-law an over-forward girl? It would be a royal match like Gandhari and Dhritarastra."

The three friends agreed on the proposal. As Kartika was away at Calcutta with the theater party, Bharat Mandal said, "Don't have the engagement ceremony without asking Kartik. There is a difference between praising Girima and having her as your life partner. If Kartika says no, then like my daughterPadma, the poor girl would be embarrassed. Why such a hurry?" Udhab and Bhairab agreed.

The engagement and marriage of Bhagyadhar and Padma were held on the same day. Girima's engagement awaited Kartika's approval. Padma became Girima's brother's wife. In the meantime, three years had passed in a wink. Padma was now the mother of a two-year-old son. The soaring mind of Bhagyadhar had now been knotted to Padma's anchal (saree-edge). He now ferried people across the river, joined Udhab's fishing group in the hilsa season. He had real love for the clever hilsa. He was as expert in following a slimy school of hilsa as he was at eating the bony fish. But the haughty Girima's marriage was being postponed from November to November as Kartika Majhi moved all over India with the theater party.

Seasons changed in quick succession. Who knows if the actor's mind has changed in the meantime! Has he been trapped by some nautch girl? Such apprehensions are false; vows Bhairab Majhi. But such suspicions are not easily evaded.

Now Kartik was performing in Surat, Gujarat. His new play, it seems, was a super hit, ringing the cash counter like mad. He had composed one or two songs for the play. He was now co-writing plays with the drama master. But the poor fellow was not granted any leave for his marriage by that master, the miserly Basu Rath. This surpasses the defense department. Bikram Balbantaray may get leave for his marriage, but this theater hero doesn't get leave!

Girima, however, seemed unconcerned with everything. But in the garden of her mind, a reticent bee was always humming, "Oh, Mother Sarala, Mother Basuli, may Kartika finally say no to this marriage! The man who Padma silently loved, with what face would I marry him? Would he come to this house as the honored son-in-law, the most important guest, and my brother's wife, the same silent lover Padma, would she treat him with six curries and nine fries? Can she playfully chide him, as per tradition? What a complex situation would arise!"

No one else but Girima knew that, since the day after her marriage, Padma had nursed a grudge against Girima. It was true that Girima was not guilty in this case, but who can stop a woman's jealousy? Girima has given up her studies for three years now. She roams around, loafing with friends, plays with Padma's son, and spends her time. But at times, a robin comes from the Himalayan forests, opens her wings, and perches on Girima's mind. A white flamingo flies off in her reverie, a cuckoo calls, and a house sparrow moves here and there to build a nest.

During these moments of imaginative flights, Kartika Majhi never appears, even for a second. He who appears is the soldier

Bikram Balbantaray, who, from childhood, had negotiated many a wave in her heart and mind. He, who now fights in Kargil and risks his life for the country. He would come home after the war. But what's the point in thinking of Bikram?

Letting her luxuriant, dark, thick hair tumble along her back, Girima sat with her face down. To kill the lifelong enemy of woman, the lice, and Udhab's aunt Malati was combing hard with a two-sided wooden comb. With the close-set teeth of the wooden comb, aunt was mercilessly dragging the lice. Just as the fish never run out even though boatloads of fish are brought everywhere from the sea, similarlythis licekilling expedition goes on every day. The shameless lice somehow or other are reborn on the heads of women.

Udhab's aunt is getting irritated. She was now old. The eyes were now dim.Yet, as her veined hands can push balls of watered rice fast into her mouth, with the same speed she runs the comb through the thick hair of her grand-daughters and great-granddaughters. And like the man plucking and shaking the coconuts from the tree, she sweeps the dandruff and lice. Once the old woman holds a head, she does not let go. Forgetting food and drink, she does her work with concentration. At first, it relaxes Girima, but she has no patience to sit for hours at one place. It's against her nature. Once her thick hair comes into the hands of the aunt, the whole afternoon is wasted.Girima becomes restless to escape her grip. The old woman, guessing her impatience, opens up the story box from the hoary past, beguiles her grandchild, and completes her work.

Udhab's grandmother Belabati, in her youth, was a tough and bold woman like the bel fruit (muskmelon). She'd disobeyed many anorthodox traditions. On dark nights, she used to go to her parents' house, crossing rivers and sea, rowing a boat alone. She had proved wrong, in the dark nights, the rule that women should not row the auspicious boat. Of course, during the day, fearing her in-laws, she used to draw her veil up to her nose, and would bite her tongue when she heard about women rowing boats.

After the death of her in-laws, whenever Udhab's maternal

grandfather would fall ill, it seems, she used to go to the waters with a group of fishermen. But people never called her ill-behaved or a termagant, rather they called her a male.But they always said things behind her back. None had the courage, not in ten villages, to speak anything on her face. The Paradip queen Bhasadhuti Devi was full of praise for Belabati, and even treated her as a sister. For this gesture of Bhasadhuti Devi, people respected Belabati fisherwoman.

If anyone said anything, Belabati used to reply, "Oh, ye male! Are you swinging your spouses on the swing, that you would forbid them the river and sea? If the fisherwoman can go to the fish market, to the road, field, and to the crematory, what is the crime in going to the ghats?"

That day, encouraged by her husband, she tucked her saree tight around the waist, and she got ready to make salt.

The news spread like wildfire that a group of women in the Kujang area had boldly come out at the call of Gandhi to participate in the salt agitation.The district magistrate of Cuttack also got wind of it.To go to Baliapat, a river had to be crossed by boat. If the boatmen refused to row the boats, what would the women do? Let them make salt in their pots and pans sitting at home! What was the need to create sensation and disturb the peace of the British government? The magistrate ordered the Sub Divisional Officer to camp near Baliapat. He also issued orders to all boatmen not to ferry women across the river. It was announced that those who disobeyed orders would be punished. The chowkidars strictly guarded the ferry ghats.

That day, hearing once again the story of Bela, Girima tied a simple knot in her thick hair. She jumped out and untied the boat from the lonely ferry ghat. When Udhab was down with fever, and the brothers had gone to the market, a lone boat was tied to the ghat, waiting for Girima.

Last year, because of Indra's mischief, there had been drought. This year, because of Indra's mercy, the rainy season had been bountiful, and even in September the river water had swollen like a belly of a buffalo. When Girima untied the boat from the ghat and eased the boat to the water, oaring it carefully, in her youthful body she felt the strength of spirits.

She felt she was the queen of the boat, queen of the river, queen of the sea, and queen of the entire universe. She did not care for anyone when she felt she was in the right. She was a girl and the daughter of a boatman too. She was rowing a boat, not sleeping with somebody, so she refused to feel ashamed or afraid.

In some distant Dwaparyug, the fish-scented fisherwoman Satyabati was rowing her boat on full-bellied Yamuna. Sage Parashar, inside the divine boat, satisfied his lust on the fisherwoman, and as a boon transformed her from fish-scented to a fragrant lady. Again, for having satisfied his sexual urge, he restored her virginity. Thereafter, she married the Kuru king, Santanu. Fie on a sage—and so lustful! At the sight of the fish-scented girl, a girl about his daughter's age, all his sage-hood had come to naught!

When the boat started moving, she remembered sage Parashar. Her rebellious mind asked Parashar, "However learned, wise, and honorable a man may be, he is only a male before someone's daughter. Can a man, before a girl, be not a father, brother, or a well-wisher? If a sage loses his mind when sexually aroused, then why blame the aimless wild youth of today?"

Such questions were never answered. Many things in life remained as questions. Thus, Girima was lost in her thoughts. At that time, the riotous young man, the ruffian Sakula Mohanty, called aloud from the riverbank, "Hey, boat woman, hold the boat. I'll go to the other bank. No boatman is available today. The ferry ghat is deserted. You ferry me to the other side. You'll get good payment."

Girima turned the boat toward the ghat. She was happy that a customer had come. That she could ferry people from this side to the other side and back could not be proven without a customer. Knowing well that Sakula was evil, she was possessed by arrogant nonchalance. Why should she say no? Should she say, "I can't do it, Mohanty's son. An unmarried woman and a wild young man in one boat. What would people say?"

Girima was confident that if Sage Parashar himself, by his magical powers and glory, tried to rape her on the boat, she would teach him a lesson. This fellow was poor Sakula Mohanty, afterall, a misguided lad of Kaliyug. Pooh! Girima turned the boat, and Sakula, with one jump, entered the boat.

Negotiating the current of the full river as the boat rose and fell, Sakula said, showing his teeth, "Remember that day you got me beaten by your brother Bhagyadhar, simply because I took a photograph of you? I have no malice toward you. Rather, I have confidence in you.If we go to the other bank, we'll be together. If we drown in the middle of the river, then we'll also be together. Why worry?"

Girima said with a smile, "Don't you know how to swim? Oh, Mohanty's son. If the boat drowns, why should you drown? I can swim the sea. It's no big deal for me to cross the river at the snap of a finger. Living on the riverbank haven't you learned to swim?"

Coming a bit closer, Sakula said, "The children of boatmen play ball with river and sea.But the upper-castes and children of bigshots bathe in their backyard with wellwater. Their bodies are seasoned with baths, with water in buckets. When floods come, those people die in large numbers. I know how to swim a little. But see how the river has swelled like the belly of a pregnant cow? Oh, how delicately slim is your waist, like the summertime streamlet! This September river is very fat."

Girima had tied her saree edge to her waist tightly. It looked slimmer than her real waist. Her nubile body was bending like raw tamarind, rhyming with the strained oars while changing the direction of the prow. She felt that Sakula's words and demeanorwere becoming indecent. But she was reassured by the fact that the lad did not know how to swim.

Straightening the oars, she said, "I vowed to teach a lesson to sage Parashara. Don't you know about sage Parashara? Kundala Panda has read several times from puranas at the Bhagabat Gaddi. I have it on the tip of my tongue."

Sakula became happy and said, "I feelyou are the daughter

of the fisher king, fish- scented, and I am sage Parashar.Only, if there was a cloud cover, the world would disappear, and I would transform you from the fish-scented to the flower-scented. If you closed your eyes, the world would be unseen. Touch the bank away from the ghat, and automatically the clouds would rush. No one would be the wiser…"

By this time, Girima was almost hissing in anger.She said to herself, "Wait, son, let me teach you a lesson. Only then would you recognize Girima, boat woman."

She then inserted the oar below the underbelly of the boat and slanted the boat sideways. When the boat tipped, Sakula was sitting. He panicked and reached out to Girima, stretching his hand to maintain the balance. Girima swiftly slipped to the side where Sakula was sitting and slanted the boat all the more. She jumped into the river holding the flailing hand of Sakula.

Sakula was half-drowned in the water at this sudden fall into the river. Girima floated a short distance away, swimming with backstrokes, and stood in waist-deep water. Then she shouted with simulated panic at the fishermen netting at a distance, "Come running, please! Somebody is drowning!"

Three or four netters jumped into the river and rescued Sakula Mohanty from the water. He had swallowed a stomachfull of water and was not conscious. It was told in the village that Tahali Mohanty's son, the owner of Studio Rati, had been drowning in the river. He had been seen by the fisherwoman Girima, who'd been taking an untimely bath in the river, and therefore, he'd been saved. The villagers praised Girima. Udhab Mangual mused, "How could the boat go to mid-river? And how did it overturn? The divine boat cannot normally overturn without cause."

Before Udhab, Bhudan, Sankhadhar, Padmadhar, Bhagyadhar, Benudhar, and other brothers and sisters, Girima confessed the truth. Her only aim was to convey that she had taught a lesson to Sakula Mohanty.

After hearing everything, her mother said, "Quiet! Never

speak this before anyone else. Sakula was drowning. This has now become the accepted truth. If this thing spreads, you would remain unmarried.I warn you. If this thing spreads, we'll not get a boy from any fisherman family for you."

Girima did not reply to her mother in the presence of her father, but she mused inside, "Am I dying to marry a fisherman's son? Where is a fisherman boy of my choice in this region?"

On the banks of river Hansua, sitting under the manguli punang tree at the newmoon ghat, Girima was contemplating the sea. Somehow, the sea entranced her.The sea entered her soul with roaring waves. Opening his arms, he took her to his lap; wet her with fondness, clasped her with love, and suffocated her.

Girima was feeling breathless like that, remembering the prize-giving day of the Kanakadurga Youth Club.She'd never known how songs were composed, or why. One day, standing on the seashore, the thoughts overflowed in her mind, and she wrote them down verbatim in the spiraling smoke that rose from the cow-dungcake. By the hotflames of the two-way hearth, she wrote,

O' Sea!
My eyes cannot measure you.
The heart does not muster strength to call you mine.
You are everybody's.
I'm one among nine rivers.
Jatadhari estuary gestures me by its hand.
That's the only way to go to you.
I'm a stream of the nine rivers.
I'm Hansua-Saomlia-Devi-Sakha-Tartara.
At times, I'm sluggish. At times, I'm restless.
O' sea, I know I'm yours.
But you are not mine, but everybody's.
O' sea, you fill my heart with sweet-salty water.
Half-mixed, two-tiered tides.
Someday, the full moon.
Someday, the dark, new moon.
As the salt forests were lost.
And lost were the mangrove forests.

So would I lose myself in your bosom.
Every day, the Jatadhari estuary beckons me.
There is no fence nor keoda-ketki enclosure.
This is my small, beautiful fisherman's village.
Abhayapur is afraid of you, O' sea!
I love my village more than my life.
Who are you to sweep away my village?
You stay where you are, dear sea.
One day or other, I would flow to you, leaving the village,
For I love you more than I love my village.
I'm the daughter of Mahanadi.
I'm not scared of earthly things.

Although Girima could not compose rhymed verse like the mourning songs, the festival songs, or the marriage songs, composing songs like the lapping, flowing river was her inborn passion. Why hers alone? What fisherwoman, Odia woman, or what woman of the world does not compose and hum songs of sorrow and joy? Who doesn't know that you need a song to lull a baby to sleep, to console a stubborn child, or to soothe your own inconsolable heart?

And the Odia woman is herself a complete song. The Odia woman laughs in songs, cries in songs, and dies in songs.Without a song, she cannot play *puchi*(a folk game for maidens), nor can she stay awake in the night of the autumnal moon, nor can she observe the *bhalukuni* festival. Without a song, she cannot even cross the threshold of her parents' house, returning after marriage, nor can she overcome the bereavement of a dear departed without a mourning song.

But had not Bhudan brother called her pure emotional outbursts *song* or *poem*, and not submitted them for the competition organized by the Kanakadurga Youth Club, the sea would have remained at its own place. And Girima, like a rivulet, would have lapped against the shores all her life. Maybe she would not have suffered as she did.

But it was quite surprising that the bright young man of Girima's uncle's village —

Chandanpur's Bikram Balabantaray—submitted a reply to Girima's poem, as if he had read it earlier. More surprising was the last day of the youth camp, when garlanding Girima and Bikram Balabantaray, the chief guest, the minister for games and youth affairs, shook hands with them and, dividing the prize money, handed over fifty rupees each and had a photograph taken of them together.

After the declaration about the prize, both were invited to the stage to recite their own poems.Girima was the first to read.Once in a while, Girima had the pleasure of reading her songs out loud to brother Bhudan, but to recite her poem in front of such a large audience was like walking up to the gallows. It was one thing to go up to the stage to receive a prize, but another thing absolutely to recite a poem in a competition for a prize. It was like asking for *bakshish* (tips) after performing a horse dance.

Bhudan had submitted her poem to the youth club, and when the news came that she would be awarded a prize in the youth mela, Girima went to the meeting, sitting on the carrier seat of her brother Bhagyadhar's bicycle. Following them, father Udhab, after selling his catch in the Erasama market, also went to the mela. Pushing through the crowd, he found a vantage point from where the stage was clearly visible.

The literature teacher of Abhayapur's minor school was also happy to sit in the front rows and instruct Girima by eye contact to go up the stage and recite her poem. The Panchayat Samiti chairman Tahali Mohanty was on the stage, looking stabbingly at Girima as if mocking her, "What song has this fisherwoman written that she has suddenly become the primal poet, Sarala Das?"

Tahali Mohanty's bluff master son Sakula—alias Mukunda—staredat her as if he would swallow Girima whole. Around his neck was hanging a camera, like bells around a bullock's neck. The fellow had a photo shop in the Erasama bazaar only to take pictures of schoolgirls and college girls in saucy poses. Superimposing photographs of unknown men with the photos of village girls, he blackmailed the parents of those girls by threatening to give those pictures to the local newspaper if they did not come to his studio. The paper was the scandal sheet of the village.

After reading the poem with her natural modesty, she raised her face above the microphone. She saw the sun rising from the womb of the sea. Like the soft, sweet light of the rising sun, the appreciative gaze of a pair of calm eyes caressed her body and face. Lingering a moment on her eyes, the look shook her virgin essence for a while. That was all. There was no further eye contact. Bikram arose from his place and went up to the stage to read his poem in his sea-loud voice.

When the bloodstream flows in Kashmir,
The Erasama Sea gets saline.
Hansua waters become thick.
The evening and morning turn crimson.
I am a soldier's son
in the lion's abode of the world.
I'm an Odia hero.
How much more blood would you drink, o' sea?
Would you drink my blood?
If blood mingles with blood,
Will not your waters overflow, o' sea?
Would not Kaliyug end?
O' sea, stay where you are.
The Himalaya calls me there.
The battlefield calls.
Hansua-Devi, Tartara, pull my legs.
I give you my word of honor, o' sea.
I would jump to your bosom from the Himalaya.
I'll be yours, entire and whole.
Stretching my hand to nine rivers,
I would tie the knot from the Dal Lake to the Bay of Bengal.

War was in the blood of Bikram Balabantaray. It was in his breath, walk, look, and also his poetry and prose. For him, life without war was a corpse. His battle arena was from the sea to the Himalayas and from Erasama to Kashmir. That day,

Girima, apart from other things in his poems, understood that this man had not merely joined the war, but had become war himself.Although she had known him since childhood, that day this man from her uncle's village looked different. It was a difference Girima had never seen in Kartika Majhi, the actor.

Her elder uncle had come.He said their village's first soldier Bikram Balabantray had earned a good name in the defense department.Soldier Bikram had enhanced the glory of this area.

Bikram, looking appreciatively at Girima, said, "Your poem is very meaningful. I thoroughly enjoyed it."

Girima replied clearly, "I couldn't understand your poem. Himalaya is far too far. Wherefrom could you pick up the nine rivers for the bosom of the sea? You took away half my prize money falsely; otherwise I would have got the full hundred rupees!"

Bikram said, looking into her eyes, "Your straight talk, your evocative poem, these make your guileless nature transparent. After returning from the war, I would refund your fifty rupees. It's a loan on me. Whatever money I have brought home has been spent. Next time, when I come on leave, I would refund with interest. Would you continue reading in the high school? Or, like the other girls of this region, is your education over after seventh or eighth class?"

Bhagyadhar cut in, saying, "There is no high school in our village. How would she go to a distant school? That's the reason no girl from our village has touched the soil of a high school. In the entire fisher class, Girima is the only one educated thus far. She has read enough."

Placing his hand on Bikram's shoulder, Bhudan said, "When you two were standing garlanded on the stage, a boy from Sakula Mohanty's studio took a picture.If he plays the villain and breaks the marriage of Girima by showing the picture to others, then our Girima would stay unmarried for having written poems."

Girima said, "Brother, you are responsible for all this. I scribbled off a few lines. You called it a poem and spread it around. The photographer boy has taken many pictures. Photographs are taken in meetings. How is he to blame? If Sakula Mohanty does some mischief with our picture, you know the village would banish us. My mother would make mince- meat of me. As such, she is afire since I came to the meeting."

Bhudan said in self-defense, "This Bhagyadhar is responsible for all this. The other day, he snatched the camera from Sakula and thrashed him. One day or other, he would have avenged himself. This meeting provided him with the opportunity. Don't forget that you are also guilty. Remember the way you tried to drown Sakula?"

Girima laughed wildly, covering her mouth with her saree edge, remembering something. Bhudan, too, laughed aloud. Bikram's curiosity ratched up a few notches.

To make the situation more mysterious, Bhudan said, adding a clever spin to his words, "Everyone knows about the fisher king's daughter Satyabati and the sage Parashar. If the fish-scented daughter of a fisherman could row the boat to ferry people, why not Girima? Girima, too, is the daughter of a royal fisherman, Udhab Mangual. Therefore, that noon, Girima released the boat into the river. Whatever was to happen, happened. The scripture says that if women row the auspicious boat, some such untoward thing would happen. Girima did not pay heed to that. Hence, the inevitable happened. Of course, Girima did the right thing. Whatever be the result, Sakula Mohanty was taught a lesson."

"What happened? What was the incident? Why don't you open up, Bhunda?" Bikram tried to provoke his childhood classmate.

Bhudan did not mind Bikram's "Bhunda. Who didn't know in this region that his name had become Bhundabecause of his father's love for Binoba Bhava? In a calm voice he said, "Wait, be patient. Why are you so excited? Why does it matter to you what happened? It is natural for you to become curious, as Girima is Bhagya's sister. But our Girima is really very naughty. She has done what naughty and mischievous girls do. She must enjoy the fruits of her action. If you are bad with the bad, the result would never be good. The age of tit for tat is over. For a girl, she is so audacious!"

On a narrow, uneven road, pushing a bicycle walked Bikram. Behind him was Bhudan, and at the rear Bhagyadhar and Girima.After raising Bikram's curiosity to the peak, Bhudan narrated, adding his own sauce, the event that had happened a few months ago.

Bikram laughed for a while and praised Girima. "Wow! This is the work of a soldier."

Bhagyadhar said, "Because you are in the army, I see that you don't see anything else in the worldexcept the soldier!"

Bikram, being a poet, was very articulate.After all, he was from an aristocratic Paika family. He said, "In everyone's blood there is revolt. He who is adventurous shows it in action. But he who is not bold fights within his own mind and revolts, but to the outside world lives a life of fear. This is a tortured world of man.It is better to be a martyr while fighting for the country. Man would definitely die one day. What's the point in trying to protect yourself by inaction?"

Hearing about martyrdom from Bikram's mouth, Girima's heart sank. She thought, *Fie, what's this ominous talk? Do all soldiers have to die? Why is this soldier eager to die? He talks big.*

Bikram resumed as if he could hear her mind. "Of course, you try to destroy the enemy before your death. If everyone dies, the enemy would rush in. This Tahali Mohanty and his son Sakula are the enemies of our region. It's now necessary to bring them around, each in his own way. Through thisStudio Rati, Sakula is blackmailing innocent girls. His misdeeds in the nearby villages have crossed all limits, but everyone is silent! Being a woman, it was brave what Girima did. Let some man do it and show that values are not dead. Girima should be the role model for the girls of this region."

Girima's bosom swelled with pride. No one had praised her so sincerely for her actions that day. Instead, the conservative people of these villageshad condemned heron hearsay. From that day; she'd been labeled a virago.

Hearing Bikram's praise for Girima, Bhudan said, "Udhab uncle, in his heart of hearts, desires that his youngest daughter should marry an educated person, not an unlettered fisherman. You know, Bikram, for a soldier like you, a fighting woman would have been the proper match. But this caste system is creating problems."

Bikram immediately said, "What is caste or religion for a soldier? A soldier is a fighting person. The country is his shield. He does not save the country, rather the country saves him. And for this reason, he sacrifices his life for the country to save himself, generation after generation. I, therefore, don't accept this caste distinction in my country."

Girima's face suddenly reddened at this statement from Bikram. In the next moment, Girima said, "Let's go, brother Bhagya. It's already late in the evening. Mother would be angry." As Bhagyadhar rolled his bicycle, Girima's thoughts were flowing over the potholed road, rising and falling until both the brother and sister fell into a ditch with the bicycle on top of them. After getting up and dusting herself, Girima said, "Why were you cycling so unmindfully? Who were you thinking about?"

"Me— or you? You put your foot on the pedal and imbalanced me. What were you thinking?" Bhagyadhar explained away his guilt.

"Let's go home quickly. I'll tell mother about how you threw me in the paddy field. You were pedaling the cycle thinking about Padma sister-in-law, wasn't it?" retorted Girima.

"I would also tell father,"said Bhagyadhar.

"About whom?" asked Girima.

"About Bikram."

Girima did not say anything, as her marriage was already finalized with Bhairab Majhi's actor son Kartika—although the engagement ceremony had been postponed time after time. The soldier, Bikram Balbantaray, entering like a missile, had now turned everything topsy-turvy.Girima knew that a woman has a free opinion, but must pretend ignorance about it.But, encouraged by the soldier; the sleeping desire of Girima has been awakened. At the long sigh of Girima, the cycle wheel rolled from the ridge to the field, uncontrolled, like her unguarded mind.

THIRTEEN

By coincidence, two letters had reached, one after the other, the Abhayapur post-office. One was addressed to Bhagyadhar, the other to Bhudan's address. Bikram Balabantaray had written to Bhudan from Kargil. The other was written by Kartika Majhi, from Surat in Gujrat, to Bhagyadhar. Udhab perceived a subtle relationship between the two letters. But the contents of the letters were different.

Bikram had written,
Brother Bhudan,

India's victory over the Kargil war is now almost a certainty. It's now a matter of a few days. I am fortunate that I have fought directly with the enemy. The place where I am fighting is a desert, but a desert of snow. Here you cannot measure the height of the mountains. And it cannot be explained what is really meant by the ferocity of winter.

The oxygen level here is low. Along with winter, the speed of the wind is so fierce that you feel as if you are being stabbed. We are alive because we have covered our bodies with seven layers of winter clothing. We are alert all the time. There has been no time even to change our clothes during the last four months. The question of bathing does not arise. You may be surprised to know that the drops of sweat which form under the clothes while climbing the mazy paths on the mountains turn to ice in no time. So to speak, a garment of snow clasps our bodies.

For this reason, my body has rashes all over, and the skin has cracked. All of us are in the same condition. It's the irony of nature that, although we are on the snow heap thousands of feet high, we don't get any water even to wash our faces. The gradients and the gales pull and push us every moment toward the caves of death.

You may be shocked to learn that matches do not burn here for lack of oxygen. You can imagine how difficult it is to breathe here! We have to contend with so many enemies simultaneously. While the bullets rain from the top, we climb up the mountains with the help of ropes, fighting strong winds and biting cold, testing our strength against our life's breath. There are many more chilling problems which I can't describe. But these spur us to encounter the enemy going forward. They never bog us down nor make us retreat.

One who hears of these from a distance may be gripped by fear. But once you wear the military uniform and shout, "Victory be to Mother India," all fear vanishes, and each soldier stands as an enemy's enemy. Except the thought of victory, no other thought enters our minds. In fact, there is no time to contemplate life and death.

It's a dream to receive or send a letter. I am keeping this letter in the chest pocket of a wounded soldier who is being taken to the hospital. Someone or other would post this letter at the base hospital. This letter would definitely reach the village. Once victory is declared, I may get leave. I hope to be in the village during the Puja holidays.

We'll stage a play. I'll write the play. The theme is The Smiles of Kargil. You perhaps would wonder, how does Kargil smile after losing so many brave soldiers? She must flow as a river of tears! But Kargil's tears every moment turn into ice at the bereavement of her children. Kargil has transformed itself into a mound of ice by the intensity of her sorrow. She appears to be smiling when sunrays touch her tears. That smile is so bright that we might be blind but for our dark glasses.

I don't wish to cause pain to people at home by saying all these things. And don't think I'm unhappy here. There is no greater joy than fighting for the country. This can't be explained-hence, let go of that. But the essence is, as life and death are the same for a soldier, so are all human beings. Here, we are all of one caste- Indian. We have one aim-saving our country. If this principle were observed in our villages, man could be saved from many an unnecessary sorrow. We'll start this reform from our village. What do you say?

I hope this year we have a good harvest in our area, a good betelleaf business, and a lot of Hilsa! Two elections are ahead. The unemployed may earn some easy money. It seems in 1999 everything would be good and auspicious after a Kargil victory. Hopefully, Bhagyadhar's sister, the heroic woman Girima, is writing poems on hilsa, bass, river, and sea. Once I reach the village, we'll have a poetry competition between our two villages.

Kartika's letter to Bhagyadhar was as follows:

Dear Bhagu,

Here in Surat, there are lakhs of Odias. The play "The D-Day is in November" has become such a super hit that the proprietor is tired of counting the money, and we are also tired of playing. Even then the demand of the people shows no sign of receding. Since I wrote this play, my clout in the theater has increased. The owner is encouraging me to write new plays. But he is stingy with money. Everything is on credit. Anyway, this year I'll come to village after Dussehra. If the wedding is not done with by November, Father would not allow me to continue in the theater peacefully. He's writing letter after letter.

Father doesn't understand that it is easier to leave the marriage altar to perform a play elsewhere than to take leave from the theater party to go to the marriage altar. He who leaves would go from the party, never to return to Surat. However, the owner has agreed. But to speak the truth, your sister is so outspoken and shrewd that to tame her I must leave the theater party and stay in the village. To leave the wife is easy for me, but to leave the theater is difficult.

Let's see. The date is in November, and whatever is fated would happen. Your wife Padma must be happy with you. Those simpletons don't need anything else after they become mothers. In a way, it is better.

Yours,

Kartika

Bhagu read the letter out loud to everyone. Girima hissed. "Hmm! To leave his wife is easier than leaving the theater? Write back to your Kartika. It is more difficult to get a good wife than it is to join the theater party. Six months a year they would be acting, and the wife would be counting the rosary in the village, is that not right? Write to him that Girima is not that type of girl, eager to marry a man like him. Ask father-though he has arranged a groom, has he arranged the right groom?"

Girima's large eyes welled up with tears. Hearing about the letter from his son, Udhab Mangual fell silent and became tense. What Girima had said could not now be changed. For a healthy and working fisherwoman, there was no dearth of grooms. But educated grooms of Girima's choice were few and far between. Yet, let this Dussehra pass. Then it would be up to the Lord. Udhab hummed a few lines from the Bhagabat.

Whatever this mind contemplates,
in time it comes as a gift.
Ceaseless Shrabana rain.

Dussehra was far away. Gandhi Das excited the whole village by saying that Victory Day would be celebrated. Golmasta burst a few crackers at the mid-village altar. The villagers gathered as if to watch a bioscope. Small things created excitement in the village, but Golmasta's crackers and Gandhi Das's announcement of Victory in Kargil spread a real euphoria in the small, narrow, calmbosom of the village. Golmasta, Udhab Mangual, Gandhi Das, Banchu Tarai, Shaikh Salbeg, Alwar, Bhudan, Sankhadhar, Padmadhar, Bhagyadhar, Sarala Das Mandal, and Dhadi Barik all embraced each other. That was the Kargil Victory Day.

It was the thirteenth day of Shravan, and the entire country celebrated victory in Kargil. But from Drona Sir's eyes was flowing an endless stream of tears. To his knowledge, three hundred and thirty-three Indian heroes had been martyred. About four hundred and fifty had been maimed and fifteen were missing. Eleven Odia soldiers had also been martyred in the war. More casualties might have occurred on the other side of the border. Victory always bloodies the celebration of victory, be it the Mahabharat war, the war between Ram and Ravana, or the Kargil war. Golmasta, in the midst of the victory celebration, was feeling unspeakable pain in some unknown corner of his heart. He had more friends and family on the other side of the border than he did in India. Many Pakistani heroes had laid down their lives. Who knew whether some relation of his had died in the war?

That day, at the small mosque and the Laxmi Narayan Temple of Abhayapur, prayer meetings were held for the salvation of the Indian martyrs. There were prayers for the quick recovery of the wounded soldiers and the safe return of the missing heroes. Gandhi Das said, "Why only for the Indian martyrs? We would pray also for the Pakistani martyrs. The heads of the countries fight, and the heads of the common people are sacrificed. After death, the souls gather at one place where there is nothing called a border. Who has the courage to draw a boundary separating Hindu-Muslim or Indian-Pakistani in the world of the Borderless?"

Everyone, however, was reassured that the first Kargil Jawan of Ambiki Panchayat, Bikram Balabantaray, was returning to his village waving the flag of victory. A week ago, his letter-sent a month earlier-had been received in the village. Bikram would come on long leave during Dussehra. His mother was seriously ill. It was uncertain whether she would survive. In the meantime, his father, it seemed, had finalized his marriage. When he came, there would first be the Kargil-Victory celebration, and then the Dussehra festival, followed by his marriage ceremony in November.

And other festivals would lengthen the list in these small villages. Mother Durga would appear this year in her most blissful form, bestowing bounties on all. But was it right to arrange the marriage of Bikram without his consent?

Udhab Mangual mused upon this question and was ashamed by his own answer. "Hey, you! Mangual! What do you think of yourself? Royalty? Successor of the Dasa King, and therefore, you are the king of all? Whatever did you think would happen? You are a fisherman by caste. Should the Paika boy's marriage have been fixed by his father, taking your opinion?"

"Let him not take my view. He, too, is a fisherman. Why should he depend on somebody else's opinion to arrange his daughter's marriage? Girima's marriage decision does not depend on Bikram's homecoming. To hope for the improbable in my old age is not the right trait of a fisherman."

Udhab was perhaps misguided by his children's words. In this region, there was no precedence of a Paika boy marrying a fisher bride. Of course, it would be different if the boy and girl eloped. But Girima was not a girl like that, and Udhab was not the father of such a girl. Bikram was not a defiant son like that. His father was a very proud man. Pride of wealth, of caste, of aristocratic lineage-and now the pride of being the father of a Kargil hero. His tail was up.

Why then delay the marriage of his daughter? If the Sendhakud boy slipped out of hand, then it wouldn't be easy to find another educated fisher boy like him. The eldest son Samkha's eldest daughter-Devi-was just a year younger than Girima. She was now marriageable. After her, Alaka and Pohala became eye-catching. Would the nieces marry first while the aunt remained unmarried?

If the niece married first, then the aunt would be stigmatized and stay unmarried. In this region, there was no tradition of the younger sister marrying before her elder brother and sister. It would be scandalous. If the younger one married, the elder was alienated. Therefore, it wouldn't be bad to get Girima married this rainy season, whether on an auspicious day or any day, leaving everything to the all-merciful Jagannath.

For Devi, the groom's family in Borikina village were awaiting the marriage eagerly. It would not be proper to give them word before Girima's marriage was arranged. Girima was volatile like the horned fish. She refused to marry Kartika, saying he was a theater man. She further said, "If father marries me there, there is no dearth of rivers and ponds in the village for me."

Even if he has to risk losing face with Bhairab Majhi, Girima's father would cancel the Kartika proposal. What else can be done? Should he throw his daughter into a river or pond? If the Sendhakud proposal materializes, it would be better to send her off, taking a chance. The problem would be over. A little learning is always dangerous; the girl has given him enough headaches.

Not so much for the Kargil victory, but at having resolved a conflict in his mind, and with the pride of having arrived at a decision, Udhab returned home, taking big strides. Fifteen days ago, the first pregnancy ritual gifts had been sent to Marua's in-laws house. That meant that she would go there for delivery. Udhab decided to go personally to Sendhakud to finalize Girima's marriage and bring Marua home.

Udhab might not be rich in terms of material things, but he has a rich heart. Despite occasional sorrow and want, there is no dearth of joy and happiness in his life. Just this year, a new boat was built, and it would be used for fishing. Bhagyadhar would take this boat to catch hilsa, and Padia would be the navigator. Girima's marriage would be held, and then Devi's marriage. Marua would give birth to a boy or girl.

Oh, for some good and auspicious works, Mother Basulei is showing the way in 1999. The greatest good work was victory in the Kargil war and Bikram's victorious return. May Mother Basulei protect Bikram. He is the pride of this area, a savior of our India. Let other things wait.

Bikram is not related to Udhab Mangual. There is no scope in the future to call him his own-but does that mean that Udhab would not be happy at his safe return from Kargil? If not, fie on his humanity, a hundred fies.While chewing a betel, Udhab spoke before Ketaki about the homecoming of the Kargil hero, and about his decision to marry Girima with Shatrughna of Sendhakud. His mind was relaxed.

Later, Ketaki stood on the ridge of the betel-leaf enclosure, looking at the vermillion-smeared western sky. Girima was standing in thigh-deep water in the pit below the ridge, staring absentmindedly at the rising stars in the eastern sky, a bunch of blue lilies in her hand.

"On whose neck would you put the garland of choice, friend?" asked Ketaki.

"On the neck of the triumphant hero," Girima answered with conviction.

Ketaki's face faded like a lily closing its petals. She said, "I offer flowers on Shiva's head and wish for the well-being of the bullish boy Shatrughan of Shendakud, friend. Forget the Kargil hero, Bikram. He is not a stud, only a bull, the carrier of Shiva. He obeys orders, shutting his mouth. Does the carrier have an independent world? He is the obedient boy of his father, of the village, and of the country. He is for everyone's happiness except his own. That, it seems, is the duty of a soldier. That he has written to brother Bhudan.

Bikram is coming, true. It's also true that he is a victorious hero. What's wrong with Shatrughan? You are so very choosy that you would be out-chosen. After you, your niece Devi, Alaka, Pohala... Would you not ease the burden from your father's head? Do you know that Uncle Udhab is deeply worried?"

Whatever she had heard from her toothless grandma, Ketaki reported verbatim to her soul-mate friend. Knowing well that her words would wound her friend's soul, Ketaki's own soul wrenched painfully. On the wheatish face of Girima, a dark cloud appeared, true, but it was not apparent from outside. Inside, though, an unseasonal rain was drizzling.

She was standing in water in the same posture, holding a wad of blue lilies with stems fresh and wild. But with a touch of defiance she said, "Who do you think is the triumphant hero? Bikram Balabantaray? Fie! Is this a victory? What has he done to take the credit for victory? If you deduct the lion's share of the heroes who died, those who were unaccounted for, and those maimed from the victory, what remains for a soldier like Bikram Balabantaray to take credit for?

"My victorious hero is Lord Shiva, who, carrying the dead body of the chaste Parbati, moved all over the universe with such devotion so that-if not in the same life-

at least in the next birth he could be fortunate enough to be her husband. That is called victory. You tell my father that I agree to the Shendakud proposal. A woman that is also born in a fisherman family is highly fortunate to eat, be clothed, and raise a family with children. Are my sisters unhappy? Why should I be unhappy? Moreover, have I given word to anyone, or loved someone? My only sorrow is that I have to take leave of you. What an unfortunate woman you are, friend!"

The shell-shaped, large eyes of Girima welled up with tears. But Ketaki knew that, having seen the play The Sati's Corpse on Shiva's Neck during the last dola festival, her friend was lecturing at her. Her tears were for herself, not for the new-moon born friend. Tears are more contagious than fire, and they infect one from the other. If you stay away from fire and there is no strong breeze, fire cannot jump to singe another. But without wind, tears affect the eyes of others. Having spoken an unpleasant truth to her friend, Ketaki turned her tearful face away and ran toward the crematory. In the evening, the shop would be crowded, and the old woman there could not handle the customers alone.

Throwing all the flowers into water, Girima stood transfixed in ankle-deep water, staring at a lone star in the eastern sky. But the lilies-by the law of nature-never drown in water until they fade out. At the center of a pond, even a single lily survives. There is no greater victory than survival, despite the million failures and defeats. Dragging her feet from the slush, she came out of water.

On the other side of the river, tickled by the cloud-drenched, sun-ray smeared, invigorating, early autumn breeze, the frolicking white grass flowers were swaying exuberantly from side to side in a tidal dance. It was as if a row of white clouds were unfolding their wings and alighting from the sky to the paddy fields.

Had autumn come early this year? Mother Durga would be

worshipped, and then there would be the kuanra punei, the festival of Laxmi. In the month of November, there was the festival of Kali, then Deepavali, the festival of lights, then the full moon night of Kartik. In December was the new paddy offering for Laxmi, the Prathamastami.

Like knots on the saree and scarf of the bride and groom, there would come to the Odia homes thirteen festivals in twelve months. Small families would enjoy the festivals, but on the head of a large family man like Udhab Mangual, there would be loads of expense, loads of worry. This was not understood by his daughters nor by his querulous middle-aged wife, Sankha's mother. So long as the strong hands of father were catching fish deftly, they would eat, drink, and enjoy the festivities with lavish nonchalance. With much effort and difficulty, Udhab earns money to afford the comforts-and how much only he knows. What is his luxury? Being clothed and fed. He has no need be lavish or enjoy. He needs only a few morsels of food. The capable fisherman has fought not only against the sea, river, storm, and cyclone, but also with his lifesince the age of six, and he has now passed the age of sixty in the Kaliyuga. The poor fisherman may not wear anything to cover his back, but at least he must eat!

Yet how much does Udhab eat compared to his struggles? Before dawn, not only Udhab, but the entire fisherman community wakes up. After the fisherman leaves the bed, the sun rises, and not before that. Whether the river, the sea, or watching the weather, unbrushed and unwashed, Udhab goes to the water. It's exactly like sucking milk from his mother up to the age of six, unwashed and unbrushed.

He carries with him a tobacco-leaf paste, drinking water, watered rice in a can, baked dry fish, salt, chili, some onion or garlic. But he never forgets to take with him a bundle of bidi (cheap, local cigarette) and his betel bag. A turban is on the head, and a loincloth is tied to his waist carefully. He also keeps in the boat a sheet of cloth for bad times, in case he suffers from fever, to cover his body.

Smoking a few bidis is his breakfast. When the slanted

rays of the morning sun straighten in the sky, the hungry fisherman's tongue salivates impatiently. The watered rice, salt, and chili beckon him. In no time, he swallows large handfuls of watered rice with chili, onion, and dry fish. Whether due to the hot, raw chili's poison or the aromatic taste of watered rice and dry fish, the devilish hunger is pacified. Thereafter, till nightfall, the fisherman has no time to think about hunger. What hunger, when he sees a school of fish in the folds of water in the river or sea?

He sells the catch of the fish at half-rate to the wholesaler and returns home. Whether it be midnight or late evening, Udhab can never guarantee. Dividing the money and the unsold fish between the partners when he returns home, he often finds his children asleep. But his wife, Sankha's mother, waits till he returns. She has no fear if he is late, but if she smells a sea storm, or if the gathering clouds look menacing in the sky, her heart sinks. Then she makes several vows to appease Mother Basulei, Ganga, Mangala, Sarala, and other deities for his safe return. Good! But expensive.

Udhab's wife desires to serve him food as soon as he steps into the front yard, but Udhab never is in any hurry. In all seasons except winter, Udhab goes to the backyard and takes a dip in the pond, whatever be the hour of the night. Wiping himself dry, he changes clothes and offers prayers to Mother Basulei. He reads a canto from Jagannath Das's Bhagabat, then he worships his belly. Hot, coarse, boiled rice with mustard fish, enriched by a dash of dried mango, or thin slices of fish floating in a sea of watery gravy, made delicate with pieces of drumsticks-or, on certain days, lady's finger from his own backyard. But big or small, every night he has fish at dinner.

In this region, vegetable for the fisherman means fish or dry fish. Once in a blue moon, on religious or social festival days, he enjoys the luxury of lentils. That's all the royal repast of the heroic male Udhab's daily fare. Only during the rains, floods, or droughts does the fisherman suffer hunger. Not only Udhab-all fishermen, farmers, and the poor. In the house of the poor-men like him-there is no room for excess rice or paddy. But there are too many bellies to feed. In Udhab's house alone, there are sixteen. Besides, everyday guests and relatives or friends crowd his house. How can he manage?

All fishermen of this region are in the same situation. The fishermen in all villages have the same business, the same lifestyle. Had he lived in the village of his birth, Bandara, whatever he would have eaten or done coming to his uncle's house in Abhayapur as an adopted son, he now eats and does the same, lives in the same manner.

There is no difference. Well, there is one difference, and that is in the heart of Udhab, which none can see. And that has made him so guilty that never does he look normally at the chest of a woman. So much so that when his middle-aged wife feeds her children, uncovering her drooping breasts, he can never look at her. When he looks, a sorrow-washed jealousy, a rolling, unarticulated regret, and a shy, helpless, about-to-cry childhood wrestles within him. These three feelings simmering inside, perhaps, have made his eyes red, and like a sudden, soft flame flickering forth from the cow-dung cake and husk smoke, Udhab sees in the flash the loving face of his mother.

When he looks at the river, his dead mother flows, alive before his eyes, with her soft murmur inside his heart. In this old age, when he takes dips in the river, he feels as if he is playing on the lap of his mother. The river is the mother; the sea, father. The vegetation, trees, men, birds, and insects are their children. The old mother, embracing, clasping, and lapping all with hands and legs outstretched, is the earth. And the gray, old sky of eternity is the old father.

The sun is the most powerful, wrathful elder uncle, and the cheerful and calm moon is the younger uncle. Because the elder uncle is very angry, no one goes near him. Looking at him with eyes raised was not possible, so the eyes are lowered automatically. What uncle is he? Therefore, people know as uncle only one, and he is the moon uncle. In the courtyard of the uncle, at night, the jasmines, tagar, tarata, malati, janhi, the night queen, henna, and the colorful flowers bloom. But, unable to bear the anger of the sun, all fade and fall, one by one, in the morning. The uncle's courtyard remains lonely and bare the whole day.

Whether man or nature, old or young couples, brothers or sisters, uncles or aunts, nephews or nieces, or other members of family and clan, this lila(drama)has gone on since the birth of man. What can man do? Man is a pawn in the lila of the universe. Man is like the solitary dancer; whichever way the dance master makes him dance, he dances. When the whistle blows, declaring the end of the dance, everything freezes, stops. Everything runs as per the old rules. The same old sky, earth, sun, moon, and stars. The old game of birth and death. The same sun sets in the west and again rises renewed in the east the next morning. When a tree is old, a new tree is born out of its seeds.

In the same order, man would come and go, would be born and die, honoring nature. This is the absolute truth. But the dead do not rise again, and the living always die. Man mingles with the dust from which he rises. This is the principle of the universe; the divine lila of Mother Basulei. But knowing it all, man becomes morose when the news of death comes, even of an enemy. He may or may not be happy at the news of birth, but certainly his heart sinks at the news of death.

Udhab that day was morose without any apparent reason. He had no desire to go to the river or sea for fishing. If he sat at home, Sankha's mother would make his life miserable. She would chase him to the sea or river. No wife likes her male to sit at home. Sankha's mother is not to blame. If the male doesn't work, he is as good as dead. Who loves a dead man?

Sankha's mother does not even understand why Udhab gets depressed without cause. If one is not ill or the children are not ill, if rice, fish, betel leaf, and salt do not give headaches, if there isno loss in business this year or no apprehension for the next year, why should a capable male be depressed? For what? Is he having a clandestine affair with a home wrecking woman? Oh! Before hearing such things, Udhab goes out of his house with his net and sits in a blue mood at the old banyan tree, in the crematory at the rear of the village.

FOURTEEN

A small village, Lavanipur, was visible beyond the ketaki fields, on the other side of Hansua. He could have touched it stretching his hand. But now, what's the point? All love and familial relationship with that village had snapped forty years ago. After the dowry was finalized, some mischievous enemy of Udhab had poisoned the ears of his grandfather that Hema was a new-moon born. That was it. The relationship suddenly snapped. Why say *snapped*?

The relationship had not even started. Only the proposal had advanced a bit. But many times, while squeezing the wet saree from her naked, brown calf, Hema was seen from the rear or front by the then-young Udhab. The fishermen often see young women, married and unmarried, with their wet clothes plastered to their young bodies. That's of no consequence. But when the proposal advanced, someone from within Udhab said emphatically that he appreciated Hema from top to toe. But when the proposal fell flat, when he knew that Hema was not for him and Udhab had no right even on the wet footprints of Hema, he could not accept that so easily. He had silently cross-examined the Maker.

Why did the faces of new-moon born lasses look so very exciting, like the full moon at the touch of youth? But he never asked his grandfather. If Hema was not meant for him, how could anyone be blamed? The fault was in the eyes of the greedy male. The matter ended there. Khulana, the daughter of the aristocratic fisherman of Chandanpur, came to Abhayapur as daughter-in-law, as she was destined for Udhab. The same fair, frail, nubile woman, Khulana Sundari, was now the mother of six sons and four daughters. A strong, solid termagant, Udhab's wife, Sankha's mother.

Udhab had no grievances in life. He was never again depressed about Hema. And there was no cause for it. Yet, looking at the other side of the river, sitting on this side, in the cloudy afternoon, the seven-hued rainbow is seen, and the moon appears, pushing the clouds. One hears in the nimble waves of a full river the soft lapping of a woman washing her clothes. Udhab fisherman's depressed mind automatically becomes euphoric. The world sees a human body growing from childhood to old age. But the mind and heart? The delicate psyche?

The spring comes and goes, but the cuckoo continues singing. Somewhere in the folds of branches and sub branches, she has her nest in the crowded world of leaves. Her warbling is not heard in the other seasons, but itis heard to man in moments of agony. At times, perched on the branches of memory, the unseasonal cuckoo calls its soft notes, but it does not excite the soul, rather makes the heart heavy with a joyous melancholy.

Welcoming spring, even the fallen leaves murmur in song. Can anyone say, placing his hand on his heart that in the varied seasons of life an unprovoked cuckoo has not called, uncalled for? Who can vow to speak-which mature tree has not been thrilled at the romantic touch of the spring breeze? Udhab, Golmasta, Bharat Mandal, Bhairab Majhi, Banchu Tarai, even Gandhi Das and the modern lads and lasses, all are bound to be wounded by the soft touch of the spring breeze and the restless warbles of the cuckoo. That is human fate.

The human mind too is strange; it derives agonized joy from scratching old wounds till they bleed. But the fisherman called Udhab, his mind is stranger still. An old fisherman's laughter and tears, joy and sadness, they move around the fish, crab, river, ditch, sea, weather conditions, rain, and cyclone. But if Udhab Mangual is to be morose thinking of all matters of the universe, who can prescribe any medicine for him? That's Udhab's nature, as if he is not Udhab, but Basuki, the mythical serpent, balancing the universe on his poor head!

Udhab thinks, "After all, you are a fish-greedy fisherman. Your head may ache if a storm rises in the sea or if conflicts arise between villagers, but why should you bother if there is a war in Kargil? Are you the prime minster of India? How are you concerned about the Kargil war? Where's Kargil, and, where are you? Even if the war is fierce, what can you do about it? And would you be depressed for such matters? As if you are a leader!"

Of course, Udhab has nothing to do in such matters, but he is destined to suffer with rising palpitation of the heart. Who can stop that? India, it is true, has won the Kargil war, but can one forget the pain of war? He has seen on TV in the village club the dead bodies of many Odia jawans sent from Kargil in body bags. Oh, they are not his blood relations, but doesn't the mind sink at that sight? Is he a man or animal?

Because Sankha's mother doesn't know or see these things, she is immersed in her world, only comprised of her husband, ten children, and a host of grandchildren, her home and hearth, fish and dry fish. When does she find time to suffer from heartaches for the sons of others? But God has made Udhab in a different mould. He suffers for others. Bikram Balabantaray is no way related to him, means nothing to him. Why then was he praying day and night to let him fight? Let him not come to the village, but let not his garlanded, inert body return in a body bag.

Udhab had fallen at the feet of Mother Basulei for him. Mother Basulei had heard his prayers! Bikram is returning alive and victorious. Let him return, marry, and live long. What worry does Udhab have? God has not only given him no sorrow; he has also not been niggardly in giving him happiness. Life is not all happiness; then why should he be afraid of sorrow? The man who moves all his life fighting sorrow, should he fear pain? Udhab was babbling to himself like this and was participating in the welcome ceremony of Bikram Balabantaray.

If waves frolic in the river and sea, on the bosom of the small villages no ripples rise. For the coastal villages, ebb and tide are regular features. Therefore, all wait for some unforeseen event.

The sensation created by the Kargil victory in these villages was far less than the excitement created by Bikram's letter from Kargil. How Bikram fought against all odds and dangers, those things grew from fact to epic exaggeration, and for his reception grand arrangements had begun in the villages. Although he did not send any more letters, it was certain from his first letter that he would be arriving before the Dussehra festival.

A welcome arch was already raised at the instruction of Gandhi Das at the river ghat. On the road leading to the village from the ferry ghat, a massive arch was constructed by the efforts of Mantri Mallik alone. That Bikram should pass through at least seven to eight arches to reach his village was the desire of Gandhi Das, and accordingly, he was busy in making arrangements for the reception of the victorious hero.

An inexplicable joy was rising in Udhab's mind. From morning to evening, everything was a good omen for him. Girima's morose mind was turning golden like the ecstatic dreams of the mustard fields in September. Bikram had not given her any word, but Bikram's safe return was enough to make her happy. She had written a few romantic songs, whatever be their quality. Girima had written only about war, snow, and the sea in her poems. Many such songs she was writing in her cardboard-bound, ruled-paper notebook, and was reading them alone for hours.

While the villages, along with Abhayapur, were busy preparing for the twin celebrations of Dussehra and the grand reception of the Kargil hero, Bikram Balabantaray, providence gave a mighty blow at their neck. The blow, however, was not equally painful to everyone. But everyone was stunned. With cries of alas and sighs, all the arches raised for Bikram's welcome were dismantled in a single day. Breaking something is not as difficult as making. The dreams cracked in a moment. The welcome arrangements for Bikram were burst like a bubble by one telegram. The telegram was, "Bikram is missing."

Who does not know the meaning of missing in a war? Udhab Mangual returned home with a heavy heart, dragging his feet. Udhab knew the dream which his daughter nourished about Bikram would not have borne fruit because Bikram was not of the fisherman caste, but a Paika. But that Bikram had become a martyr in the Kargil war, was it in anyway less than lightning on his head? Would not his daughter Girima die alive, getting this news?

Of course, Girima knew that her dreams would never see the light of day because man's living enemies were a legion. Caste, religion, big-small, high-low, so many obstacles, boundaries, and fences. Girima might have been opening up her mind in her sleep, but she never revealed her mind during her waking hours to anyone. Udhab, as her father, knew her mind. His wife knew only the bellies of her children. She had no time or concern to understand their dreams and aspirations. According to her, what was the meaning of mind for a female?

While entering the courtyard, Udhab met Girima face-to-face. The father and daughter looked at each other like numb strangers. Girima, mustering courage, and without any bashfulness asked, "Is the news true?"

"Better to wipe the name of the missing person from your mind," Udhab answered somewhat rudely, and entered the house, face down.

It's easy to count the stars, but not the days awaiting a promised event. Whether promised or not, it's easy to count flowers. Compared to counting days for the coming Dussehra, it was easy for Girima to count flowers. Her time was spent moving from pond to pond, and tank to tank, plucking lilies. Being born in a fisherman family, her leisure time was not endless. But in the world of fish and dry fish, the lily too was a part of the September Khudurukuni, an Odia festival for unmarried girls. Not bothering about month or time, auspicious or inauspicious day, Girima, entering into ankle-deep water, was counting the pollen of lilies more than searching for fish or crabs. From September to October, from October to November, like the fondness of the twelve-month heart, the lily too was a twelve-month flower, blooming all the yearlong like the twelve-month sorrow. Girima was also sad about her friend.

Ketaki that day was distressed for herself. That betel-chewing passerby was not coming anymore. That day, through some investigation, Ketaki could know that he wouldn't come again. He was working with some contractor of this area, and therefore he was taking this road. The contractor's job was over, the camp was dismantled, and the unknown passerby's walk to Ketaki's garden was also over. But why was Ketaki sad? What were the chances of being elated again, looking at the passerby? Nothing, yet she was happy seeing him.

But could Ketaki deny the strange kind of relationship which made her unhappy-not seeing him? Like making a betel with a clove tucked in it and handing over to a customer, Ketaki sealed the unknown relationship with the passerby and handed it over to the past; and by the time she sat down, shaking off the past, she saw that her fingertip was stained deep red with lime and catechu. No worry. In a few days, the color would fade away from the tip, and the hand would be clean.

No one can see the heart of a woman, thank God! The vermillion on the forehead of a woman is the only color. It is better if the colors inside the mind are not seen, for who cares for those colors?

The news of Bikram's disappearance, like a lash of lightning, struck Ketaki with the fire of sorrow. She knew that her friend would be plucking lilies. It was not unlikely that she would drown herself on hearing this news. Forgetting her own sorrow, she ran to the betel-leaf plantation enclosure area. On the ridge of a slushy ditch, looking at a lily, Girima was standing under a lone star in the sky. That day, somehow or other, she had not collected lilies. Girima had not even stepped into the water. Before Ketaki could speak, Girima signed at her for silence and pointed a finger at the mound near the betel-leaf plantation. A cobra couple was dancing with raised hoods in the lime-turmeric, mixed-saffron rays of the setting sun.

"Auspicious or inauspicious?" slipped from the mouth of Ketaki.

"Auspicious; not inauspicious like a lone star. If you are lucky, then only you can see a male and female cobra playing together. They have been playing for an hour. I'm looking at them, all attention. Have you seen this before? You are a voice of doom. Why should this be inauspicious?" Girima said absentmindedly.

"But friend! A telegram has come today."

Girima quick-swallowed the rest of Ketaki's words and interrupted. "I know. It has spread all through the villages. Many have been missing in the war, and he is one of them. Let it go."

"One chapter has ended." Realizing Girima's strength of mind, Ketaki tried to console herself.

"Ended? Or has it begun?" Girima said.

"What has begun?" asked Ketaki.

"Sad days. Bad times are ahead. The prophecy says this, father was mentioning." Girima heaved a long sigh. The sun went down all of a sudden.

September was about to end. On the dawning autumn's grass flower fields, October had advanced the first diamond-dust like drops of dew. Yet the coastal villages looked forward to the honey-month spring festival, and men and women, old and young, wait longingly for the month of March to come. By the oars of the south wind, the chaiti tide rises from the bosom of the sea. The saline waves flow into the rivers, and again the sweetness of the river water returns in the rainy season.

At times sweet, at times salty, and at times salty-sweet, water flows in the nine coastal rivers as the sea and river mate on the east coast. This is life. Seasons of joy and sorrow come and go, festivals come and go, man comes and goes, but man's love for each other remains, never fades, lingers as memory. The dusty childhood games, the soft bathing hours, they lose themselves in the womb of time. But the past is never lost.

Do words really fade away, fade away the visible reality, the face of the moon, rays of the sun, and whole lifetimes and human births in this twelve-month, six-season, self-wounded whirlpool? If everything really fades and disintegrates, how then does tonight's pale moon appear again tomorrow in its pristine glory? How do new flowers laugh when today's flowers fall and perish? How does this year's spring return next year? After the waves return through Jatadhari estuary to the womb of the sea, how do they rush in again on full moon or new moon days, raising their foamy hoods? Man dies every day. How then is it that man's name is never wiped off the earth? When sound flies and fades, how is the echo heard like a reply?

In Udhab Mangual's perception, nothing is ever lost. Udhab's parents and fourteen generations have been lost in the maws of time. Yet they are very much there in the unwritten history of his clan, culture, traditions, and festivals. In life's indelible, untorn pages, they have been recorded automatically. For that, Udhab has not taken the trouble of learning the lessons by heart. Also, he has not repeated their names, holding slate and chalk. Everything has automatically dissolved in his blood, has entered into the minds of generations. From the old records of time, their names have faded long since. But they have not faded from the history of this village, or from memories.

Udhab was thinking many thoughts in a state of depression. Where have the previous generations of Kundala Panda, Banchu Tarai, Narku Routray, Tahali Mohanty, Magbul Mian, Dhirendra Manna, Magana Bhoi, Kichaka Pradhan, Dinakara Mishra, Dhobei Sahu, and Bharat Mandala gone? Where were their fathers born, their fathers, and their fathers? And where have they gone, leaving everything, after working hard to save for the future, to settle their families, to spread new clans in this old world, entrenching their roots deep? Man is never everywhere all the time.

Udhab has no record of when, how, or for how many millions of years, the human race has been nomadic. But Udhab knows this much-that even if man settles at a place during his lifetime, the universe is in the mind of man, and the entire universe is his home. Man thinks it safe to live within a certain geographical perimeter, true, but he is never happy. For security, geography provides the boundary, but for freedom, history has provoked man to go beyond the limitations and limits any way he pleases.

Man has created the order and discipline of country, state, district, block, panchayat, ward, street, family, and home. For his comfort and convenience, man alone has divided not only man and the earth, but also gods and divinities. His quest for pleasure has been his bane, the basic cause of his sorrow. In the guise of God and religion, man has poured on fellow men his hate, violence, anger, and other poisons. He has killed and is killed. O' what bloodshed!

This human race has experienced all. Like the python of the forest, he has tolerated everything. He is a pachyderm. Like all men, many people of this region have withstood the cruel outbursts of violence, have come away leaving their homestead. They have left behind their brothers, friends, families, property, and golden harvests. Crossing the borders of language and geography, they have come away to build new homesteads, new lives, new villages and cultures in far-flung areas.

In strange, unfamiliar territories, they have settled and grown. The human settlements have spread like canker growth in fields, riverbanks, sea coasts, and crematories. They have adopted different callings for existence. Even then, there is no respite. No respite from hate and war. No respite even in the thrills of victory; this was because of the mourned dead. Who had anticipated that, even after the country's victory in war, such a thunder would strike the forehead of this region? Who anticipated that the welcome arches for Bikram would be struck down by a single telegram?

On the day of victory, Bikram's name was added to the list of missing soldiers at number sixteen, which meant Bikram was no more. Sighing deeply to dispel the sad thoughts from his mind, Udhab became all the more morose. But Udhab was not a man to be cowed down by depression. He rose, tightening his waist, to start his dream project, his cherished lifetime ambition of building a boat. Through the dirt road, running piteously through the marshlands, he moved toward the riverbank.

The wild, naked sun, taking dips in the marshlands, was napping on the bed of reeds. Bending in knee-deep water, Bharjan Mallik was cutting the reeds. If two reed mats were not knitted for this year's winter, the cold days would be torturous. These all-eating children might not have morsels of food in their stomachs, but there was no dearth of excreta. The reed mats were to stem the field of filth. The urine-soaked mats didn't last a year. The emaciated old Kanduri was not able to tie the reed bundle and lift it up to his head. The old haggard might not survive this winter, but look at his greed! Coming out of the water, Bharjan raised the bundle to the old man's head, and as he descended again into the water, he felt a sudden pain at the base of his thigh. Bharjan dismissed the pain, as he had noticed a horn fish playing in the water for some time. Leaving the reeds, he was after the fish. In the slush, moving like an eel, he was about to catch the horn fish when the nasty fellow stung him. Holding tight the blood-mixed, injured finger, Bhjarjan came up.

Mantri's mother was returning home, carrying a bundle of twigs on her head. Asking for a bit of fire from the Sahu house, she had come home and lit the hearth. If she made some curry soon, the children were waiting to eat hot rice. After Mantri became the crematory-devil, Bharjan had lost the right to be a bonded slave in anyone's house. He was a daily-wager now. Every day, the belly needed rice, but it is not written anywhere that he would be hired every day. One night, he had lifted a measure of paddy from someone's farm. Boiling the paddy, Mantri's mother had gotten some rice.

The boys are greedily waiting to eat hot, cooked rice. Want destroys character, otherwise, her husband would not have turned thief. Nowadays, seeing the plight of the children, Bharjan steals some paddy from someone's threshing floor, or a banana bunch from someone's backyard, or small fish from someone's fish basket. What's the way out?

Sucking the stung finger with his cleft lips, he tastes his own salty blood, walking fast toward home. Mantri's mother's eyes fall on him.

She asks, "Why do you limp?"

"That bastard horn fish stung me, and with that, my leg was twisted in the slush. I'll tell you a secret. If one or two reed mats are not made this year, the children would shiver in winter. If the cold pounces on them at home, let them all go to the burning ground. You dreamt that one would be a minister, and that boy is basking in the burning pit. Let these also enjoy the warmth with their elder brother. Let them eat the rice offered to the ghosts. My worry would be over. Let all of them live like devils. What joy is there in living like untouchables?"

Mantri's mother has been observing for quite some time the layers of frustration on Bharjan's face. The banishment of his son is eating into his vitals. The woman is helpless. She has neither time nor strength to quarrel with her husband. Where is space in her mind for other thoughts except the worry of keeping the children alive? The children are moving, but shabby and dirty, and for that she has no regrets-but, being a mother, how can she tolerate her children turning into corpses from hunger and starvation? Is her heart so very small because she is an untouchable? Is she less fond of her children? She quarrels with her husband, standing there. Bharjan still has strength in his fish-stung hand. He strikes his wife in the midst of a field in the presence of others. Fie, fie, the man is deserted by all morals.

Udhab Mangual moves fast with his fishing group toward the sand dunes on the riverbank. Saying, "Stop, stop," he comes between the wife and husband. He doesn't ask why Bharjan beat her or what the matter is or who is at fault. He knows that the quarrel would be fiercer if questions are asked and explanations sought. He knows that in the maws of want and poverty, this is the daily routine of husband and wife.

He calls Bharjan, "Come with me. My new boat would be ready in a few days. You would do errands. If nothing else, you would bring tea and snacks from the shop. Hey! Don't worry, your caste would not matter. What better caste we are born into?"

With the joy of getting a job without effort, Bharjan swells and, looking straight at Udhab's face, says, "See, Mangual, my due wages you have to give. Don't bargain like others. Don't delay payment, and do not cheat as the others do. Since the day I started as a daily wager, I know everyone in my bones. Everyone is a villain. My son, they say, is eating the flesh of dead bodies. But these people eat the raw flesh of the living poor. Those who enjoy the sweat-earned money of the poor, are they not sucking the blood of the poor? If I am a thief, are they not armed robbers?"

Mantri's mother interfered and snubbed her husband. "What are you telling, and to whom Mantri's father? No one gives you a job. Mangual has offered a job out of pity, and you are throwing tantrums? Is Mangual a cheat? Has he ever cheated anyone? Why are you biting the picking a fight for no reason?"

Udhab signaled to Mantri's mother with his eyes and said, "You be quiet, Mallick's wife. Bharjan is saying the correct thing. Who in this area does not exploit the shabby poor? How long should he tolerate sealing his mouth? Bharjan's indignant outburst is a good sign. Now, one after another would open their mouth. Only then a change would come."

Bharjan followed Udhab Mangualwith slow steps. A few half-cut reeds were floating on the water like half-dead snakes. To Udhab, it looked as if his new boat were floating on Hansua waters. In the life of a poor fisherman, to have a new boat is like building a ladder to heaven-maybe a thread short. To cajole a sulking wife is easy, but to navigate and control the aft of a boat is not easy. The dry sheets are very resistant. Warming and leveling those and bending the fore parts takes almost a month. Udhab was lucky that the real obstacle in boat making was overcome. After bending the fore and aft, to fix the side boards was more difficult. That too was done without much strain. Like the clever hilsa playing in both sweet and salty waters, in the boats of this region, the rasalila (love-drama) was performed both in river and sea. Therefore, instead of iron nails, Udhab had fixed bamboo pegs in the joints so that the boat would be worthy of both river and sea.

Now if tar was painted on the boards, only an auspicious day would be waited for its release into water. His five sons' lifetimes would be served by this boat. But Udhab thought they ought to have learned the art of boat making. If you spend your own lifetime well, the lila of the world would not be over. The grandchildren and the future generations also must spend their lives. Life must go on generation after generation. Udhab believed that if he had not taught the technique of boat making to his children and the other young men of his village, he would have gone to hell. Only for that reason, at his old age, had he made a boat in the presence of his fishing group. Otherwise, his life would have been spent smoothly with the old boat. The end is near, and how he knows it!

On the Shiva Ratri, people stay awake and pour water and milk on the head of Shiva. The day following would be better for the release of the boat. But this Shiva Ratri is far away. Udhab has decided to consult an astrologer to fix a date for him, immediately after the Dussehra festivities are over. It would be better if the release function were over before the harvesting season in late November. This year, all his auspicious ceremonies are lined up, back-to-back.

Dame Luck seems to be favorably disposed toward everyone this year. In fish, betel leaf, and paddy, everyone is expecting a bumper crop. If only Girima's marriage were over, Udhab's worldly responsibilities would end. After that, he wants to be a disciple of the Naked Sadhu and spend the rest of his life listening to and discussing the Bhagabat. Udhab always thought that it would be better to die in harness when your limbs were functional than to be a veranda-vegetable, eating from what others earn. But is his death in his hands? Why then worry about that so early?

FIFTEEN

On the narrow forehead of Abhayapur, smaller than the tiny bird-like boats floating in the vast sea, all the events of the universe-accidents too-happen like seasons following one another. The same happens in 1999, the last part of Kaliyug.

What else is the universe? Is there any village called the Universe somewhere? The Maker has designed the universe with small and big villages together. Abhayapur, in the vast universe, may be a paltry piece of land, like the hoofmarks of cattle; yet who would call the rest of it-developed, undeveloped soil, hills, and sea without Abhayapur-the Universe? Is it not, therefore, advisable not to consider Abhayapur small? Forget the events, the accidents, and untoward things that have happened in the world this year. No less have been the combined calamities that have happened in Abhayapur, in the district of Jagatsinghpur, and in Odisha.

Near the crematory grounds, sitting in a circle around the holy fire of the naked sage, were Gandhi Das, Drona Sir, Udhab Mangual, Banchu Tarai, and a few other market-returning passersby. Mantri Mallick was singing with closed eyes playing the dhudki (lyre):

O' wise man! Speak the secret truth.

In which lotus is the bee imprisoned, O' wise man?

Udhab's mind was attracted toward that tune, as if he were the honey bee and was impatient to spend the rest of his life chasing that secret truth like the newborn calf running behind the cow. The world no longer pleased him. Everywhere, a sadness had spread after the news of Bikram's disappearance in the war. With that, all kinds of unfortunate events began happening, one after another. Gandhi Das was describing the calamitous events that had happened in Kaliyug, chronologically. The others, like a herd of lambs, were nodding their heads with unblinking eyes. It was not clear whether it was helplessly or in ignorance. Without excitement or sadness, keeping his tone and voice level as far as practicable, Gandhi Das was providing a running commentary on calamities of 1999.

"On the Sripanchami, mother Saraswati's worship day, on the twenty second day of the first month of 1999, the Australian missionary Staines Sahib and his two innocent young sons were burned to death by miscreants. They attacked by pouring petrol on and setting alight the missionary vehicle while the family slept inside. Oh! In the entire universe, has such a horrendous incident happened anywhere?"

"No, no, never," breaking the silence, the shocked listeners of Gandhi Das said.

With a long sigh, Drona Sir drew an oblique line on the holy fire, changing the direction of the flame. And he spoke, raining fire.

"See our own Odisha. Our boys died at Kargil eating bullets. Their body bags came by airplane and were sent to their parents. As the whole country, with the world supporting our cause, awaited the result of the war, some self-centered leaders dreamt of election victory and power. Victory in the election is more important for them than the victory of the country. The political chair is more important for them than the capture of Tiger Hills in Kargil. In our Odisha, in the meantime, two chief ministers have served, and a third one is now in power. When the battle strategy for Kargil was being planned, the House of People was dissolved by one vote! The border was insecure, the freedom of the country was in danger, but the politicians created instability and a crisis in governance. Should we call this the last phase of Kaliyug or the last throes of man on earth?"

Before Drona Sir concluded, Gandhi Das said, "Before the Kargil victory was consolidated, the date for the parliamentary elections was announced. And listen to what a few leaders said during election campaign to the vote-disillusioned, unlettered people. 'Brothers! The value of your one vote is worth more than a million rupees.'"

The parliamentary elections had recently ended like the first festival of October. A new government had been formed at the center. But to what purpose? What changes had come to the old lifestyle of Abhayapur? Where were the elected leaders? Why were their hearts not bleeding for this region?

Udhab sang in his usual manner:

They occupied their seats of power.

The wise became the beast of burden.

Gandhi Das, said, "This is the style of elections. This year, for our unemployed youth, is a golden harvest. The Assembly elections are ahead. Let's see what improvements happen in the village, but I have misgivings. If Bikram is missing, is it not the responsibility of government to trace his whereabouts? One who was lost fighting for the country, would his father search for him?"

From behind was heard the laughter of Mantri Mallick, sounding like a burst of Chinese crackers. Everyone looked at him in amazement. This was that crematory-devil Mantri, who had been banished from the village by Kundala Panda? This was that Mantri, whom all said was foolish, useless, a halfwit? Who didn't know that Mantri was the unelected leader of the youth of the village, and that he had laughed at the news of Bikram missing?

Udhab said, angrily, "This is not a matter to laugh or to mourn. When Bikram's news spread, even a villain like Tahali Mohanty blinked his tearful eyes. I've seen. But you, Mantri, you are laughing? You be damned. I thought you were different, but I see you have become more heartless than the corpses, living in the crematory."

In the meantime, Dhadi Barik arrived, sweating and panting for breath. He stood and said, "Don't you know that Mantri has become stark mad now? He kills the living and propagates that the dead have come back from the abode of death. According to him, Bikram is not dead, and no such telegram has come. He says to go and ask in the telegraph office whether the wire was not in the name of Sumanta Balabantaray of Chandanpur."

"Yes, a telegram has come. But where is it written that Bikram Balabantaray is no more?" Mantri shouted.

"It is written that he is missing. What's the meaning of that? "said Dhadi Barik.

"Have you read the telegram? Who the hell are you? You are that hypocrite Tahali Mohanty's yes-man. Have you now become his wife's yes-man?" Mantri laughed boisterously. Dhadi Barik's eyes were always red like the crow pheasant. It wasn't known whether this was in inebriation or because of an inferiority complex. But intoxication and inferiority complexes are like Dhadi Barik's hair and nails-the more you clip them, the more they grow.

Dhadi screams in his nasal voice, "The chairmanship monopolized by Tahali Mohanty for the empowerment of women has now been reserved for women. But that does not mean a bullish man like Tahali Mohanty would become a woman. Without Tahali here, the Panchayat committee is irrelevant. Therefore, Tahali Mohanty's wife Kalabati Devi was asked to contest, and she was elected. Now Kalabati Devi is the proxy of Tahali Mohanty, and she is our chairperson. Husband means master, god, and authority on all rights. Thus, for records, Kalabati Devi is the chairperson. But the de facto chairman, the ultimate authority on everything, is Tahali Mohanty.

"When the ministers and super ministers come from Bhubaneswar and ask where the chairperson is, it means they ask for Tahali Mohanty. Whatever he was doing when he was the chairman, he does the same now. Only, on the dotted line, Kalabati Devi signs, grunting and groaning. Kalabati Madam, as usual, bows to the guests from under the veil and goes back to the kitchen. She treats the guests with varieties of dishes. Tahali Mohanty enjoys his power, as usual, and the work goes on smoothly, and the seats reserved for women also stay reserved.

"Who loses what in this arrangement that this crematory

devil mocks at me? In eighty percent of the seats reserved for women, the husbands are all-in-all; in this small block, if a chairman's post is managed by her husband, why is it giving you sleepless nights?"

Gandhi Das sighs and says, "In our country, politics means divide and rule. Scheduled caste, tribesman, and women's politics were prevalent, now Hindu, Muslim, Christian, and family are added to politicking. The caste and clan of the deities are also now being researched. Who should you complain to? Gandhi Mahatma has supported the division of the country so that man would live following the path of peace and non-violence, whereas the same division is opening up ways of further division of branches, sub branches. The meaning of divide and rule politics is to cut to pieces the human race."

Drona Sir said, "It only remains to be seen when the tenth avatar of Vishnu, incarnation of God, holding a twelve-hand measure sword, would make mincemeat of the human race. Only on the heaps of destruction the flag of "God is one and the human species is one" would fly. Wait, it's not far away. The words of malika would come true. Total socialism would be established on the rubble heap of civilization. This is inevitable."

Golmasta said, "Why a twelve-hand measure sword? In 1999, Kalki Allah would appear with a ninety-nine-hand measure sword. God knows! Man does not know the date of his own death; how would he surmise the death of Mother Earth?"

"Hey, you mullah Golmasta mian, what do you say? Well, who is this Kalki Allah? You have destroyed the Hindu faith of god Kalki, an incarnation of Vishnu. You have made him a Muslim? See, you have worsened the situation. The loss of the Kargil war has not been compensated. The soul is wounded. If you speak like this, a riot may break out. You withdraw your words and atone for them, or else leave Pakistanpara village and return to Pakistan." This was the thundering voice of Kundala Panda. Finishing his prayers at Kali temple, standing at a distance from the crematory, Kundala Panda had been listening to the entire conversation. Finding an ugly meaning in Golmasta's Kalki Allah, he used an uglier word, riot. His life-long principle was to extract wrong meanings from statements, and to think of ways of atonement.

Gandhi Das stood up as if touched by a fire, and, looking at Kundala Panda, said, "Panda sir, the riot word which you have used-for that, you have to expiate. To threaten Golmasta with banishment is also a sinister crime. You must withdraw that sentence. Otherwise, you can't remain here as the village priest. Golmasta has the same right on this soil of the village as you have. You may be the priest of this village; Golmasta also has right as a member of the civil society. He always thinks well of others. I warn you-"

While the priest was thinking whether to curse or not, Mantri Mallick sang out, playing his lyre:

> O' rat of the mind,
> You are a ganja addict.
> Never could you understand the cat,
> O' rat of the mind.

Dhadi Barik rose up to the priest and whispered, "Sir, these people are starting a movement; they are violating the caste barriers. The scheduled castes, Dalits, and Muslims are now their priests. You destroy them by your curse. Root them out from the beginning. Why quarrel with the gods?"

Perhaps Kundala Panda was doubtful of his powers to curse. Therefore, avoiding the issue, he asked, "What is the truth? Bikram is missing, or he's really become a martyr?"

"Who knows whose son is dead or missing? A telegram came with the address of Sumanta Balabantaray."

Hearing that, the fertile mind of Tahali Mohanty guessed why a telegram must be bad news. "If Bikram's body is not flown in here, we must assume that he is missing. Tell me, priest sir, what can be the meaning of missing? Moreover, the proof that Bikram is no more is given by Sumanta Balabantaray's action. After receiving the telegram, he sat gloomily for a while and, instead of finalizing the date of Bikram's marriage, postponed it.

That day, the entire family was in grief. Does this not mean that it was news of Bikram's death?"

Panda, instead of answering, retorted, "Who gave so much news about Chandanpur to that slimy tout, Tahali? How could Tahali know that in Sumanta Balabantaray's house that day, no one ate anything? This is strange indeed."

Patting his own skin-and-bone chest, and with some self-confidence, Dhadi Barik said, "Who else gives news? With Dhadi Barik around, who gets hint of the inner circles of the ten blocks here? That day, I went to Chandanpur with a letter. I sensed an eerie, stunned silence in Sumanta Balabantaray's house, as if somebody were dead. The mental condition of the old couple was miserable. Getting the telegram, the old man postponed his son's engagement. He was broken down. May God spare others from such sorrow. Sumanta Balabantaray's clan is lost, sir."

"Oho Dhadi, you have not given up the habit of exaggerating things. When a crow flies away, you say a child flew away. Do you know what the significance of a telegram is? I know. Bikram wired his father not to fix up his marriage. It seems he has not made up his mind for marriage and cannot come for this year's Dashrath would come in November or December-not to marry, but to bring about some reform. Reform! Unredeemed brat! Hey, culture is inborn; the Brahmin, Dalit, and Muslim are born with their culture, and would also die with it. Again, a Brahmin would take birth as Brahmin, and a Dalit as Dalit. This is the meaning of culture. And what other culture or reform is there? Culture is not a dress that you can change or clean with soap. To change the culture which is in the skin, bone, and marrow of a man is sheer bluff. Because of victory in the Kargil war, Bikram thinks that he has become a destiny-maker of India. But at the insistence of Tahali Mohanty, the inauspicious things which you have spread, now face them."

"Sir, who am I? If the chairman is the villain, he would reap the consequences. I am just a puppet; however he makes me dance, I'll dance. The poor man's wife is everyone's sister-in-law. I know everyone would blame me-"

"Okay, okay. We'll do something about this. Tomorrow is an auspicious day, and this year we would have a bumper paddy crop. Let the festivals be over, and then we'll see. You just be patient."Panda asked for a loan of two rupees to buy betel from Ketaki's shop. The betel bag was empty. He showed it. The money bag was empty, and that also he showed Dhadi Barik.Instead of two rupees, Dhadi reluctantly proffered one rupee to the priest and said, "In this Kaliyug, I don't see any good coming to the people who worship the Brahmin and gods. That's why people don't pay the priests nowadays."

Panda tucked the rupee on his waist, and said, "That bird which soars high knows what transpires there. Everyone is not open-fisted like you and me, Dhadi. Give me a betel. The betel made by your wife is tasty. Who would take betel from that new-moon born, unmarried Ketaki, and destroy his merit? Now, I hear, she's having an affair with some spoiled lad from some village! What betel would she give me? See how I teach that lass a lesson. I called her during the evening prayer at the Kali temple to bless her, but the silly girl replied, 'A lonely Brahmin is inauspicious. When you are alone, your blessings give negative results. I don't need your blessings.' What commitment or restriction does the unmarried woman have, that she would tie up blessing in her saree edge? Oh, she is really a female cobra, a witch!"

Kundala Panda moved fast toward home, and Dhadi went in the opposite direction. To lose one rupee was a bad omen for Dhadi Barik. It was also a bad omen to propagate Bikram's death while he was alive. Such evil things do happen when Kaliyug approaches its end. But the crop situation this year was so heartening that Kaliyug might not end in the near future. The fortune teller also had predicted that Mother Durga this year was disposed favorably toward this region. Let all untoward things change their course to other regions and other homes. Dhadi did not care for those things.

After the new government is formed at the center, the state government is anticipating trouble. The Assembly election is certainly not far away. For Dhadi, that is auspicious. What's the meaning of one party for Dhadi? He would follow the political party that enjoys power. The leaders have no roots. They are always floating. Dhadi, after all, is a small fry, a party worker. He has no other aim except to earn his keep. As many elections that much gain. To compensate a thousand times the rupee he has lost, this is his unarticulated vow on his way home.

Ringing the bell of his bicycle, the postman is returning from Chandanpur. Hearing the sound of the bell, Kundala Panda turns back. Dhadi Barik too stops and waits. When the postman comes close, he asks, "From which village are you returning at this odd hour? The delivery time is already over."

Pulling a face, the postman says, "Bad news has come. Sumanta Balabantaray's son Bikram is missing. Perhaps he has been taken by the Pakistani army as a prisoner of war."

Kundala Panda says, "Then this Tahali Mohanty is really foul-mouthed. He spread the lie of Bikram missing, and now it is true. OH, at last, one from our village has become a martyr!"

Dhadi Barik says spontaneously, "Oh ho, man is saved from one danger. I was worried after spreading the false news about Bikram, but the matter has come true. A missing soldier may escape from other enemies, but not from the hands of Pakistanis. It's doubtful whether the Pakistanis would return his dead body."

The postman says in a sad voice, "Bikram may return. All missing heroes are not martyrs."

Kundala Panda replies with a smile, "Are you mad? The Pakistani soldiers after the Kargil defeat are like wounded tigers. Would they return the captured soldiers? If he returns, the body would be in flowers. That's what normally happens."

The welcome arches to receive their hero had been dismantled at the falsely spread news of Bikram missing, but the authenticity of the news broke the confidence and patience of the loving villagers. When the Hindus and Muslims live happily in Erasama like brothers, is it proper for the Pakistanis to capture and brutally kill a patriot like Bikram? Is it justice? The beginning of Kargil war would be played out again in this village!

The unknown passerby disappeared on the trodden path.

For Ketaki, the passerby was unknown, unheard of, but for the passerby, the road was known and familiar. While going on his way, if he took a betel from Ketaki and paused for a moment, distracted by the fragrance of Ketaki, how is he to blame? Ketaki is at fault. Why did Ketaki give the ingredients of love in the betel, tucking it neatly with a clove? Why did she add the redness of her lips to make the catechu colorful; and why did she carefully cut the areca nuts of her virgin dreams to make the betel more tasteful? Moreover, why did she deliberately make the village people see how she was handing over the betel and her heart in an enticing manner to an unknown man? These things are noticed automatically.

However you try to keep it a secret, the feelings are seen, if not the heart. But Ketaki never bothered about that. Because Ketaki knew that the man had no lascivious thought for Ketaki. It was Ketaki's own decision how and for whom she would prepare betel, and what ingredients she would put in it. Ketaki also knew that the unknown passerby would not take that road every day. If the mind changed, the focus of the mind shifted, and as a rule, the route also changed. Ketaki would not bang her head in desperation nor commit suicide for this.

For Ketaki, her life was dear. Whatever be the situation of life, it was sweet-

not expendable, but livable. When Ketaki's mother was dying daily for nothing, she was pleading, "Don't beat me. Don't kill me. I want to live."

What pleasure had her father given to her mother in life and death? For nothing, she'd been defamed. Poverty, sorrow, ill-treatment, and a lowly life; yet she'd been pleading, begging to live. Since those days, Ketaki had known that one's own life was the most precious; the others come next.

What was then strange about a mother snatching food from her child's mouth for survival during the great famine of 1866, in the ninth reginal year of the King of Puri? Her own belly was the womb of the child as well as the cave of the demoness, hunger! The child which a mother brings to the world and protects with love and care, when time's joints break, the same child is sacrificed to the demoness of hunger. Oh, how beautiful and ugly is this creature of nature, man!

Ketaki sighed and became absentminded looking at the heavy, indifferent face of the September sky. Her heart rankled for her friend, Girima. Who knew what was fated for her? Bikram Balbantaray had won the war, his father had fixed his marriage elsewhere, and the news of his missing from Kargil had been spread, on hearsay, by Tahali Mohanty. And finally, again, the rumor went on that Bikram was alive, that he had only wired his father not to finalize his marriage. All these made Girima almost a stone.

Her feelings were not reflected on her face, as though Bikram was an unknown passerby for Girima. He went his way, Girima would find hers. Maybe the two paths would meet or cross each other on some fateful road, but there was no chance of the two paths meeting and widening to go forward. A sprightly girl like Girima was now sluggish like a lazy stream. Good! Whatever is unfated, hoping for that means sorrow. Maybe, if she married that hefty young man of Shendakud, she would again flow ecstatically.

In the life of a young woman, sleep has nothing to do with dreams. The night fading into morning has nothing to do with the shattering of dreams. All the blooming flowers of the nightfall on the ground, denuding the tree, yet flowers again bloom in the trees, fruits swell, ripen, and regenerate life. The life of women is exactly like this. Butthe news conforming Bikram's disappearance dealt a stunning blow to Ketaki's friend. Ketaki was making betels with swift hands for the afternoon customers. In a palanquin, a bride was on the way to her in-law's house, sobbing and singing the ritual song of farewell to her home and village. The bejeweled, turmeric-polished hand of the bride clasped her father's hand tightly through an opening of the palanquin. Wiping his eyes with his scarf, the father walked alongside the palanquin, up to the river ghat, to board her on the boat and bid her farewell. The bride, remembering her mother's anguish after she'd sat in the palanquin, started mourning again.

"Like the betel-maker cutting the betel-nut, O'mother! My demonic mother-in-law would cut my head, O' mother!"

The bride sobbed bitterly while waves of grief engulfed her like the tides of the river water. Ketaki ran to her, leaving the shop. She asked the palanquin to stop so that she could console the bride. She opened the palanquin door. On such occasions, it is not necessary to know who the bride is or who you are to the bride. Everyone has the right to console a wailing bride who is going to her in-law's house in a palanquin. Similarly, every woman has the right to stop the palanquin and see the bride coming to the village, and assess the ornaments adorning her body. Whoever sits in a palanquin is everyone's daughter or daughter-in-law. There is no mine or thine in such cases.

Raising the betel-leaf shape face of the mourning bride, Ketaki breaks down herself, instead of trying to console the other woman ha! The mothers-in-law, even today, are like demonesses.

When the tear-flooded eyes met the eyes of Ketaki, the bride again starts weeping with the farewell song, "The wavy breeze, the street-roaming days. A holy dip in the Ganga, the sight of sages! Eating the mahaprasad, have you come? O' my friends! Where would I get a chance to see you again? O' my friends!"

The moments of farewell of a bride are unique. The words and songs on such occasions are all practiced and rehearsed, but at that moment, tears flow with genuine spontaneity. For the moment, the tears are true. The moaning becomes the true voice of feeling. The trees, birds, and witches also cry at the farewell moment of a bride. The two women, unknown to each other, shed tears, clasping each other's necks.

A few passersby gather there. A few women from the nearest streets also come running, wiping their tears. The palanquin bearers now separate the two women, and start off again, singing rhythmically their ritual song, "Up and down, night and dawn, ditch and swamp, softly tread."

When she returns to her shop, she sees Udhab Mangual, sitting tired and spent on the wooden bench in front of the shop, wiping his eyes with his scarf, looking at the fading sight of the palanquin. Seeing Ketaki, he said, "Your friend too, in a few days, would go to Shendakud village, snapping all ties with the village. After her, Devi and Alaka. My house would be empty. Without the daughters, the house is a stump, dry and joyless. Songs, laughter, tears, and festivities, everything goes with them. What else except sweating for money, eating, and growing old? But I'm thinking about you, my Keti."

"Let it go, uncle. Are your worries so few that you lift boulders from the road to put on your head? Why worry about me? I'll be sitting here and seeing off brides and consoling them. And I'll be the first to see the daughters-in-law coming to the village by this road. One day, I'll grow old suddenly, and I would burn to ashes in the crematory. It would not be too far for me." Ketaki vigorously cut the betel-nuts to escape from her sadness.

In the evening, from a distance, was heard the drumbeats announcing the death of an unwidowed woman. Ah ha! Which fortunate woman died with the red vermilion on her forehead? Couldn't wait till the Dussehra month was over? Who died? From which village?

The unblinking eyes of the people gathered near the shop and looked in the direction from which the dead body was coming with more curiosity than sympathy, as if it was first time someone had died. As if natural deaths were an unnatural event. Udhab Mangual had sympathy, but no less curiosity. In front of the corpse carrier, the unfortunate husband of the short-lived wife was crying, head down, throwing parched paddy and small coins as part of the last rite.

Udhab thought, Birth is the first step of death. Then, step-by-step, there was a journey toward death, which man called life. Death creates more sensations than life. Man's feet do not slow down listening to the first cry of a babe, but they stop when hearing the death chant. As if death was not natural, was an unforeseen, unnatural event! Ah ha! What has happened? Which unfortunate fellow left, ending his lila on earth? What injustice of the divine is this? Death astounds and stuns. Who died? How did he die? How tortured was he by death pangs? Did life go out through the eyes or the mouth? Was he accompanied by the messengers of Yama or the ambassadors of God?

The middle-aged, rickety, diseased, lean man who was walking, throwing parched paddy and coins, was of Labanipur village, a captive son-in-law. It was Mandara Behera, holding whose hands? The new-moon born Hema, who had escaped the unmarried state by a stroke of luck! Looking at the half-dead husband of Hema, Udhab was certain that this asthmatic, sickly man would have found his way out to the other world in his prime, had he not married a chaste Savitri-like woman, Hema. Udhab forgot to extend his hand to take the betels. Taking big strides, he went toward his home in the opposite direction of the funeral procession. The tobacco-mixed betels turned wooden in the hand of Ketaki after the inadvertent rejection of Udhab Mangual. Bikram was not dead, only missing. Getting such auspicious news, why Udhab uncle became so very absentminded Ketaki couldn't comprehend.

SIXTEEN

The rolling, rising moon, swimming in the flowing, wavy waters of Hansua, urged by the nippy October breeze, was zestfully playing with the river ghats on either side. The silver-plate-like moon, falling from the sky on still waters, broke into smithereens by the terrified swimming of the mischievous fish. Whenever Girima extended her hand to scoop the whole moon from the water, a fish from nowhere jumped into the bosom of the moon and scattered the image! Rising from the waters, the wet moon sticks to the fearless bosom of the sky. Just like Girima, the riverside moon is also whimsical! Udhab Mangual watches both the river and his daughter and wonders, Does the river care about shattering dreams?

When you take a boat and throw the net into the sea, you would get a catch of fish, big or small. Bartering the fish for rice from the fair or market is a windfall for the fisherman. The local fishermen are never satisfied with any other curry or vegetable except fish. Fish curry and dry fish fry would make the rice balls jump into the mouth. Energy enters the body, and blood flows in the vein. In exchange for fish, if you buy salt, clothes, mustard oil, and kerosene, the house is full. Besides, the angel of the house, the fisherwoman, grows hot chilis and eggplants in her backyard, white gourd, pumpkin, and other creepers on the roof. And seasonal spinach and other vegetables. On the sides of the pond, along the streams and wasteland, the Maker has sown varieties of healthy, edible greens. And in the backyard, you have your own kitchen garden.

So to speak, the rural poor have no want. He may be a small farmer or a fisherman. He may not get rice during hard times. But he is never short of vegetables and greens. If nothing else, there are pickles, lemon, and chili in the poorer homes. If there is no want of rice and curry, then why save money to alert the thief? Is it not sheer foolishness? The scripture says:

The money you earn taking pain
Is of no use for happiness.

Yet because of feminine greed, gold or silver jewellery is more or less in every home. Not so much for decoration, but for hard times; to sell or mortgage to save the prestige of the family.

That was the seventh day of worship of Durga. The auspicious eighth day was knocking at the door, again to add to that the beginning of Sankranti, the movement of sun to the next zodiac sign. A very auspicious day. In every home, baking cake, worshipping to Goddess Durga, and joyous festivities were on. It was evident from the seventh day arrangements that this year the Dussehra festival in Abhayapur would be celebrated with lavish enthusiasm. Normally, because of a large Bengali population in Erasama, the festival of Mother Durga was celebrated on a grand scale. Again, Abhayapur's Durga Puja was famous in Odisha, for the special reason that the celebrations were organized by the All Village Durga Puja Committee, whose chairperson was Sheik Ghulam Mustafa, alias Golmasta mian! Even staunch Brahmins like Kundala Panda, Danakarna Mishra, Panchuki Panda, and others could never oppose the chairmanship of Golmasta.

The seventh day ceremony was observed with great joy. On the eighth day, Durga's eyes were to be unveiled. By the benign sight of the merciful goddess, Odisha would have prospered. But what did happen? What was this divine punishment on the destiny of Odisha? It was the seventeenth of October; all arrangements had been completed for the worship of Mother

Durga. But instead of the arrival of Durga, dark, ominous clouds and a cyclone loomed large in the sky like the Mahisasur- a large, mythical demon-rushing in to destroy Odisha.

It was proved that the year 1999 spelled doom for Odisha with floods and cyclone. Earlier in the month of shravan, seven coastal districts had been licked by the vile tongue of the flood. Then this terrible cyclone on the eighth day of the festival. The evil eye of the cyclone was more focused on the districts of Ganjam and Gajapati. Destroying the pandals, hacking the limbs of the earthen icons of Durga, it had razed everything to the ground. Ganjam and Gajapati were reduced to rubble heaps by the conscienceless cyclone. The speed of the wind was 150 Kilometers per hour, and with that, the sea roared into the land, swallowing villages and cities. Sucked clean were the homesteads, enriched by the long years of sweat, blood, and toil. The cities and villages of the south coast were devastated. Man, cattle, houses, harvests, trees; nothing was spared by the heartless cyclone. Those who were spared cried for help and rescue from rain, wind, and hunger, surrounded by water.

From the Gopalpur seashore, the boatmen and fishermen villages were washed away. The relatives and friends of Abhayapur fishermen were sucked into the mouth of the Gopalpur sea. Thousands of men who never foresaw the future were waiting for the Dussehra festivals, and, losing their homes and hearths, families and friends, they all looked up at the wrathful sky for mercy. Hundreds of lives were blown apart by the cyclone. Not only Ganjam, Gajapati, Berhampur, but also Puri, Keonjhar, even Dhenkanal districts lost many lives at the hands of the deadly cyclone.

Here in Erasama block, Ambiki Panchayat, including Abhayapur and ten or fifteen adjacent villages, the Durga festival was going on as usual. In Cuttack, the old capital of Odisha, and Bhubaneswar, the new capital, Dussehra was celebrated unmindful of the devastation in Ganjam and other districts. Seeing the pomp of the celebration, none could imagine that about a half of Odisha's population was enmeshed in such a calamitous situation!

Listening to the bad news of the Ganjam cyclone over the radio, everyone was dejected. Sitting in the clubhouse, they watched the heartrending scenes of devastation. They enjoyed those clips on TV like watching a tragic play in a theater. They saw with bleeding hearts how helpless was man, surrendering to nature's fury. They wished for the salvation of the dead, and they prayed for divine mercy on the survivors. They also cursed the cyclone in the south for having reduced the celebratory joy of the eastern region. They prayed to the spiritual powers not to give this kind of misfortune to others. What else could they have done?

Yes, they could have done what Sheik Ghulam Mustafa did. All were present at the Durga pandal in the village fairgrounds. Some of them were entertaining the avid listeners by narrating sensational things about the cyclone in the south, mixing fact and fiction for dramatic effect. The worships and rituals of the goddess were going on. The chanting of the mantras by the priests and the accompanying music of cymbals, conch shells, drums, and other instruments were rising up to the sky. The devotees were appealing to the goddess to give them wealth and prosperity. As per the tradition of the area, Golmasta and other Muslim families of Pakistanpara were present, along with other devotees, and they too were appealing to the goddess for good harvest and business. This region was famous for Hindu-Muslim unity. The Muslims never formed separate lines for Devi worship. But this year, it was contrary to the tradition.

Golmasta was standing apart with a small group. In that group were Muslims, Gandhi Das, and a few Hindu youth. That queue did not ask for anything from the goddess. Golmasta appeared serious, pained, and worried. Gandhi Das was standing dumb, perhaps thinking of the future course of action. The cymbals fell silent, the fire offering started. The devotees were bowing to the goddess. In the gap of that silent appeal to the goddess, rising above all selfishness, stood firm Golmasta.

In a thundering voice, he announced, "Stop this pompous worship of the Mother Durga. Let the puja, this year, be confined to lamps, incense, and fruits. Let the money collected this year for the festival be donated to the Ganjam cyclone relief fund. Our brothers are dying there, and here we are celebrating! When our children die abroad, do we have festivities at home? Answer my question."

The devotees stood uncertain at this thunderous announcement of the Pakistanpara Muslim, Golmasta. While Tahali Mohanty, Kundala Panda, Panchuki Panda, Kumpani Soin, and other leaders were immersed in devotion to the goddess, the unexpected stern announcement created another cyclone.

How does this Pakistani Muslim dare? Perhaps, this Muslim fellow was searching for an opportunity to disturb our faith and worship; yes, there was a cyclone in Ganjam, the images of the goddess were broken to pieces, but does it mean that the entire world should stop worshipping Mother Durga? The goddess broke into pieces by an act of nature, but should man, knowingly, keep the goddess un-worshipped?

Tahali Mohanty asked, "Had there been a cyclone in Ganjam during a Muslim festival, would you have stopped the religious procession?"

"That's a different matter. Why discuss something which has not happened? This is inviting a quarrel. Let us consider what has already happened. Golmasta is saying something reasonable. In our neighbor's house lies a dead body. Would it be morally proper if we indulge in festivities? Therefore, let us donate the unspent money to the Chief Minister's Relief Fund. Let this year's Durga Puja be observed with austerity," Gandhi Das announced, without rhetoric.

While Gandhi Das said this much, supporting Golmasta, the people of Abhayapur and the nearby villages formed two groups and were prepared to fight. Some of them without understanding anything took sides, and, to enhance their importance, they started shouting. From verbal duels, the matter would have gone up to physical fights-had there not been heard the shouts from a crowd of people coming out from the narrow lane behind the Durga pandal.

A group of young men appeared to be beating somebody mercilessly with sticks, and shouting, "Die, you! Die, you scoundrel!"

Whoever he was, had he been an elephant, he would have been decimated by such violent beating. Which poor fellow on this auspicious day, near the pandal of Durga, reached God? No one was trying to protect the young man. Rather, they were provoking the young group. From the crowd, at times, was seen the agitated, cruel face of Alwar, Golmasta's grandson, and at times, the calm faces of Benudhar and Bhagyadhar, the sons of Udhab Mangual. Many other known faces were also seen in the crowd. Sometime back, those faces were known faces of Abhayapur. But now those faces were divided into Hindu faces and Muslim faces.

Where the matter related to Tazia (a Muslim festival) and Durga pandal reached lathi (sticks) and bloodshed, there, leave alone Abhayapur, even the great country India gets divided. Golmasta had experienced it himself. In spite of their friendship, at the slightest provocation, Golmasta and Udhab had mutual squabbles over Hindustan and Pakistan. Everyone knew this. Kumpani Soin and Dhadi Barik rode a motorcycle and rushed to the police station.

If the police did not interfere, the Hindus of Abhayapur would be finished. The Muslims were raw butchers. They had knives, swords, even bombs and explosives. Abhayapur would certainly be destroyed. Trying to help the cyclone-devastated Ganjam people, here the fire of communal hatred would spread from Abhayapur to the entire district and maybe from the district to the whole state and country. In India, 1999 would be counted as the year of riots and mass destruction. There was no other way of controlling the situation except to arrest Golmasta and Udhab Mangual.

This statement of Narku Routray made it clear that the election was in the offing. The basic strategy of elections was to provoke a riot and control it, to burn houses and call the fire brigade, to cause great harm and loss to people and then demand for compensation. In the last Parliamentary election, Tahali Mohanty and Kumpani Soin's party had lost miserably. Before the Assembly election, if a riot could be manipulated, the event would work as a major weapon in the election campaign without any doubt.

Although everyone knew that the Mahabharat war had originated from a sporting event, that a humanitarian approach to help the victims of the Ganjam cyclone victims would lead to an inhuman riot between two communities who had been living in harmony over the years was unthinkable for the senior citizens like Golmasta, Udhab Mangual, and Gandhi Dashed they advanced toward the trouble spot to bring about an amicable settlement between the feuding groups, a batch of political opportunists stopped them. They warned these senior people not to budge an inch before the police arrived. Like the lightning flash followed by thunder roll, in a few minutes a police vehicle was seen on the village road. With the police was ex-minister and a future contestant, Narku Routray.

Like a demon appearing by the magical chants of a sage, Mantri Mallick suddenly appeared at the troubled spot. Around his neck was a long, three-layered snake, whose lifeless head was hanging over his chest, down to his knee, and the tail was on his back. Dancing wildly, Mantri was screaming, "See this powerful group? Sweating and groaning, they were beating this helpless, innocent, non-poisonous snake for an hour! Hey, if you are real heroes, why don't you finish the poisonous serpents of this village? You are showing your prowess on these water snakes? This one at least was killing our enemies, rats and frogs. While the poor fellow had half-swallowed a frog, you hit him!

"I, Mantri Mallick-the crematory-devil to you-say openly that because of these few ignorant lads in this region, everyone's food would be hit. The Maker sees all. This water snake had called once or twice on everyone's house. What harm had he done to anyone? He was everyone's friend. For me, he was a daily guest, friendly and loving. How quiet he was, how innocent. If you are so very manly, then kill the satans moving amongst us!"

The last sentence Mantri Mallick said referring to Tahali Mohanty, Narku Routray, their hangers-on, and the Brahmin priests. Two policemen jumped off the jeep and captured Golmasta and Udhab Mangual, who by then had become quiet and were standing still. Like the bride and groom locking their hands on the altar, the hands of Golmasta and Udhab were handcuffed. The blind policemen tied them up in inseparable ties; both Iswar and Allah. Laughing like a madman, Mantri threw the dead snake on the jeep.

Clapping, he said, "Yes, take the real rioters. Before dying in custody, they are already dead. Only, for them, the two groups of Hindus and Muslims coming from two sides of the road were dancing tandav. It is the dance of destruction of Lord Shiva here! There was competition as to who would kill the innocent. Now handcuff the culprits. See, you all? Our efficient police officer is taking credit for nabbing the rioters."

Releasing both Golmasta and Udhab Mangual, the police jeep returned honorably, negotiating the bends, twisting and turning. Without the police handcuffs, Udhab and Golmasta were imprisoned in their own thoughts.

Divine wrath is more on Utkal than human insensitivity. Banchu Tarai thinks that this soil is the soil of floods, droughts, cyclones, famines, and epidemics. The Pathans, Moguls, Marathas, Portuguese, and the British invaded Utkal, ruled and looted, made the people destitute and used them as bonded slaves. Their rule ended one day; they left with their loot. But on this blighted land, Indra, the god of rain's rule and misrule, never ends, at times beneficent and often malevolent. If Indra is more bountiful, the Odia dies, and when he is vengeful, the Odia also dies. On the sacred Akhyaya Tritiya, an auspicious day, praying to all deities, Banchu Tarai sowed whatever seeds he had saved from last year, the small and big seeds, high and low, in marshy lands everywhere. And he waited for the mercy of the rain god. He hoped that if the benign eyes of Indra fell on his lands, he would have a bumper harvest.

Sowing, transplantation, and other stages of crop

cultivation this year were finished timely and properly. The extra seedlings around the clusters too were transplanted elsewhere early. Weeding, cutting the grass on the ridges, and manuring were completed quickly by Banchu Tarai, as the weather and luck were propitious.

As soon as October arrived, as per the law of nature, the ears came out, and by Dussehra and other festivities, the fields had turned green up to the horizon, blurring the lines between the paddy fields owned by different villagers. In another week, the paddy flowers would blow.

If a stray cloud floated awkwardly in the sky, Banchu's palpitations grew. If it rains now, the wind would beat the stems and the paddy flowers would fall off. If by the time the paddy starts milking and God becomes vengeful, it would mean starvation. Yet the symptoms of cloud movement suggested that there may not be any deviation this year.

Banchu's family situation was tight. Bipin's mother was dull and sluggish, but very tolerant. So tolerant that she endured labor pain, tightening her lips. None have heard of her screams, although she has given birth to ten children. It is she alone who has shouldered such a large family like mother earth! Her body is made of watered rice and spinach. No one has seen her eating curries. She raises her nose in fake dislike at half of the things of the world. She wants her children to eat. That's the truth. She would prepare cakes and goodies, serve everyone, but she would eat a half or a quarter. She would feign acidity or indigestion.

But this year god Indra is so calculatingly pleased that the expenses for the whole year may come off well. Bipin's mother now looks shabby. By this paddy harvest festival in December, he must buy her two beautiful handloom Maniabandi cotton sarees. December is not far away. Whether this year the threshing floor would hold the sheaf of paddy stalks is doubtful. Beating the stalks, separating the straw, the paddy is to be carried and buried underground. But the good fortune of burying extra paddy is rare since his grandfather's time. The expenses are mounting; the prices are rising like moon-tide. Girima's marriage is scheduled for this December, and he has said in advance to take paddy on loan. Let him take. What worry this year?

Banchu Tarai is calculating, closing his eyes, how many measures of paddy he would keep for Bipin's marriage, how many for the nuptial of his daughter, how many for household expenses, how many he would loan out to Udhab Mangual, how many he should keep for seeds, and what measures could he sell. This year, it was not only on Banchu Tarai that the mercy of Indra was so lavishly poured. Good fortune came to the paddy fields that the big and small farmers were dreaming grand dreams about; whose accounts were perhaps, available with the Creator. The same sky, the same earth, the same human labor, but above all there is one, the Creator. At his command, the world is full, and also is devastated. Man is only a medium, a plaything. Last year, the parched earth had been cracked open; this year, the crop bursts out of the same earth. But why worry? December is only a month away!

On his way back to Ambiki from the Erasama fair, Bhairab Majhi changes his route from the Nagari bridge toward Kiada. Udhab Mangual was walking on the temporary road to Ambiki with Banchu Tarai and many other market-returning men of the coastal villages. Some of them had heard a rumor in the Erasama market. Someone had raised an alarm in the market that a thousand times more destructive cyclone than the Ganjam cyclone was rushing toward Erasama from the Paradip sea. It would move from Erasama to all parts of Odisha, and Kaliyug would end.

"Why? For Odisha, there is Lord Jagannath. For the Erasama region, there is Mother Sarala. Jagannath of Kujanga fort, Mother Basulei, Grameswar, the saints of several seats are there. Why worry? They would certainly protect us. So many cyclones have come to Odisha in the past, but Kaliyug has not ended. It seems Kaliyug would reign eternally. Don't you feel so?" asked Banchu Tarai.

Udhab replied, "What do I know? Gandhi Das returned from Bhubaneswar today. If we ask him, we would know whether there is any truth in the rumor. But whether true or false, we have no way out. Whatever is fated would happen. I had heard from my grandfather that about hundred and fourteen years ago, it seems, there was a dangerous cyclone. It was called Sunia. Do you think this cyclone would be more devastating than Sunia? Somehow or other, I don't believe this. But I have heard from Drona Sir that Sunia was a terrible cyclone."

"What is the Sunia cyclone?"

"Come today to the Bhagabat seat in the evening. Kundala Panda has sent for the village people to discuss about a yajna to be performed. We would hear about Sunia from Drona Sir there."

"Has the Odia ever been terrified by the cyclone that you worry so much? The elections have frustrated the Odia. Unstable politics and frequent elections have done more harm to Odisha than the cyclone," somebody said from behind.

Mangual looked back to identify the half-recognized voice. He became happy and said, "How are you in this area, brother Behera?"

"My eldest son-in-law is working in the Erasama Block office. I had some work with him. November is knocking at the door. December is not far off. I have to make arrangements for the marriage. My eldest son-in-law is like my eldest son. All responsibility is his. I thought, since I'm here, let me call on you. Let us finalize the dowry. How many tolas of gold? Expenses for the procession, motorcycle, color TV, wristwatch, pant, suits and shoes, and so many other things. My son is not a boatman or a netter. He works at the Oswal Company. You never speak a word about this. Do not blame me later. I'm telling you."

Suppressing the enthusiasm of Girima's future father-in-law, his would-be relative, Udhab said in a frustrated voice, "Let December come. Let's tide over this cyclone. What I heard at the market has disturbed me so much that the mind does not allow me to think of any auspicious thing. The cyclone would rise from your Paradip sea and spread over all sides. That was the announcement over the public address system. Haven't you heard?"

"Why do you bother about the government warning? These

are the prior indications of the election. Please, you mean to tell me that the heart of the government is crying for people like us? The microphone says leave your huts, you need to go to the strong buildings at high places. How many good buildings are in this region where all the people can be accommodated? How many cyclone shelters are here? Do you think people would leave their money and valuables? Okay, let me take leave of you. At least I have met you. If you say so, let the cyclone blow over, and then we would settle the matter. But I tell you, there would be no big cyclone. A fortnight ago, there was cyclone in Odisha. Do you think it would come again? Do things happen like that?"

"That's also true. In our area, the predictions of fake astrologers come true, but government's weather forecasts never do. Whatever promises are made by government for the improvement of this area prove to be false. This cyclone alarm is like that. Had it been true, the government would not have merely alerted people, doing nothing. Where is government preparedness compared to the intensity of the information to the public? The sense of urgency which the British government had during Sunia, a hundred fourteen years ago, where is that urgency of the present government?" someone said.

"This is a black government. After occupying seats of power, they concentrate on black money and black deeds," said Udhab Mangual.

"Hey! Ours is the state of the dark god, Jagannath. If our leaders serve the black culture of the state, we must congratulate them. You all are small oysters. How can the significance of black art enter your skulls? "Saying this much, the future father-in-law of Girima changed his course.

Udhab's mind and consciousness were stuck at the news he had heard in the fair. Taking longer strides, he said, "Then walk fast. We'll try to understand the correct picture at the Bhagbat house. Is it true that a cyclone of great magnitude would rise from the Paradip sea? The cyclone has its limit. The sea too has its limits." Udhab was crossing the ridge while talking, controlling the load on his head.

Banchu Tarai said, "Who is within his own limits, hey? Price rise has crossed limits. Sin has crossed limits. Man has crossed all limits. Why not the cyclone? The sea is always eager to cross limits; only because of daughter Laxmi, the Goddess of wealth, the sea roars but seldom crosses the coastline. In our region, this year, Mother Laxmi has appeared in the form of a golden harvest. The winds may cross limits, but how can the father of Laxmi, the sea, cross limits? The father's heart for others may be stubborn, but for daughter it is all milk and honey-love soaked ambrosia."

"How then did the sea lick off the fishermen villages in the Ganjam cyclone?"

"The fishermen have looted the sea since their birth. The sea looted once. But the sea would not touch the golden soil of Erasama. I bet. You would see."

Contradicting each other's statements, the market-returning people not only beguiled the tedium of walking long, but also blew away the rumor of cyclone and, cutting across twilight, turned their obedient, habit-bound feet toward their own village routes.

Drona Sir and other elderly persons, that evening, gave a graphic picture of the Sunia cyclone, and the people of five to seven blocks of Ambiki, including Abhayapur, listened as if they were listening to some hair-raising story, and appeared to have enjoyed the terrible details. All of them thought that such divine punishment was only for those who were lost in the womb of the past.

"After the Sunia cyclone, so many other flood-cyclone calamities have been happening in Odisha, like ritualistic recurrences of festivals of death. What precautionary steps have been taken by our government?" This question was raised by the young groups.

Tahali Mohanty enthusiastically said, "To hell with the past. If the predicted cyclone actually hits this year and damages life and property, you all take my word; if our party returns to power, we would change your fate by relief work. The elections are around the corner. Why bother?"

"Your government? Who is your government? Do you have a party worth its name? In the Parliamentary elections, all your party candidates were decimated. The results of the coming election are crystal clear," someone commented.

Tahali Mohanty said with a mischievous laugh, "Whichever government comes to power after three months would be our government. If the government changes, how can our party loyalty remain unchanged? We know that the present government would be thrown out. Let it go. Whichever party forms government, if cyclone devastates this area, foreign aid would come in millions. Why do you fear?"

"If no Sunia-type cyclone has recurred during the last hundred fourteen years, somehow or other I can't believe that a more powerful cyclone would hit Odisha in a day or two. This is a government bluff. Besides, how can the cyclone again come to Odisha after just ten days? Have two cyclones ever hit the same place one after the other?" Dhadi Barik said confidently.

Someone from the party in power said, "You are unnecessarily worried. What powers do you have that you would stop the cyclone if it hits? Go, eat and sleep in peace. Our chief minister has not neglected the measures against the cyclone. Meetings are going on to plan out strategies in Bhubaneswar. Our chief minister has great faith in God. You would see. If this cyclone is heading toward Odisha, our chief minister would change its course toward Bangladesh by his occult powers."

A joyous note rose from the self-imprisoned villagers gathered there.

Someone asked, "What's the name of our chief minister, hey? In the last few months, so many chief ministers have fallen one after another that our unlettered minds fail to remember anyone's name."

Gandhi Das shouted, "What's in the name of a chief minister? They are all the same. Before coming to the power, subjects. After grabbing the power, kings. Like Bikramaditya one, two, three, if you say chief minister one, two, three, everything is understood. Getting his name by heart, are you going to count the rosary a hundred and eight times? Everything is the chair. If a cowherd sits on the throne of Ujjain, he becomes Bikramaditya. Any Tom, Dick, or Harry, fool or un-fool, sitting in the Utkal state chair becomes chief minister."

"In the Kaliyug, if you pray and count the rosary in the name of God, nothing results. But if you worship the chief engineer, chief minister, or chief manipulator, you get results. Those who do not do that, they are born wax-headed like you, and they die wax-headed. Our chief minister, appeasing the chief manipulator, is now the head of such a big state. All chiefs have their occultists. To blow apart the cyclone, our chief minister is now closeted in Bhubaneswar with three tantrics. You are unnecessarily worried," Tahali Mohanty said.

"Victory be to chief minister the third!" From the innocent faith of the cyclone-apprehending villagers, a chorus of ecstatic joy drew a straight line of fearlessness on the crooked face of the cyclone.

Welcoming the future, some Kaliyug lad shouted at the top of his voice, "Victory be to chief minister the fourth!"

A roll of laughter arose, churning the bellies, and hissed away all fears.

* Legendary emperor of ancient India.

SEVENTEEN

Pale sunlight filtered through the trees all through the day; not causing trees to droop, but the hope, courage, and faith sank from time to time. The thick shade of the clouds had made the earth morose. Drawing semicircles with a plough, Banchu Tarai was sowing ragi. What's this madness? Does anyone sow off-season? Each season has its own harvest. Doesn't the veteran farmer Banchu Tarai know this much?

Udhab Mangual, while tying the boat tight at the ghat, shouted from the riverbank, "What are you doing, O' Taraie, in this off-season? Haven't you heard that a cyclone is advancing this way? Moreover, it is now end of October!"

Tarai arose with the ragi basket and came up. On his face was a coat of fear and frustration. Udhab had never seen such a bloodless, drained face on Tarai. Coming up to the riverbank close to Udhab, Tarai straightened his back, and his eyes roamed around the paddy fields. Tarai's hopes were looking up to the sky in the wavy grace of the green field. At this time, if that cyclone hit, the paddy flowers would fall off. The womb would burst. All the dreams of the year would be blighted corn.

"Oh! I had thought that this year would yield such a bumper harvest that for full five years there won't be any dearth of food. It would be divine injustice to the poor people if really the wind builds up into a cyclone. I thought if the village and houses blew apart, what's the point in saving the handful of ragi? If the mother earth gains something, let it be; I have nothing to gain. If the paddy crop goes, would these ragi seeds save my life? Honestly, Mangual, my mind is not working anymore. The little money I had saved to renovate the house, with that Bipin bought a motor bike, constructed prawn farms. Now both the prawn farm and the house would be destroyed. In Bipin's prawn farms, there are fish worth six lakhs. If the sea rushes in, all that would go." Banchu Tarai's frustrated voice poured down like a cloudburst.

It was now drizzling. The dense, entangled boughs of trees cast shadows in the intense sunlight, looking like sluggigh water-laden cow dung. Holding Banchu Tarai's hand, Udhab took him to the shade. He sat down on the ground and asked Tarai to sit down. In an encouraging manner, he said, "Have patience. I have worshiped goddess Basuli today. I have prayed and worshipped to all deities. What sin have we poor people committed that the sea would rush at us? Yes, there may be a cyclone. What's new about that? Why fear the crocodile living in water? For long years now, we have harvested chafe instead of paddy, and we have lived up to sixty-five years.

"This time we would also survive. Our children too would survive till the end of their tether. As our children are superior in knowledge and technique to their parents, they would live longer than us. Is God so very deceitful that He would toy with us? Never have such misgivings, brother! Man's faith is the opium for the gasping patients in dangerous times. God would appear in our faith and give us the strength of the lion to fight calamities. The way the cyclone news has been exaggerated, if it comes true, to fight we would need the heart of a lion. If you lose faith now, you would fail, I am telling you."

Banchu Tarai gave a wry smile. In that smile was the pale glow of lost faith. It was not a true smile, rather a wisp of smoke from a lamp put out. He said, "The wind speed that is being rumored would blow apart elephants. Who cares for the lion? Our Bipin has heard at Bhubaneswar. I believe it, and then again, I disbelieve it. Everyone is half dead."

"Who's not half dead? But we have to face everything. If we men lose heart, what about our women? Shall I say something?"

"Yes, speak up, and tell all."

Placing his heavy hand on Banchu Tarai's back to reassure him, Udhab said, "We don't know whether we can sit and talk like this tomorrow or the day after." Banchu Tarai looked unconcerned, as if whatever was to happen had already happened.

Udhab said, "Listen. Whatever man does, he reaps its consequences. If you cut your tongue yourself, who's there to protest? Your son did the prawn farm, therefore you could not renovate your house. And there, all of you felled trees, cleared the mangrove forests, and paved the way for the sea. Now all gates are open for the sea. What's the point in worrying now?"

Grinding his teeth Banchu said, "We would die, certainly, but mercifully these Bengalis would be cleaned up, I am telling you."

Udhab bit his tongue, looked balefully at Banchu, and said, "Fie, what's this mindless thing I hear from you? Is there any distinction between Odia and Bengali before storms and cyclones? It's only man who makes all kinds of divisions. Bharat Mandal, Bhairab Majhi, and the other Bengali families who live with us with their families and children, they are all of our village, we're so friendly with them. What's their fault?"

"Okay, listen to me about their crimes. They have occupied large areas but have built very small houses. Even their paddy fields are not close together. Their fields are far away from each other's. Barring a few coconut trees, they have not left a single tree standing on the ground. Only field and field, harvest after harvest. And then, carrying the produce on the sea route, they do business in their country and get rich. When the cyclonic winds blow furiously, the spaced houses would be hit with great force. The sea would roar into their open and spaced houses and clean up the Bengalis.

"All the three coastal villages in our ward have been set up by Bangladeshi refugees. Oh brother, we don't have that much land in our own ancestral earth as they have. In our four wards, while there are two hundred and fifty houses, each Bengali family has almost one village area in his possession. Don't you know that whenever a cyclone comes, it hits these isolated Bengali houses first? As man is the only support of man, likewise close and contiguous houses support each other. Only when the jungles and bushes break do they hit the houses."

"The Bengalis are not my enemies. I'm not the only one saying this. I went to the block office today. There, I heard Narku Routray lecturing about this. The matter touched me. The isolated houses would be blown away like chicken feathers, he said. The cyclone would be on a violent scale."

Udhab's round face suddenly appeared larger than his real face. His thick lips swelled like ripe, bitter gourd. The nostrils of his wide nose fluttered like the gills of a fish. The eyeballs spun like a wheel. The salt-and-pepper whiskers twitched intermittently. This was the most violent incarnation of Udhab. In a thundering voice, he said, "Like the myopic, self-immersed men of the Narku Routray tribe of politicians, the Bengalis would be destroyed. And we too would be finished with them. The true worship is nature worship. Do you think it was for nothing that our ancestors worshipped rivers, mountains, and vegetation? And these people, they worship only the chair made from felled trees, not the wooden planks of the deities, nor the chairs in which the teachers sit-only the seats of power to intimidate the poor and helpless.

"For chairs of power, they stake earth and nature, gamble on them. You know pretty well that, handing over an election chit to the gullible people, they deal off illegal land and virgin forests to mafia leaders without any qualms of conscience. For a single vote, they may even stake their religion. The election for the state legislature is ahead. Routray must have brought a few more Bangladeshis to rehabilitate them here. Government would spare some more land for them, handover election slips, buy votes, and rule over them. Thereafter, how do they care whether the Bengali refugees survive or die? The refugees are also thorns in the eyes of the villagers, poor fellows! Their misery is endless."

"True, but who bothers about that? They pretend innocence, knowing everything. Come, let's go. We are the fruit gatherers, why bargain for the orchard? Even thieves and scoundrels would not come to our rescue. Also, this is not the time to waste on gossip. Do you think the cyclone would be devastating?"

"Not I, but three government astrologers are saying this. Not ordinary astrologers, the select few tantric scholars. They are doing some tantric rituals to ward off the cyclone. Therefore, I am worried, but my mental strength is not broken," said Mangual.

"Wouldn't it have been better had they changed the course of the Ganjam cyclone toward Andhra Pradesh by their tantric practices? Where were those ganja-smoking tantrics at that time? The poor Ganjam people would have survived." Banchu Tarai was getting agitated.

From behind, he heard the satirical voice of Gandhi Das. "The same tantrics tried the whole night to ward off the Ganjam cyclone. After all, they are human, and they must have dozed off for a while. In that blank moment, the cunning cyclone lashed at Ganjam. The cyclone is the true devil."

In sorrow and frustration, Gandhi Das roared with laughter. Udhab and Banchu were now standing on the tottering ridge of belief and disbelief. Although the head was untouched, their legs were already deep in the waters of fear. Undulating between hope and hopelessness, they had to return home, regardless of whether the cyclone would lash out or blow away. They must prepare to encounter the next morning and fight for life. They couldn't fight if they lost hope.

After such a long time, Udhab understood that Banchu Tarai was not sowing off-season ragi out of madness. He was sowing hope. The earth was the hope. The earth was faith. The earth was the only friend in times of need. If the cyclone blew off the ragi seed in the end, it would return to the earth again. If the floods carried Udhab away, finally he would go back to his dear Abhayapur soil. It would be the same if he mingled in the Bandar village earth, blown by the current.

In life and death, man is a creature of the earth, not of the sky. Who can ward off man's hope in the faithful earth, which is more trustworthy than the sky? With that hope, even if man becomes a recluse, he does not fly in the sky-he settles his feet on the earth. A lump of earth creates the foundations of endless hope.

Udhab became restless, believing the rumors of the impending cyclone. He could not sleep. But in his feigned sleep was open the eye of agony in his bosom, from the searing of his son, Gadadhar, in the last cyclone. Udhab has not uttered his son's name since. But his wife moans loudly for her lost son twice or thrice a year. For women, crying is cathartic. But for rock-solid men like Udhab, the medicine is stoicism. What breaks the heart should not tear up the eyes.

His wife cannot fathom the depth of sorrow in Udhab's heart, let alone anyone else. Udhab, on the other hand, consoles his wife, saying everyone has to go at some time or the other. He says, "Forget about him as I have. The reckless lad threw caution to the wind, ignored his ancestors' warnings, went out to the sea on his boat, and was swallowed up in the devastating cyclone at sea."

The Mangual clan has lost many a male member to the sea over the years. Oh God, whose curse is this? The net for a large family man is so very tight that it does not loosen till the death wind blows. Udhab can weave one net after another, but he cannot escape the net of worldliness.

Udhab's major worries were the old men and women. His younger grandfather and uncle were sick. His aunt was a cripple. His younger grandmother was bedridden, limbs immobile, a gone case. What would they do? What would the old men and women of the village do? What would the pregnant daughters and daughters-in-law do? Also, Sankha's mother is not what she once was. Her filarial leg has almost finished her.

After Girima is married off, she would turn into a lump of earth in a corner of the house. How long would the woman work hard? Udhab's second son's wife has already made arrangements to give in marriage granddaughters Devi, Alaka, and Pohala. Poor woman! Would she save the marriage trousseau or the daughters and nieces from the anger of the cyclone?

Udhab's worries are for everything, from the ox yoke, chicken enclosures, rice paddy bags, and dry fish pots to the nets and hearth. No worry is less than the others. In a few days, the new boat would have been waterborne. That one boat would have served the generation of his sons and grandsons. If the cursed cyclone destroys the boat, Udhab would die alive. If Udhab's limbs are broken to pieces in the cyclone, no worry. For that, medicines are available. But if the boat is destroyed, Udhab cannot make another in his life. Not only the children and family, but also a tradition would be orphaned.

Udhab had completed construction of the boat with his skill, sweat, and love, coating it with a layer of his endless dreams for future generations. The villagers were amazed at seeing such a boat. Although a fishing boat, Udhab had carved on it the inherited and well-preserved art of several generations. It looked like the merchant ship of the sadhabs of ancient times. After a great deal of consultation with astrologers, he had selected the name Satyayug for the boat.

That day, Udhab did not even think of taking the boat to the sea. He'd returned earlier from the river and roamed around the village like the lads. Whoever he saw, he asked, "Where would you go if the deluge comes? Where would you take shelter since there are no brick buildings in this village? The government has announced over the radio-only to free their conscience of any guilt-that you go up the terrace of buildings. The worries of the government are over. Our worry begins now. What shall we do?"

Everyone had the same answer. "Where else shall we go? Whatever is fated would happen. Let's see when the time comes!"

Udhab asked the trees, the boats whether they knew about the impending cyclone. Nah, they don't know anything. Again, he asked and said, "So be it, if you don't know. Most of the people of this area also don't know that an unprecedented cyclone is on its way. The few who know do not believe that the cyclone would be ferocious like the tsunami. Where would they go, then?"

They did not give any reply. His handiwork, the Satyayug, lay mute on the sandy bed near the stream. In the exciting sea breeze, the trees were shaking their heads, saying, "No, no, we do not know anything."

Udhab could guess from their demeanor, whether tree or boat, that they had nowhere to go. Where would they go, leaving their birth soil? That was the situation of all the poor of this area-where to go? They didn't have buildings like the big shots in Manijanga Bazar, Jagatsingpur, or Cuttack. They would go there to escape the fury of the tsunami!

If they survive don the village earth, if they died on the village earth-that was their fate. Half of the tension goes if you leave everything to fate. Udhab, too, like his own handmade boat, the known trees and bushes, and his dearest village Abhayapur, surrendered everything to its fate and waited for the likely onslaught of the cyclone.

And the deluge was on its way.

Before a cataclysmic time appears, man has to encounter various tests. The deluge is the most horrendous test for man. Those who have the strength to rise from devastation have survived when deluges have wrought destruction. Only, after the deluge, comes the Satyayug.

Whenever man becomes selfish, materialistic, and violent, the evil within him takes the form of the deluge and destroys man. The earth never gets destroyed. It's man who gets wiped off. After the deluge is born a new man, a being pure and noble of the age of truth. Then why worry?

Gandhi Das may die, but man never dies. Gandhi Das was speaking as if explicating a truth. In Mathuri Sahu's teashop, gossip continued over the rumors about the cyclone. Gandhi Das, however, was speaking philosophically, the meaning of which perhaps he alone understood. The other village folk, sipping their tea noisily, were pretending to understand. Befitting the context, Udhab Mangual recited a few lines from Bhima Bhoi's Chautisa:

> The storm winds would blow for seven days.
> Time shall snatch away things.
> Soldiers would be marching with stumps.
> Time is fast moving to show such things.
> Don't fade into the valley of death.
> He who survives shall be the seed on earth.

Listening to the lines of Bhima Bhoi, everyone thought of himself as one of the selected future seeds. And, for that, they were promising many offerings to God. Rationalizing the small and big sins to themselves, they were making a mountain of the mustard-seed-sized merits and were enlisting themselves in the catalogue of rare meritorious men. All of them, however, had the sinking feeling that they were all sinners, big or small, and were apologizing to the Unseen without letting others know their confessions.

Silently they were praying, "O' sin-cleansing protector of the fallen, God! Please pardon us this time. Please save us this once. After this, we would not commit any sin, crime, adultery, violence, or any hateful blunders again. We would not even entertain in our minds evil thoughts for others. We'll never do any harm to another living being. Forsaking all the seven deadly sins, we would spend the rest of our lives serving the sick and helping the needy. O' Lord! Give us the final chance to live." All, in their several ways, were praying in this manner.

The chairman, boss Tahali Mohanty, was whispering, "I was never so vile, O' Lord. These politics are the source of all evil, all sinful deeds. Unless you are a schemer, hypocrite, and manipulator, you can't survive in politics, O' Lord! Knowingly we commit sins like the farmers going to reap the corn, knowing pretty well that the heat would be unbearable. We are guilty, true, but the main culprit is today's politics. Please forgive me this time. I'll never ever take the name of politics."

Dhadi Barik, like spitting pan, spat out all predictions and said, "Huh! Don't you know that the day the radio warns of heavy rain and high winds, that day the humid air stands still? That day, only the heat rises to boiling point. Let go of your worries. Go home, eat, and sleep. Let's see how the weather turns out tomorrow."

Some people nodded their agreement to this. But Kundala Panda was apprehensive that a deluge may occur. He warned everyone to be careful and explained the reasons why.

Kaliyug has a longevity of four thousand years. Yet four

hundred years on either side may also be added to Kaliyug. It means Kaliyug may drag its reign for four thousand, eight hundred years. Shrimad Bhagabatam mentions this. By 1985, Kaliyug was supposed to end. But, according to sage Hadi Das's Laxmidhar Bilash, the Kalki incarnation has already started and must end by the year 2000.

"Then there is still one more year to go. Why fear?"

Gandhi Das said, "The end of Kaliyug comes when the administration tilts because of the weight of the crown. In our Odisha, that time is passing. Therefore, who knows whether Kalki would have the patience of waiting for one more year?"

"Why are you saying such disagreeable things, Gandhi Das? This government would go. A new government would come. Everything would be alright. Kaliyug's reign would be extended by five more years. Let's postpone our discussion. Should we wrap ourselves up and sleep before death comes?" said Dhadi Barik.

Tahali Mohanty came walking up, and, putting the folded edge of his dhoti in his khadi shirt pocket, sat tight in a wooden chair. Everyone looked at him with hopeful eyes. He had come straight from Bhubaneswar, alighting from the bus and crossing the river. The correct news might come from him.

Kumpani Soin asked, "What's the weather forecast?"

"Who has control over the weather, hey? But it is said that, six days ago, a low pressure was building up in the Bay of Bengal, six hundred kilometers away from Paradip. It may reach Paradip, and by midnight tomorrow, it would go over to the Khulna district in Bangladesh or Haldia in West Bengal. Therefore, there may or may not be a cyclone by tomorrow. If our stars are powerful, the cyclone would change its course and may go in any other direction, not touching this area.

"Of course, getting the news of the cyclone, Narkeswar Routray has already left for Bhubaneswar with his entire family. He has sent word to face the situation with patience. He has advised to forsake the rural habit of panicking on hearsay of danger, and just be ready with courage and patience to encounter the cyclone. The top-level officers in Bhubaneswar do not believe that the cyclone would blow at a speed of two hundred kilometers. Would the cyclone come riding a rocket? You are all panicking for nothing."

Kundala Panda, while entering the compound of the Bhagbat altar, declared, "Come to the altar, stopping all rumors and gossips. There, the prayer is going on, arrangement for prasad also has been made. Let there be a mass dinner. The next morning is the first Thursday of Kartik-the Rohini and Margasira stars would come together. Tomorrow is the twenty-eighth. We would calculate astrologically tomorrow whether the day after that, the twenty-ninth, would be good or bad. At least all of us can have a mass prayer this evening. No one can reject the power of prayer. Let's see how audacious the cyclone is. You, don't fear. Tomorrow, early in the evening, I'll collect the sacred water from Grameswar Mahadeva, and, going in a boat into the sea, I'll sprinkle with the conch shell the sacred water from one end to the other end of the sea and tie him up by the powers of mantra. You'll see that the sea may go anywhere but cannot touch the borders of Ambiki Panchayat."

"In the name of God," Golmasta said in an anxious voice, "don't mock at the sea! The cyclone is on its way. How do you plan to go into the sea? Don't you care for your life?"

Kundala Panda said, "I'm the chief priest of the area. It's my duty to imprison the sea by the powers of my mantra. Otherwise, fie on my priesthood, fie on my sacred thread. You're Allah's servant. How can you understand the power and glory of the sacred water of the deity's feet, the sacred thread of a Brahmin, and the power of the mantra?"

In Kundala Panda's voice there was no arrogance of a Brahmin today. There was the auspicious timbre of faith. If he went into the sea, would this priest ever return? Who would release the boat tomorrow evening? When Banchu Tarai asked those questions, forgetting all his grudges, Bharat Mandal declared, "I'll not go to the river ghat under any circumstance."

"Okay. I'll fend for myself. If there is a boat at the ghat, a boatman would be there, seen or unseen. Why worry? In the sea of the universe, there is only one boatman. On the sacred soil of Sarala Das's Odisha, what boatmanship you are talking about, you Bangladeshi Mandal!"

Reciting the mantras, Kundala Panda moved forward toward the compound of the Gaddi. Behind him a line of fearful men was drawn, like the border line of Kaliyug under the shady cover of clouds, toward the compound of the Bhagbat Gaddi. But Bharat Mandal sat like an anthill in that darkness. Born in India, he was now ripe enough to die in India. Yet he was still a Bangladeshi here. His father had left Bangladesh out of his love for India, but he and his entire class could not get a country. In that darkness, his eyes got moist. Luckily, there was no light to see his tears.

The grim Thursday morning was fearfully awaiting an unforeseen deluge. The sky was dark and grim like a funeral ground. There was no stir of life; no clouds, no air, not even a leaf stirred. The sun was not visible. But a bloody layer of clouds covered the sky and had the day terrorized. No one had seen earlier such reddish clouds in the sky. The sky, as it was, was looking at the earth with painted eyes, and was warning the earth to be alert.

It seems the pre-cyclone sky thus suffocated the entire earth up to the horizon. Yet, normal life in the villages of Erasama block was not at a standstill. At the lowing of the returning cattle, a gush of north wind was pulling and tearing the red, patchy sky and flinging the pieces to the bosom of the earth. All of a sudden, gusts of lashing rain started. The rain was the lifeblood of the farmer, the breath of the fishermen. The people of the area were not afraid of the rain, but the violent speed of the wind was creating wild fear in the minds of the helpless villagers.

The Panchayat Samiti radio was broadcasting regularly that a cyclonic storm would blow over the area at a speed of two to two-hundred-and-fifty kilometers per hour. With the cyclone would come a tidal wave three times the height of a man. The government had warned the villagers living in earthen houses to move to the concrete buildings in the area, but half of the villagers of this area were not aware of that warning. Those who had heard the warning had no time to make a move. They were worried about how to move with their families and belongings and where to take shelter. In this helpless situation, who would move unless the cyclone winds blew in full fury?

After trimming Kundala Panda's coconut trees and walking with a load of a few dry coconut branches on his head, Karji Behera said in a defiant manner, "Oh! We have seen so many cyclones and storms. How would this threaten us? The fearful warning of the blaring mics is for the big men who have buildings, vehicles, helping hands, and servants. It's for them. We are used to plucking coconuts, cutting the dry branches even during severe storms, and carrying the dead branches home on our heads.

"Panda is very clever. Lest the coconuts be blown away in the cyclone, he has used me the whole day in taking the coconuts down. There is not even a small, raw fruit on any tree. Taking out the coconuts, ripe and green, cutting down the banana clusters, digging out the potatoes, he has dumped those in his house in such a way that there is no room for anyone to take shelter in his house.

"But Panda's wife is a kind-hearted woman. Giving me a bowl of ricewater, she said, 'Karji, if the sea rushes in, come with your family to our house. At least we have our cowshed. Our cattle are not harmful like my husband. You can take shelter there till the cyclone subsides. There is no untouchability in the cowshed, do you understand? Your houses are in low-lying areas and would be drowned even in a heavy shower'"

So saying, Karji Behera laughed. In this region, he was the only scheduled caste who climbed trees to pluck coconuts, that too without using the rope trap in his feet. Kundala Panda says, "Karji is a monkey." Karji does not bother about such comments. He thinks, "At least there is a shelter".

The cowsheds of the Brahmin locality are on high land. If the sea rushes in, how far would it come? And how high would it rise? At least it would not rush in from the sky! And our Kundala Panda is not a small man. Giving charge of the house to his eldest son Panchuki Panda, paying some money to a boatman, he has gone this evening into the sea in a boat to tie up the sea by the power of his mantra. That morning, he'd collected a pot of sacred water from the Grameswar temple. When his wife asked him not to venture into the sea, he said, "Here I go and come, no worry. I'll just tie up the sea and return. If I don't venture to do this, who's there to help these hapless people? The Minister, MLA? They are now sitting in Bhubaneswar."

"Is the sea afraid of you? Or is the sea at your beck and call? Or you are venturing into the sea to save the village people at the cost of your life?"

When the Pandit's wife started sobbing, Panda very cleverly consoled her saying, "What haven't I done for God? What haven't I done for the people of these villages? How many flowers haven't I placed on Shiva's head? What amount of sandalwood paste have I not smeared on his forehead? How many tons of sweetened milk have I not poured on his head?

"Mounds of prasad I have offered him. I have built temples, flown flags in his honor, and performed yajna. Are these not enough for God to listen to my prayer? Even if all blows away, God would be there, untouched by nature's fury. The temple would be there. The Bhagabat would be adorning the Gaddi as usual. The flag would be fluttering in the breeze. If God survives, would his priests not survive? If God wishes, the sea would be reduced to a palmful of water. You just wait and see what trick I wield. Do you think only cooking is an artful trick? My dear! In order to survive, man has to perform many gimmicks. You don't worry."

"Okay. Why worry, then? If the sea does not rush in, who cares for the wind and rain?" Pandit's wife was convinced. Narrating the melodrama of the Panda household, Karji stepped up his pace. The rain was growing in intensity.

Someone in that darkness sang out from Achutananda Malika, "It'll gather in the north and pour in the south. None would survive in the east."

Another, from his broken memory, added, "And disappear shall the earth."

Someone from the front sang, "The three realms are rudderless if you try to control O' Ramchandra! Nothing would be stable."

Banchu Tarai was almost running southward behind his son, Bipin Tarai, in that bellowing north wind. He was appealing to his son, "Don't go to the prawn farm tonight, my son. Let the prawn business go to hell. The little one, Baia, is there already, and, again, you too! You know the prawn farm is close to the sea!"

Bipin said fearlessly, "Nothing would happen. Have these villages ever feared the sea? You please go home, Father. Mother must be sick with worry with the children. After the wholesaler takes his share, I'll be back in two hours with the rest of the prawns and Baia."

Banchu Tarai again pleaded, "Both brothers must come back soon, for your mother's sake."

At this time of impending calamity, Bipin had a laugh in his belly. "How cheap these mothers are in these rural areas! For small things, the mother is the wager. Oh, are the mothers of the educated townsfolk very costly! If leave is not granted to employees, they would arrange to send telegrams from their homes. 'Mother serious! Come immediately.' Ha! 'Mother serious. Come soon.' But, honestly, for mother at least, I must return from the prawn farm soon. Otherwise, there is no logic that the villages are safer than the prawn farm."

An infernal darkness is swallowing the earth. He was afraid of going alone to the prawn farm. He thought of calling Bhagyadhar Mangual to come with him, since he'd been asking for a long time for some tiger prawns. He could have given him some had the merchants left any. But today it's doubtful as to whether all those fish merchants would come. Although many have advanced money, some of them might not turn up for fear of life.

If Bhagyadhar were given the bait of tiger prawns, he might run behind Bipin like a calf behind a cow. Greedy fellow. The fisherman catches big fish but eats small crabs. But how is he to blame? In a large fisherman family, often even the prawn shells are not available to prepare a curry. In the fish godown, the owner sells the shelled prawns. In today's world, even the shells could reap profits. Only the outer shell was everything. Who has the time to gauge the inside? Piercing the darkness, Bipin takes large steps toward the prawn farm.

In this village, if a crow flew, it would be exaggerated, and the rumor would be that a child flew. Along with fears and apprehensions, many rumors were afloat about the cyclone, and in that confused emotional heat, the fog of anxiety was receding a shade. Moments were fleeting, oblivious of the precipice of fear. Before nightfall on Thursday, while Abhayapur was reeling under the lashing wind and rain, right at that time, not one but two rumors shook the foundations of Abhayapur village.

By even time, Golmasta's grand-daughter Masuma had not returned home, and there, Kundala Panda's grand-daughter Ganga was also missing. Both were friends, but not so intimate as to have gone for ablutions like Juno's swans. Where had they gone? Now was not the time to search for Ganga and Masuma. Someone whispered this in the ears of Tahali Mohanty. He was not too worried about the cyclone because, in the meantime, he had constructed a double-storey building near the school. He was busy shifting his household valuables to the first floor, using his servants. Moreover, his house was near the village market on highlands and was standing firm on high foundations.

Tahali Mohanty came outside his house on that cloud-cast evening. It was his normal habit to walk in a serpentine fashion, even on straight roads. Therefore, the umbrella on his head was moving from side to side as if possessed by a devil while he was walking on the ridges, snaking his way forward, negotiating the wind. For duty's sake, he must survey the position in some ward. The real chairman, Sakula's mother, is, after all, a woman. Would she come out in such threatening weather?

He alerted everyone that, on such murky days, the devils may kidnap the young married and unmarried women. It was also not unusual for the characterless girls to exchange garlands in some temple with wayward guys and marry, exploiting the opportunity of the panicky situation. Two of those scandalous girls had already absconded with two ill-famed boys. It was rumored that they would marry in some temple, exchanging garlands. Then they would go to Cuttack and register their marriage. Fie-fie! This region would go down the sea.

"Who? Who?" the villagers eagerly asked, oblivious of the cyclone.

Clearing his throat, Mohanty said, "O' Dhadi, why don't you speak?"

"Do you think, in this calamitous time, I would speak of those sinful matters?"

The children of Dhadi Barik, by that time, had already taken shelter in the solid building of Tahali Mohanty. Dhadi, therefore, was self-assured.

Contracting his eyebrows, Dhadi said, "Let the bastards go and die in the storm and floods. Let this village be purged of them. O-ho! They flouted caste, clan, and religion! Why should not the sea then transgress the shores?"

"Why don't you say who flouted the clan? Why should the villagers drown for them?" a worried Karji Behera asked. His thoughts were stuck on the safety of his wife and children. Even then, pausing for a while, he was curious to get to the root of the matter.

Dhadi said, "Oh, that bitch! Masuma has run away with Gandhi Das's son, Bhudan, to Kanakpur. They would return, exchanging garlands in the presence of Goddess Sarala! Okay. Now, you tell me, should we allow them to enter this village if they return? The other one is that shameless Brahmin girl, Ganga. She has run away with Banchu Tarai's son, Bipin. When this matter was raised earlier in the village Panchayat, those three hypocrites Udhab Mangual, Bharat Mandal, and Bhairab Majhi laughed away my words."

"Hey Dhadi, Banchu Tarai's son, Bipin, has just gone ahead of us to his prawn farm, and Udhab Mangual's son, Bhagu, went with him. Where did Ganga come from, hey? It's nasty of you to spread rumors against others' daughters. All of us have daughters."

While someone was saying this, Tahali Mohanty interrupted, "Don't you know! Ganga has been in the prawn farm since noon. Do you think that we're saying this without seeing or knowing anything? If that were not so, why should Bipin, instead of going home, go to the prawn farm at such a time?"

"Then those two would die there. Jatadhari estuary is not far away from the prawn farm," one intolerant villager said.

Another villager from Barada said, "Whoever has run away with who, let them survive. If they have gone to the temple, then whether Muslim or Brahmin, the girls would definitely survive. If Ganga has gone to the temple near Bipin's prawn farm, may God save her. Kundala Panda has gone to charm the sea, and here his grand-daughter. O' God!"

The whole sky was grim red, as if someone had collected the rags of clouds to mop the sky with blood. While Sankha's mother was straightening her back after mopping their courtyard with cow dung and mud, as it was a Thursday, she was shocked to see the blood-red sky. Before the auspicious arrival of Mother Durga, usually she painted jhoti with rice paste on the walls putting a red mark on entrance, before Ma Durga's eyes are unveiled. The mother never thirsts for blood when such red marks adorn the home walls.

But today, on Kartik Thursday, who has asked for blood, that some unseen hand has painted the whole sky blood? O' Mother Sarala, you are our only hope. For how many shall Sankhas's mother worry? As a large family man has endless wants, a mother of many children has a world of worries.

Look at Bhagyadhara. Like a madman, he has followed the obsessive Bipin Tarai to the seaside prawn farm. How does it matter to you whether his business thrives or dives? Under whose care have you left behind your wife and children?

The youngest one, Benua, also went for duty, just gulping a few morsels of food at noon. He had gotten the job of a level-crossing gateman at a small bridge between Paradip and Rahama a few months ago. Not that it was a new job, but the nature of the boy is such that he would stake his life whatever job you give him. Sankha's mother made a sobbing appeal to the boy not to go for duty in this beastly weather. Did he obey?

No. Rather, he replied, "My job is to guard a small bridge at a level crossing, but don't think it is a small job, Mother. It's as important to open and close the gate, watching the movement of the trains, as Bikram Balabantray's fight was in the Kargil war. Can you ever play with the lives of men? So many lives depend on my work there. Moreover, I count my earning every month. Does the government nourish me to sleep at home like an invalid, taking the plea of heat, rain, flood and drought? Listen, in this type of cyclone, it seems even the tracks blow away. Whole trains turn turtle and get derailed. If some such thing happens, who would inform the government?

Sankha's mother's heart sank at her son's words. She said, "Hey, Benua, if there is an apprehension that the rail tracks would be blown away, then how would you be safe in that fragile tin shed? Who would come to rescue you there? At least there are people around us who would help each other."

Hearing this, the wise-beyond-his-years Benua gave his mother a real lesson. He said, "Do you understand, Mother? You have simply given birth to this human creature. You are blinded by motherly love. But you never really know him. If it comes on you, you are responsible for yourself. No one would come to the rescue of another. When it is impossible to save yourself, how would you save another? As I am helplessly alone at the level-crossing gate, you are also alone here.

"God is our only hope. You did not allow me to join the army, lest I should be martyred; now you don't allow me to go for duty, fearing that I might be blown away in the cyclone. Tell me, wherefrom would you get a danger-free world for your children? Listen to me. The cyclone would not be as severe as it is being publicized. Had that been so, the government would have closed all schools, offices, markets and stopped traffic, also cancelled the airplanes today, on the twenty-ninth of October, 1999

"When everything is functioning normally, why do you think the government has plotted to destroy everything? You think of that, and don't worry. I'm going for duty. I only came to see you for a while. Violating level-crossing duty is dangerous. The lives of hundreds of people are in my hands." Benudhar left, consoling his mother.

Udhab silently heard everything from Sankha's mother. He thought, *if this boy had joined the army, he would have earned good name. He has the solid character of a fisherman—honest, loyal, brave, and dutiful. In fact, when the government has not declared the twenty-ninth as a holiday, by what logic would he not go for duty? At a forlorn level-crossing, he is absolutely alone. But, oh, who is not alone in this world? And who is really alone in this world? Is Benua alone when there is God?*

EIGHTEEN

Sankha's mother worships the 330 million deities, but has not understood this much. She has a head only to bow down before the gods, but no brain to appreciate the deeper meanings. What can you say? That's the female mind!

Udhab's male head, wishing all the best for his son, bowed before the 330 million deities and finally the old Pir, as if his son had gone to war. Would he come back alive? Such a nagging doubt was smarting his benevolent father's heart.

But God knows why, he chastised Sankha's mother, "Why are you sobbing at your son's departure for duty? How could Bikram's mother hold herself, sending her son to war? As if you alone have given birth to a son! Why not you go and pack up whatever rice, sugar, and provisions are at home? God only knows where so many of us would take shelter?"

Udhab Mangual had just returned from praying at the Bhagbat Gaddi, Mother Basulei's temple, and the Pir Sadhu. While returning, he'd been chased by the wild wind, wind that had been like a hissing cobra. The intensity of the rain had increased in the meantime. Was there any method to this wind and rain? Someone was saying at the Gaddi that, after the Kargil debacle, Pakistan had sent this devastating cyclone to India using black magic. It is also heard that Pakistan may direct half of this cyclone to Bangladesh. Pakistan is also the enemy of Bangladesh. But is this the way to treat your enemy?

When Udhab reached home, he found his wife touching

her head on the central doorway, praying for the welfare of Benua, Bhagyadhar, and Marua, and crying over all of her worries and fears. To add to the stress of the household, Bhagyadhar's son, Kapila, was now shivering with high fever. He'd also developed rigor. No medicine had any effect on the boy.

Kapil was the apple of the eye of Girima. Instead of his mother's lap, the boy was having an uneasy sleep in the lap of Girima. Padma, dragging the boy to her lap, cried and made the boy cry. Uncle and aunt, the old couple, are grunting in their geriatric pain. One after another, so many fears and apprehensions, so many futile solutions to a million helpless problems, all creep into the mind of Udhab like wild canker growth. And his wife herself is in constant trouble with her heavy, swollen feet.

What can poor Udhab do? In every home there is sickness, disease, want, frustration, and pain in uneven measure. As the others would face the cyclone, Udhab too would have the same face-off. What would be the point in weeping and wailing? Udhab was irritated.

"We are not alone, having so many problems in this crisis. Why are you confusing me by crying? Be patient till this dark night passes. The night frightens more. When the sun rises, you would see. All fears would go. Leave everything to Mother Basuli."

At that moment, giving her feverish child to Girima, Padma complained before her father-in-law, "See, Father, how he has gone to Bipin Tarai's prawn farm at this bad time. In this inclement weather, the prawn merchants won't come. He would therefore sell the prawns cheap. Buying prawns from Bipin at cheap rates, he would come in the morning so that there would be a feast at home. He did not listen to my request not to go. Even mother could not stop him."

Udhab's heartfelt trepidation. His head started aching. In such cyclonic weather in 1982, Gadadhar had gone to the sea, defying everyone. And that boy had not returned. Bhagyadhar today had gone to the prawn farm, two to three kilometers away from the sea- just to buy prawns at a cheap rate. Being a fisherman, he was so greedy! It was all fate. Who would be to blame? Honestly, ever poor fisherman's son ate tiger-prawn curry to his heart's content? For other fishermen, prawn is not food, but business.

There is no choice but to wait till morning. Bhagya may not care for his life, but does he not have any sense of responsibility for his wife, children, father, mother, pregnant sister, and grandparents? Ha! Udhab had been born to look after uncles, grandparents, and grandchildren till his decrepitude drags him by the nose. Udhab raised his hands, praying for the well-being of Bhagyadhar, and slept on his back on the bed. Crossing his fingers on his chest, he patted his apprehensions.

Although Bipin's prawn farm is near the sea, is Abhayapur far off the sea? The storehouse of Bipin is made of brick and mortar, hence comparatively safe. If God has taken him there, nothing to fear. Whatever God does, it is for the well-being of man, Udhab consoled himself.

Finally, he was calm, thinking that the cyclone would not be as devastating as it has been predicted. Udhab tried to sleep, closing his eyes, but he was still looking open-eyed at the ceiling. Girima was coming down from the inner roof, having stashed a wooden box there.

Udhab asked, "Did you keep gold and silver in that box, dear? Your mother has buried a box at the head of the hearth, dumping everything there for a long time. What invaluable things have you kept there?"

In an assured voice, Girima answered, "My poetry book and pen I have sealed in a polythene cover and put in that box. I have also locked it. Have no fear. Even if water enters, the letters would not be washed out. If the poems fade away, it is not easy to write them again, Father. On the other hand, gold ornaments can be made again if lost. True or false? And if water enters the house, how many hand measures would it rise? It would never go up to the ceiling level. Mother has also kept her gold in the same box, digging it out of the earth near the hearth. If the flood comes, it would first of all sweep away the house and floor and then the ornaments. What do you say?"

In a worried, delirious babble Udhab said, "Now the most

invaluable things are our lives. I don't know how to save all the lives of such a large family. If the sea rushes in at mountain height, who should I try to save, and for how long?"

Just at that time, a wall of the cowshed fell down with a thud. Rain and wind gushed into the courtyard. Outside, the wind was roaring ferociously. The flutter of panicked birds in the backyard trees sounded like his own pounding heart. Man does not know what is in store between two steps. Even then, man has so many future plans, as if his head were anointed with immortality. Two days ago, the weather and time had been auspicious. The hoary old chakunda tree in the rear of Udhab's house had been the safe haven for many a bird who, leaving their twig and leaf empire on the tree in search of food, returned to enjoy sound sleep. They had, perhaps, not heard of the government warning of the impending cyclone or, even if they had heard it, they had no care for government and their superficial warnings.

But, listening to the footsteps of the deluge in the fury of nature, deciphering the rhythms of revenge in the loveless silence of the earth and in the roar of the sea, the birds had alerted their younglings, "Be careful. The cyclone is approaching fast-an unprecedented cyclone, the deluge. This old chakunda tree cannot give us safe shelter anymore. Come, let's go. Before the end comes, let's fly away toward safety."

By that time, sensing the signs of danger, the moon and stars had already left the treacherous sky to some trustworthy realm of a safer world. The night, therefore, was praying for rescue under the blanket of murky blackness. Studying the calamitous fate of men and the creatures, the sky was shedding clamorous tears the whole night. Just as the doctor does not give up hope till the patient's death throes shatter his confidence, likewise the old battered chakunda tree was not giving up its pride.

Shaking its branches, it was consoling the cluster of birds. "Be brave, I'm here. I have tested the veins of so many storms and cyclones and lived this long, up to my hoary age. Have I ever measured my length on the ground, forsaking the birds who had reposed their faith in me? Don't you know how deep my roots are? You scream wildly because you do not know. Have faith, and cling on to me. Bowing my head before the cyclone, I'll negotiate the danger.

"When you know that, at the time of real danger, there is no one to protect you, it is prudent to surrender to even a bad, harmful enemy to ward off the danger, my children. If you survive, then only you can fight the same dastardly enemy tomorrow and win and tame the enemy. You just endure this danger with fortitude. This cyclone is testing your patience because it has no patience at all. It would rush in as a conqueror with sound and fury and would not bother about anyone's loss or destruction. And, after creating a large area of waste, it would go its own way with the same nonchalance. Has anyone seen a cyclone blowing for a month or year? If a tree does not break, has anyone seen the wild wind returning to throttle the tree again?"

Thus, consoling the birds, the tree shook its own branches and leaves in slow rhythm. Listening to such comforting words, the birds were reassured for an hour or so. And where would they fly away in such a dark, windy night? But by about midnight, when the wind speed increased, the ravens in their harsh ka ka ra ra calls warned the other birds, "Go fly away. It's not safe. Leave this region and go wherever your wings take you."

Without waiting for anyone, the panic-stricken birds shout warnings to everyone while deserting the birthplace of their ancestors, the old chakunda tree. They abandon the tree to the heartless cyclone and fly away in search of unknown shelter. Following them, the birds on other trees also fly away in groups.

The birds have their own scriptures, and they alone know the lessons. Each one of them is a foreteller. All of them read their invisible futures. The scripture of the birds is nature. Because they read nature's mood swings, stars, and times in storms and cyclones, fewer birds die than humans and animals. The animals understood nature better than men.

But the birds can fly, as they are endowed with wings. The animals can only run-but how far would they run? If the sea rushes in, they cannot fly away to the sky. Therefore, if they do not run away in time, they would have no choice but to surrender to death.

In the dark, the roar of the turbulent sea from the Jatadhary estuary sounded like the angry hissing of a king cobra. It was as if not one, but the whole trio of the sky, wind, and sea had all turned into thousand cobras and announced the end of Kaliyug in a thundering voice. "No one would survive!"

The sea was hissing and roaring, gnashinghis teeth." I'll devour, devour. I would devour everyone whole. You have destroyed my empire. You have eaten away my forests, devastated the beautiful nature around me. I'll devour you all, waste your villages, empires, civilizations. I'll play the destroyer. You have to suffer the consequences of your actions."

Udhab wondered whether the sand dune, the one by the side of the four wards, would shelter them. The wards were comprised of twenty-five-hundred people, and were five kilometers away from the village marketplace, in front of the Ambiki Panchayat office. Since evening, many people had gone there. Those who had not gone, fearing the rain, they must move there by early dawn. But would this dreadful night ever end?

Alas, adjacent to the sea, near Abhayapur, there were few villages which were more vulnerable. Ninety percent of those villages were of Bangladeshi refugees. And there Bharat Mandal was a senior leader. Those leaders who had issued unwritten permissions to them to fell the jungles and set up residence, all for votes, and who had been empowered by their votes, all of them must be enjoying sound sleep in their well-protected homes in the cities. Who would come to their rescue in this time of death? Near their villages, there were no trees or sand dunes. Their only shelters were the earthen houses. Whatwould they do when the sea rushed in?

The dogs, sensing mortal danger, started howling and began a deafening, choric wailing. Hearing that, Udhab's heart raced. You are worrying about the refugees because you live in Abhayapur, but where would you take shelter? Do you think that only the refugees would be blown away, and the people of Abhayapur survive?

"No, no. God, let everyone live. Save all." In that darkness, Udhab was praying with folded hands.

By that time, the cattle, lowing wildly, appealed, "Untether us. Free us. You cannot save us."

In that darkness, Udhab shouted, "Hey, Chakara, Padia! We'll be guilty of murder. Free the cattle."

Without waiting for his sons, Udhab himself untethered the cattle. Whichever cow he touched, he ran his hand on with tearful eyes.

"Go, my darlings. Now your fate is yours. You have not sinned, nor are you guilty of any bad deeds. But you are going to suffer the consequences of man's sins. May God save you." Tears ran down Udhab's cheeks, and they were washed away by rainwater. What rubbish! Self-preservation is impossible. Being an old man, he cries like an effeminate fellow!

The chakunda tree cannot hold anymore. After a few moments, it would be separated from its birth soil, and, with a cracking sound, it would fall down, no doubt about it. The mynas resting on the tree were not able to fly away; like querulous women scrubbing a new pot, they chirped expletives at the conscience-less cyclone. The parrot couple belonging to Girima, flapping their wings in the wildly shaking cages, was searching for ways of survival. Girima, finding her way in that darkness, opened the cage. The parrot couple flew away, chiming with Udhab's prayer, "O' wielder of the disc, save us," and flew into the dark night traceless. Similarly, the soul, severing all ties and forsaking the earthen body, flies away.

Udhab's pet chickens were screaming in the night the same refrain. "O' wielder of the disc, save us." But Udhab was realizing that the wielder of the disc had fired this cyclone to destroy the sin and immorality of men. How can he save anything, and why? When the creator becomes the destroyer, causing the deluge, who else can save them now?

In fact, the din which the birds, animals, trees, and shrubs together raised that night was not a fearful voice to save another; it was a choric prayer for survival. All prayers are not always answered by God. But that does not mean that God is cruel. Had he been cruel, how could so many dreadful nights end? But sometimes, when misfortune strikes, God turns into stone. But even stone melts. Seeing the sad plight of his creatures, if the stone-turned Kaliyug God starts melting, maybe, who knows, this night would end in a hopeful dawn.

The sun would rise, piercing the clouds. The cyclone would change its course toward Haldia of West Bengal and the Khulna district of Bangladesh. Oh! There too, this all-destructive cyclone would wreak havoc.

Let this cyclone devour no one, and God save us too! Udhab's fear stood before him like a ghost, with mouth wide open, and with a sinister laughter flowing like the roaring tide of the Jatadhari estuary. The thudding fall of earthen walls was heard, as if the earth's bosom was being pounded by the sky.

Touching and probing in that darkness for his flashlight, fearful Udhab called his sons all at once, "O' Sankha, Chakra, Gada, Padma, Bhagya, Benu…" Oh! Gada's name came out of his mouth in his panic. Gada's memory did not tear up his heart so much as his own fear of death.

The eldest Sankha had gone to Ramtara, his father-in-law's place. Bhagyadhar was at the prawn farm. Benudhar was at his level-crossing gate duty. The other two sons came out. The rainwater had already entered the house. Udhab, during his lifetime, had not seen all the walls of a house collapsing, nor the breaching of the riverbanks. Whenever floods came, the upper regions were damaged, and floods subsided. What wrecking cyclone has come now, that all houses in the village are falling down, one after another?

From his own house and from outside, the wailing screams are now rising. All children, old men, women, and young men are screaming for dear life. Putting their valuables in bags or tying them in towels, carrying boxes in their hands, they are all getting ready to go to the Ambiki Bazar sand dunes. But dawn must come. How to move in this infernal darkness?

Udhab decided to carry his aunt like a bundle of clothes. He told his sons, "We'll go, carrying the old ones on our backs. The women would carry the children. We'll think of the trunks and boxes later. After leaving the old and the young at the dunes in the morning, we'll take the trunks and boxes."

Udhab had already released the cattle and goats. But instead of running away to safety, they stood dumb, looking at the water. But that was not sea-water. Why were they afraid of rainwater? How much would it rain? Not a man's measure or two? Why such panic?

If knee-high water enters the house, we'll go up the inner ceiling and spend the night without getting wet. We'll see what to do in the morning. Udhab suddenly developed great faith in Kundala Panda. He had gone to charm the sea, taking the water from the feet of Grameswar. The men of Kaliyug might defy the divine orders, but the sea is of Satyayug, not of Kaliyug. It would not defy the great Brahmin. What would the sea gain by swallowing the poor people whose only property is these thatched houses, where they live moment to moment? Would the sea fill her belly and soul with this?

Sea, you are the fisherman's rice, fish, wealth, life, and everything! How can you be his death? Yes, Meghanad and Gadadhar defied you, and you took them. God doesn't tolerate anyone's arrogance. But the innocent villagers who are devoted to you never step into water before worshipping you. Why should you destroy them?" Thus, Udhab was mumbling his prayers. His agitation was visible to him in that darkness.

The guests and relations who had come for the universal Durga Puja, the Mahalaxmi Puja, his daughters and sons-in-law, son and daughter-in-law, grandchildren, and the elderly people together were twenty-eight in his own house. All of them were now standing in water by then. Uncle, aunt, and grandma were hanging on the backs of Udhab and his two sons like untidy bags. The fearful children were stuck to their mothers like dead lice.

Marua was in an advanced stage of pregnancy, with her belly hanging like the cloud-laden sky. Lifting her with difficulty, the others made her lie down on a big wooden box. She groans intermittently in pain. Udhab knew that she was not groaning commensurate to her pain. Yet that suppressed groan was so distressing that Udhab was not hearing the thunder roll. He was only hearing the earth-piercing groan of his daughter.

Udhab said, somewhat irritated, "Are you not able to tolerate the labor without groaning? Do you think the rain and cyclone would subside if you groan? We can go somewhere only at dawn."

Udhab's wife screamed a protest. "What an insensitive man are you! How can she tolerate labor pain with closed mouth? Alas! What shall I do now? Howwould my child be relieved? O' Mother Sarala!" Sankha's mother had another round of sobbing. But she was silenced by a single shout from Udhab.

Outside, the sky broke into two with a roll of thunder, mingling with the rain. It seemed as if the whole sky fell down. It poured thick, wet darkness on the stricken earth. Girima, with the two-year-old Kapila on her shoulder, was standing like a warring demoness, tucking her saree at the back. She was comforting the child. The child was crying ceaselessly, so agonizingly long that the others felt suffocated. Oh! Everything was concentrated in this moment! Cattle and men were all standing, stunned, in knee-deep water in their respective places. Luckily, the roof overhead had not blown away!

Not only Udhab, but also people in all the villages were praying to the cloud deity, the sea god, the wind god, and all the 330 million deities in heaven. They were praying for only one tomorrow to dawn on the palm of the earth. Their prayers perhaps moved the gods. The cyclone in the night was less wild, and the sea did not rush in.

At last, from the miserly sky, an unwilling morning dawned hesitantly. That cloudy and grim morning was the greatest boon on the offering plate of the earth. It made the distressed human beings reassured and grateful to God. Udhab, standing in knee-deep water, raised his palms full of water as a token of gratitude to the scheming sun hidden in the clouds. Imprisoned by the clouds, that morning's sun was darkening the earth like the evening in slow degrees because, by then, he had joined hands with the cyclone and was part of the deluge plot.

Lashed by the rains the whole night, the tired villages were taking the Mahakartik holy dip. It was water and water wherever one looked. Perhaps the cyclone had changed its course! Almost all the walls of the houses in the villages had fallen. Was the rainwater and river water rising or receding? If it was receding, how then had the water level risen from the knees to the waists of his five-hand-measure-tall sons?

From everywhere came shouts. "The water level is rising, rising!" Udhab made everyone climb up his large, thatched roof. The children and the old people were not able to withstand the force of the wind. They were unsteady. Bringing a long rope, Udhab tied seven-fold the roof with coconut trees.

He felt as if Satyayug had come after the end of Kaliyug. But where was the real morning? This was only a fake morning; a disguise of the fatal night. The murky sky of that morning hung down on the earth like the belly of a pregnant buffalo. But the all-destroying sky was not delivering the sun; it was only churning within with the pangs of labor. A long, unbroken strand of hair of the fierce demoness cloud had covered up the nascent sun like a hairy, dark blanket.

The inebriated wind was unrhythmically churning the sky and was making the hefty trees dance mortally at its fingertips. About ninety percent of the trees, weakened by the sweeping winds, had surrendered since midnight. Long ago had the strength of the youthful trees waned? But the strong, tenacious, stubborn trees were fighting till the end.

As time advanced, the rising, orgiastic wind started blowing as if possessed by spirits, at tremendous speed, and vowed to destroy the arrogant trees. The tree leaves severed from the branches were flying in the dark sky like the broken wings of insects. The wind had become a sharp knife and was carpet-cutting the leaves from the branches just like women used the chopper to remove coconut leaves from their ridges

Before their eyes, the tall coconut trees were twisted like snakes and fell on the ground. The coconuts were severed from the trees and flying in the air as if shot from a catapult. The screaming wind was shaking and twisting the trees in the flail of the sky like housewives while separating the broken rice husk in a flail. The earth was churned cruelly at first by the north wind, then the east wind, and now the south wind. The furious roar of the wind shook the earth up to the horizon.

Clinging to the treetops, roofs, and terraces, the panicky people watched helplessly the wild dance of the deluge. Dispelling the planets from their orbits, shouting with blood-chilling ferocity, the cyclone was rushing toward Erasama like a rogue elephant. As the Almighty rubbishes the arrogance of the powerful, as Bhima's mace smashed the mighty thighs of Duryodhana after Mahabharat war, the cruel, powerful hands of the killer cyclone were crushing the trees and the ancestral houses and possessions of man.

The self-willed rain was blindly raining havoc on the deluge-battered humans. Skin was pierced by the sharp needles of windy raindrops. The humans had no power even to open their eyes. Blinded by the rains, all were groping for their veins of life. What was ahead? Life or death? All was dark; no dust, no smoke. Was this rain or fog? Sky or the sea? A wall was descending in the void like white smoke or condensed fog. How could a wall descend? It was beyond comprehension.

It was as though the cyclonic whirlwind was plucking out the sky and twirling it fiercely like a weapon, striking it on the heart of the earth. It appeared as if the sky would be smashed to powder and the sun, moon, planets, and stars would be thrown away from their orbits and would fall on the earth, blasting her to pieces. The sun was struggling hard to free itself from the large cobweb of clouds. The cyclone-stricken clouds were scratching and bruising the sky and the sun.

At about eight in the morning, the cyclone had a lull in the space between the eastern and northern winds, maybe to regain its breath. The fatigued sky was softened for a few moments. As a block of breathless cloud receded from the sun, a strange yellow light spread everywhere; the water level also appeared to be receding.

Relieved by the lull, the people who had taken shelter at high grounds came down, forgetting the crisis, to place for safekeeping in high places their hard-earned money, food grains, trunks, and boxes. They ran to their houses. If someone ran to protect and preserve the land-related documents, another went to take his pregnant cow to a high place, and yet another went to dig up the buried wealth. Another ran to bring to safety his old parents, who had stubbornly refused to leave their birth soil.

But Udhab Mangual and his family did not think of coming down from the roof. Stricken by the needles of rain all through the night, they were all shivering like coconut leaves. The village was like a choppy sea because of the rain. Yet the sea, so far, had not transgressed its limits. The two-toned water blown by the east wind from the sea-river confluence was negligible. But while Udhab thought that the cyclone had subsided and there was no fear of the sea, he saw a gray, smoky second sky rushing toward them, uncaring of the dark, cloudy sky overhead.

Looking in that direction, everyone was stunned. Looking at the demon-like ash mountain that was rushing toward them, why should anyone have imagined it to be the sea and not sky? No one had the presence of mind to gauge the speed of the south wind shaking the entire sky. To start with, it was two hundred kilometers and steadily grew to three hundred kilometers. The south wind was roaring like a death knell. The tin roofs were flying like torn paper, the battered leaves like dust particles, and men and cattle like torn kites. One after the other, the lamp poles were falling down, broken and twisted.

While the hapless humans were fighting for survival in the gale, at the selfsame time, the Basuki snake holding the earth turned on its side. The seawater, with a deafening battle cry, rushed in to swallow the sun, moon, and planets. Who cares for mere humans?

The sea was turning like a disc, almost touching the sky, at times blue, at times foggy, and at times the waves, like harpoons, were blinding the eyes. It was felling a thousand heads, trees, sand dunes, earthen and concrete houses, the rich and poor, old and young, Brahmins and Dalits without discrimination and was dragging everything to its maws through the Jatadhari estuary. The concrete houses in which humans had found shelter; the same houses crushed the refugee humans in a trice.

Oh! Not one or two, everyone was floating in the bottomless flood. Oh, what did the sea do at last? The fisherman had thought of the sea as life, and, in the end, the same sea took their lives. Man had reposed faith in the houses. The same houses crushed men to death.

On the rooftop Udhab was sitting with his family and many, many such hapless humans. Again, the sea rushed in up to ten kilometers, driven by the east wind. And by the north-wind-driven sea, the homes and hearths of the ancestors were twisted and torn. By the south wind, villages were dragged to the mouth of the mighty beast. Roaring like a demon, a twenty-five-foot-high wave rushed into the village, dragging and swallowing everyone in its path.

Last night, Chakara and Padia had removed with great difficulty the pregnant Marua from over the box to the roof. Now she was having acute labor pain, and her groans were overwhelmed by the ferocity of the cyclone. Like the bamboo bushes bending and straightening by the force of the wind, the thighs and legs of Marua were rising up with shooting pain as she tried to tolerate and absorb it, to surrender the enemy in her belly to the cyclone. She was lying on her back, hair loose and disheveled. In the next moment, the conscienceless cyclone and the cold arrows of the rain defeated all her efforts toward freedom by again throwing her limp legs on the bald roof. Thus, the struggle of Marua and the unborn in her belly continued.

Gradually, the rooftop was covered by water. A family member saw a tree nearby and climbed up, holding a branch. By the time Udhab's family heaved a sigh of relief, watching him climb up the mango tree, the tree caved in. He was swept away, along with the body of the aunt on his back. They were both drowned.

At this critical time, the two thatched roofs were turned

over by the fierce south wind. All twenty-eight persons tied by the unseen thread of blood floated away, each according to his or her fate. Not only they, but also thousands like them were floating away to the mouth of the sea. The strong current carried loads of men, cattle, buffalos, goats, and sheep away. Wives slipped away from husband's hands. Children slipped away from the laps of mothers.

Udhab's entire family was lost to the sea while he looked on, panic-stricken. Snapping the ties of blood, one after another, they slipped away from the tight fist of Udhab. An expert swimmer as he was, he still floated, watching the doom of others. Udhab was floating, holding the hand of his granddaughter, Devi. Falling into a whirlpool, and after going under three times, Devi too was ripped free of his hold. Her "Grandpa, hold me!" appeal was dragged into the current.

Udhab was dashed against the trunk of a coconut tree that was standingnose-deep in the water, seemingly praying for survival, raising a few bare branchesskyward. Udhab held tight to the neck of the tree. His hands went limp, his legs nerveless. Before he knew whether he was dead or alive, the tree's trunk was twisted, and it fell into the rising water. Udhab was incapacitated by the tide and was pushed under. Udhab was sinking toward the hissing roar of the Jatadhari estuary. The expert sea-swimmer, giving up all hope for life, went motionless for a moment.

But in the next moment, some unseen inspiration enlivened his three-score-and-six years of fisherman's energy, and he rose up to the surface of water and started swimming in the unending sea. Whoever wished to leave halfway the last battle for life? At that moment, Udhab saw a tottering boat near a tree trunk. It wasn't merely a boat-but hope. Expending all his energy, Udhab brought the boat under his control. Praying to the boat, he climbed into it and searched for the oars.

A roof was floating away near a massive tree. Udhab pulled a bamboo pole from that floating roof. How he could muster that strength, God alone knows, but he rowed the boat to save the strings of floating humans. Udhab was a boatman. Having a boat, his hands intact, and an oar to boot, if he did not do his human duty, would God ever forgive him? He did not bother dwelling on the fact that he had no wealth, cattle, family, or God's mercy.

Not just Udhab Mangual, but almost everyone kept on fighting the last battle for life without caring for victory or defeat. In this fight, victory is victory, and defeat is also victory-because, in that moment of struggle, none aimed at victory. The only aim was to fight till the last breath and to go down fighting, shaming death. After rescuing hundreds and taking them to safe, high land, Udhab's boat fell into a whirlpool and upturned. While floating away toward eternity, Udhab transformed death into battle.

Merging into the sea, the river Hansua blew away everyone's hope for life. When pregnant Marua slipped from the roof and was swept away by the current, Girima too lost her hold on Bhagyadhar's son, Kapila. Shouting, "Kapila! Sister! Kapila!" Girima swam, negotiating the waves, and caught hold of a leg of Marua. But like a slimy fish, Marua slipped away. Girima too was swept away uncontrollably.

The heartless wind swirled the two sisters like a spindle. Marua's heavy body disappeared in the water. The two sisters were carried by the rushing flood in two different directions, Marua toward the Ketaki bushes and Girima toward the mangrove forest. Girima by then was not shouting, "Sister," or," Kapila," she was simply repeating, "Mother Basuli."

She had no strength in her limbs to swim. The Hansua River that the boatman's daughter Girima had swam in during the spring tide and the September frolics, today showed no sign of any bank or shore, although she spent all her energy searching. By that time the clan-destroying sea, with waves four man-measures high, had already swallowed up rivers, tanks, pools, and the villages of the area. Girima was not swimming anymore. She was floating. She did not know where the current was carrying her.

Like the denuding of Draupadi in the court of Duryodhana of Mahabharat epic, the sea was taking away the clothes of all men and women using the cruel hands of the merciless cyclone. The waist knot was opening up, the buns and plaits of women were turning loose, hands and legs were sagging sideways like the dead branches of a tree. Girima saw men floating; not men, but bodies. She did not care whether she had clothes on her own body. She could not know whether she was alive, but the stormy hands of Dussasan were dragging her toward the hall of death. When she tried to hold a thorny fence, her grip was torn free by the push and pull of the cyclonic wind. She was forced to release her hold.

She grabbed something else in her left hand. Not thorny, but round, rough, and strong-skin, like the arm of a warrior, with muscles straining. Who was this unknown warrior on whose hand or arm Girima's cold palm was stuck, lifeless? Girima had surrendered to the sea long since. She was pulled toward the belly of the sea by the murderous waves, strong like a hundred Kauravs. On the other side, she was being pulled by the unknown warrior. She did not know where. The defeated soldier who has surrendered to the enemy, why does direction matter to her? Her only sense of direction was toward her fate. Girima kept on floating without making any effort, vacantly, as she lost consciousness. By that time, a sea of distance had been created between her family and her village, like the distance between this life and the after-life.

While an unprecedented cyclone was blowing outside, in Marua's blood, flesh, bones, and entrails, another cyclone was raging. The sea was churned by the gale. Her own abdomen was churned by her own flesh and blood, inside. Marua had come to her father's house for safe and easy delivery. But who knew that, like an evil spirit, the cyclone would rattle up the sky, earth, and sea? While floating away, her bun was loosened. Yes, it's believed that if the bun is not opened, the babe cannot be delivered. It sticks to the umbilical cord inside and takes life away.

Marua then had no fear, nor felt any pain from being blown away by the cyclone. Her labor pain had rendered all other pain, fear, and anxiety insignificant. In fact, her labor was the only calamity, and she was fighting with herself to be free of that. Without a midwife, how could she deliver her first child? She felt somebody tying up her spread-eagled legs and holding her heavy body tight. Somebody was turning her around, holding her long hair. Thunder, lightning, and the deafening roar coming from the estuary-none could lessen her spasmodic pain.

A trial of strength was going on between creation and destruction. Could this deluge deflect a bit the time and stars of the arrival of a human child? No! Tearing her up a hundredfold, creation finally was freed from destruction. The cry of victory was heard over the deluge. Raising its birth cry, the babe stuck to the umbilical cord at the protective thighs of the mother.

The mother and the child were safely laid on the Ketaki forest. The dear Ketaki forest of her parents' village had made her sleep peacefully, and had promised to never wake her up again. Incessant tears were flowing from the Ketaki petals. The birth cry of the newborn announced the arrival of a human child. It sounded like the conch blowing the sound of victory. But there was none around to hear that victorious conch sound except the deluge.

When the speed of the wind increased gradually, Benudhar felt that the wind was sharing a funeral feast with the villages and trees. He was getting excited because, staying in that lonely shed by the side of a small station, he was alone, witnessing such a big cyclone. He was proud of that. No one else would know what form the cyclone would take here, in this totally open earth. Returning to the village tomorrow morning, when he would describe the strange deeds of the cyclone in this deserted place, everyone would look amazed. He would tell how, singlehandedly, he'd fought the cyclone, closed and opened the gate at the proper time, controlled the speed of the train, and staking his head, hadput on track the train that had blown away.

When he would describe these things, all would slight Bikram's war experience at Kargil. In Kargil, there were hundreds of soldiers with Bikram. There was heroism in that war, yes, but the heroism of fighting the cyclone all alone was not there. Therefore, by the time Bikram returned from Kargil in December, Benudhar would have become a real hero in the Erasama region for having fought alone the cyclone of '99! At the least, Benudhar Mangual's frustration at not being able to join the war would be neutralized.

Wherever the eyes reached, one saw the bent stalks of half-ripe and half-unripe paddy plants in the paddy fields. Elsewhere, there were only vast grazing fields bordering on the cremation ground on the other side, the place that had been the salvation of souls from the nearby villages for thousands of years. In that open crematorium, it seemed, the souls rose to heaven along with the funeral flames. Again, if they so pleased, they descended down and, in their birth-places, played in mischief.

At times, when the night snored, Benudhar got frightened. He dispelled his fear by whistling like the train. On the left-hand side of the grounds can be seen a bend of a stream, like the uneven parting of a woman's hair. A little distance away from the stream are four-to-six memorial tombs for the dead, standing like the studded hairpins in the bun of the cremation ground. On the other side of the river stream, like smeared paintings, were a few closely built small villages. Various were the names of the villages, peculiar and arrhythmic. In times of difficulty, if you called out for help, help was a far cry, and your call would echo unanswered. In this godforsaken place, Benua's day friends are the grazing cattle, and the night friends are the chirping birds in the isolated trees. Although the trees in the darkness of night looked like ugly ghosts, the chirping birds often dispelled fear.

But that night, struck by the cyclone, half of the birds flew away to unknown places, and the other half fell dead. The morning of the twenty-ninth, shaking the earth vigorously, uprooted the large trees, which lay supine on the ground, pulled and pushed by the elephant trunk of the cyclone. The wind, at first applying the bulldozer, smashed the small shed of Benua. Grinding its teeth, the sky shot arrows from above. It was hitting and kicking with powerful thrusts. The unseen hands of the cyclone were twisting the necks of anything that stood on the ground.

Benua, as it were, was standing like a lone soldier in the battlefield". Certain that he would be blown away by the wind; he tied himself tightly with a long towel to the level-crossing pole. Whoever was nearby was seen running far off, running for dear life toward the Shiva temple. Without knowing or recognizing Benua, they shouted, "Who's standing there to die? Come out, come out. The cyclone's evil eye has fallen on Erasama. It's rushing in at a speed of two-fifty-to-three-hundred kilometers! The world would end. See, the rail tracks have started shaking! Why are you inviting death?"

Benudhar stood, sulking. Those who were running toward the temple, none of them were on duty like him. Benudhar was doing his duty. It was time for the train to come. Crossing the rail lines, groups of fear-stricken men were running helter-skelter to save their lives. Benua would close the gate in a few minutes. Otherwise, the train would crush countless men. Benua knows how a little carelessness could result in a disaster.

The train lines go over a bridge at a short distance. The bridge collapsed with a cracking sound, and the twisted rail tracks hung perilously, like the loose ribbon on a girl's braids. If the train comes now, it would be dangerous. He must stop the train any way he can. Benua would never run away from duty like these self-centered men. He can't commit such a sin.

Untying his red towel, he got ready to wave it to stop the train. He had to move away from the gates. Suddenly, a whirlwind came, rushing in and blowing everything in sight; trees, houses, men, and cattle. Twisted and turned, an electric pole dashed to the ground and blew away the thin body of Benua, smashing it against a concrete pole on the other side of the tracks. His skull was reduced to a pulp. His face was sliced off. His bones were broken into a million pieces, flesh into bits and shreds. His youthful blood was diluted by the pouring rain.

The strong arms of the cyclone lifted his battered, lifeless body and dumped it at the head of the hanging bridge. No one knew that the dutiful Benua had been martyred fighting the cyclone, alone, at the place of duty. There were no relatives or villagers to even identify him. Neither was there his innocent, dusky, dutiful face to identify.

NINTEEN

Man regrets many things in life. There is none who acts rightly at the right times and has no regrets in life. Ketaki was regretting that day, as she'd never learned doing the right thing at the right moment. If she escaped from the grip of this killer cyclone, she would definitely learn that which she should have learned right from the age of going to the river for a bath. What was the point in regretting now? Death was already knocking at the door.

Her friend, whether you call her naughty, mischievous, masculine, or whatever, had been right. Many a time she had thrown Ketaki into the river from the riverbank. Ketaki had survived drowning many times because of her fate. At noon one day, about a month ago, when Girima's marriage had been finalized with the Sendhakud boy, the two friends had been sitting on the riverbank eating sour lemons with salt and green chili. Suddenly, Girima had said, "Let us jump into the river."

"Why? Are you immorally pregnant? Why should you jump into the river?"

"Fie, what shameless things you say, friend! Why should I be pregnant sinfully? In this village, there is no such lover boy that Girima would lose her sense for. Even without that kind of pregnancy, if we jump into the river for the heck of it, who would lose anything? What happiness is there in a woman's life, that we would live the same mundane life everyday till death?" Girima asked.

Ketaki looked with stern eyes at the raw-pumpkin-complexioned, round, smooth face of Girima, and said, "What happiness is wanting in your life? In a few months, you would go to the village on the other side of the river. You would not be born in Abhayapur and die there, like me. Why then should you jump into the river?"

Girima said, "O' dearest, is going to the village on the other side the only fulfillment in a woman's life? If that doesn't happen, everything is lost? Does the Ketaki flower bloom in all those villages on the other side? Does sweet fragrance rise in all those villages on the other side?"

Ketaki replied while sucking away all juice from the lemon to the bare skin. "Listen, friend, don't think taste is only in sweet things. The sour things also have a taste. In the face-puckering sourness of this lemon, is there no taste? Why then are we sucking away at it feverishly? Sitting here, stealing those lemons from others' backyards? Everything has sweetness. Sweetness is the essence of life. Sweet and sour depend on your moods and mindset. Rice, curry, karamanga (starfruit), all would taste sweet if you eat them with love. Otherwise, they would taste sour and bitter. In the end, even life would be sour for man. Love is such a thing that the sour, bitter, salty, and hot-everything would be sweet and sweet. Life is the art of extracting sweetness from things sour."

Girima said, "Even sweet tastes sour to me. Therefore, I'll jump into the river. You are my closest friend. We can give up lives for each other. Therefore, I would take you with me and jump. How can I leave you?"

Suddenly, she grabbed Ketaki and jumped into the tidal river. She swam and frolicked in the water playfully. After Ketaki, who had never learned swimming, was about to drown, having drunk a bellyful of water, Girima dragged her by her hand to the shore. She rolled with laughter shamelessly.

While comforting Ketaki to normalcy, Girima said, "Are you not ashamed, my friend? Our village is in the tangled net of nine rivers and the eternal roar of the sea. Children much younger than you are expert swimmers. You are an adult, yet you are afraid of the river? Except you, there is no other girl in this village who has not learned swimming. If any marriage proposal comes for you, it would break only for your inability to swim. Man does not live by only making betel for others. With that, one has to swim many tidal rivers.

"Okay. Forget other things. If floods come, won't you die first? Only for that did I push you into the river in cruel jest. And I have saved you from drowning. But you did not learn even to stay afloat until today. Today I had planned to teach you swimming by forcing you into the river under pretense, but you stayed immersed in the lemon juice and rose up to emotions, feelings, and love.

"What rubbish! What is the meaning of love in our lives? Whatever fate throws at you, you must love it, dying every moment. Yet life is the best of all. I love my life. You love yours. Whether the village this side or the other side, my life is mine. Why should one talk about losing it? But you should learn swimming. In our villages, every year, storms and floods visit as relatives visit our homes."

Interrupting Girima that day, Ketaki said with defiance, "Yes, I definitely love my life. But my lifeline is my innocent, carefree twelve-year-old brother, Ainthu. He has become an expert swimmer even at this age. On his wings, I swim many a river. So, what would I accomplish, learning swimming at this age?"

The two bosom friends had been conversing like this only a few days ago, sitting on the riverside. Today, Ketaki was regretting remembering that. Had she really been a swimmer like Girima, today her heart would not have been palpitating like this. If the sea rushes in Ainthu could swim away to shore somewhere, but that Ketaki would die, her friend had said only yesterday.

Ketaki had not murmured. Her house had not been thatched this year. The gale had already blown away half the roof, along with the bamboo beams. Ketaki had none to protect her. Ainthu could climb trees and could swim expertly. God would help him somehow or other. But what would Ketaki and her grandma do? The betel enclosure of her ancestor's times was a possible shelter, as it was on high mangrove grounds. Between the sea and the betel enclosure was a thin deodar forest.

With that hope, Ketaki went to the farm with her grandma and Ainthu on Thursday evening. Incidentally, Masuma too went with her to the betel enclosure for safety. They had taken a small packet of puffed rice and jaggery. The other valuables she had put in a wooden box, and she had locked it. Tying the key in her saree edge, she had tightly fixed it around her waist. She'd had a sense of relief. The inside of the betel enclosure at that time was somewhat warm.

Ketaki explained to Ainthu, "Listen, if the sea actually rushes in, we would climb up that peepal tree. We would also lift up grandma together. The peepal tree appears to be quite strong. And the old Pir is worshipped on that tree. It would never be uprooted. Moreover, the sea would never enter our sacred farm. Why should anything untoward happen then?"

The betel enclosure was shaking like coconut leaves in the roaring wind. Ainthu was staring at the face of his sister, frightened and stunned. Tiredafter babbling inanities, Grandma, by then, was leaning on the farm wall mumbling prayers, eyes closed. From the roof, water was leaking incessantly on the four, who were taking shelter there. Their bodies were numbed by cold. The only hope of the four creatures was the morning to come.

Masuma had gone to Ketaki's betel shop at noon on Thursday. The panicked gossip of the cyclone was quite an amusement for her. She could not believe that the sea would actually rush in and destroy the world. She thought the waves, after playing puchi (a folk game of maidens) on the village roads, would leave behind multicolored oysters, and that a long line of green-eyed sand crabs would lengthen on the smooth bosom of wet sand. Masuma would collect a lot of oysters, and crab creole would also be enjoyed that day.

She accompanied Ketaki when she returned home after closing her shop. Masuma had come away from packing things with her mother. What daughter is not averse to being an errand girl for hermother? Yet, packing and placing packets on the false roof with Ketaki was a pleasure. Sister Ketaki was very tidy in her ways. While packing and hiding for safekeeping the odds and ends, darkness, rain, and wind came together frighteningly. With Ketaki, Ainthu, and the old woman, Masuma too went toward the betel enclosure, carrying a few packets.

She was fascinated by the idea of spending one night at the betel farm because she had heard that, on stormy nights, the princes from the snake world came and frolicked there. And it seemed they did not harm anyone. They disappeared after dancing to their heart's content. Whether the cobra prince came or not, she could spend the rain-soaked night listening to fairy tales and scary tales-stories from the old woman.

Without any worry, she stayed that night in the betel enclosure. There was a heavy downpour. Eating rice flakes and jaggery, they were sitting inside, their shivering bodies close-pressed. It was not from the rain, but because of the tale-telling. The story was of the betel creeper coming up from the underworld. In a shaky voice, the old woman went down memory lane and spoke about her old man, her mind receding into the days of her never-to-return youth.

Her story ended, and Phelgm choked her voice. Her breathing became noisy, and her chest palpitated fast. In an undecipherable voice, she said, "Then-" And she stopped.

Everyone was saddened, thinking of the old woman's end in the story. The old woman's body was cold like ice. The breath ceased. The palpitations of the heart were not audible. Her toothless mouth was open. The three young people sat, with fear and sorrow, like statues.

As the betel enclosure was on a high, sandy place, the rainwater was flowing down. But after midnight, the wind speed increased. The walls of the farm collapsed on the three people taking shelter. While thinking about escape routes from the farm, they saw the sea stand on the chest of the betel farm. Ketaki and Masuma were swept away on a part of the devastated enclosure fence. Ainthu somehow or other climbed up the peepal tree, holding the aerial roots. Falling into a whirlpool and revolving for a minute, Ketaki and Masuma were swept off in two different directions.

Thereafter, maybe after a few hours, Masuma discovered herself on the head of a tamarind tree. She did not know that the tamarind tree was of the Dhobei jungle. She prayed to Allah in gratitude for her magical survival. Once upon a time there had been tigers and bears in the Dhobei jungle, even thieves and dacoits had their headquarters there. Nowadays, even the calls of the crow and cuckoo were not heard there.

On Masuma's back there was no skin. Throwing her on the cane bushes, the hands of the cruel cyclone had tossed her around vigorously. The thorns of the cane bushes had scrapped off the flesh and skin from her back. On it, the saline waves of the sea stung like lime on a wound. Masuma's tender heart could not gauge the height of the rushing sea. The incessant lashing of the rain, like date palm branches, was scouring her wounded back and face. The stormy hands of the cyclone had snatched away the striped cotton saree from the lean body of Masuma and had hung it on the cane bushes. But she had no shame for her naked body at that time. Hunger and the pain on her back had made her oblivious to shame.

The sharp, cold arrows of the rain stung her eyes like needles. Her eyes closed. She was shivering violently all over-not out of fear or hunger, but out of cold. Her hands were going limp on the tamarind branch. Bottomless water below. After some time, half- opening her eyes, she searched for some light of hope. She could not hold on to the tree much longer. She lost consciousness.

Just behind her legs, in a hollow at the bifurcated, thick branch of the tree, was sitting a ghost! Ghost or a Dhobei dacoit? Masuma's hands loosened their grip. She fell down into the void and fell on the ghost. The blasting wind was lashing at her and the ghost. The rain was crueler than the ghost. Masuma grasped the ghost tightly. Whether to save Masuma or himself, the ghost too released his grip on the branch and holding tightly to Masuma, fell down to the fathomless sea. Thereafter, both Masuma and the ghost, freed from hunger, pain, and fear, sank down toward the pearly depths of the sea.

Alas! It was not a ghost, but a man who'd wanted to save Masuma! For Masuma, he'd lost his grip on the branch and died.

Before her last breath, Masuma uttered,"O' Allah!"

Mantri Mallick, from the beginning, was a carefree master. Hence, except saving his own life, he ought not to have bothered about saving others. But on his head was the load of the youth of the village. Wearing a palm-leaf, sombrero-like hat on his head, he'd been moving from one end to the other end of the village since Thursday morning.

"Be alert! Be careful! A high gale would blow. The sea would rush in. Go to high places or take shelter in big buildings!" Mantri shouted this warning the whole day.

Many people knew about the oncoming cyclone in the Dalit and Muslim settlements from Mantri Mallick's warning. Mantri somehow was worried about his parents, brothers, and sisters. He was, after all, a disowned son, a cremation-ground devil to boot. But Mantri knew that the Dalit streets were in such a low land that, even during normal rainy seasons, it got waterlogged, walls collapsed, and houses got inundated. In this situation, if the sea really rushed inland, the Dalit streets would be wiped off the face of the earth. He was visualizing it in detail. Who knows what arrangements had been made by his father?

He had not been on speaking terms with Bharjan since the day he'd declared before everyone, "Mantri is dead for me. I disown him."

Whenever the father and son came face to face, they went their own way without looking at each other's faces, as if strangers. The villagers thought, meanwhile, that the father and son might have forgotten each other's faces. But this father-son relationship was such an earnest relationship that none forgot faces. To avoid seeing Mantri's face, Bharjan was not even taking the cremation ground route at the end of the village. Mantri was not even cremating bodies from the Dalit streets.

Only after hearing about the oncoming cyclone did Mantri warn everyone, shouting, "Be alert!" in the Dalit street. But he never looked at their thatched houses thathe'd left in childhood. Why should he feel for that which he no longer belonged to? Why should he tie a knot in the snapped rope of illusion? Mantri knew that he was dead for his father, but not for his mother. For his mother, he was the adored child forever.

He'd been a guileless, mad fellow. Hiding them in her torn saree-edge, she would bring curries or sweets given by others on festive days, and either place them at a corner of the burning ghat or give them at his house. Mantri never refused. Some other mothers and aunts also sent him cakes and sweets on festive occasions. But why did he eat first what his mother brought? Why did the ordinary fried spinach, prepared by her, taste different to him? A mother is a mother. Mantri does not think deeper than that.

Standing on the road, Mantri simply wants to know where his nine siblings and his parents have thought of taking shelter before the cyclone strikes. Then he consoles himself thinking that what the other families of the street would have decided, his father too must have thought of that. What concrete building does Mantri have that he would call his large family to take shelter?

At that time, hearing about Mantri moving on the street, his mother came out of her hut. She gave him some holy water and ran her hands all over his body. In a choked voice, she asked, "Mantri, have you eaten anything yet? Because of this incessant rain, our hearth is cold. No cooking since morning. Knee-deep water inside the house. Who knows what's ahead? But, my dear son, where would you stay when the cyclone blows and the sea rushes in? Your small hut would blow away like a leaf. O' my mad darling!"

Mantri retorted with some irritation in his voice. "Where would all of you take shelter?"

Mantri's mother spoke with enthusiasm. "We are going to Kundala Gosain's house. His cowshed and backyard are at such high grounds that the seawater would not reach there. Although the cowshed has a thatched roof, it has brick walls. And how high would be the sea waves? Kundala Gosain has said that he has opened his backyard, cowsheds, and even the veranda of his building for all of us.

"Your father has gone to pluck coconuts from a few trees

left by Karji Behera. When he returns, we would pack and go to Gosain's place. Do you know, my mad son, we all thought that Kundala Panda was a stone-hearted man, with no feelings for the poor and destitute. He is cruel to the untouchables. Since the day he made you the crematory devil, Inever felt like bowing to him.

"But, dear! He is a wonderful man. Risking his own life, he has gone with the holy waters to tie the sea. He sprinkled holy water in every street. In a bag, he was carrying the prasad of Grameswar. He gave parts of it to whoever he met on the way. He called me aside, and, giving me a bit of it, said, 'Give it to your crematory devil son. He would not take from my hands. I know. But I bless him. Mantri's mother, let the boy live happily here. A boy like him is rare in these ten villages. His only flaw is that, whether guilty or not guilty, he would not bend down to the Brahmins or respectable people. The thing he did that day, of course, he did unknowingly.

'But, tell me, should I not have gotten angry? Which man would not? If a crow suddenly releases excreta on Bharjan's head, would he not shoot it down with his catapult? If I expelled him from the village, would he have apologized, falling at my feet? Had he done that, would not my anger have subsided? Anger, after all, is the very devil, and the wrath of a Brahmin is a super devil. That's my flaw! But I am telling you the truth, Mantri's mother. I love that lad.'"

Whether Mantri Mallick had faith in the spiritual powers of Kundala Panda, he had great faith in divine powers. Therefore, he had some faith in the holy waters of Kundala Panda. But he had more faith on Kundala Panda's assurances. In such a critical situation, Panda might not have lied, he who had gone in a boat to the turbulent sea, risking his own life to charm the sea. It was a different thing whether he would divert the cyclone, but it was not a joke to take such risks for the welfare of the villagers. There was no other priest in this region like Kundala Panda who thought about the welfare of the people.

Mantri, in his heart of hearts, bowed to Kundala Panda. He decided to fall at his feet and ask for forgiveness once the threat of the cyclone blew over. He would say, "Gosain! Whatever has happened was not intentional. Had I known that you were sitting under the tree, I would not have done such a silly thing!"

Mantri told his mother, "You all go with the children to the house of Gosain. I am going to my hut. My hut may be fragile like a broken seashell on the sands, but the crematory-edge banyan tree, where the food pots for the dead are placed, is so wide, tall, and strong that there is no building stronger than that in this village. In the island, on the other side of the river, stands the old ghost-infested abandoned building of the Zamindar; this tree is older and stronger than that.

"My wish is to sit in the hollow of the banyan tree and watch how the cyclone plays with his twelve hand-measure sword, riding the dark horse of the sea, and how he would hack the sinners! When the cyclone subsides, I'll describe the whole thing to everyone. Like that pot-offered banyan tree, there is no other dependable shelter in this village."

At that time, Bharjan Mallick came, showing his dry and bare date palm branches like chest bones, carrying on his head two coconut boughs. At close quarters, his face looked very depressed. Had it been some other day, Mantri would have left the place, making an about-face. Bharjan too would have shouted at his wife, seeing the crematory devil, saying, "Don't allow this chandal in the house."

But that day-he did not know why-Mantri looked at his father from top to toe and stood immobile. He was thinking, how many years have elapsed in the meantime that my father looks so emaciated and old?

Bharjan's face was all skin and bones, and the cleft on his upper lip had widened. And that comparatively large tooth behind the widened wound had untimely fallen, making that blank space look like an open tunnel from which was seen the blankness of hard work, sorrow, and hunger. Bharjan's face appeared much diminished. Not distorted, but morose and defeated-his face, eyes, and everything.

Being the eldest son and having become a banished devil, his father was still working at this old age. So hard that, even in this stormy weather, he was plucking coconuts and climbing the trees. And, out of greed, he'd carried a few branches to put on his hut. Would the cyclone respect the dignity of these coconut branches?

All of a sudden, tears filled the stony eyes of Mantri. Wiping his face with his towel, Mantri turned toward his hut. Even before the cyclone came, this stubborn stone of a man of long years had been reduced to pulp.

Unsure whether to speak or not, in a halting voice, Bharjan called him from behind, and said, "Listen! Take the holy water from mother, the holy water of Grameswar temple. He alone can save, if at all. None else except him can save us. This cyclone would be more severe than the '71 and '82 cyclones. The wind speed would be murderous. This time, it is the apocalypse. Kundala Panda, Panchuki Panda, and Danakarna Mishra all have predicted."

It just slipped from Mantri's mouth, "I've received the holy water from mother. You all go immediately to Gosain's house. Otherwise, you would not get space."

"And you?" Father's anxious voice.

"Don't worry about me.I have to inform other villages urgently, or else, like skinlice, all Abhayapurias would stay put in their own places. Let me go."

When Mantri glanced at his father again, the long years of self-denied eye contact went haywire. Both stood looking at each other intensely, tears welling up in their eyes. Neither were guilty of anything. Whatever had happened was unfortunate. As fate is unseen, man often blames it all on fate to cover up his own guilt. Mantri did not want to waste more time thinking like that. He was anxious about the whereabouts of the hot-headed Ketaki. Like straw on the camel's back, the lass had one decrepit old woman and a useless lad.

While Mantri was stepping back, he was saying, "Ok. I am leaving."

Bharjan, showing his father's concern, said, "Do whatever you wish to. But keep yourself safe. Self-survival is the only priority. Do you understand?"

"Yes, yes. But you be alert. Anduntether the cattle. Otherwise, after the cyclone, Kundala Panda would accuse you of cow murder and make you expiate."

From his long experience, Mantri had understood that Kundala Panda was not as bad as a man, but his judgement had no life beyond the scriptures. Whether the religious books had meaning or confusion, he would not deviate. Moreover, Kundala Panda had his own scriptural judgement. Therefore, it was not certain how many people would be made to atone for this cow murder after the cyclone.

Mantri Mallick ran straight towards Ketaki's house. The roof of Ketaki's house had blown away, but a lock was hanging on the front door. Where had she gone at this odd time? In this village, Tahali Mohanty's was the only concrete house. All the people of the village could not be accommodated there. There were two temples at the two ends of the village. Those had already been overcrowded with shelter seekers since evening.

Where had Ketaki gone? Should she not have informed Mantri?

But why? Why? Why should she have informed Mantri about where she was going to take shelter? Was Mantri Mallick the village Zamindar or her guardian? Let her go; why does it matter to Mantri whether she lives or dies? The wind is rising in tenor. To save himself, he moved toward the banyan tree, side sweeping the drenched darkness. Many birds by then had taken shelter on the liberal branches of the tree. Looking at his own hand-made hut with affection and sadness for a while, Mantri climbed up the tree. And, being one with the vultures and hawks, he waited for an uncertain Friday morning.

While Bharjan Mallick was picking up coconuts for Kundala Panda, a few mynas in a nest were crying. Perhaps their parents had flown to safety, sensing danger. Bharjan's mind was disturbed for the orphaned mynas. Alas! These would die. But what could he do? Should he have taken them home and fed them rice and milk? But what home does he have, a sheep pen?

If he does not go to Gosain's house with his family, he may not survive. He's carrying the fearful cry of the mynas in his mind. But at least these mynas are at sky height. Even if the tall waves of the sea come, it is impossible to touch the head of the coconut trees. The mynas might survive if the wind subsides. But there is no sign of the wind falling.

Kundala Panda, while going to freeze the sea in the evening, had said with pride, "I've seen many a cyclone. I've also seen the ocean all my life."

Gosain could mock at the sea because his house was at a high place. His cowshed was also very strong. The height at which man must live above the cattle, his house was at a much higher place than that. And it ought to be. Living with the cattle, Bharjan Mallick and a few other poor families could survive the onslaught of heavy rain all through the night. Do not the people of Bharjan Mallick's street live an inferior life than the cattle? Therefore, no one had the least misgiving in spending the dangerous night with the urine and dung of the cattle in Gosain's cowshed. For the kind gesture of the Gosain in giving them shelter at such troubled times, Bharjan was praying for Kundala Panda.

The wayward rain showed her gimmicks to the hapless people all night. The matter would have been over, had it rained cats and dogs. The morning would have wiped off the water from the sun's face and woken him up. But the dark clouds had spread over the entire sky like a limbless body and had made the morning worse than the night.

Kundala Panda's eldest son, Panchuki, moving his hand on his flabby belly and rubbing tobacco paste on his teeth, was showing off pompously. "Do you see, Bharjan, how the cyclone was diluted by my father's mantra? It stuck to the sky like a leech but could not do any harm. Did the ominous propaganda of government come true a bit? Could the cyclone create havoc? The sea merely roared but could not enter the village. These are the effects of father's mantra.

"Father must be returning now. See how the wind is limping like a lazy bullock! Now it would certainly calm down. When the sky is clear, you all would return to your homes. Before you go, Bharjan, clean up a few more coconut trees. Whatever the wind took away is gone. The remaining coconuts you pluck. Who knows what's ahead?"

Was this a Brahmin or a butcher? Yes, a butcher. He has his prawn farm. The smell of fish comes from his sacred thread. The wind now was gathering speed, and this man is worried about coconuts. My children, bitten by mosquitoes and rolling in cow dung below and the lashing rain from above, are tortured like anything. There, the symptoms are clear that the cyclone would now grow violent.

This Panchu Panda is already middle-aged, but look at his mind. O' did the earth crack somewhere? Did the sky fall or the earth blast into two parts? From the front, with loud thunder, rushed in another smoky sky. In front is the Jatadhari estuary, and a little away is the age-old Bay of Bengal. How could another sky come from the estuary, rushing toward the village, leaving the sea behind?

Yesterday, the pregnant swell of river Hansua was visible. Today it is not. Everywhere the sea and more sea. The river was drowned and gone in the night. From all around, suddenly, came the death cry, "O' father, O' mother, O' my life's life! Water is rushing in. Let's go away.O' God, O' Jagannath, Mother Basuli, O' Ma' Sarala, save us, save us."

The village was sinking. Someone was climbing a tree, another the thatched roof. Men, women, children, old people, all at once turned into tree climbers and sea swimmers. The water rose above the level of the cowshed. Bharjan climbed up a palm tree in a trance. On his shoulders were sitting his younger sons, holding his rough hair. Was a grindstone tied to his neck or what? What was this fatal curse at such a moment?

In the morning, out of curiosity, he had come to see the children. Seeing the water level rise, he'd lifted the eight-year-old son of Panchuki Panda to the roof on his back. And he'd also lifted his children to the roof. Frightened, watching the roof totter before the water reached it, he climbed up a palm tree with his younger sons on his shoulders. Before his eyes, beneath the palm tree, strings of cattle and men were swept away to the womb of the sea. His wife and six children were swept away toward the Jatadhari estuary. Known and unknown faces were lost in the roaring ambit of the murderous waves.

Straining under the weight of three children, Bharjan had gone up the tree, and he was jumping up the tree in keeping with the swelling waters below. Now he was at the treetop. Wherefrom had such strength come to the arms of incompetent Bharjan? How could his limp legs muster such strength? His legs were entangled in the floating branch of a tree. Swirling in the whirlpool, the tree appeared to pull his legs down.

Unconsciously, Bharjan hung from a branch of the palm tree and tried to disentangle his legs from the floating branch. On his back was hanging, like a bag of ice, the hefty Brahmin boy. His hands were tight around his thin neck like a lock. Sitting on his shoulders, his two emaciated sons were moaning in fear. Bharjan's shoulders were bursting. He could not remember ever having cared for or embraced these two unwanted ninth and tenth children. Today he has become their protector and was carrying them on his shoulders as he climbed up the tree.

The skinny children were getting heavier as time advanced. The sharp edges of the palm branches had already started drinking the blood from his palms, as if somebody were slicing layers of flesh from his palms with a sharp instrument. With a jerk, he brought the children from the shoulders to his arms. He felt that his palms would be cut off at his wrists. He was not able to hold on to the branch. His hands were slipping.

The sea is rolling her tongue below. Whoever comes her

way, the sea pulls them to the mouth through the estuary. Many reputed swimmers, floating with their mouths open, eyes open, have been swept off into the sea before Bharjan's eyes. In a few moments, Bharjan too, with three small children, would suffer their fate. He too would float, dead, with the countless bodies floating now. However expert one might be as a swimmer, he cannot escape the deluge.

TWENTY

In the final hours of Kaliyug, everyone would perish. But no one dies without a fight in a war. Even the novice who does not know the art of war does not bare his chest before the enemy. Each according to his knowledge, intelligence, and strength, fights till death overpowers. This rule of war applies to life also. Everyone is a warrior. Even he who does not fight an enemy fights against his death until his last breath.

Bearing the weight of three children and made heavier by his own fears, he has climbed up sky-high; almost! Keeping the mad sea down below, he is safe; almost. The seawater is not rising, not receding either; only rumbles and rolls, shouting to swallow and destroy. Had his hands been sawed off by the palm branches, he would have surrendered himself to fate and the sea by now. But his palms, which have fisted death, have held on to his life, fighting with the sharp teeth of the palm tree branches.

Oh! Around his neck is hanging, like the deadly snake, the Brahmin brat, Debu, perhaps an enemy from some previous birth, as if he is begging for his life to a Dalit and also sucking his life. And there, slowly slipping from his shoulders, have stuck to his arms his two flesh-and-bone children, like dry streams of his own blood. These children are mere curses, come without rhyme or reason to the mother's womb, and are born easily but do not die easily. They are curses. Their living is as painful as their death.

The poor have a stubborn obsession with prolonging their lives, and with the same obsession they live till they get old. Except the pleasure of loving life, do the poor have anything else which is painless? No, the hands cannot withstand any more. The raw flesh sawed off from the hands is worse than the pangs of death. Because it is Bharjan, he has tolerated so much pain. Any other father would not have hung from palm branches with children on his shoulders. As Bharjan is slow-witted and passionate, he is suffering this torment.

The children scream in fear, "O" father! Our hands are slipping. Don't leave us. Don't leave us. We'll die, father!"

Bharjan, in panic, lost his grip on the branch. He hung like a cut branch. Both the children fell into the water like small, raw coconuts, with a splash. The elder one, clinging to Bharjan's hand, was pulling him downward. Bharjan, in panic, threw the life-sucking enemy away. Saying, "Go, you bastards, die," he cut all ties from the children. The expert hacker Bharjan suffered death pangs, as he could not be an expert in throwing the two brats earlier. He was finally saved from death when he cruelly threw the children away.

They were not children, but deadly burdens. This was not the time to regret his actions, throwing the children into water. Bharjan, now clinging to the trunk of the tree, was thinking how to save himself. The Brahmin boy was still sticking to his back, with his hands and legs almost limp. Is the fellow dead? He could shake off the live children, but to shake off a dead one was not easy.

His sons gave a final, deathly call. "Father!" Then they were lost in the water. Jah! The miserable brats are now free. Bharjan's hands had no more strength to hold onto the trunk. With the flowing blood, his strength too had oozed out to mingle in the water. He had no strength in his hands and felt as if his palms were gone.

He was falling, with eyes closed for fear of death. That ominous Debu too was falling down, sticking to his back. Perhaps he was dead, and therefore unresponsive to the fear of death.

Bharjan thought that he would die in a few moments. But he had to endure the debilitating fear of death. Before encountering the horrible face of death, he fell into space with the dead Debu on his back-but not into water. He fell face down on the large roof of a rooted family, uprooted and blown away by the cyclone.

Debu was sticking to him like a leech. Bharjan's mind was blank. Gradually, the world, family, children were receding into a black void. He'd been fighting for survival the whole day. There was some assurance floating toward nowhere. Spread-eagled on a floating roof, his eyes were closed. Thereafter, he had no way of knowing whether he was dead or unconscious.

Bhairab Majhi was a reputed swimmer. All his six sons were also swimmers. His three daughters were also one better than another in swimming in the river. He had a vast tract of land beside the banks of Saonlia River. Six large living quarters for the six sons, six ponds and three hundred coconut trees. Including children and spouses, they were forty-one members. Together with father's quarters, they closed the doors of the seven quarters and prayed to Mother Durga and Mother Sarala for protection.

Bhairab Majhi had explained to everyone how to break the waves and rise up and up in case the sea rushes in. As a determined boat, at sunrise, negotiates the ebb and tide of the sea and carefully stays afloat, similarly one must swim when the sea rises landward. Majhi had explained graphically to his sons, grandchildren, and the sons-in-law who had come as guests to enjoy the Kumar Purnima with the family. He was worried only for his second daughter and eldest daughter-in-law, Bhagabati. The second daughter was arthritic and did not know swimming. Bhagbati was slow-footed and too obese to walk properly. How could she swim?

Majhi had taught them a few tricks. But as no one was sure whether the sea would rush inland, none were afraid. Majhi's radio, at that time, blared, "The cyclone is moving northward toward Haldia in West Bengal and Khulna in Bangladesh."

Majhi thought, perhaps, that government had appeased the gods and had made such arrangements. Bhairab Majhi comforted everyone, "Sleep peacefully. The cyclone has gone in its course. Let's see in the morning." But Majhi did not know that the morning would be darker than the night. He also did not know that in the life of his family there would not be any morning again. The strong walls of Majhi's large house smashed to death all their fears and the rest of the dawns in their lives.

Golmasta, after completing his morning prayer, had urged villagers to seek shelter in the mosque, as it was on high ground. He pushed his family toward the mosque, chased by the fear of death, but there was no space for even broken rice on the veranda. Not getting any space in the mosque, he raised everyone to the roof and tied the roof tightly to the thick branches of a mango tree.

Son Salbeg had been out searching for Masuma since the prior evening. There was no trace of him. He was not worried for him. But where was his darling Masuma taking shelter? She'd left at noon, informing her mother, "Just coming." Where could she have gone? Maybe to Girima's house, or Ketaki's betel shop, or else to Karji Behera's daughter, Benga. Her mother was apprehensive and also angry with Masuma for where she was in such a horrible time. She was angry with herself because she'd let her go, and was also angry with her husband. Her brother had come to take his nephew and niece. Why had Masuma's father refused to let them go?

Why had Aklima Bibi not allowed Masuma to go, even when Salbeg advised? She'd thought Masuma might help her in packing things. And what help had that useless girl rendered? But where has she gone? Her father had gone out searching for her and he too is out somewhere. With the worries of saving the lives of so many children, her own life, and on top of that the worry for the daughter and her father, Aklima Bibi was frantic. Anger, fear, regret, rain and sorrow were all making Aklima Bibi cry streams of tears that were falling on the soaked roof.

She was desperately waiting for Friday morning; the father and daughter would definitely return. They must have met, and they must have taken shelter somewhere in the murky night. If Allah saves, who can kill? Why kill? What harm has Aklima Bibi done to anyone? Like a hen covering her chicks with her wings, Aklima was sitting on the roof, covering eight children. Sitting on a nearby roof, Golmasta was thinking, how could so much water rain in one night?

The mosque was overcrowded. Almost all of them were Hindus. About half of Pathan Street's residents were on trees and roofs, accepting their fate. Sitting on the roof, Aklima Bibi was abusing and cursing the people who had taken shelter in the mosque in language one cannot hear. The mosque had really been built by Muslim contributions, to offer prayers to Allah. But did that mean that, at this dreadful time, the mosque belonged only to the Muslims? Could Golmasta, at this time of danger, say to those people, "Vacate the mosque because you are Hindus. If all space of the mosque would be occupied by you, where would the Pathan street people go?" Can anyone say such inhuman things?

Of course, when Golmasta invited everyone to the mosque, he did not know that there wouldn't be any space for his own family. OH, alright then. It's all Allah's wish. When dawn broke out, Golmasta sat on his knees and prayed in a loud voice, "Allah ho Akbar." A slice of light pierced through the clouds; his fear and dilemma were gone. "It's Allah's wish! If he saves, who can kill?"

In thought and action, Gandhi Das was always a free thinker. He had defied many superstitions and restrictions of the society. Therefore, in regards to the rumor coupling his son Bhudan and Masuma, which had, for a moment, diluted the horror of the impending cyclone, he did not care a fig for it. If Bhudan actually married Masuma, what was wrong with that? But he knew that Masuma did not have that kind of relationship. Moreover, he had asked Bhudan to stay in the Sarvodaya office at Cuttack for the night, to do whatever was necessary for the registration of Sabuja Setu as a voluntary organization.

Bhudan would try to remove all illegal prawn farms from this area and create a mangrove forest between the sea and the village. That alone would save the village and the poor. This was his resolve. Gandhi Das, as his father, could not believe his son to be a transgressor of his own resolve. And how could this Tahali Mohanty get such unconfirmed news of a scandal? This rogue had not changed his nature even at this deadly hour. Who cared for him?

Gandhi Das knew that his son was safe. But where had this innocent Masuma gone? During the last five years, Bhudan had preserved in a box every one of the rakhis, the sacred thread tied on brothers by sisters that Masuma had tied on Bhudan's hand. Gandhi Das himself had locked the wooden box and put it in the false ceiling. But four unmarried daughters, his wife, and youngest son-where would Gandhi Das safe keep them? He saw in the unusual darkness of the much-awaited Friday morning the anticipated, horrible form the cyclone was assuming. The terrible form was that of the demon-killing Mother Durga. But would this cyclone kill only the bad and mischievous? Would the guileless innocent be spared from its hands?

Gandhi Das thought of a novel way out. The roof was tottering on water by that time. If the speed of the cyclone increased, he knew the roof would nothold. If the sea advanced, it would push it somewhere. He tied his children and wife to the coconut trees tightly with ropes. He told the children if water came, they should hold the tree, crablike. The seawater would come and go as the waves did.

"If you withstand that, closing your eyes and ears, there is no fear. At times, you need to be tied up. Voluntary acceptance of a bind at times is a kind of freedom."

After doing that, Gandhi Das felt free of fear. Bestowing his and his family's responsibility on the trees, he became indifferent. Like the tree, he became a piece of wood.

At that time, Kumpani Soin, closing all doors of his concrete building, was praying to God with his family. He thought of inviting Gandhi Das and his family to his house. But ego stood in the way. Who needs shelter? Gandhi Das or Kumpani Soin? Why did Gandhi Das not come to his house with his wife and children? Had they come, would Kumpani Soin have chased them away at this dreadful time? But look at Gandhi Das's ego. He might die, but would not take refuge in Kumpani Soin's house. His honest head would not bow down! If he takes shelter in the concrete house built with ill-gotten money, his body would be desecrated. Let him remain honest. There will be none in his home. The crocodile has dragged him to midstream, but look at his arrogance, even in the teeth of death!

But Kumpani Soin was ill at ease. His servants and bond slaves had taken shelter in his house with their families. Yet, being his brother, his own blood…should he go and drag them all to his house? He faced a dilemma as to whether to go or not, dilemma between sympathy and arrogance. Before the dilemma between the thoughts of self-interest and the concern for blood ties was resolved, in rushed in the gale, rain, and the sea.

As the eldest son of the Mandal family, and having taken a large share of his father's property, Utkalmani Mandal was living in separate quarters. The other six children, with their families and property, were living in the partitioned portions of their father's house. Utkalmani Mandal, panicked by the government's irresponsible propaganda, shouted expletives at the government to ease his own palpitations. Doesn't the government know that, in the nearby five villages, there is no concrete building?

On the west side of the village, there is the famous Mahabir temple on a slightly higher ground. There, the villagers were jostling for a foothold. The temple compound was looking like a messy carpet of heads. It would have been better to have reached there earlier. A slow-witted man suffers like this. On the other side of the village, there is the temple of Mother Ganga. Although a small temple, it is situated on lowlands; hence many people might not have gone there. Hopefully, there would be space to take shelter.

The stormy winds were rising by the moment. At midnight, the walls collapsed. Torrents of water rushed into the house. At midnight, a panicky Bharat Mandal called his brothers living in the old quarters, but there was no response. He immediately took his family out, and in that hellish darkness groped his way toward the temple of Mother Ganga. In such deadly times, no one waits for others. Each man suffers his fate alone.

When they came near the temple, Mani told his wife,

Mandodari, "You be in the temple. Let me tie the boat securely and come back."

Sobbing, Mandodari said, "Let the boat go to the hearth. Which is first? Life or boat? If you are going to the riverbank, take us all with you. We'll die together. That is better."

Mani Mandal reacted violently, and said, "You would go, or I'll show you what I am!" He sent his wife to the temple. "It's a matter of one night. If you make life more valuable than the boat, tomorrow morning when the cyclone subsides, what would the children eat? The cyclone would not have its dance of death for a month or two!"

What is fear for a male? Utkalmani is an expert tree climber, swimmer, runner and boatman. If the high tide comes, can he not save himself, that he would leave his boat an orphan in the hands of the cyclone? Leaving his family behind, Mani Mandal ran in that dark night toward the Saonlia river ghat as if possessed by some spirit.

Asking her seventeen-year-old daughter, Sundari, and the younger sons, Nidhi and Bidhi to enter the temple complex, Mandodari ran behind her husband, piercing that darkness-as if she were running behind the king of death to ask for the life of her husband! Actually, she was not running to get back her husband's life. She was running toward her home.

She had left behind on a shelf a packet containing gold earrings, a gold chain, silver bangles, and a silk Khandua saree which she had purchased, saving each pie, for the marriage of her daughter, Sundari. If she did not bring it, then either the sea or thieves would take the packet. Daughter's marriage had been fixed for December. Could she make another ornament in the rest of her life? She would also bring a small packet of flattened rice. If there was no food, you could not live on air on higher grounds.

The three children were shouting from the temple veranda, "Mother, mother, don't leave us!" and were running behind her. Mandodari, in that darkness, saw only the ornament packet, not the children. She was thinking, I'll just go and run back. Will the sea rush in within this short time?

The mother and children, wet all over, entered the house. But they could not come out. At that time, it was not the cyclone that was raging outside, but the demoness of death, hungry for lives.

The schemy night dawned on the innocent village. But what is the meaning of such a dawn, if darkness was not dispelled, fear was not reduced, and the speed of the wind did not abate? The morning appeared more fearful than the night.

The cyclonic wind was blowing at a speed to tear up the earth, with an aim to powder the sky and with the determination to annihilate creation. Whoever came in its way was finished-tall trees, electric poles, stones, pebbles, earth, water, and its creatures, fish, and crab. None had any respite.

The chips heaped for the repair of the Saonlia Bridge rose in a pile to the sky, and fell, scattered with the speed of an arrow like the sparks of fire from a box of firecrackers. Cattle, sheep, goats, and men were flying in the sky. Who was there to keep an account of who fell where, who was smashed to smithereens? The water from the tank of Bhairab Majhi was thrown twenty feet high, and the fish, crab, oysters, and leeches were thrown up and smashed down outside. Even the waters of Saonlia rose to the sky, and all creatures saved in her womb over long years were cleaned up in a trice. The cyclone had no mercy on anyone.

The symbols of rooted aristocracy, of Nanda Mangaraj of the Khandayat street, the beautiful palanquins stacked against the high veranda-all were so ruthlessly thrown into the sky that people closed their eyes at seeing them. The cart-wheel kept on Dhanu Mohanty's veranda flew like a plate and fell God knows where. Mandodari was stunned to see a few boats rising up along with the river water and crashing on sandy grounds to a thousand pieces like a broken earthen pot. She cried aloud for Mani Mandal, not knowing what had happened to her husband who had gone to secure the boat.

With her also cried the seventeen-year-old darling daughter, Sundari, "O' father! Where have you gone, father?" At that moment, the cement roof of the new office room of the contractor building the Saonlia Bridge was dislodged as a whole and flew toward their house. Seeing that, the mother (and children, crying 'O my mother!') went out, not caring for the waist-deep water. The flying cement roof straight away fell on their thatched roof. It smashed the roof, along with the half-broken house.

Anyway, they were saved at least from one danger. But during calamity, if one danger passes, several other dangers line up like the messengers of death before you. But man tries to surmount the dangers till the fatal one comes. Clasping the three children, Mandodari was consoling herself that it wasn't so easy to snatch away the children from the mother. Would God be so unkind? But where had the father of her children gone?

The early bathing hours must have passed. But the darkness enveloping the sky had not brightened yet. The wild cyclone was perhaps tired of fighting hard. Even a giant would be tired, fighting with such fury. Did they hear the call of Mani Mandal? The mother and children, walking on the banks of Saonlia, stretched their eyes toward the Hansua River, hoping for Mani Mandal's return. But the helpless creatures became breathless with fear looking ahead.

The cyclone was mad once again. A wounded sky overhead was still lashing cold rain from above. There, crossing the casuarina fence, one more ash-smeared tempestuous sky was thundering down from the east. Mandodari had never seen such a demonic sky; who had ever seen twin skies? It was not possible to distinguish between the real sky and the demonic sky. As if the sky and sea, in their conspiratorial alliance, were running to press the earth from above and below and from front and rear.

Before they could guess anything, the saline tide came rushing from the front. Lifting the children to a floating roof, Mandodari herself climbed on it. The mother and children were floating toward infinity. There was no other thought left in their minds to worry about Utkalmani. Hundreds of roofs, thousands of men and animals were floating. The east wind was chasing the floating roofs toward the fathomless womb of the sea.

There was no way to jump off their roof to safety, as they

were surrounded by water. Below them was unnavigable water, and on the water, hundreds of floating creatures; some dead, some half-dead, and some dying. Everyone was at the threshold of death. Before her eyes, people known to Mandodari were being swept into the sea.

Some of the dear ones, like irresponsible humans, were floating on their backs with their mouths open. They were free from the struggle for survival. Mandodari had thought that the floating roof would anchor somewhere. If they touched soil, their lives would be saved. She, however, could not believe that all those who were floating would all die. If some of those would survive as future seeds, why should not the roof carrying her children find safe harbor somewhere?

Mandodari was cursing herself. She would have survived had she not turned away from the Mother Ganga temple, prompted by greed. Her three children would have survived. Because of her own greed, she'd sealed the destiny of her own children. Only for her had the children left the safety of the temple. Now they were floating on bottomless water.

The cyclone was churning the sea-water from east to west and from north to south. If the roof was moved once to the right by the east wind, it was again turning toward the left by the north wind, exhausting the sheltered people. Mandodari was holding the children, lying face down, and was hoping to overcome the crisis. Suddenly, the tide rose to the height of two, and a gush of the south wind spun the roof and overturned it. The three children were thrown out of the protective shield of the mother and were swept away. Was Mandodari trying to save herself or the children? Her mind was not working.

At that time, blocking all her worldly worries and ties, stood before her the spectre of death. She was praying only for herself; save me, save me, save me! Some angel's hand at that time fished her hand out of the water. When she opened her eyes, she was in a boat. All three of her children were also in that boat, with thirty or forty other men of the village. That stout male who'd held the oar tight and stood challenging the fury of the sea was none other than the savior boatman and navigator, Utkal Mandal, her own husband, who did not look like the father of her three children, but like God.

Old age does not threaten as much as oldness. Bharat Mandal had known that he was old for a long time. But oldness had not debilitated him until last night. He had realized in his bones that he had no strength or courage to save all members of his family from this calamity. For that, he could not muster courage to take Kundala Panda in his boat to charm the sea. He did not even know on whose boat Kundala Panda went to tie up the sea by the power of his mantra. In one night, in his hands, head, and chest, the soot of oldness had settled. He was worried more about how to save his own life.

When the dawn of October 29, 1999 came, Bharat Mandal lost his bearings. He had not seen in his lifetime such a vicious morning, diabolical sky, or tempestuous wind. As his house was on a bit of high land, the water had reached only up to the veranda. Not much water had entered the house. All night, his entire family sat in darkness, closing all the doors and windows. No one spoke a word. The swishing roar of the wind was heard through the chinks of the door. The house was shaking to its foundations. The sprays of water entering the house were numbing the courage of everyone.

Bharat Mandal was reciting the Hanuman Chalisa. Outside, Kalki avatar was grinding its teeth, and the mighty trees were breaking with loud, cracking sounds.

The room in Bharat Mandal's house that had unburned brick walls and a tin roof had eighteen adults and children jam-packed in it. Padma was remembered at that time. Also remembered were Padma's son, and Padma's grandson, Kapil. The other daughters were married in far-off Midinapur, and Bharat Mandal comforted himself thinking that they were safe. Meantime, the radio had announced that the cyclone may turn toward Midinapur. His fears were receding and rising again, causingtrepidation in his heart. Would his daughters at Midinapur be saved from this cyclone?

Old age, sitting on his neck, made his lifelong manliness ineffectual. No one had the time to think about others. The deluge had come to the doorstep. At one stroke, the doors and windows broke, creating a yawning gap through which entered the gushing waters of the flood. Outside, all space was smoky; all space was a sea. The straw from the roof had already blown away. The tin sheets, like torn paper, had flown into the sky to the void. Nothing was overhead. Except the raised hood of the cyclone, there was nothing overhead.

The children started wailing. The cattle lowed. The trees, swimming in the sky, were screaming and falling spread-eagled on the earth. The walls of Bharat Mandal's house fell with a splash, since the doors and windows were already gone.

The world was gaping at his house. Except water and wind all around the house, there was no trace of any human habitation. He was always alone. Today, his loneliness frightened him more. Where would they go? Except the roof, there was no other safe place. Everyone climbed up the roof with their children.

At this moment, the sunlight, faint and nascent, fell softly on the watery world. The rain paused for a while. The wind too rested somewhere, perhaps to get back its breath. Life returned while going away. Had the cyclone, deviating from its course, gone somewhere else?

It was better to dig up from the floor the hidden money and ornaments now. Alighting from the roof into knee-deep water, Bharat Mandal searched for something, bending on all fours, braving death.

TWENTY ONE

Wiping off the fate line from the forehead of Erasama, the water level was rising constantly.Bharat Mandal during his lifetime had seen many cyclones and floods. He was never afraid. Who is afraid of the crocodile while living in the river? Bharat Mandal's fourteen generations had been boatmen of river Padma. His forefathers had rescued in their boats the flood-afflicted people in so many floods. Bharat Mandal is also no less an expert in boatmanship than any of them. But today, his wits gave in as the cyclone and floods together thrashed him from above and below.

No one knew, in the early bathing hours, why the sky was menacingly dark. It was the sea rushing inland. The sea was not alone. With her, the nine rivers, tanks, and ditches all together were in a hurry to swallow Erasama. A seven man-measure high wall of water rushed into the village in the blink of an eye. The ululations and prayers of the villagers changed into screams of panic. But the screams were lost in the marching roar of the merciless sea.

In one push, Bharat Mandal's oldness vanished from his joints. Without caring for his age, Bharat Mandal rushed out as the water entered, and he untied his boat. In a way, Bharat Mandal was old, but in another way, he had greater strength than the incompetent youth of today, more energy and verve in his body and mind. He wished his sons were stronger and more self-reliant, but they always wanted to be under his care and guidance. Would he live forever?

Mandal did not choose to be quiet and selfish at this misfortune of the villagers. He had confidence and faith in his own boatmanship. He also had enough faith in the strength of his arms. But he could not trust the east-west, north-south whirlwind movement of the cyclonic wind, nor the mindless tidal waves. But a boatman does not jump into the river when he knows that the boat would sink. While navigating and oaring till the end, he dies or survives. This is the principle of a true boatman.

At first, he took his wife, three daughters-in-law, and the grandchildren on the boat. His two grown-up granddaughters and two useless sons, all these eight creatures were looking like cold, lifeless corpses. Without looking at them, he fished out of water his relatives and sat them on the boat. He must leave them first at some high ground and then think of the others. The boat could not withstand the weight of too many people.

Praying to Mother Sarala, Kali, and Basuli, Bharat rowed the boat using all his strength of body and mind. He turned the boat toward the nearby sand bank. If no space would be available, there was the high school and the new double-storey building of Danakarna Mishra. If that would not be available, he would drop the human herd on any high land that met his eye. Again he would come back, turning the boat, to rescue others.

At that moment, he saw his eldest son, Utkalmani, seating about fifty men and women in his boat and rowing as if one possessed. One stubborn obsession was driving his son. The stubbornness with which a boatman stakes his life against water. It's not found in any other man. How strong is that stubborn commitment that only a boatman understands, and yet he cannot explain why. It is a feeling native to a boatman. Maybe it's the obsession in his blood. As the water did not know why she was playing with lives, Utkalmani similarly did not know why he was hell-bent on making the impossible possible.

If you seat fifty people in a boat, you would drown. Why was Utkalmani so foolish? If Utkalmani today was possessed by his innate desire to save the villagers, let him show it. It's not undesirable to strive for selfless service. But he could not believe that the boat could hold its course with the weight of so many people.

The lives of so many people were now in the hands of his son, Utkalmani, because he had the oar in his hand. At this moment, man was nothing; the lifeless bamboo pole was the savior. Yet, was man any less arrogant, knowing well that too much pride had done in Lanka? Until the death wind blows, he does not come to his senses. Utkalmani, perhaps, was thinking that his hand was everything.

The tide was pulling the boat while the wind appeared determined to blow away the oar from his hands. In such a situation, naturally, man's hands are the be all and end all of life. But if the wind blows away the oar, what can the hand do? Bamboo frames from the roofs were swishing overhead, blown by the wind, as if the sky were throwing javelins from all directions. It would be no wonder if the oar was blown away from his hand.

Bharat prayed for Mani's hands to be replaced by those divine hands of Lord Krishna that had thrown the Sudarshan disc to cut the heads of the evil people in the Kurukshetra war. Whenever a hand struggles to save helpless people that hand does not work as a human hand. It becomes the hand of God. Otherwise, how could his three-score-and-more-years-old, half-dead hands rise powerfully like youthful hands? How could the strength of hundred lions energize Bharat's body, and from where? It's all God's play.

As Bharat's boat moved toward the highlands, he called out, "My dear Mani, I would come back after leaving these people and join you. Straighten the boat toward the right. Mother Basuli would protect you. Bravo, Mani, bravo!"

Mani just glanced at his father. While controlling his boat, he saw his father's boat upturning. His family and clan were swept off in different directions.

Breaking through the waves, Bharat Mandal shouted for the last time, "Bravo, Mani, bravo. Never lose your courage, dear!"

Thereafter, only the swish of the cyclone and the hissing from the estuary was heard. With the downpour from above, Mani Mandal's strength was also flowing down to the heart of the tidal waves. The boat fell into a whirlpool, the oar fell short of the depth, and the boat did not respond to his efforts. Although the hand and oar were there, about fifty-five lives hung on a thread.

The whirlpool had formed a wheeled battlearray. Like Abhimanyu, the lone boat was sucked into it. Waves after waves, like the seven warriors, blocked all escape routes. The boat bent to one side uncontrollably. Within the twinkling of an eye, many from the boat fell down and floated away, and with them all the three children of Mani. Mani'swife screamed aloud, seeing that. What woman would have patience when she sees all her children being sucked into the sea?

Mani Mandal brought the boat under control, grinding his teeth, stopping his breath, and sweating blood. The children were screaming for help, raising their hands, and were drowning. His wife was shouting, "Save my children, save my children!"

When Mani turned his boat toward the children, the thirty-five people shouted in a chorus, "Save us, save us."

Mani Mandal was torn. There, his blood's blood, his children, had floated away a bit far. And here, the boat was tottering. To save three, if he went there and fell into the whirlpool, about forty lives would be lost. It was not easy to sacrifice certain lives for the uncertain ones. A few had already come swimming nearer the boat. Lifting the people near at hand, he said, "Be patient. I would leave you at the high land and then think of other things."

"Victory be to Mani Mandal! O'God, let all good things happen to brother Mandal. Let him grow and prosper."

Never berating the cyclone, the good wishes of the people frenzied the wind. Mandal did not have the courage to look at his drowning children. The voices of the three children were heard no more. Here, his wife, beating her chest, was attempting to jump into the water. Some people were holding her, saying, "Saving many lives in the month of Kartik is a great virtue. All good things would happen to brother Mandal. Godwould protect your children!"

Rowing the boat toward the high land, Mani Mandal thought, Ha! Auspicious things would happen to me! The result of virtue in the month of Kartik has already come. Before my eyes, my family, my clan, including my father, have already drowned. My children have been pushed toward the estuary. What good would happen to whom?

The people on the boat were lavishing their blessings on Utkalmani Mandal. His wife was unconscious.

"Oh, I am saved! At such a critical time of sorrow, of life-and-death confrontation, instead of encouraging me, she's making me nervous and weak."

"Brother Mani, you are our god! You are our destiny-maker. You are not a man, but an angel! We cannot repay your debt in seven births! You just leave us at the high land, and then take the boat and fish out your children. They are children of a fisherman, they must be floating, cutting the whirls.O' God, protect the children."

Mani Mandal was not listening to anything. He was no more a boatswain. He was transformed into an oar; strong, dutiful, and stoic. He who does not hear anyone's laughter, cries, praise, or blame, he has no rise and fall of the heart at someone's death or another's survival. He has no feelings of thine and mine. The principle of the oar was to take the boat to the shore, not to capsize the boat. Saving a drowning person is not within the capacity of the oar.

Mani Mandal, like a man deified, brought boatful ofpeople from the village and left them on high land, again and again. After ferrying people several times, Mani Mandal turned his boat toward the clan-destroying whirlpool, hoping that his children might be found. No other panicked call was heard from behind. The men left alive had already gone to high places. Those who were floating, yet not calling for help, they were beyond all rescue. They had gone, fighting with the waves, to the highest place from where there is no return.

Gaining consciousness, Mani Mandal's wife was simply cursing and abusing her husband. "God! This demonic father fished out his children from water only to eat them. O' God! For him, the villagers were top priority, and his own blood were strangers! O'my children dear. O' my life's life. I never knew this man was such a stone! O' my dear ones, why did not God take me?"

Mani's wife could not find the apt language to pour out her pain and bereavement. To condemn the stonehearted father, her language was inadequate to the task. But how do two eyes pour out all the agony of a battered heart of a mother? The eyes, therefore, were no more shedding tears. Only the heart continued to wail in silence. The people on the boat had consoled Mani's wife. She was quiet in her pain. They were deifying Utkalmani Mandal, but the deities are always unmanifested. Relegating to the background his wife's condemnations and the high praise of the villagers, Mani Mandal, following the echoes of the mortal screams of his three children, jumped into the water and gradually disappeared in the confounding waves.

Business and cyclone were in a strange encounter. Before crossing the real danger of the cyclone, the ferry ghat owners were working, staking their lives. By early evening, when he reached Bhagyadhar at the prawn farm, Baikuntha was fishing with his throw-net. The fish merchants had given money in advance. Therefore, closing their eyes and ears to the cyclone warning, they were sitting at the prawn farm, riskingtheir lives. Their hawk eyes were brightening when the net rose from water. The sooner they got the fish, the sooner they would drive away to Cuttack or Bhubaneswar with the fish.

The radio at hand was giving out the news about the course of the cyclone and the speed of the wind continuously. Keeping aside the prawn for Bipin and Bhagyadhar's nocturnal feast, the rest was packed, and Bipin sent Baikuntha with the packet to the village saying, "You go soon. I have told mother that tonight there would be prawn curry. There are a lot of guests at home. Also, there was a surplus of fish. The Jagatsingpur merchants, for fear of life, stayed at home. They had not advanced any money. Therefore, how does it matter to them if we lose money? Luckily, two big merchants who had advanced money have not turned up. We caught fish for them. They did not come. Is it not a fact that our fish would rot? And their money is also forfeited.Alright, you go. The rain and wind are rushing fast."

"And you! Would mother spare me?" Baia was on the verge of tears.

"Hey, we would cook here and eat. We would return within two hours, after making arrangements for the safe keep of things here. Bhaga's son is ill, my sister may deliver tonight, brother Sankha is in his father-in-law's house.Do you think we would stay in this sea-facing prawn farm? See, fishing is going on even now in all prawn farms. Can we do business if we fear?"

Bipin sent Baia to the village with the fish. From the freshly cooked, boiled rice, hot smoke was rising. The hot and spicy prawn curry was fresh and blood-red.And to add to that, hunger! Bhagyadhar had never eaten so much prawn at one meal. Nor had Bipin. If the business thrives, who eats prawn without selling, whether he is a fisherman or not? Defying the rain and wind, they ate prawn to their heart's content. Even rice was eaten up to the neck. They had no room for water.

The storm was dancing to its own tune on the asbestos roof. The rain was beating would fully. Eating up to the neck, the six of them slept, tired and heavy. Bhagyadhar too forgot his son's fever and his home. He thought of going to the village before dawn. Even if the forecast about tidal waves was true, nothing would happen before morning. Better to sleep for a few hours, for God knows how much energy had to be spent in the morning. Bhagyadhar slept, praying to God. Bipin started snoring as soon as he touched the bed.

Before the morning was dragged in by the storm winds, the six of them got up in shock at early dawn. By that time, the asbestos overhead was already blown away. Rainwater was pouring in through the dark hole of the roof. Gathering the cooked prawn and the money in a big polythene bag, Bipin tied one end and put it on his shoulder. Better to go to the village before the darkness lightens. But the intensity of rain and wind had increased to such an extent that it was not possible to come out of the room.

Last night, some of his friends from the nearby prawn farms had come to Bipin's place because it was comparatively well-built and at a higherlevel. Everyone's heart sank seeing the condition outside. At about eight, when the direction of the wind changed, they all started toward the village. The sharp rain was tearing up their skin. When they could not proceed further, they entered a washerman's house nearby. But by the time they changed into dry clothes from their bags, the washerman's courtyard had knee-deep water.

"The sea is rushing in, O'God!"

Crying, all of them started running toward high lands. The sand from the casuarina jungle of Sahadabedi village was going down. They were falling down from time to time in the water. Jumping over the kewra bushes and running toward safe ground, their legs and thighs were torn. But that pain they did not feel in their race for life. The teashops and grocer's shops by then were already under water. The walls of the shops on the side of the road for the car festival had fallen left and right.

A cabin was being swept off as a whole, and on the cabin, about seven to eight people were also carried along by the current. Within a moment, they floated toward the smoky estuary and were lost in the smoke. The sea, as it were, was turning the water into gaseous smoke by its hot, hissing resolve to destroy everything. The sky, sea, and earth were all one, nothing was decipherable. It was as if the three realms were determined to ring down the last curtain on Kaliyug!

Bipin, Bhagyadhar, and forty to fifty others could save themselves going up a high mound through the cane bushes. As the tall, stout trees on the mound had fallen, they were lashed and beaten by the death-dealing wind and rain mercilessly-but there was no fear of death under the broken branches and trunks of the trees. They watched in awe as the young trees were uprooted and the swishing water entered their haven, driven by the wild north wind. The south wind carried fast the floating people into the sea. The south wind was so much fiercer than the north wind that some children were forced out of their mother's hands and dashed against the trees before their mothers' eyes. All of them sat like mute stones.

The south wind blew from 8:00 a.m. on the twenty-ninth to 10:00 p.m. on the thirtieth-in unabated fury. The south wind alone destroyed life and property on a massive scale. Bipin and Bhagyadhar, like a pair of twins together, were hit by the rain and wind the whole day. Dead bodies were floating face down toward the estuary the whole day. At first, when a twenty-five-foot high tide came sweeping fast from the Jatadhari estuary, the foamy tide threw to Bipin and Bhagyadhar a thin, nude woman. Bipin and Bhagyadhar were sitting, faces down, with eyes closed. It was impossible to keep their eyes open in the blasting rain and wind.

The naked woman was lying unconscious before them. Both Abhayapurias opened their eyes a blink. The others like them were praying, closing their eyes. Sometime later, getting back her consciousness, the woman babbled, "O, my child, my child!" and tried to jump into the water. The two friends pounced on her and forcibly prevented her. Whether mad, unwanted, or unsearched for, life after all is life. It has its own value.

Although before their eyes the carnival of death was celebrated, no one was able to do anything. But how could Bipin and Bhagyadhar leave a mother to die? An old woman sitting there took out a saree from her bundle and threw it on the woman. The madwoman immediately put it on her body, not to cover her shame, but to protect herself from the cold. The old woman had come visiting her daughter's house with some sweetened parched paddy for Kumar Purnima! With her, her twelve-year-old grandson. Somehow, from somewhere, they had come floating to shelter there. The sick, feverish child was shivering in the cold.

Some bidi addicts took out matchboxes and dry clothes from polythene bags, and, burning the clothes, tried to foment the child. The old woman sat, holding the boy in her lap. All were starving the whole day. The boy was restless no more. Maybe he was feeling comfortable. Eyes closed, he was lying still as wood. The mad woman was massaging the boy's body softly the whole day, tirelessly. The cyclone abated at 10:00 p.m., but there was no sign of the rain and cold wind subsiding.

The night was terrible. The number of shelter seekers was growing hour by hour. About seven or eight snakes, coming out of the water, took shelter in the bushes while everyone was looking on. From a tree in the mound, about half a dozen snakes were hanging. But all of them were pale and weak, being stricken by the rain and cold wind. Some of the timid in the crowd were praying, "Om! Namo Shivaya."

Bipin's clothes were all wet. From his curly, luxuriant hair, water was dripping, and he was shivering in the cold. He had given away the dry clothes in his polythene bag to someone else, large heartedly.

Bipin expressed his gratitude to the pitch-black night because the night had covered the naked, dead bodies all around with a black shroud, and it was crying bitter tears ceaselessly. At that time, he felt that he was shivering not out of fear, but fever. He'd been suffering from malaria for the last few months. Taking medicines for malaria, he had also developed dizziness. His vision was blurred. But the fever came and went like the ebb and flow of the tide. Bipin had neglected this, intoxicated by the fish business of the prawn farm. On the small sand mound, by this time, people were packed to capacity. Floating from different places, they were stuck there by a stroke of luck. How, no one knows.

The woman, who had turned mad after losing her children, had been caressing and pressing the numb body of the old woman's grandson all day. Perhaps she could sense that she was caressing only a body, from which life had already gone since evening. She was quiet, thinking that she was caressing her own child.

Sensing the coldness of death, she suddenly said, "My child is no more. Why should I live?" and jumped into the water in the darkness.

Behind her was heard the scream of Bhagyadhar, "Hey! What are you doing? Wait, wait! Your child is alive!"

Before Bipin could say anything, he heard two splashes in the water in close succession. Then everything melted into the choric din of rain, wind, and tide. Had Bhagyadhar done such a suicidal thing? Drinking the poison of darkness, could he come back alive from the water thickened by the soil of the swallowed-down villages? Tomorrow morning, if the road to the village was found, and at the end of the road, if the village was found, and in the village, if Udhab Mangual or his daughter-in-law were found then, if they asked, "Where has Bhaga gone?" what answer would Bipin give? Of course, an answer to such a question he may not get a chance to give to anyone. Who does not know that no one has the authority to ask such a question to the deluge?

And was this the time for the fever to hit Bipin? He was thinking of home and the warm bed at home. He remembered the nursing hands of his mother. Had he been home, his mother would have weighed him down with bedding and blankets. Rubbing hot mustard oil on his palms and feet, she would have chased away his fever. But would his house be there? Four man-measure high water! Would it have respectfully left intact their house of seven generations? Oh! These annoying chills were not allowing anyone else's concerns in the mind except his own.

Baikuntha too was moaning, "Uhu, ah! O' mother, O' father…"

At this time, someone took his shivering body, covered his body with part of his own clothes like a warm shawl, and caressed his hands and feet. When the fury of the rigor grew, he fully embraced Bipin's body. Into Bipin's nostrils wafted the scent of an unknown hair oil. Although it was a strong scent, it was sweet and comforting. The body clasping him, perhaps, belonged to somebody's mother, wife, or daughter, but Bipin felt God had sent his mother to nurse him because the warm intimacy he was experiencing could only be the touch of a mother. Bipin does not yet know how a wife's nursing feels, but how can the touch of a wife be as warm as a mother's touch? Bipin knows that mother's unconditional love is thicker than a wife's love ambrosia.

When the shaking stopped and the body felt solid and whole, Bipin could feel that it was the body of a young woman's tight embrace, whose calm sincerity was gradually becoming deeper to make him sleep in comfort, to take away the pain from his body. Whoever the woman was, that she had held his body in close embrace with motherly love, moved by his condition, he had no doubt about it nor any embarrassment. He would see the face of his savior in the morning and would take her to her village. He had no choice but be eternally grateful to her.

Bipin did not know when he flew into his dreamland. When his dream-laden sleep got disturbed by the weeping of the old woman holding the corpse of her grandson, he knew that all night he had slept under assured safety. The night ended at the right time, but when Bipin woke up, the morning was no morning. The early bathing time was standing like a criminal, not daring to show her face to an unimaginable world of sorrow and bereavement after the deluge.

Bipin at first searched for Bhagyadhar. There was no sign of him. OH, last night Bhagyadhar had jumped into the water after the mad woman, like an unfortunate person. Then he searched for the mother icon who had given him warm comfort under her saree all night.That woman had disappeared.Maybe she had started walking in a directionless world, searching for a path leading to her house, family, and a new destiny. Ah! He would not get a chance to express his gratitude!

Bipin got up in a hurry. The packet containing money was safe in his pocket. But another polythene packet was lying near him. He picked it up to see what it was. There were a few pairs of silver earrings, a talisman, a bead necklace, and with those, a few balls of Pir's prasad. Bipin recalled that such earrings were worn by the Muslim women. They meant that woman was Muslim. Lastnight, Hindus and Muslims had been one in love and compassion.

Carefully, he lifted the packet. Fromit was flowing out the distinct fragrance of attar. Therein, he could decipher the affection of her being and the aroma of her heart. Where and how would he search for that woman? How would he return her property? Bipin could never return the wealth of love, respect, and gratitude which he has saved in his heart for the woman. All debts cannot be repaid. Bipin, moreover, did not know what to give to repay the debt of unconditional compassion. All remain indebted in life to many people in many ways.

For the last thirty years, since his birth, although he has seen Hindus and Muslims living in amity on Erasama soil, for some unwanted reason, Bipin could not accept the Muslims as his own brothers; as if this soil was meant for Hindus only. As Golmasta, Sheik Rahman, Salbeg, and others forcibly live on this idea, it is not possible to tell them anything or tolerate their presence.

But one night of the deluge had dispelled from his bone and marrow all misconception. Now he could understand that this soil belonged to all. He who loves this earth, the earth is his. He who does not love the soil is a renegade. The deluge had proved that there was no other religion than love.

Bipin touched his head to the packet. Taking a bit of the offering, he expressed his gratitude to Pir, as he could see another new day on this beautiful earth because of Him. But when he looked at the foot of the mound, his eyes closed. Is this his beautiful world? Yellow-clad, golden Erasama!

Sankha Mangual's heart swelled with joy, looking at the moon-faced twins. At the same time, the aggressive sea was rushing in withthe rogue-elephant-like storm, in unison. Seeing this, even the bullish male Sankhadhar's heart sank. When he was getting ready to return to his village, a mountain-high sea rushed in. The villages where waist-deep water collects when a toad urinates, those villages were no more villages in a wink, but instead the rising deep. The people did not have any time even to think where to go. Seeing the sea in front, their eyes closed, and when they opened their eyes, they were floating in the vast sea.

In the dark roar of the sea and the fast breath of the cyclone, the agonized screams of thousands of people were lost. One could not hear his own screams. Sankha saw that, sitting on his father-in-law, Bhima Behera's, roof, eighteen people from his in-law's family, including his wife and the newborn twins, were swept off into the sea. Whether due to good or bad luck, Shankha held on to something in panic as they were being pulled into the sea along with others.

A drowning man pins his hope even on a straw. But that was not a straw; it was a long-broken lifeboat of a ship. Where the lifeboat was taking him, he did not know-towards life or death? Wherever it was, Sankhadhar had no choice. To float only was his helpless duty; hereafter, his fate.He was losing consciousness and gaining it back intermittently. Like that, he stuck to the base of a bamboo bush. There he lay, nerveless. For how many ages, who knows?

He felt few snakes sliding over him. But the snakes too were searching for a place to survive. For them, Sankhadhar was only a heap of earth because he did not have the stir of life. He had no thought of those who, before his eyes, went to the sea. He knew where and how they were. Why should he worry about them? His worry focused on the four children he had left behind at home under the care of his parents.

Perhaps they were safe. His father, Udhab Mangual, would not have thrown his four children into thesea.Somehow, his father would have saved his children.The faithhe had in his father was never in anyone else, not even God. What did God do to his wife and his innocent children? What crime had the two-day old children committed before God? If He were to take them, why did he give acute labor pain to his wife for three days and nights? Who could question such cruelty of the Merciful?

At that time, Sankha saw from inside the broken lifeboat that it was Ganga floating on the sea. Into the python mouth of the Jatadhari estuary were entering so many people known, unknown, friend, enemy, and blood relation, of this village, that village, that no one bothered. The floating world of people was self-immersed. Who knew how Ganga came into the sea and why? Ganga herself did not know. That day, the cyclone rumors had so excited the adolescent mind of Ganga that she'd run around the entire village.

Here and there, clusters of villagers had been gossiping about the news. Whensomeone said that the cyclone would rise from the east, Ganga had gone and sat facing east on the edge of river Hansua. She had not been aware when it became dark. The rain had poured, and the cyclone roared. When she heard footsteps behind her and rose to return home, she saw a political goon standing like a messenger of death. During elections, such lads grow like mushrooms in the villages. And they fade away after the election.

A group of political workers had come from somewhere. An election had just ended, and it was heard that another election was in the offing. Therefore, such workers were seen here and there. No one knew their names, villages, or addresses. Even the leaders who hired them do not know them. Ganga was the darling child of a rooted Brahmin family. Looking at the boy, she could know that such daredevil lads do not care for the cyclone, the law, or death. But as he appeared malicious and evil, Ganga's heart sank. Without thinking of consequences, Ganga took steps backward and fell into the river. The boy jumped into the water after her. At that time, rain and storm raged wild, and they swept away Ganga to such a distance where the hands of the boy would never reach.

But misfortune comes in hordes. To escape from one ogre, Ganga slipped into the river, but there she encountered another giant, the sea. There, when she tried to avoid going through the Jatadhari estuary, she fell into the clutches of a known giant, one who, fishing her out of water, carried her whole virgin body on his back and, swimminglike a buffalo, went in search of an island where there would be no deluge-whether life is there or notanda, who had unconditionally surrendered to the deluge, surrendered herself to the giant and became free from all tensions. She did not have to fight for life now because the giant was fighting with water for both of their lives.

Sankhadhar was only looking at her in a state of shock. Despite his wishes to save the soul mate of Girima, the raw virgin Ganga, he was not able to save Ganga from death. Fighting with the water, the giant figure raised his head once, raised his hand, begged for rescue, and then went limp and lowered his face. In a moment, he was traceless in the mouth of the sea, holding Ganga.

Like a breach in the embankment, Sankha's chest cracked inside and was flooded with sorrow and pity. Alas! Had not Narku Routroy's wanton swimmer son, Arjun Routray tried to save Ganga, maybe she could have been saved. This lad, it was rumored, had strangled a girl to death after raping her. Maybe her curse had fallen on him! He had, perhaps, a prawn farm. Perhapshe was swimming for his life, caught in the night by the sea. Alone, the poor fellow perhaps could have saved himself.

But what did he not do to save Ganga! Because of his father's black money, the fellow had fallen into bad company and developed evil propensities. Otherwise, he was not really bad. May his soul rest in peace. And poor Ganga! What could Sankhadhar have done? He himself was at the mercy of the bottomless sea!

TWENTY TWO

Deluge and destruction do end because the Creator creates and recreates daily, never destroys his creation every day. He destroys only when man defies and insults creation.

Mother earth was crying for rescue. Therefore, Varuna, the Sea God had thrice vowed to destroy the earth. The sea god of Kaliyug, keeping his promise, had been carrying only three weapons in his ninety-nine hands; cyclone, typhoon, and tidal waves. Launching those weapons, the lord of the sea observed the ritual of massacre for thirty-six hours on the tolerant earth. Sacrificed were merit, compassion, and the world of joy in the ambit of the deluge launched to decimate sin! In the war of Dharma between the Kurus and the Pandavas, only the Kurus were not destroyed. The five innocent children of the Pandavas were also sacrificed in the righteous war.

This is the consequence of war and deluge. The god of destruction, with only three hissing puffs of rage, had finished them all. The first hour of the black twenty-ninth had blown away the home, hearth, and future of men; the foundations of thousand years of civilization had been uprooted by the moral revenge of the Overseer. The harvests of love, the fruits of labor, and the sweat of centuries were wiped off in a few sunless hours. The foamy fury of the wrathful Sea God stood victorious on the slushy earth for four more days.

The roaring havoc of the deluge, the sound of cracking trees, houses, and hope, the ululations and pitiful prayers, screams for survival, as well as the Jatadhari estuary's wrathful banter for human lives were all silenced. Finishing everything, the deluge, after thirty-six hours of devastation, was perhaps tired, and stood shocked at its own handiwork in waist-deep saltwater in the village road-or whatever was left of it. Before the dawn of Saturday, the thirtieth, the fate of the villages of Haripur district, torn between hope and despair, was already sealed. The night ended and the sun arose, but there was none to see the sun rise. Those few who had survived, for the mall quarters were dark. The scarlet glow of the rising sun appeared like the funeral fire to them.

Does the dawn ever come like this? There was no chirping of birds; the crowing of roosters was also silenced. The shouts of frolicking children were not heard on the village roads. The field-going farmer's song was not heard. The bells on the necks of bullocks were not heard. The baby prattle of the calves was not heard. The tinkling of the anklets of women going to the bathing ghats was silent. The temple bells and the "Allah ho Akbar" of the mosques were not heard. There was no stir in the air, no fragrance of jasmine and champak floated in the morning air. On the whole, there was no earth, no soil. How could men, animals, and trees be there?

Many a cyclone had come in the past. Many trees had been broken and uprooted, but the bamboo bushes and cane bushes always stood stubborn. But this cyclone was so devastating that, in the entire Haripur region the bamboo, cane bushes nor kewra jungles were spared. About ninety percent of the villages in Jagatsingpur district were treeless, birdless, lifeless, and flowerless wastes.

That day's morning could not find a lump of live soil to put her sacred feet on. Therefore, a naïve morning, fearful and dumb, was standing on the rotting flesh of thousands of dead bodies. The 1999 cyclone had blown away villages. All vegetation from the Dhobei and Jatadhari forests had fallen victim to the fury of the cyclone. Except the coconut stumps, the other broken and uprooted trees were beyond recognition. The seawater-swollen corpses were beyond identification. In fact, the entire world was unrecognizable for the survivors here and there.

After one-and-a-half days, the saline tide had withdrawn her guilty feet from the dead bosom of the villages. After the water receded, wherever one looked, one saw only heaps of bodies of men, women, children, animals, and birds. A few concrete buildings stood barren amid the rotten, eye-gouging horror of the earth. And in them were wailing a few lucky people who had unluckily survived, losing home and hearth, golden harvest, and an entire lifetime. Abhayapur was totally decimated by the dreadful tidal waves.

The Gajalaxmi festival was over. The immersion ceremony of goddess Laxmi would have been observed after worship of the soil. But not only the broken earthen icons of the goddess, but the earth herself was immersed in the deluge caused by seawater. Not satisfied by eating golden yellow harvests, backyards full of lush, green vegetables, boxes full of money and jewels, thousands of men, cattle, and houses, the all-consuming saline tide had eaten away even the fertility of the soil before receding.

Like the all-swallowing, vile leaders well-versed in the art of smiling to please others by their complex manipulation of death, life, fame, and infamy, the all-destroying saline tide, showing her fury before innocent humans, had returned to the bosom of the sea baring her naked, foamy teeth. The thrashed and raped earth was lying face down, having lost a world of men, property, vegetation, family, friends, and the aristocracy of inheritance, of values and valuables.

Those who died fighting, they attained salvation. Those who survived not by encountering the cyclone, but out of sheer luck, their suffering was worse than death. Taking shelter in a few strong buildings spared by the deluge, in temples, treetops, and on a few thatched roofs or stuck to the joints of broken trees, the survivors had no food for the last three days. Beaten by the cyclone and winds, lashed by the pounding rain, and stung by despair and the biting cold winds, they were half dead.

Helplessly, they ate whatever they laid their hands on. There was not a drop of drinking water in the wasted villages. They had no hands to collect the falling rainwater to drink because the hands were numb on the tree trunks, bamboo poles, or even buffalo and snake tails. Yet, life was so desirable. The incorrigible hope of survival was irresistible, even knowing well that the days ahead would be despairingly miserable. Man lives for himself. To demonstrate the truth that life is most desirable, destitute had already started their survival ploys as per their capacities. Inspired by self-consolation, not by others' assurances, they had the willpower to await the moment of rescue.

Stars that glow in the night sky fade away in the morning. This is the law of nature. Whatever creatures are born on earth all perish one day or other. This is the law of the world. It may be amazing how so many creatures are born on earth, but it is no surprise how they die. Born on this mortal earth, even angels die. This is always true. There may not be any rebirth when one dies, but die he must. But it was astounding that so many died on the same day in the same manner.

Is it true that all Erasama people who'd died had died in the same manner? It is true that all of them are together lying on the death-bed, but each one of them fought for life in his way and died a death of his own. He alone knows what form of death he saw and how long he fought, expending all his energy. He alone knows. The ferocity of his struggle was writ large on the horror of his death. The faces of the dead, their open eyes, bitten tongues, the swell of their veins, the loosened buns and plaits of women, the sliced- off skin from their muscle, the death throes of their battered bodies, and the postures of their final surrender betrayed all untold stories.

It was obvious that all did not die in the same manner. Each death here was a rare, heroic feat. In someone's fist, a bunch of grass. Someone's legs were entangled in bamboo joints. Another's hair was wound around kewra bushes. Somebody's hair stood on his head in revolt or fear. Someone's eyeballs were out of the socket in his all-out fight against the elements. Someone was buried under a wall. Someone was hanging dead from a tree branch. Someone was lost in the sea. And someone was spread-eagled on a paddy field, like he'd been watering the parched plants.

Someone had fought with the crumbling walls, another with the wind or the cloudbursts. But fight they allhad. All were separated from each other and again were united in the feast of death. Naked, open bodies, open eyes, open mouths, limbs twisted and almost cut off from the body, the death blues on their lips, limbs and bodies painted with their dear village soil and saline slush, strings of worldly humans were lying like orphans after their futile fight with death.

There was no one to assess victory and defeat after the battle was over. But as they were all fighters, they were all victors in the war of life, although dead. Who has the brave heart to call their fighting spirit effete and insult their sublime fight, although all of them were conquered by death? The heartless deluge was still raining tears of repentance over the victims of her own cruelty, thereby intensifying the agony of all.

The sea returns, but fate never does. What fate or future does a dead man have? What's there after death? The sky, earth, air, sea, river, vegetation, sun, and clouds, all of them had conspired a malefic nine-planet constellation. The 1999 cyclone was a spent force after causing the Armageddon. The sea had returned after wiping off the fate line from the brow of man. A slice of the earth was separated from the world in the dance of death.

No roads were there in the villages. Not a single electric pole was erect. The lights were out. Not a lamp was burning anywhere. Without any discrimination or partiality, the deluge had blown out the lamp of life in every house. Not a single house was spared. No fertile land, no ripe harvest, the divine fruit-filled coconut trees were not there. Even the concrete buildings of Ambiki Panchayat were not spared. Only standing, stump-like, were the stunned temple at the head of the village and the graves of the crematory, proclaiming the two eternal truths of God and death.

All our todays and tomorrows become yesterdays, in course of time, and become our pasts, disappearing from memory; the living men become ghosts and spirits. The relationship between man and man becomes the fading shadow of memory. Life, whatever the manner, turns into death. Experienced truths become stark lies. What was here four days ago, who was there, even the eyewitnesses doubted their beliefs! A frozen line was drawn between earth and sky by the tragic end of the merciless deluge. As if there were no villages, houses, trees, life, nothing. There was only an unending stretch of horizon cutting in circles the earth and sky. And within its perimeter, only salt-infested, despondent earth as far as the eyes reach.

Like the cold, bloodless, indelible fate line of a dead man's hand, the detached horizon, deep on the brow of the wasted earth, was manifested, distinguishing the earth from the sky. Except that fate line, there was nothing else on the ill-fated earth. All good fortune and misfortune were equally wiped off the brow of the earth. The foamy hands of the sea wiped off the earth herself. Searching for the earth, one got only cadavers, rotten bodies, and the hateful leftovers of the deluge.

Cut off from the entire world, Erasama was lying unconscious on the exhibition ground of death, begging for respite from misfortune. At that time, the democratic government of a rooted race, the saviors and destiny-makers of the people, safe in the palaces of the capital, were singing, "Give us alms! Give us aid! Save our souls," extending their begging hands before the entire world.

The news spread with lightning speed from one end to the other end of the world. "Half of Odisha is obliterated from the surface of the earth. Jagatsinghpur district is devastated. The Ambiki Panchayat is gone."

Luckily for the government, the villages living with the pride of uncompromising self-esteem were all voided in the cyclone. Otherwise, they would have protested, "O' friend! Safeguard your own prestige! The cyclone has impoverished us, but does that mean it has made beggars of an aristocratic race?"

It was beyond the ken of man to assess the damage caused by the supercyclone. Who could estimate how many died and how many were missing? Relegating that estimate, the government was calculating the amount of aid not in lakhs but crores. Even if thousands of crores poured in as aid, that would not compensate the loss. The three forces: Army, Navy and Air Force were working with self-sacrificing dedication to rescue the victims from inaccessible places. The relief packets were dropped in blind abundance. Many a voluntary organization extended their helping hand.

From the different states of the country, from foreign leaders, charitable organizations, rich and sympathetic people, relief materials were heaped in the capital. The capital and the Erasama block office turned into big markets of food, clothes, medicines, drinking water, and shelter-building materials. The victims thought in amazement, there were so many states in our country! Are there really so many countries in the world? And so many philanthropists and kindhearted persons are there in this world?

In the aftermath of the unprecedented cyclone, the government, instead of being overwhelmed, were confused and worried, not knowing what to do with the aid. Are the victims worthy of receiving such rare commodities in the name of relief? He who extended his ungrudging hand of help to save Odisha from this divine wrath, who was he? Was he the savior of all, God himself? Many unanswerable questions arose in all minds.

People were heard talking, "Relief has come from the moon! Why worry at all? After getting the blessings of the moon deity, the broken waists of electric poles stood up straight. The moon shone from the lampposts. The main roads were cleared for the movement of trucks. The helpless people heard relief had come from the moon. Maybe the chief minister of the moon has sent relief!"

"Who is our chief minister, our charitable, brilliant CM?"

"You don't know who our chief minister is? Fie on you! Our CM is the moon himself!"

"Why do you call the moon our CM? This would insult our deity. He is our life-giver, our destiny-maker!"

"Hey, nowadays, the ministers are the deities! It would not please them if you don't offer flowers, sandal paste, and sweets."

"Therefore, it's the same whether you call the deities ministers or the ministers deities. So, we are honoring the moon deity by calling him minister. He is the life-giver, our savior."

Opening the relief packets and gulping the food, the simple, hungry, cyclone-hit people were praising the moon amid rolling tears. The victory slogans for the moon by the dumb cyclone victims amused the people of the world. Whenever a packet fell down from the sky, the people were bowing to the moon. Some people thought that this was possible because of our religious, stargazing chief minister's merits. Or else where is moon, and where is Erasama?

Sitting in an army van, passing through infernally dark Cuttack city, listening to people on the way, and bowing a thousand times to the moon god, alighted in the Manijanga market the Kargil hero. The road ahead was not motorable. Road closed. It was only eight days after the cyclone. Even if God himself had descended, he could not have eased life so soon after such devastation. Why blame anyone?

The Kargil hero, Bikram Balbantaray, was different from the jawans of the three forces, as he was an integral part of the Erasama soil. He had joined the army eleven years ago. Coming on leave three years ago, he had searched for his lost days spent in his village. When he got the news of the cyclone, he did not believe that not just humans or houses, but entire villages and acres of golden harvests were flattened together, rendering the fertile earth a waste land. The road, without the trees on the sides were bald, while a mountain of broken and uprooted trees was heaped on the roads.

Seeing the corpses lying in grimy clusters, biting the earth, Bikram could not believe that his near and dear ones, known friends and acquaintances, would be alive. He could not muster courage to search for his relatives. Better if they were untraced, at least a false, comforting hope that they should be alive may kindle expectancy. It was not easy to face the cruel truth of searching for them and finding them dead. Bikram had shot many enemies dead on the other side of the border. The sight of strings of dead bodies had given him heroic pride. The strength of a hundred lions had generated in his body, counting the heads of dead enemies. Bikram, for the first time, was dumbfounded seeing the rotting bodies.

In these dead bodies, possibly, might be rotting his parents, brothers, sisters, friends, and who knows how many others! Bikram had already heard that his village was no more. All the people had been swept into the sea except a twelve-year-old boy, Sana. The boy survived by sitting at the top of a tamarind tree, munching for four days raw tamarind stems and leaves. Now he has been rescued and lodged in a tent along with other survivors. Besides Bikram, Sana is the only other future generation of his village. But where is his village?

Yet, Bikram Balbantaray has not given up hope. He is a soldier. He knows that defeat is certain, but giving up hope is not in his horoscope. He is hoping to meet at least a relative, friend, or known person. He would get a slice of his village soil; his own birth soil would be regenerated. As the reddish buds have started faintly smiling on the broken branches of trees, measuring their length on the ground, likewise life would start smiling. If not today, certainly tomorrow, life would smile on this salt-coated earth.

As he is advancing through dead bodies, broken trees, cankerous thorns, and bushes, his sense of despondency increases with every step. Erasama is a fair of dead bodies. Passing through the devastated villages from Manijanga market to Jagannathpur, he felt as though he were inching forward through a quake-hit area. He could not see even a wall standing anywhere.

He did not come across a crow, crane, or a vulture, could not hear the lowing of the cattle. Bodies were spread along roadsides, drains, and fields. Everyone was almost naked. Snatching away their clothes, the cyclone had thrown them helter-skelter. In the fields were lying slushy and shabby petticoats, blouses, bedsheets, and household items.

A pale smoke was rising from all directions. The nauseating smell of burning bodies, along with the rotten smell of bloated bodies in water, added to the bleaching powder sprinkled on them, created a sense of world-weariness. Putting on face masks, gumboots and gloves, the volunteer groups and cremators were burning the bodies feverishly. Groups of army jawans, hordes of volunteers, different religious organizations, and social workers were so enthusiastically busy in burning bodies and nursing the unfortunate survivors that it was difficult to assess that the number of the dead was more than the number of the living.

The dead bodies had no power to assert themselves except to pollute the air. Using hooks, chains, and ropes, the cremators were heaping the bodies, dragging them from water. And, putting tyres and pouring kerosene on the bodies, the cremators were celebrating the festival of fire. Self-satisfaction was proportionate to the number of bodies they burned. Watching this, many a half-burned skeleton flashed a toothy, mocking smile from the ashes. There were no priests or mantras for the moksha of their souls. There was no ritual, no sons or nephews to light the funeral pyre. Instead of sandalwood, ghee, and incense, all were reduced to ashes, burning with useless tyres and kerosene. Finished, lost and gone from form to formlessness.

Hindus, Muslims, upper caste, lower caste, Bangladeshis, and Pakistanis were united in those ashes. It was a socialism of deformed secularism. In the Kurukshetra war, the Pandav and Kuru soldiers as well as sinless commoners must have died like this, embracing each other in the feast of death.

Yesterday, where the golden harvest had swelled from the bosom of the earth, there were mingling in the soil the rotten bodies of men and women. It's the law of nature that mortal bodies would ultimately mingle with the earth. To save the living and cleanse the environment, the first duty of civilized man was to burn the bodies; not out of respect, but fear. The Erasama market was a market of voluntary organizations. The health workers and officers, relief distributors, the police force, army, top-level bureaucrats, journalists, photographers, and the onlookers were raising a din to a deafening pitch.

Relief materials were heaped up on the premises of the block office. Those who had survived the lashing rain and wind, they came wading through slush and chest-deep water, rolling the dead to the sides or stepping on them to the block office to receive a fistful or two of smelly rice. But where would they cook that rice? Where were the utensils? And drinking water? Everywhere there was the stink of death of relatives and unknown humans; in the air, water, sunshine, rain, and the rest of life ahead.

Help was pouring in from the whole world, but the state government was not able to deliver relief from the block office to the affected villages. The people in authority looted the relief materials, while the cynical politicians politicized the cyclone. Relief had created, after the supercyclone, a cyclone of human greed, a deluge of human inhumanity. The victims required shelters over their heads and food for the belly. The other things lost in the deluge could never be compensated, even by God, never mind about government. Who cares for the government?

A rally of hungry men at the block office shouted, "Give me, give me, give, give, give." Bikram was breathless at the pitiful appeals of men. He knew that the cyclone had destroyed houses, but he could not believe that the cyclone had transformed the golden earth into a veritable hell! The farther Bikram moved from the block office, the more his despair intensified. As his legs took him toward Ambiki Panchayat, he became all the more dumbstruck.

Between sky and earth, there was nothing but blank loneliness. Drawing a circle around that loneliness, the destitute horizon was searching for a wholesome world, where some unlettered woman was waiting for the appointed day, drawing lines on the bosom of the sky. On the horizon were only a few denuded stumps of coconut trees that did not have branches or leaves or stems, let alone fruits, raw or ripe! A proud earth was lying forlorn, like a field after the game was over. Only yesterday she had been fertile.

Wherever one looked, one saw only tear-filled, rotten ponds in the houseless villages. On the banks of those putrid ponds, the eyelashes of leaves on the cyclone-ravaged, dying coconut branches were staring at someone in the orphaned quarters. There was no stir in the branches, even when the breeze blew. A few unconscious, emaciated coconut trees standing limp, along with the tearful ponds, were the only indicators that once there had been a village there, houses, and the familiar rhythms of life. No joy of life was wanting in that innocent, rural world.

But today there is no village, no old trees, anthills, kewra jungles, high, aristocratic verandas, palanquins on those verandas, jhoti-painted walls, anything that could have identified the villages. It is now a strange world on which the killer cyclone has created a macabre equity in death, despair, and destruction. In short, standing on an earth which is no more, Bikram Balbantray is searching for his roots, his present, and his future. But he encounters only a past, formless, severed, and dead.

Although he has come with an army unit for relief and rehabilitation work, he cannot be entirely selfless. He is, after all, a man of flesh and blood, whose past, present, and future was in these villages. He had his home, parents, relatives, and friends in this waste of an earth. He was supposed to come last month. Had he come, he could have seen them all. All could have seen him. He could not come due to his ill luck. He could not keep his promise made to his friends.

Now he sees everything has disappeared. He is not fated to see the vibrant life of these villages ever again. His village was the most beautiful in the world, and how dear to him the people of his village had been! He'd been nostalgic of his village even in the tented fields of war, but he had never experienced such soulful intimacy for his village. Everything was priceless to him after losing his inherited bearing. He had never even dreamt of reaching a world of void, searching for his home. No, no, such things never happened, except on the day of judgement, the doomsday!

Maybe Bikram has lost his way. If he finds the way, at least one village, one jhoti-painted wall or one dear soul he would encounter. Forgetting the others, he is searching for his village, arguing to himself that the home deity is first, and then the public deities. Under the open sky, amid the houseless, rotting corpses in the fields, the hero Bikram is standing in despair. He'd thought the sky had a border; that border is the horizon of the earth, the limiting boundary. But human agony is borderless. Whose sorrow is more intense? One whose twenty-two family members have been swept off into the sea, or one who has lost five? Whose filial bereavement is more? One Karna's death for Kunti, or the hundred sons' death for Gandhari? No. No mathematical computation could be made of the loss of children.

Droughts and floods destroy one harvest for some people, but here an entire lifetime's hopes and aspirations have blown away. Even God is not competent to compute the loss and sorrow of the people. This was worse than thoughtless carpet-bombings by the worst enemy. Bikram expected that the people of his village would be wailing when he would reach home. But such calamity makes stones of human beings. Who is there to cry for whom? Maybe the trees and vegetation would have wept over such sorrow of man, but here there are no trees to cry, even for their own decimation.

The ripe stalks of paddy, face down on the muddy fields, were turned into black fodder, along with the stems, in the saline tides. Hundreds of swollen bodies were lying amid that ruin. These festering bodies would enrich the soil, would enrich the future generations. If, by a stroke of good luck, some of the progeny of these dead men were alive, orphaned like him, maybe in the marrow of the new paddy, these would enter their blood.

One day, some son, while tilling the soil, would discover the skeleton of his father, mother, or brother. He won't cry at that time, but would fear. And with a fearful scream, he would run away, leaving behind the plough and bullocks. With palpitating heart, he would go to a sorcerer to exorcise himself, and he would wear a talisman around his left arm. Fie! O' despicable is this human life! Bikram recollected a couplet from Bhaktacharan Das's Manabodha Choutisa,

You look pretty like a painted doll
But tear and see inside how rotten is it all!

How deeply had they seen life, our forefathers! In two lines, they had said the greatest truth of life.

Bikram did not search for roads anymore, as there was no road in sight. What is required to walk; feet or road? Which comes first? Human feet or man-made roads? Roads do not create feet. It is man who fared forward through canker growth, and it became a road. Making roads in the pathless forests, man advanced to know and conquer. Man does not depend on a road to advance in life. This is the indomitable spirit of man. As man does not want to be defeated, he is victorious. And destitute Bikram is on his feet.

Bikram's colleagues were working hard to clear the road for the relief trucks to go to the villages. Bikram moved forward, knowing well that he would not get his village or parents or relatives.

If the sky rains, the estuary-bound river water is sweetened. If the eyes rain, the weight of misery is lessened from a sorrow-bound life. Washing the face with tears, and placing sorrow in its own sanctum sanctorum, like a divine symbol, man again turns toward life and world. Life does not stop stumbling on sorrow. It flows along its course despite all misery.

Bikram was walking along the muddy pathway through paddy fields. The dazed feeling of the deluge was still pervading all quarters. Bikram was reminded of past events. But he understood that the past remains only to cause pain. The memory of the good times of the yesterdays would only intensify agony. The past cannot be wiped off like tonsuring the head for the dead relatives and observing obsequies. The unfortunate leftovers of the cyclone in Erasama would spend the rest of their lives stung by the memories.

Red-hued leaves had started smiling, throwing away their sorrow, on the broken branches of the fallen trees. Although they appeared like new leaves, they were not new leaves, but the same old sorrow-and the tearing red eyes of sorrow.

In the Pachera market, there were no buyers, no vendors, only the clusters of festering bodies rotting like goods gone bad. The stink was suffocating. Bikram had somehow developed a stubbornness to fight the foul smell. He crossed the market, jumping over the bodies. The Dhobei jungle was totally ruined.

Where had the mountain like trees flown away to? As the forest was a wasteland, the Chandan pond of Chandanpur village was clearly visible. In that lily-blossoming pond were floating three lotuses; some loving mother's three beloved children were floating, bloated, in the pond, rotting in the living tears of dead eyes. Stonehearted Bikram's military heart felt like bursting into pieces.

Bikram's feet paused at the Jhulan Mandap. He was overjoyed, thinking that, at last, he had found his dear village-although he knew that, once he found his village, he would be devastated and shattered. Just then, his foot fell on a rotten body. Bursting from the chest of the body, a bone pierced his foot. While removing the bone, crying in pain, Bikram could identify the body by the silver ring on one of the rotten fingers of the corpse. This hand, the ring, the body, and the bone of the rib cage were his loving sister, Bimali's!

The body, luckily, had a blouse on. The lower part of her body was half-buried in the mud. Although there were no crows, vultures, dogs, or jackals to pull out flesh and bones, there was no dearth of thieves to pull out ornaments from the body. Those sinful rascals had pulled out the ornaments from the hand, neck, and nose, injuring those parts of the body. Crueler than the cyclone were those men who had come in a group, in a boat, and had dug out the money and ornaments buried under the floors in the houses of Bharat Mandal and Bhairab Majhi.

Bikram had heard such heartrending stories at Erasama bazaar. Bikram looked at his sister with stoned eyes. The thieves, in a hurry, had left behind the silver ring, as her dead, swollen finger, perhaps, had not eased quick removal. Otherwise, he had no way of identifying her. The seven-day-dead faces were not only unrecognizable, but also horrible to look at. All bodies were stinking masses of horror.

This was his only younger sister, Bimali. How beautiful had been her oil-of-turmeric-polished, aromatic body and face, how fragrant her bun, like a champak in full bloom-and the Kewra-scented, pan-red lips! As charming as a black bee on a sunflower petal was the mole on her fair left cheek. Today, all those things were damn, rotten lies, as if ink had fallen on a beautiful painting! Alas! How unwanted lay his loving sister, Bimali!

He could not cry, holding her. The body was too far gone. He could not even think of burning her body, picking it out of the scattered dead. He stood motionless for a while, not knowing what to do.

Bikram now turned to find his concrete house. The brick and mortar of that building had been purchased with hard-earned, honest money. Somebody pointed the house out to Bikram. Going ahead, he saw a concrete building leaning to one side. Under it had taken shelter Bikram's father, mother, and some other villagers. Bimali had come out to buy some biscuits for her one-and-a-half-year-old son. At that time, the roof had given way. Bimali had been saved from that disaster. But the tidal waves had thrown her dead body into the fields. Bikram heard everything from the same man. Many such deaths had become stories and legends, which eyewitnesses narrated and people listened to eagerly.

Hunger in the belly is man's worst enemy. When the belly is full, the other enemy is the hunger of the mind. The deluge-dazed bellies of people now are hungry. Bikram too was hungry. He saw smoke rising at a distance. Abhayapur was only three kilometers away from Chandanpur. In between was a large kewra jungle, nothing else. But smoke rising meant there were houses. Maybe there were a few lucky survivors. Udhab Mangual's was a well-to-do house. Strong walls, high veranda. Had all of them survived? Maybe rice and fish were being cooked.

The roof was not visible, but the smoke can be seen. Hope flickered in Bikram's mind. He rushed toward it, not caring if there was a path. He thought whoever's house it may be, even in Bharjan Mallick's house, if rice was being cooked, he would put a leaf on the floor and eat. Then, tightening his belt with the other jawans, he would busy himself in cleaning the roads, burning the bodies, and serving the victims. He would forget that he had a past in this village. There is no better good fortune than forgetfulness in such times.

But is man so fortunate that, like spit cleaning the chalk letters on the slate, he can wipe off the past from the tablet of his memory? The mind is like a stone wall on which is carved, with chisel and hammer, the story of happy days. A story that is not easily forgotten. The broken stones falling off the Konark Temple do stare at you unblinkingly with the carved art of eight hundred years ago. Likewise, memory of life's experiences stay fixed and undamaged in the broken pieces of ruined life. In course of time, it stops bleeding, but the blood never dries up. It's only man who lives enmeshed in his memories.

Man never loses the I in him, his superego, even after losing everything, hence he creates an illusion of a personal world, claiming all that he sees and feels as his own. That illusion sustains him through all his agony, and it also kills him. People were saying that all the twenty-eight members of Udhab Mangual's family had been wiped out by the cyclone. Only Sankha was luckily spared. He was like a madman, searching for the bodies of his wife and children. He also ate in the relief food centers. After getting some rice in the belly, shouting, "My son, my daughter," he jumped into Hansua River while everyone was looking at him, dumbstruck, and was swept away by the strong current.

Is this not maya? Could he get his children? Then why did he jump?

TWENTY THREE

All the unfortunate men and women, who, having lost their children and dear ones, survived the wrath of nature, ate amid the piled-up bodies around, ate free food at the relief centers, and fought for relief materials despite the unperformed obsequies. When the whole sky falls on your head, you do not bother about the thunder falling on your head. As there is a slice of earth under your feet, you do not commit suicide, despite the sky falling on you. Rather, you harden yourself to survive and brave all dangers. On the contrary, you jump into the midst of danger with greater resolve to live.

On the other side of the Jatadhari estuary, the sea was quite restless, whereas the horizon was quiet and unmoving. There was not even an iota of difference between the pre- and post-deluge horizon. Rather, because of the void created by flattened houses, villages, and vegetation, the vast spread of the horizon was manifesting its true infiniteness in deep measures.

Bikram immediately cast off his I and discovered within himself that he had become one with the universal agony. He was freed visibly from a strange kind of stasis, and it was as if the doors of the boundless and immeasurable vastness were being opened up for him. Unconsciously, Bikram's mind lapsed into a meditative mood. Inside his mind the worries, anxieties, agony, and emotions over the past calmed down. In a wondrous light, beyond the ken of the mortal eyes, his whole universe was resplendent. In that light, he could read a line of poetry in his heart, "Life is a flow, like river Hansua, which does not dry up even after falling into the estuary. After reaching its destination, it continues flowing to merge in infinity."

In the mustard-scented breeze, where the aroma of the sweet, ripening paddy ought to have been dancing, there from the wasted plots a nauseating, rotten, fishy smell was pervading the air. Added to that, the stink of sorrow and despair had so thickened the air that it was suffocating. The sweet-smelling blood of men who'd enchanted the living for a lifetime smelled foul to the life-loving people the moment their vital breath ceased. They tended to vomit, tearing their throats, and also evince hate.

Mandodari did not know this earlier. The heart was no more willing to even touch the near and dear ones whom they embraced with love just last morning. The call of the soul was not forthcoming. Therefore, seeing the bodies of the relatives, the rest who were alive sat like wood and stone. But Mandodari, hoping against hope, was searching for her three children and husband. Although she knew that she would not have the good fortune of meeting them alive, her woman's heart prompted her to think that, maybe, they were stuck somewhere after floating for some time. Maybe a bit of life is still there. Many people have escaped the jaws of death.

If her luck is sturdy, maybe her children too. To think beyond that, Mandodari is not able to fortify her heart. Her husband, Utkalmani Mandal, has become a deified man and must have got his place in heaven. Why should she search for him? But her daughter Sundari, sons Jagan and Balia? Are they rotting in hell?

The light festival of the full moon night was far away, but here at midday, the cremation fire festival was going on. How her full house of yesterday had become a barren void, how her children and husband had been swallowed by hungry tides. Mandodari remembered everything. And that memory was scouring her heart. Her blooming garden village, her heroic husband, and her three children, more valuable than pearl, emerald, and diamond-disappeared like burst bubbles.

Poor Mandodari has become bone-tired, moving through swampy fields, searching for them the whole week. On top of that, this blasted hunger. A woman losing her children and husband for nothing also gets hungry. What worse irony of fate is there than this? Tired and almost dead, Mandodari is sitting in a strange world where there is not a single unbroken tree; no branch extends to the sky the loving offering of fruits and flowers. Her clothes are torn to shreds.

The body and limbs have cramps. The demonic hunger in the belly makes Mandodari oblivious of her sorrow. She is pulled toward the relief center. Yet she pauses, and thinks. Is she a daughter of a beggar's family that she would stretch her hands to beg for food? Her feet do not move.

A middle-aged man asks, shivering, "Are you going to the relief center? Do not delay. Here all are destitute. The relief officers also eat there, despite the stink of the dead bodies. If you delay, you may not get anything."

Hesitating, Mandodari says, "I have to go. This blasted hunger has no caste, no prestige. Here, the haves and have-nots are lining up to eat. The cyclone has reduced everyone to the level of beggars and relief eaters. What shame anymore?"

Mandodari starts walking again.

The feverish man says from behind, "Get a fistful for me. When food goes into the belly and the fever subsides, together we would search for your children. All of my family found the grave pressed under the brick wall. On the day of the cyclone, I went to Manijanga to receive the ritual gift of a dying old man. When returning, I fell in the mouth of the storm. God saved my life. But going home, I heard that my world had been finished. Now the only worldly worry left is to drag this body and live.

"My sons did not worship the deities, although they were Brahmins. Therefore, they operated prawn farms, earned good money too, built a brick house. While going to receive the gift, I thought they were safe; the cyclone may take my life on the way.

But such is my fate, that this old man survived, and they were all wiped out." Tremors and sobs together made the old man breathless.

Mandodari said, "What kind of greedy man are you, gosain? Even on the day of the cyclone, leaving your children, you went to collect gifts at such a long distance?"

Hiding his face in his knees, the gosain said, "You could not recognize me, Mandal family's daughter-in-law! I am Danakarna Mishra of Bandana village."

Mandodari ran like the wind to the relief center. Danakarna Mishra hated himself. He thought of how silly man is, that he thinks of a Brahmin as a deity, that after such a devastation he still thinks that God exists. The Brahmins are of a higher caste, and their blessings come true! The gosain who could not bless his own children, she, falling at his feet, asks for his blessing to get back her children from the other world? O' what a helpless creature man is!

And this helplessness of man is being exploited in so many ways by the masters, kings, politicians, priests, astrologers, tantrics, and faith healer cheats. Danakarna Mishra is one of those cheats. Today, when everything has been proved false, this simple woman has not realized? Poor woman! With what faith she has run to get food for him! Let her go get food for him, and let Danakarna Mishra's life be saved. But he cannot bring back the lost children of this mad woman.

Is Danakarna Mishra any less helpless? He is more helpless than this fisherwoman. Poor woman, how dearly she has reposed faith in lies. Danakarna Mishra has been adding poison to the simple faith of these people by giving them false hopes.

While bringing hot khichdi tied in her saree, Mandodari ate a part of it, stung by hunger. When the fire of hunger was doused, the fire of her children's sorrow started burning in her entrails. Alas! Had they survived the cyclone, her children too would have eaten the goodies. The kindhearted donors are distributing so many things: bread, rice flakes, jaggery, paratha, and steaming hot khichdi! Like their father, her children were very fond of khichdi. The youngest son pined for a piece of bread. As the children of well-to-do families are fond of food, her eldest son had been very fond of rice flakes and jaggery.

Oh! At least they should have survived for a few more days. They could have died after eating good food! Mandodari is shocked by her own thoughts. Foul mouthed, ill-mannered! Are you a mother or a witch?

When Mandodari stood near the gosain, he anxiously stretched his weak, palsied hands, and said, "Give me, give me! O' this hunger is unbearable. Why did you delay so much? I would really die if you delay further."

Seeing Gosain's hungry face, stretched hands, and reading the appeal in his eyes, Mandodari came back to her senses, and she felt faint. She has eaten a portion of the khichdi on the way, as she was famished. How can she feed her leftover food to the priest, being a fisherwoman? Her children would be cursed. Would she earn more demerit and sin? And here, if she does not give him the khichdi, and he dies, then she would be guilty of Brahmin murder! One way or the other, she would be committing a sin. Poor woman. She could not decide what to do.

But seeing the famished condition of the priest, her woman's heart rankled inside. In a sobbing voice, she said, "O' Gosain! I am a fisherwoman. Losing my senses due to hunger, I have eaten a portion of the food. How can I serve my leftover food to your holiness? I am a bad sinner, Gosain, please tell me what to do."

Danakarna Mishra, in a more appealing voice, said, "You are a fisherwoman by birth, but being born in a Brahmin family, I am a low caste person by my deeds. You do not know what sins I have committed. My sins are tearing me apart. And with that, this demonic hunger has made me forget caste and creed. Give, give me that khichdi. Let me survive. Then I would tell you all. Before I die, I would confess all my sins before you. You are Mother, goddess Laxmi, the giver of food. You are a Devi, Mother Sarala. I am your hungry son. Would you not save my life? I am a chandal. I would tell you, tell all. First of all, give me something to eat, my mother."

Mandodari was moved by the distressed words of Mishra. Forgetting sin and merit, she spread her saree before the gosain. From Mandodari's dirty, mud-stained, fishy, and tear-soaked saree, the priest ate with a clear conscience the leftover khichdi as if he were eating temple prasad. Mandodari had never felt such fullness in her belly from feeding a hungry man who was not her child or husband. She could have given, raising her hands, had there been even some surplus in her world of wants.

Alas! Had she brought some more khichdi, the gosain could have eaten with relish to the full. Tomorrow, she would bring separately for the gosain. The gosain could have eaten a bit more. He did not leave behind even a grain of rice!

By the time the fire of the belly was doused, the blasted rigor attacked his uncovered body. The rain-washed cold wind was attacking his body. Shivering, the gosain said, "I have no merit left in me to bless you my child. You have saved the life of a sinning chandal by feeding him. I am reaping the harvest of my sins. My sins would not be purged only with this suffering. I have to rot in hell, my child! Yes, this is hell. Is Erasama anymore the world of man? He who dies, he attains salvation. I am alive to suffer hell. What I have done, even the chandals would never do. O' God!"

Mandodari could not know whether the gosain was shivering out of fever or from heartrending sorrow and regret, hiding his unwashed face in his knees. She was upset for the gosain. In a soft voice, she asked, "What crime have you committed, Gosain? You are not a man even to hurt a fly. What sin have you committed? Everything has been done by the Maker-this cyclone, the tidal waves, this massacre of man. How could you have stopped all this, Gosain? What is the way out for man when God punishes?"

"Man! Man is no more human, O' Mandal's daughter-in-law. I have myself become inhuman, although such a staunch Brahmin. Tell me, whose sanity has not been blown away by this cyclone? Listen to my story. My sin would be lessened if I confess.

"I discovered myself on a branch of a broken tree when the

cyclone subsided. The tree had fallen half in water and half on land. The rain was lashing from above. The body was getting numb." Saying this much, the gosain shivered more vigorously. He could not speak.

Stretching her hand toward the bundle of the gosain, Mandodari said, "There may be some dry towel or dhoti in that bundle. Let me cover your body with that. Let the rigor calm down, and then you would speak whatever you wanted to."

Gosain pulled out the bundle from Mandodari's hand. Shaking all over, he said, "Do not open that bundle, you Mandal's daughter-in-law! If you hear what I have done, you would not call me anything but the devil. That day, climbing down from the tree, I denuded a young woman lying in the field. This mind of man at times loses its sanity. What I did at the prompting of my body that day, damned be my life."

"O' fie! The body's demands at this old age? What-what did you do, Gosain? Do not say any more." There was reprimand in her voice.

"You listen, Mandal's daughter-in-law. Let me unburden my heart. Half dead by this rigor, cold wind, and pounding rain, that day I disrobed a dead young woman's body and made her entirely naked. With that saree, I covered myself. Thereafter, without looking back, I walked forward. I did not see the naked, dead body of that woman. I am speaking the truth.

"But now I feel that, although this old Brahmin has not seen the nude body, these fake young social worker groups must be looking at her. Alas, what a beautiful, shining face she had! Her long tresses were spread over the field like the waves of the sea. A gold stud was dazzling on her nose. A little distance away, two young lads were lying dead, clasping each other. Perhaps they had taken shelter on a tree, and when the tree was uprooted, they floated into the field. A bit of the saree of the woman was in a death grip in one of the boys' hands. Maybe they were brothers and sister."

"What? What did you say, Gosain? Luxuriant tresses, a gold fly on the nose, and two young boys?" Like mad, Mandodari tore open the bundle and pulled out of it a red cotton saree with black stripes. Then, clasping the saree on her chest wailed, "Sundari, Sundari! Oh, my darling queen! O' my love! Where have you gone? Where did you go, my Jagan, Balia? Why did not the god of death take me instead?"

Then she suddenly calmed down, as if water had doused the fire, and, looking like a demoness, said, "Chandal! You have denuded my daughter. God would never spare you. You would die of cholera. Your clan would be lost, you devil. No one would live to offer you water at the time of death, you heartless gosain."

Shivering viciously, Mishra fell down on the ground. The boy who was watching this drama in a state of shock had never been looked at charitably by Mishra all his life because he was that rogue Sakula Mohanty, whose main source of income was blackmail. Taking pictures of young women clandestinely, he used to blackmail them. Everyone knew that he had raped and killed a girl working in a voluntary organization and thrown the body into the river. His father, Tahali Mohanty, had bribed the police to suppress the crime of his son.

The same Sakula Mohanty was saying, "O' Gosain" and holding the weak body of Danakarna Mishra, almost burning with high fever. By that time, Mishra's teeth had locked and his mouth had gone limp. When Sakula Mohanty thought of giving a few drops of water in his mouth, there was no water worth giving anywhere near, nor was the gosain alive. The bird of his soul had flown away from the rain-battered, burning body. The gosain had no more hunger, thirst, pain, or sorrow.

Sakula Mohanty had not cried seeing so many dead bodies, but seeing the death of the gosain, the boy's eyes welled up with tears. Bowing at the cold feet of the gosain, he shed a few drops of hot tears. When he looked up, he saw Bikram Balabantaray standing there with a few photojournalists. Bikram was cross-examining them. Sakula ran and embraced Bikram Balabantaray.

Ecstatic, in joy, he said, "All would have been so happy knowing you are alive. They are no more alive. What has happened to our sacred villages, brother?"

Bikram tightly held Sakula's palms and caressed them with a sincere touch. He had no words to speak. Looking at the dead body of the gosain, Sakula said, "How to cremate the gosain's body? After all, he was the priest of our village."

Bikram said noncommittally, "The earth cremates all. For the earth, there is no distinction between Brahmin, Dalit, Muslim, money lender, or sharecropper. To understand this, are you waiting for a more devastating cyclone? Gosain would be cremated like the others. Civil, military, government, and non-government organizations are busy burning bodies. Let us concentrate on the living more than the dead. Otherwise, they too would turn into corpses.

I just saw Kundala Panda's body. The sea has thrown him into the kewra jungle. He is bloated like an elephant, beyond recognition. His son Panchuki is alive, his nephews are alive, and son-in-law is also alive. Who cremated his body? Everyone is now caught by the relief storm. I told Panchuki Panda about his father's cremation. Do you know what he said? 'I would do the obsequies if I am alive. The relief materials are being looted on the way. If you do not go personally, you do not get a fistful of rice.

'The capable are taking things in various ways. This year, there is no chance of any sheafs of paddy coming to the threshing floors. If we, who are alive, do not save rice and dal for the future, we too would die eventually. Moreover, government has taken up the work of burning bodies. Why should we lift up the rotten bodies? Father dying this way pains me, yes. It's very painful. But who asked father to go to charm the sea? Did he listen to anyone?' Of course, Panchuki Gosain shed a few drops of tears for his father. What more could he have done? And, in fact, it is now beyond us to cremate so many rotten bodies. The Ananda Margis are doing this work sincerely."

Shocking Bikram, Sakula Mohanty ran to the cameramen standing there, screaming, "Are you humans or devils? Do you not have mothers and sisters at home? You are taking pictures of the naked dead bodies of our womenfolk? Selling these pictures, you would earn money? What do you think? The people of these villages are now destitute? Therefore, they would keep quiet even if you insult their womenfolk?

"As long as one young man is alive here, you won't be allowed to do that. You think all are dead, and you can do whatever you wish and publish any rubbish you wish? Why, the Kargil hero Bikram is alive, I am alive, and many more are alive in these villages. We are alive to safeguard the prestige of this area. You leave this place, I say."

Sakula was chasing away the journalists like a rabid dog. Bikram thought, "It was perhaps easy to hate this boy when he was living like a characterless debauch. The boy has a soul now."

Man turns into a ghost after death, but when man's past, present, and future die, he becomes a living ghost. Udhab Mangual, perhaps, had fallen into the ditch of death for thousands of years. No one was able to locate his body; therefore, his name was not in the list of the dead. Many like him had not been identified, and hence were not listed as dead. Udhab's soul did not want to be identified. He wanted his friends' bodies; Golmasta, Banchu Tarai, Bharat Mandal, Bhairab Majhi, Gandhi Das, Kundala Panda, Magan Bhoi, et.al., to be identified and cremated together.

The people who could not embrace each other while alive because of the caste-religion divide, let them turn to ashes together, united in death. But in the competition to burn the bodies, who could have identified anyone, lifting the shroud from the face?

Udhab did not remember how long ago he'd been a ghost. Did not remember who had killed him; man, God, or the devil? He only remembered the bloody massacre of the ninety-nine-hand sword of Kalki. Udhab hummed, thinking that he has survived. Who can kill who the Almighty saves?

Then his ghost laughed hysterically. Huh, if the Almighty saves, how can the powerful kill? The Almighty is the most powerful. He saves, He kills. When the creature entangled in the net of illusion falls into the hand of the powerful, he surrenders to the Almighty. And when he gets the protection of the Almighty, he thinks of himself as very powerful. Swelling his chest with pride, he says, "I fought, survived, and saved the world."

As Udhab had turned into a ghost, he did not wail seeing such a great cyclone. Rather, he thought, well served. It serves man now that Kaliyug has been ended. Toward the end, Kaliyug was riotous and wild. It did not care for values or authority. Every day murder, loot, corruption, prostitution, rape, and whatnot-all has happened in the single life of Udhab Mangual. When milk boils over, it enters the hearth. When man grows violent and wild, he enters the ditch. And when time gets disjointed, it enters into the maws of eternity. If eternity does not swallow this arrogant, violent, self-centered, greedy and wild Kaliyug, another Satyayug would never be born.

But where? Where is Udhab Mangual's Satyayug? Where are the seeds of Satyayug, his children and grandchildren? He had shaped them as the seeds for Satyayug; truthful, honest, dutiful, and patriotic. Udhab's ghost from the ditch gave an earth-shattering cry, and first called out the names of his sons. Maybe they are lying unconscious among the dead bodies! Listening to father's loving call, they would respond by saying "Father!" definitely. They are children. Why should they die?

Udhab called out the name of his youngest son. "Benudhar! Benu! Benua! O' Sankha, Chakra, Gada, Padma, Bhagyaaaa!"

Udhab's ghost became quiet. Udhab again called out his darling daughter Girima's name. "Girima! Girima. Girima, Ma, Ma, Maaaa!" His call mingled in the calls of, "Mother!" coming from all directions, shouted by orphaned children. The head of the ghost turned. Udhab's ghost could not remember now any name or village of anyone. Transformation of life makes one forget the names and addresses, tied up to the new bloodline. If one is not born again as a jatismara, a person having memory of past lives intact, a father cannot even recognize the face of the son.

Udhab's condition was worse than that. But Satyayug? His boat, Satyayug, cannot perish! Udhab cannot forget Satyayug! He has spent his entire Kaliyug in diligently makingSatyayug!

It is said the perseverance of one lifetime becomes the culture in the next birth. How could he forget Satyayug? Sons, grandchildren, family, and clan were dead and lost in the deluge.

Not only his, but everyone's. But if Satyayug was also dead and lost, what was the significance of this deluge? God creates the deluge only for the dawn of Satyayug. If Satyayug is destroyed, then he would not have the hand or strength and the present life to build another Satyayug.

The ghost arose from the ditch of death, muddy and slushy. He remembered that someone had handed him over a boat and oar. In a state of frenzy, he had fished him out of water and placed him at the high ground where the buffalos rest. Then the gale had snatched away the boat from his hands. The tidal waves, spinning the boat seven times, had thrown it into a pit. While being swept away, Udhab Mangual had fallen into a death hole and died.

After who knows how many days, his ghost rose from the death hole and ran to search for the Satyayug. While running, he met the heartbreaking sorrows of his mortal life. Jumping like newborn babes only yesterday, his three grandchildren were floating in the rotten water. The emaciated children were bloated up. Their doting mothers and grandma, at first, would have been very happy seeing their children well-fed and fat, and then they would have started wailing. Then they would have died of shock.

Good, very good that none of them were alive to see these things. Udhabhad not had any time when they'd been alive to clasp the frolicking children to his chest and playfully kiss them. Today, there was no way to go to the river or seaside, leaving his bloated and dead grandchildren. No boat, no prop, nothing. No work, no life or living. Udhab could not show his love to the bodies of his grandchildren before the sea pulled them to its belly.

Udhab's ghost gazed at his floating children, focused attention on Padma's son, Kapila, and released slushy tears from his dead eyes. Udhab's wife's striped, pitcher-bordered saree was hanging down from a branch of a palm tree. How could the poor woman reach the top of the palm tree with her elephantine legs?

The British came here to loot wealth, silk, and fineries. They looted the wealth of this region to their heart's content. After the country became free, the leaders, officers, contractors, and businessmen had looted, each in his own way, the wealth, greenery, jungle, and the sea. In many ways, they had denuded this region.

This time, the cyclone had looted the vegetation and wealth and had made this part of the world an empty shell. Of course, thousands of hands had been proffered to help the victims here: food, clothes, blankets, polythene, medicines. But who could restore this soil to its pristine health? Where from would come the endless, unfading clothes of vegetation to cover the shame of this naked earth? What sin had Udhab committed that, even after becoming a ghost, he sees the naked earth and the naked women?

Tears don't flow from his ghost eyes anymore-thank God! Or else another sea of tears would have swept away these ghosts of villages and the dead bodies. It would have served well! But his eyes are dead. The eyeballs are still. The heart is a piece of wood, the mind a stone. Is it the good fortune or misfortune of Udhab's ghost that he was able to identify and recognize the bodies of his loved ones, here and there?

Golmasta, Bhairab Majhi, Bharat Mandal, Banchu Tarai, and Kundala Panda had lost their lives in their own ways. They were festering in the fields. Banchu Tarai had died clinging onto a wooden box. Inside it were documents and land deeds. Kundala Panda's hand was stuck to the divine water pot. Bharat Mandal was open fisted all his life; he had fallen on all fours on the river sand with his palms open. People were saying, when he saw his son's boat pull into the Jatadhari estuary, he had left the oars of his boat. Bhairab Majhi was lying face down on a tin box supposedly containing money and gold. But the box had been empty.

This time, he cried earnestly for a long time, and then challenged the roaring waves of the Bay of Bengal, visible beyond the Jatadhari estuary. "O' Sea! What do you think of yourself? Stronger than the earth, superior to the earth? Ha, ha! You yourself have spread your body, leaning on the earth! Don't you know that the foundation of the earth is at the bottom of the seven seas? You haven't gauged the strength of the earth. If the earth wishes, it would lift you up and sprinkle you on the vast expanse of the universe like cow dung water at one go, and it would raise towering mountains in your place.

"However mightily you may hiss and fume, you cannot swallow the earth. You cannot destroy the earth, for the earth is fortified by human hopes. The earth feeds and strengthens man, and man empowers the earth. Such is the unbroken bond between earth and man. Today, where the saline water has made the earth infertile, there fertile soil will regenerate on the breast of this hoary earth. The harvest that went rotten, the corpses which spread foul smell, the same would enrich the new earth. The earth would be more fertile. You would waste your energy like this from time to time and watch with unblinking eyes how the rejuvenated earth would burst into new harvests. The sky may be miserly for man, but the earth is not. She is always reborn for human sustenance."

Udhab's ghost did not give up. Before his eyes were heaped up like a hill the mighty, uprooted trees. If the other ghosts like him joined together, they could build hundreds of boats and rafts. The ghost hummed lines from the Bhagabat, "Studying each elemental character, I have straightened the oar."

Thereafter, the ghost, with a thudding jump, disappeared into the heap of the broken trees.

Udhab Mangual's journey to salvation had started from hell. It was not possible to compute how long he was tortured in that darkness of the hellhole because, after he shrugged off his mortal life and fell into hell, all sense of time, star, and arithmetic were lost to his memory.

Udhab Mangual had lived long, but could realize the meaning of life only at death, and he started appreciating and loving the rare privilege of being born human. He loved the entire universe. He was convinced that no one and nothing was evil in God's creation. He therefore accepted his rebirth as his salvation and wished to love the world afresh.

In his whole life, he had never laid foot in Lavanipur village. That village was forbidden territory for him. Of course, this ban order had not been imposed on him by others, it had been the decision of his own conscience. The village where a woman named Hema, although a new-moon born, was living happily with her husband and children, it was beyond dignity for the man who silently doted on her to cast his shadow there.

But now, in the world of Erasama, there were no villages, no habitation. There were more dead bodies than living. The few who had survived were not only destitute in terms of family, but also had drowned their intelligence and judgement in hunger, sorrow, and bereavement. Since Udhab was a ghost, he was not obliged to obey his conscience. Hence, he wandered into the village with Hema's fragrance, hoping to find a piece of earth instead of a sea of dead bodies. He remembered that, with her bangles and vermillion mark intact, Hema had gone to the other world to the accompaniment of the drums meant for an unwidowed woman. As Hema's brother had died untimely of an undiagnosed disease, her husband was living in Lavanipur as captive son-in-law with his family. He was the only hope of his brother-in-law's widow and their five children.

Forsaking his own fate, somehow or other, Udhab thought that maybe, by chance, someone or other of Hema's children, husband, and relations might have survived. The world knew that, in the '99 cyclone, Abhayapur, Chandanpur, and Lavanipur of the Ambiki Panchayat had been obliterated. Udhab's ghost had moved around Abhayapur, Chandanpur, and had seen them all-lost and void. Now Udhab had no house or family, and Udhab himself was not there, so to speak. But that didn't mean that others must be destitute in the world. He would not get back what he had lost, but he cannot wish the same fate for others.

Udhab knew that Hema's bangles were strong and resistant to widowhood, but her diseased husband was not fit for anything. Could he have saved his wife, children, and dependents from the fury of the cyclone? It's doubtful whether he could have saved himself. Does Udhab Mangual have no responsibility for the lost world of Hema? If somebody does not stand by a person when he is in difficulty, all his good deeds not withstanding, he cannot be counted as your own.

Like a speck of dust on the seashore, Lavanipur is a tip of land in Erasama. Even that tip of a village was not there. The soil of Lavanipur had turned into a crematory. And in that, the corpses had begun to putrefy. The known faces were poised on the verge of oblivion. Udhab knew many people of this village. But he had never seen Hema face to face. For that, the ghost stood unmoving like wood. Where? Where are they all? Has Hema's entire family gone under the sea?

A few days ago, man had been pursuing his fate in sea, water, paddy, fish, and betel leaves. Today, the few who had survived were searching for misfortune. What worse misfortune was there than searching for their own, turning and staring at the festered bodies? If the faces of the relatives were identified, instead of the joy of discovery, the anguish of loss suffocated the survivors.

Some half-witted woman, staring at the bodies, was calling out the names of her sons and daughters in a voice that echoed up to the horizon. But there was no response from her children. The mad woman's call was echoing, and she was wailing so heartrendingly that Udhab's stone heart too was bursting. O' what is this human tie? What maya is this? Although the human soul is unattached, like a glowing drop of water on a lotus leaf, man's mind is too attached to be indifferent. Let this madwoman go on searching for her children like this; let her not find them, that's better. She would find only their rotten bodies, if at all, and then what?

A short distance away, another shadowy figure was searching for misfortune among the dead, and he was standing helplessly, ruing his failure. Udhab gazed at the shadow, going nearer, and saw that he was the cursed husband of Hema, Mandar Behera. This man had never been a rival of Udhab, nor was his enemy. As he was a retarded, incompetent fellow, no one had been willing to give his daughter to him in marriage. But the family needed a woman to do the household chores. Therefore, his uncle and aunt had given the burden of a new-moon born woman to the father-less orphan.

This naïve man didn't even know that one Udhab Mangual, a hefty male from Abhayapur, had fished out of the Hansua water the reflected image of his wife Hema, and, making a statue of her in his heart, would worship it all his life. This tolerant husband of Hema was such a simpleton that he couldn't have nursed any grudge, had he known about Udhab's love for his wife.

At the end of the road of life, Udhab has come to perceive that arrogance, irrational jealousy, and stubborn obsessions alienate man from man, making him lonely. Man suffers untold agony shutting himself up in his own dark dungeon. Had Udhab opened up the doors and windows of his mind and purged himself of his dark jealousy, he could have had a true friend like the faithful husband of Hema. At least he could have cried himself to a calm solace, holding Hema's husband to his heart. Can Udhab not cry his heart out, clasping this guileless man to his chest? Can somebody refuse a drop of ambrosia offered by another at one's dying moment? Does it not compensate the fire and brimstone of a lifetime?

Udhab's ghost stood before the skeletal frame of Hema's husband like an indifferent shadow. The man didn't flinch at the sight of the ghost. Because he alone could recognize this Mangual from Abhayapur, he felt somewhat reassured. Looking at the dried-up face of Udhab with unblinking eyes, he said in a choking voice, "Udhab bhai, had H-H-Hema been alive, such a blighted curse wouldn't have befallen this village. The deluge gushed in because a pure, auspicious woman like Hema left this village. None of my children are spared. Hema had said at the time of her death, 'My children are now in your hands. You'll forget my death, looking at their faces.' You tell me, brother, looking at what shall I forget her loss? Hema loved the entire earth. In this Hema-less earth, where is life anywhere that man would live? See how the saline water has made this earth dark coal? The earth is also dead, Udhab bhai."

Udhab's ghost came to his senses. He was not searching for the dead bodies of Hema's children. He was searching for the soil-a fistful of live earth-in which he could see his thousand births.

But where is the earth in these once green-robed villages? Is this earth really dead?

In the patchy darkness of the fading evening, seeing two dark shadows among the corpses, a few volunteers were heard shouting, "Ghost! Ghost!" Udhab's ghost, pulling the hands of Hema's husband, started running. Yes! When you turn into ghosts, you would find living men and live earth. The rest who pose as good souls for the photographers and indulge in the relief gimmick, they can only find the dead and the inert and receive accolades.

The two shadows merged into the darkness. In the widening hour of the night was heard a tapping sound coming from the ruined forests, a sound that caused the mortal fear of thousands of unpurged souls in the hearts of the living dead. Maybe, in this domain of the ghosts and goblins, more devastations were gushing in! If the wind whistled, fear. If the wind is stilled, fear. The survivors in all villages, including Abhayapur, had only fear and more fear. Would the rest of their lives be victims of fear?

TWENTY FOUR

Bharjan Mallick was returning, taking slow steps, after tying up a packet of food collected from the Free Relief kitchen. Where would he go? No home, no village, no wife or children. So much khichdi is being distributed, but he has none of his own to eat it with. The pathetic cry of his two little boys-"Father, Father!"-rankles his heart. After getting the food, the death of his little ones pains him even more. It was not death, but murder. Being a father, he has killed his own children. None but he himself knows that he was the murderer of his two sons.

Even during the desperation of the cyclone, trumpets of his praise were heard, for he had released his two sons from his shoulders in order to save the son of Panchuki Gosain. Whoever heard of his sacrifice lavished praise on Bharjan. Panchuki Gosain had given up hope for his son, Debu. He'd been almost insane, not finding his son even three days after the cyclone subsided. Kundala Panda's body had stuck to the kewra jungle-but instead of making arrangements for the cremation of his father's rotting body, Panchuki Gosain was searching for his son.

The day Bharjan had returned from the other side of life, with Debu on his shoulders, that day, before embracing his son with joy, Panchuki Gosain had embraced Bharjan. He'd even been prepared to touch Bharjan's feet when he'd heard that, to save his son, Bharjan had sacrificed his own sons to the sea

Bharjan had stopped Panchuki Gosain crying, "No! No."

Shedding profuse tears, Panchuki had said, "In which birth what were you to me, Bharjan! For that, you did such a great thing! You are an angel of this area, although born in a low caste family. There is no other selfless man in this region like you. Does anyone make such a great sacrifice for another's son? How could you sacrifice your own children? I couldn't have done that. I would have saved my son, offering the others' children to the sea. Your name would be recorded in the history of Erasama.

"The history of the '99 cyclone would not be complete without the story of Bharjan Mallick's courage and sacrifice. What can I ever give you to repay your debt? Today, all are destitute. Everyone is homeless. This Brahmin is fated to be your debtor all his life. O' Bharjan, I bless you to be born again in our village as Bharjan Mallick, and be my sharecropper. I would be born as Panchuki Panda again only to repay your debt. This relationship would be unbroken, life after life. Maybe in the next birth I may be free of your debt. In this life, I declare myself as your debtor. You have saved my clan. You are no man, but an angel."

That day, the joyous blessings of Kundala Panda's firstborn, Panchuki Panda, on the rebirth of his only son, Debashis, fell like a curse in Bharjan's ears. Why should Bharjan be born as a sharecropper of the Pandas, life after life? If there was any merit in his sacrifice of his own sons to save another's son, why shouldn't he be born as a brother of Panda in the next birth?

What merit had Panchuki Panda earned in his life that he would be born again as the same Panchuki Panda, and Bharjan would be born as his incompetent slave? Kundala Panda went to charm the sea by his spiritual powers, could he do it? Let not Bharjan be born again as someone else's servant. Let Bharjan in his rebirth be born as an animal or bird or tree, but not in a caste-ridden society of man. But who can say, except God, that his prayer would be answered?

So many people were swept into the sea! Why was Bhjarjan chosen for grace? Bharjan should have suffered the fate of others. But Bharjan's sorrow was too heavy on his heart. Others could endure the pain of losing some or all members of their families. But Bharjan could not, as he had thrown his two sons into the water to save himself and Panchuki's son. It was as if he had strangled his sons to death. Had Debu, instead of hanging from his neck on the back, sat on his shoulders, he would have thrown him too.

Bharjan is not at all a kindly, brave, sacrificing, and god-like person. Bharjan is a hangman; he not only fells coconut branches, but also humans when the need arises. He could smash and kill anyone when his own life is in danger. How could these men, who have returned from the doors of Yama, not understand this, and praise him for his so-called sacrifice? They were simply adding salt to his wounds.

For what joy or happiness was he alive? Can he ever be happy over anything? Can he laugh anymore? Man is a strange animal. He doesn't live for joy or sorrow. He lives on for the sake of living. Perhaps there is no greater fortune than being alive. Inebriated with life, he tolerates all misfortune, bowing down his head. But there is none more unfortunate than Bharjan.

It seems Bharjan would get a lot of money. Seventy-five thousand rupees per head for his dead wife and children! Including Mantri, nine of his family members were gone in the sea. Put together, it is the property of a king or Zamindar. What would Bharjan do with all that money? Moreover, how would he enjoy that wealth that he would get for the death of his own wife and children? It's one thing if the children are swept into the sea, and another that he threw his children into the sea.

Bharjan had not gone insane yet. But he would go mad when he got the compensation for the death of his children. He has decided to give half of that money to Debu because he had fought death with Debu on his back. Debu had survived certain death. Had there been no deity in him, he wouldn't have survived. Maybe Debu is the seed of Satyayug! Maybe he would live to do well to the world-would destroy evil.

The rest of the money, he would donate to the Mamata House - the home for destitute children. Government had dumped the orphans in a cowshed-like house, and had named that swampy house Mamata House, a house of compassion! In that house are mosquitoes, darkness, hunger, sorrow, and pain, no compassion. Bharjan, therefore, has made up his mind to donate half of the compensation money. He knows that by this act his sins may not be expiated, his heart may not stop bleeding, his tears would not stop flowing.

But the tears of the orphans, so like his own children, may dry up. They may have some healthy blood, getting something to eat. Lakhs and lakhs of money; so many things could be done with that kind of money. But would he actually get that money? Bharjan has heard that, to get that money, there is red tape, politics, running around, bribing, and unnecessary paperwork. Everyone from top to bottom must have his share. So much money! So much relief! The fortunate ones cannot tolerate the unfortunates getting such relief. Bharjan's mind has already renounced this ugly world. He wonders why the deluge, instead of finishing everything, has left behind some sinners.

Yet it is heard that some money would be given to the destitute. If Bharjan donates that money, people would say he is selfless and charitable like the great King Karna of the Mahabharat. But Bharjan knows he is not Karna, nor a charitable person. Had one or two of his family survived, he wouldn't have given even a farthing from the compensation money.

Now some distant relatives from far-off villages come to invite him to their homes. They were never supportive of him in his bad times. Bharjan many a time had returned empty-handed from their doors in his time of need. He was never given a drop of rice water to relieve his weary body. Now they are eager to take him home, unasked. They now queue up to take him home to take care of him in his few, last, dying days. Bharjan has understood the secret of their love and care.

When Mantri did that unfortunate thing and polluted Kundala Panda unwittingly, then all of them had threatened to cut their ties with him if he kept Mantri in the house. Today, they are shedding crocodile tears for Mantri and the other dead children. At this grim hour of sorrow too, Bharjan felt like laughing. Seeing the different forms and shades of this creature called man, Bharjan's closed inner eyes were opening, one after the other.

Getting back Debu, Pachuki Gosain looked indebted and lowly before Bharjan for a few days; was speaking sweet-plum-pudding-like words. But now his Brahmin superiority had surfaced again. Despite calling him an angel under the weight of gratitude, he felt that he was the master, and Bharjan, after all, was his slave.

A day ago, Panchuki had sent for Bharjan. Asked him to clean up the mess of broken trees from his backyard. But Bharjan straightaway said no to his face. He had no strength in his body and soul to toil again. For whom would he toil and slave himself in another man's house? He had no awe or fear for the gosain or anyone else, as he had before. He had always been a self-respecting man, and today, what care or ties did he have?

Forgetting Bharjan's great sacrifice, Panchuki was annoyed, and, looking at him with stern eyes, he said, "Hey, you untouchable Bharjan! It's true that you have saved my son, but that does not mean that you are not an untouchable, nor not my slave. Agreed that you had a great misfortune. But how long would you sit in idle sorrow? You have mourned enough, but now you must again work for your keep. Hey, where is the time in a sad house to observe mourning? Hearing rumors about getting compensation, you are so defiant. When you really get the money, I think, you would not care for gods.

"You were never such an insolent man to answer back in my face. You never stood facing my father, and now you answer me in my face? Don't you know that I'm the priest of this area after my father's death? Don't think the compensation money for which you are waiting with such bold hopes would come so easily, my dear! You just wait and see what farce you would face this time for the compensation money. If you'd rather stay within your limits, we'll help you in expediting it. But, you monster, you don't even recognize me. Why are you so arrogant, and for what?"

Bharjan did not give any reply. He was not under any

obligation to give a reply. He sat silent, holding the packet of khichdi. He remembered the time of the first relief distribution after the cyclone. In his ward, a long queue of hungry destitute were waiting. A few upper caste people had broken the queue of the Dalits and had lined up forcibly. In that queue were standing Panchuki Gosain and some other Brahmins.

Bowing to the priest, he'd said, "What's this, Gosain? Standing in the Dalit ward, you'll accept cooked food and old clothes? It would be a load of sin on our heads. You, please go home. I'll bring you whatever relief they give. While we are here, you would stand in the queue? Are we dead yet?"

Panchuki Gosain had been a different man at that time. Standing firm in the line, he'd said, "After this cyclone has leveled all the Brahmin and Dalits, upper caste, lower caste, rich and poor, what is this caste-non-caste now? All are of one caste now. All are destitute, hungry. Why any distinction between big and small?"

Bharjan had seen many an example of the gosain's liberal temper. Sitting together in one line to eat with Dalits and low caste people in the free relief kitchen, they had eaten together at the time of sorrow. Yet within a few days, the same Panchuki Gosain had made an about turn! Now in his house are stocked bags of relief rice, ten to twelve blankets, and what not. Plenty of utensils. More than required polythene for his cowshed, although his house was of brick and mortar.

There were thousands of people lying in the open in sun, rain, and cold! Not even a small piece of polythene was given for them. Children and old people had already started suffering from cold, fever, and cough. Who knows how and when some of them would fall dead? Who cares for them? Bharjan Mallick hasn't gotten a polythene sheet till now. Let them not give. He has no desire anymore to pitch a tent. There is no tree anywhere to take shelter under. Better to kick off as soon as possible, lying exposed to the sun and night dew. Death is better than suffering the loss of the family for the rest of the life.

Bharjan never knew that he had so much love and

attachment for his family. He had never spent a joyful day of conjugal life with Mantri's mother. He had never looked at his herd of children with love and pride because of the pangs of poverty, ill-treatment of the society, and the blasted curse of daily toil for bare survival. Far from being a loving father, he'd been almost tyrannical with his children. Instead of blaming his fate for not being able to give away in marriage his grown-up daughters, he was blaming the poor girls. Not being able to counter the hunger in his children's bellies, he was thrashing his helpless fatherhood on their backs. Making Mantri's mother pregnant every year against her wishes, he was abusing her for giving birth to a bunch of children, like a herd of pigs. He was also abusing the gods and deities for Mantri being alive in the crematory.

But after his entire family had been wiped out, he understood that he was evading his own impotent failure by maintaining a false image of himself. He loved soulfully all those people of his village who misbehaved with him, treating him like a pest. Today, he was not only mourning for his wife and children, but also for all those who never gave him anything but hate.

Mantri was so ill-fated that the ghosts of the crematory had not eaten him up, the sea had. Mantri was such an expert climber of trees, such a good swimmer in the sea. But all was wasted before fate. Many a great warrior had fallen in the killer cyclone. Mantri, after all, was nothing, a mere untouchable brat. Wherefrom would he get his Mantri now?

As the days passed, his sorrow intensified. The NGOs and leaders did not understand that relief kills hunger, not sorrow. People jostled at the relief centers to take whatever was doled out; torn clothes, smelly rice, and rubbish. Bharjan wanted to thrash them away. But he was empty of all desire. Sitting on the ruined platform of the village, he was lost in chaos of thoughts. He'd never known earlier that he had the power to think about so many things. Like the body, why doesn't the mind diminish in its capacity in the face of sorrow?

"Father!"

It was as if somebody had raised a thatched roof over his

head all of a sudden, as if leaves had grown on a denuded tree, as if shade had spread over his burnt fate, as if fresh blood had rushed in his dead veins!

"Who?" Bharjan stood up, holding his khichdi packet.

"Father! You're alive? And the others?"

"O' my Mantri, Mantri, my life's life! You are alive! I've searched for you all over. Where were you? How were you saved? If your mother were here, she would have got Kubera - the God of wealth's treasures, my child! Unfortunate woman, couldn't know what happiness is-in the end, was swept away in middle age, and took with her the unfortunate. Left me behind to suffer."

The father and son, in tight embrace, wept a sea. Even then, the tears were uncontrollable. The deluge had united the lifelong estranged father and son in a wave of desperation. So much was lost, so many broken hearts were united, but they never knew that the relationship between father and son was intense, so broad and deep. They felt as if they were never separated from each other-Mantri was never a disowned son. Whatever had happened in the past was due to false ego and a posturing of social compulsion. All that was for show, superficial. But deep inside, the bond of blood endures. Gradually, both calmed down, looked at each other from top to toe, and thought, oh, how the poor fellow has suffered!

In a hurry, Bharjan placed the packet of khichdi on the broken platform. Lovingly, he said, "You look hungry since ages, my child! Come, eat this fistful of khichdi. Let life flow in the body. I don't know why, but today the soul didn't ask for food. All of you crowded my mind."

Mantri was hungry. He'd had no time to go to the relief kitchen. He ate a fistful. Fed his father with him. Father and son ate together from the same leaf plate, maybe after so many births. No one spoke about how they'd escaped the clutches of the cyclone and how they braved the sea, for all had experienced the hair-raising moments of their fight with death. No one had any less fighting spirit than the other.

Mantri didn't ask about his mother and the other brothers and sisters. Looking at Bharjan, he knew where they were. Mantri wanted to go in a hurry. But where would he go? For what urgent work this crematory devil of a son had no hunger or thirst?

Bharjan blocked his path, and asked, "Where are you going? Let's go home. I'll not allow you to go to the crematory again. Let me see what anyone can do to me!"

In the midst of all that sorrow, Mantri laughed, "Home! Where's home? Where are my mother and brothers and sisters? You know father, standing in this vast crematory. You don't want me to go there! Fearing Kundala Panda, all of you made me the crematory devil. Now this entire region is a crematory. Wherever you look, all are crematory devils. Heaps of bodies everywhere. Wherever you look, the funeral flames hit your eyes, fire and smoke rise up to the sky.

"By good luck, Kundala Gosain has been saved. He could not be a crematory devil. Becoming a corpse in the clusters of dead bodies he has made everyone a crematory devil. So much so that even his sons and grandsons are now devils. In his own backyard are floating strings of bodies. You need not be sorry for your crematory-devil son anymore. I've been away from home since childhood. Don't drag me to the illusion of home, father.

"One day, I took the responsibility of a small crematory. Today, a large crematory is spread before my eyes. You can well understand my responsibility. This barren cyclone has not spared a flower anywhere to offer the burning heaps of the dead, abandoned like heaps of filth."

When a tiny tot learns to walk in this new world, taking tottering steps, the father follows behind, lest the son should slip and fall. When the son grows up and walks with firm steps, taking long strides, at that time too the father follows, taking nervous, aged steps, lest he should fall down himself. At such times, the father has already left behind the vast world of right and wrong, where there is no way of finding what is lost, joining what is broken, and fixing what is disjointed. But before the son lies the endless world of building, joining, and fixing. Following the son, one feels like getting back the strength in one's limbs. The call of the son's world echoes in heaven, earth and the netherworld.

That's the fate of a father. Walking behind Mantri, Bharjan was feeling happy. In the bottomless sea of sorrow, Mantri was moving like a lifeboat, steering clear of the floating corpses. Turning the faces of the dead, Mantri was identifying them like a man driven by some alien power. Mantri had been eccentric from his birth, but he became totally insane experiencing the devastating cyclone. Such madness was significantly valuable while recovering from the deluge. Therefore, Bharjan had no sorrow at this total madness of Mantri.

The cyclone had bolted the time-worn banyan tree to a stump but had not been able to uproot it. The hundreds-of-years old roots of the banyan tree had pierced the dark depths of the billion-year-old, aristocratic earth. The cyclone had been breathless, shaking it, but the roots never gave up their pride. It stood like the clan-destroying Dhritarashtra in the Kurukshetra war, clinging onto the earth. The hanging roots of the tree were blown away. The branches were all gone. And the few left were bereft of leaves. All around reigned an eerie baldness.

But the banyan tree did not appear to be worried about that. Standing in the midst of the old ruined platform, it was perhaps waiting for the time when, one by one, Gandhi Das, Kundala Panda, Danakarna Mishra, Panchuki Panda, Bhairab Majhi, Udhab Mangual, Dhadi Barik, Banchu Tarai and many others would come. Where were they now? Such a great calamity happened, yet no meeting was held! These small villages of Erasama never wait for the sarpanches or ward members. In the tradition passed down from generations, the village elders solved all problems of the villagers.

The sarpanches and ward members would rather create problems but never solve any. Their role is politically acknowledged for government grants and things like that. But in the villages, they are counted as one among the common villagers. If they are given importance, the simple lives of the villagers would get entangled in the political nets. Therefore, even today none waited for the sarpanches and ward members. A meeting could be held with the five to seven survivors of the villages. What would happen in future, and how could this earth be regenerated? Some decisions could be made.

But who is where? Supporting himself against the broken platform was standing only one old man whose roots had penetrated the earth to immeasurable depths. He looked like old Gandhi, but he was not Gandhi Das. Of course, seeing whatever had happened, was happening, and likely to happen, he had turned into Gandhi. In these times, Gandhi meant only a statue. He who was real in the past, his work and fame too was in the past. He was no more, his life and work irrelevant.

Because in the reign of the non-Gandhis, Gandhis are not only sacrificed, their ideals and values too become expendable. These days, those who follow the principles and ideals of Gandhi become victims of violence; get victimized by non-values, just as Gandhi was. The man who had turned Gandhi and was standing in the middle of the platform of what once had been a throbbing Abhayapur, like a statue, was observing everything silently. He too was waiting for those who had already become the past. He was waiting for a future of possibilities.

Like a small island in the rubble heap caused by the cyclone, there was seen from among the soldiers the living face of Bikram Balabantaray. On his face was etched by sorrow the resolve to fly the flag of victory in the morose sky of defeat. The statue, as it were, was reinvested with life. Bikram came running and embraced the statue.

"Sir, sir, you are alive!" Saying this, he wept aloud. After such a long time, the soldier chest of Bikram melted and flew down as tears. Here, no one cried for another; at least let this one cry. Crying is not a weakness. It is strength. Crying for another means he had the desire and empathy to wipe off another's tears. That was enough.

Drona Sir was silently stroking his back. He knew that his emaciated, weak body was capable of consoling the strong military body of Bikram. Bikram too knew that. For a long while, no one spoke a word. Like shriveled stumps of trees, they sat close to each other on the yawning cracks of the platform.

Then Bikram said, "Sir, there is no one here. Nothing is here. What shall we do? All are orphans. Who can support another?"

Sir said in a calm voice, "Today the orphan would be the support of the orphan. Otherwise, no one would live. Does dependence on government relieve sorrow? Does agony get solace from rice, dal, polythene, and old clothes? Does naming the cyclone as supercyclone neutralize super sorrow? This year's Deepavali was the darkest. There was no one to offer water to our honored ancestors. Who cares for the ancestors when no one can give a handful of water in the mouth of the living?

"See, Bhairab Majhi's son Kartika is alive, Bhudan, Baikuntha, and Bipin are alive. Mantri Mallick is alive and burning dead bodies like a madman. Why worry when they are alive? Some others maybe, are stranded somewhere. If luck favors, they would come searching for their village. My children, grandchildren, and great-grandchildren have been swept away. Who knows where? But I haven't been reduced to a stump.

"Kundala Panda sacrificed his life to save this village, at the dictate of his own faith. Benudhar Mangual, the watchman of the railway level-crossing, became a martyr. Utkalmani Mandal and Bharat Mandal lived here as refugees, but they died only for the people of these villages. What sacrifice hasn't Utkalmani made? Narkeswar Routray, Tahali Mohanty, and many others of their ilk; selfish, miserly, corrupt, and scheming, have opened up their homes and yards to people irrespective of caste or religion. They have given shelter to all.

"Under the strong roofs of their houses built with black money, quite a few of these villages have survived. Opening their granaries, they have cooked rice and dal to feed all of them. Had they locked up their houses, many more of these villagers would have been dead and gone. We always looked at them with crooked brows, taking them as heartless and evil. But even in them, there is no dearth of humanity."

Listening to Drona Sir, Bikram calmed down. Hearing that Kartika, Bipin, and Baikuntha were alive, he moved in the direction of Gandhi Das's house. But he paused to think. Whose house? What home? No houses are there. All are homeless.

Instead of searching for homes outside, if he would search for homes inside the hearts of the survivors, he would find homes, villages, and blood relations. For the new leaves of hope to emerge, time must be given to unite the love of the soil, perseverance of the kernel, and patience of man. The deluge happened in a night, but for creation a whole lifetime is spent. Whatever life is left ahead, let that be spent in the worship of creation-what harm is there?

The two faithful coconut trees, the trunks that the Gandhi Das family had been anchored to, were swaying, slightly bent in the wind. The sea-water, rising up to their noses, had left them bare and ugly. Not even a small, raw coconut had been spared by the heartless cyclone and the sea. The trees had surrendered everything to the sea, but not the family of Gandhi Das.

How could they have sacrificed them? Gandhi Das had himself planted the trees. Again, he himself had tied tight with a jute rope himself and his family members around the trunks of the trees. Only Bhudan had escaped the death-trap, as he had gone to Cuttack. A few days after the cyclone, he'd come walking all the way from Cuttack, stumbling and rising, and finally identified his homestead by the landmark of the statue of Brindavati, the basil leaf goddess, in his front yard on a cement platform in the blessing mode, sitting on one knee, raising her right palm, dispelling all fear. Bhudan felt as if her saree reached out to wipe off the sweat from his brow and the worry lines from his forehead. Half of Kumpani Soin's brick house too was standing firm; the other half was broken off by the wild sea.

Except the middle two sons, luckily the rest of the family of Kumpani Soin had survived. Those two sons had been on night watch duty at the prawn farms, and they were swept off into the sea. The prawn farms in this area had been the doom of half the population. Seeing the dead bodies of his father, mother, brothers, and sisters tied to the coconut trees, Bhudan had stood like a dead body himself. How could a sensible man like Gandhi Das think that the twenty-foot high death waves of the sea would return without touching them?

The sea returns everything except life.

It was true that Gandhi Das and Kumpani Soin always differed on ideology and principles. But the whole family could have survived had they gone to his house at the time of danger. Gandhi Das could not sacrifice his ego, and Kumpani Soin, his pride.

When Gandhi Das, being a younger brother, did not seek shelter with his family, why should he have invited Gandhi Das? As his house was built with black money, Gandhi Das's character would have been blackened! What logic? But so many upper caste and lower caste people had taken shelter in his house at the time of crisis. Did Kumpani Soin invite them all?

Even the women were not any less intolerant and arrogant. Bhudan's mother and Kuber's mother would not give up their pride. The elder sister didn't invite, nor the younger one go with her children to the brick house. Had Bhudan been in the village, forgetting all conflicts, he would have chased his mother and children to his elder uncle's house. He had come from Cuttack, walking all the way despite the lashing rain and beating wind, wading his way through thorny bushes and stinking bodies. He didn't have the patience to wait till the roads were cleared and became motorable.

Walking ceaselessly for two days and seeing the diabolical face of the cyclone, Bhudan had reached his village. He had no strength even to mourn the death of his parents and brothers and sisters. He stood like a pole, burying his feet in the mud. At this time, Kumpani Soin's eldest son, Kuber, came running from his house and clasped him. The brothers, forgetting the long disaffection of the two families, cried in unison the same tuneful sorrow of loss and pain. Kumpani Soin too had tears in his eyes watching them from a distance.

Bhudan ran to him and cursed him in anguish. "Uncle! You being here in your big strong house, our entire family was lost! How torturously must my father have died, mother, brothers, and sisters! I know how my father has suffered because of his principles, but how could you tolerate the decimation of his entire family, clinging tenaciously to his ideology? Why didn't you drag them to your house at such a calamity?"

Beating his chest, Kumpani Soin mourned regretfully, and reprimanded himself. "I'm a devil. I couldn't give up my arrogance. My heart goaded me a thousand times to brave the cyclone and go out to pull them all in. But my arrogance stalked my way. Being my younger brother, if Gandhi Das did not think it wise to take shelter in his elder brother's house, why should I, unasked for, have called in an honest and principled man to my house built with black money? I'm speaking the truth, believe me. When my conscience got the better of my arrogance, and I was anxious to open the door and call them all in, the wind speed had increased to such a pitch that, instead of opening the door, all of us had to push the door from inside to save it from the force of the wind crashing it open.

"Otherwise, all of us, including the house, would have been blown away. A part of the window had already got broken. The wind blew up half of the house. Luckily, there was no one that side. The sea has swept off the big copper pots, boxes, and also the documents and sale deeds of the land and other things. Now, if I hit my head, I have no way of getting Gandhi and the children back, my child. Fie on my manliness! If Gandhi didn't come because of his pride, what fame have I achieved?

"The rest of my life now would be mired in guilt and regret. The two prawn farms I had made on government land, using black money, in the same prawn farms my two young sons were offered to the sea. I got the wages of my sin; what did the sea get by taking my hefty boys? How are they guilty of anything?"

Who would have weighed whether Kumpani Soin's filial sorrow was heavier, or Bhudan's sorrow at the loss of his parents and family? All were sinking under the weight of their own misery. Bhudan looked at the dilapidated compound wall of his courtyard, sighed deeply looking at the fenceless farmland, and said, "Had father been here, how happy he would have been! He always used to say that, one day or other, this dividing wall would vanish from this ancestral courtyard; the ridges and fences would be removed from these farmlands. Everything would be leveled as before. The minds would unite if the land and soil were not divided. All of us would again live happily together."

The cousins consoled each other, holding each other's hands, and waded through slush and mud near the coconut trees. They tried to untie the rope stretching their hands. The rope snapped, and the strings of rotten corpses fell into ankle-deep, slushy water. The excruciating sorrow could not suppress the nauseating stink of the bodies. Both tied towels over their noses and stared at the rotten bodies of their near and dear ones.

Bhudan spoke in a despairing voice. "Everyone doesn't have the good fortune of lighting their parents' funeral pyres. I am one of those unfortunate ones."

Kuber consoled him, saying, "It's not possible to cremate these bodies. Wherever you look, only water and water. The condition of the bodies is not conducive to carrying them to a dry place. Let them all mingle with the soil of their homeland. Gandhi Uncle always loved this soil. The soil would cremate him and would gain sanctity. We have no choice."

Bhudan again sighed deeply, and said, "What shall we do now? Wherefrom shall we start? My mind is not functioning."

Someone answered from behind, "You must always begin from the end. One generation is gone. We must begin the new age from our village. We're all in the same boat. You have your Kumpani Uncle and Brother Kuber. I've none, but so many of us are still alive. How can we say there is no one to help us? Are we nothing to each other?"

Kuber turned back. The sorrow was behind him. Before him was standing the Kargil hero, Bikram Balabantray. Bhudan embraced Bikram. In a choked voice he said, "Bikram! You're alive! How could you survive? You were supposed to be dead! The news of your death had spread in these villages. Oh! How painful was that news!

"Bhagyadhar, Udhab Uncle, Girima, Bharat Uncle, Bhairab Uncle, Golmasta Uncle, my father, Kundala Gosain, Ketaki, Mantri Mallick, and your parents-all, all had mourned for you. Were they alive today, how glad they would have been, seeing you! They are all dead now. Had you sent a telegram that you were fine, they wouldn't have died with the pain of your death in their hearts."

Bikram knew that his family and clan were all gone. Yet, when he had the names recounted by Bhudan, his face darkened. Saddened, he said, "I was never lost, my brother. While on duty, I was injured by a stone falling from a mountain. In a border village which was half Indian and half Pakistani, I suffered for a long time. A Muslim family of that village nursed me back to life, and when I was cured, they brought me to the camp. Everyone thought that I was missing; hence they sent a telegram to my father.

"Who said that I was dead? When I thought of sending a telegram, the news of the killer cyclone had reached the borders. I'm here now not on leave, but on duty. I've come with other jawans to cremate the dead of this region, to clear the roads, and to rehabilitate the cyclone victims. But who realizes that I too am a victim? My own misery is limitless. My parents suffered the pain of my death while I was alive, and with that sorrow, they were crushed to death by their own roof. I didn't have the good fortune even to see their dead faces. From that viewpoint, you are luckier than I am." Bikram cried uncontrollably.

Bhudan laughed a laughter worse than weeping. He said, "Yes, brother! We're in such a state that even misfortune could be counted as good luck. I'm lucky that I could see my parents in this condition."

Kuber said, "See, Kartik Majhi has lost his parents and his whole family. He couldn't find the corpse of anyone of his family. Returning from Surat, eight days after the cyclone, he was searching for the bodies like a demented man. When you meet him, you would understand his mental state."

"Kartika is alive, then?" Bikram stretched his gaze toward the home of Kartik Majhi. There was no trace of the seven-blocked house of Bhairab Majhi. Bhairab Majhi's home lay like an empty world, wiped out by the seawaters.

TWENTY FIVE

The theater hero Kartika had been delivering love dialogues confidently before the fathers on stage, to the applause of audiences, and while acting, he'd been slowly mustering courage to confront his real father about the affairs of his heart. When the time came to stand like a brave bull before his father, this blasted cyclone had finished everything like a born enemy. Ah-ha! Does the end of conflicting thoughts come like this? Destroying the conflicts of hope and ambition, what credit did the cyclone gain?

When Kartika turned toward his village road from the Erasama bazaar, his chest started hardening like stone. The heart bursts at the death of a dear one, but when the clan, family, and villagers are dead, the heart hardens into stone. Receiving the news of the cyclone when he left Surat, he prayed, "May everyone be safe," and he was not worried. Now, after seeing the doomsday devastation, he was, in fact, dumbfounded.

For whom the fear? Standing in a paddy field full of corpses, moving his eyes around tree-less blankness, he changed direction from east to west and north to south and searched for his village, moving like a whirlwind. He couldn't see any landmark to direct him.

And where had the others gone? His Padma, who had loved an actor like Kartika, only to suffer frustration and loneliness and finally settle with Bhagyadhara? The other unfortunate ones, Girima, Ketaki, Masuma, Renu, and other fateless men and women were born here, maybe to die together. Is to be born together and die together good fortune? Kartika went on asking countless questions to fate, God, and life, whose reply echoed in the wailing tone of the unfortunates. Give, give, give.

Today is the last auspicious Thursday to worship goddess Laxmi after the harvest. The creative Odia women, even today had painted on the broken walls pictures of hope, mixing the rice paste, jhoti, with their ceaseless tears. The cyclone had blown away the houses, but wherefrom would it have gathered the strength to blow off the traditions of a thousand-year-old culture, the sacred nuances of life, the loving traditions of a rooted race? Kartika paused at the jhoti on broken walls. Now is the paddy-worshipping hour.

To Mantri Mallick's ears, the ululations of the closing ceremony were like the wailings of death. Today was the last day of Mantri's search for Ketaki. Mantri finally found Ketaki; unfound, she was torturing Mantri, but found, she shattered Mantri. Looking at the face of Ketaki, he turned into stone. Like the dead lips of Ketaki, Mantri's lips turned blue.

Since his own escape from the cyclone, he'd been turning the dead bodies to find Ketaki's face. But he'd never wished to find the dead face of Ketaki. He wanted only one live face among the heaps of dead faces. He was searching for Ketaki's fresh, simple, and bright face. He identified her by seeing the silver bangles on her inert hands. He found her after so many days; but was it a finding?

Ketaki's adolescent, sickly, fit-for-nothing brother, Ainthu, was found alive stuck to a tree branch, begging for life, simpering like a baby bat. Two days after the cyclone subsided, people rescued him. Mantri has kept Ainthu close to him. The twelve-year-old boy refused to go to the Carewell Home. Crying, he'd said, "Why should I go to an orphanage? My parents died long ago, but I was never an orphan because my sister Keti was alive. If she is dead, you are there for me, brother Mantri. You were the protector of our house. How then am I an orphan? Were you only a brother to my sister? And none to me?"

Relations and family men, none came running to take the orphans to their laps. Yes, they came at that time when some service organizations came forward to adopt these orphans. From nowhere came uncles, cousins, and distant relatives to volunteer, "Our nephew, our niece, how can they be orphans as long as we are there?"

"Then how were they identified as orphans with you all being there? Why didn't you keep them with you?"

The answer to this question was very simple, "We were lying in the open in sun and rain. The Carewell Home maybe was worse than a cowshed, but at least there were walls, roofs, and rice, and dal. The day we have our own houses, we would take them home. We'll take all responsibility."

Not only that, there was also a virulent competition between the uncles and relatives as to who should be the guardian of these orphans. Mantri Mallick knew the real motives; the orphans would get 75,000 rupees each for parents. Once that money came to hand, these orphans would be used as bonded slaves. Even after the super cyclone had exposed the super truths of life, self-interest sat on the minds of man as an unshakable obsession. The big shots who came running from the cities, they were for the upper caste orphans, not to adopt them, but to use them as unpaid servants.

Mantri's questions haven't been answered. No answer is available today, and he is sure no answer would ever come. He has the strength to defeat the orphan-hood of one orphan, Ainthu. But he doesn't have the means of neutralizing the orphan-hood of the world, for he is not God, but a mere crematory devil. Ainthu sought his help, and he accepted the responsibility, and that is all he is capable of.

Luckily Mantri, not Ainthu, saw the decayed body of Ketaki. The boy could not have stood the shock of seeing the rotten body of his sister. It is one thing to accept the fact that his sister was no more, but quite another to witness the horrible truth. This boy, who'd been nurtured by his sister, had cried enough, believing that his sister had been swept away by the sea. Why punish him more than that?

The Anandamargis were dragging Ketaki's rotten body, along with others, with an iron hook, in order to burn them together. Pouring kerosene on the bodies, they were tirelessly burning the corpses. Mantri appreciated their work to keep the environment clean. But he could not tolerate the sight of them hooking Ketaki's body.

He ran, screaming at them, "What do you think of yourself? Is there no one to cremate their own? Are all dead in your view? Or you have no regard for those who are alive? I say, leave that body-that one wearing silver bangles. I would cremate her."

One volunteer asked, "What are you to this body?"

"Me! You want to know what I am to her? I'm everything to her," Mantri answered back.

"Everything means what? Brother, husband, friend, family?"

"I'm from her village. She was an adored young woman of our village. I may not be her brother or family, but can you say that I am none to her? You people-don't you have your village? Do you think, beyond the family, none can be another's own? You are entirely self-centered people."

They left the corpse. One body was less from their list. They thought where was such a selfless creature till now?

A city journalist said, "After such a long time, I saw a young man interested in cleaning his own house. The youth here, eating their fill in the free kitchens, are playing cards on broken verandas. They never remove known or unknown bodies lying before them. Their hands are too limp even to pour kerosene and throw a match. When asked, they say, 'Are we scavengers, to remove and burn the bodies? If we burn bodies, clear the roads, and build houses, what would the government do? Only beg from the countries and the world, collect relief, and eat away basmati rice, biscuits, blankets, and even tarpaulin and polythene, but then get all the accolades?'

An onlooker said, 'The lads are saying the right thing. Poor fellows, they fought with the cyclone, lost their families and homes. They have no strength anymore in body and mind to burn the dead, to clear the roads, removing broken trees. Can anyone easily overcome such a great shock? Poor fellows are shocked.'"

Standing near the lifeless head of Ketaki, Mantri screamed again, "Who the hell are you, such kindhearted gentlemen? How many young men of this region have you seen, that you speak whatever you please and write whatever comes to your mind in the newspapers? The relief drama is going on at the Erasama block office. People are clamoring, 'give, and give.'

"Has any one of you lifted a corpse from the rest of the villages? Have you gone to Abhayapur, Chandanpur, Pakistanpara, Nagari, and other villages to see how the few surviving young men are working? Do you know Bikram Balabantaray? Although he has come with the army contingent, he is a man of this soil-a Kargil hero. He is our leader. Go and see how he is working and making others work."

Supporting Mantri Mallick, someone said, "Have your Ministers placed their sacred feet on our soil to date? Yes, now they would come. The election time is fast approaching. They needed a cyclone before the elections. Go and preach to them-let them not come to our village to ask for votes. If they come, we'll bash their brains in, one by one."

Mantri's sorrow at the horrible death of Ketaki had turned into passionate anger. He was hissing to bite.

"Ah-ha! Please don't mind, gentlemen! At the death of the dear ones, some have become dumb and some have gone insane. If they find God, they would take out their anger on him. When that chance is not there, on whom they would take it out?" one volunteer said.

The journalists were not irritated; they too were shocked at the devastation and mass death and had sympathy for the victims. Stroking Mantri's back, one of them asked, "Well, young man, what's your name? Your judgment is very sound. I never knew that young men like you are here in these villages. Please excuse us. Would you please tell us your name?"

"Name? What would you do, knowing my name? Publish it in your newspapers? Take my picture, garlanding me? What would we gain by that? See, gentlemen, there are no flowers in our villages in any tree. Ketaki's body would be cremated without flowers. No sandalwood, no ghee, nothing is there even for symbolic rituals. Well, brothers, burn her along with the others, pouring kerosene. Let her ashes mingle with the dust of our village. It's beyond my ken to do anything else for her. God knows it, even Ketaki's soul might be sensing it."

As Mantri's tears were about to fall on the rotten body of Ketaki, the Anandamargis hooked away her body. Kerosene was poured on the heap of bodies; the flame rose to the sky.

Happiness ends, misery ends, wealth, calamity-all end. But sin never ends in the world. Mantri knew this. Yet this world had opened her lap to sustain life, not death. In the broken branches of the fallen trees, crimson leaves were now smiling. A lone bird was building a nest with twigs with all sincerity. In the rotten waters, the blue lily was slowly opening up her innocent petals. The hope to live was rekindling in the minds of unfortunate men. Mantri Mallick would also live, he would let others live. Mantri vowed.

On a mountain of broken trees, like the wood-framed pictures of the subtle needlework of the Odia woman, was stuck an open notebook, wherefrom a cluster of characters, written with a red ballpoint pen, was winking like crematory flowers. Where life and property have vanished, there, who cares for mere letters?

A tin suitcase was stuck at the tangled branches, openmouthed on its back. Bikram Balabantaray, with the other army men, was cutting the trees to clear the place. As the broken trees lay blocking the road to Abhayapur, the relief trucks were not able to reach the village.

The road was damaged, and, at places, there were breaches and holes. Even the footpaths were inaccessible. Although not army men, Bhudan, Alwar, Bipin, and other young men were working to clear the roads. Bhudan's eye fell on the notebook and the open suitcase near it. He stood amazed. Removing the broken and twisted branches, very carefully he retrieved the notebook from the debris. His face brightened as if he had rescued a dear one from the pits of death. Dusting off the notebook, he pressed it to his chest, caressed the torn leaves of the notebook.

In a voice choked with love he said, "Bikram! See, my sister."

"Your sister?"

"Yes. My golden sister, Girima."

"Girima! Where? Where is Girima?" Bikram's fast-working hands had stopped. A hope had kindled his eyes.

"See here! Our Girima's poetry book. How carefully she saved it in this suitcase! Many times, she read the poems to me. I have read all that she wrote; her life's poems. The sea has left it untouched. The sea could not wash away these letters, our Girima's magical alphabets of the heart."

Not Girima, but Girima's songbook! Bikram couldn't decide whether he should be happy or sink into sorrow. He saw that Bhudan, who was ecstatic at discovering the notebook, was crying. Bhudan was insensitive to sorrow and pain, seeing the dead bodies of his entire family. Whereas, holding the song book of unfortunate Bhagyadhar's sister, he was crying as if he had seen the dead body of Girima. How pure and wonderful are the ties of these rural folks' hearts, how soft and smooth are the cords of their relationship!

Bikram softly touched the notebook, like taking a garland from another hand. He felt as if he were touching and holding, for the first time, the hand of that song-writing girl. A strange sensation arose in his heart, and then melted away. Is this the dead hand of Girima? Girima is not there; the heart was not brave enough to speculate whether she was living or dead. Let there be no Girima, nor her hands, at least her handwritten letters are there.

Man fades away and dies. Words never fade away, never die. The words are Brahma. The first known poet of Odisha, son of this soil, poet saint Sarala Das, has faded away in six hundred years, but his words, written on palm leaves, have not faded. His songs have not been lost. His Mahabharat and Chandi Puran have not faded in time. Those letters are in the hearts of the Odias.

Girima is the daughter of the same soil. If she is dead, so be it. Man is born only to die. Now she is gone. This is the way of the world. But her letters are alive, and that is good luck enough. Joining the torn pages, matching the letters, Bikram read slowly like a learner. Maybe this was Girima's last poem.

> Warrior,
> You can fight ice and snow.
> But can you fight the sea?
> Tell me, for my sake,
> Placing your hand on your heart.
> In ice, you find the cold dew of the heart's core.
> In the sea, you have the saline tears of eyes.
> Can you taste the tear streams
> Without shedding your heart's blood?

He couldn't read further. His eyes streamed, his chest was suffocated. In a half-educated girl, such oceanic depth! And such pearls in the bottomless sea? No, it's not possible to assess those; to get the pearls of the fisherwoman, you have to wait for another birth.

By the time he finished reading the poem, he felt as though he had returned from the depths of thousands of years. Had returned from where, who knows? From what unknown corner of history, crossing many births? And for what-to live a new life, to build a new world? Like the honey in the pores of the beehive, Bikram didn't know that such honeyed hope seeps endlessly through the words of love. Man lives when he collects the honey by enduring the sting of pain like the sting of the honeybee. If he cannot, life becomes a living hell.

These are the two paths before man. There may not be anyone to show the way to the army man, Bikram.He has the letter of love on torn paper that has escaped, unscathed, the jaws of the deluge, the letter that can fill nectar in the sorrow-soaked notebook of life. Sorrow is never an impediment while being swept away on the sea of nectar.

While repairing the roads with a few lucky survivors, the

seeds of the Satyayug, Bikram thought, this cyclone has not only destroyed houses and trees but, particularly, has broken into fragments the age-old tradition of the joint family in Odisha. Despite the self-immersed, self-centered life pursuits and modern materialist culture, the joint family in the urban and rural areas had always been vibrant and thriving with loving togetherness.

Blocks of rooms, broad courtyards like liberal hearts, around which the seven brothers and their seventy family members danced, holding each other's hands like the beams of houses brushing against each other. They spent many a beautiful full-moon night singing "O, virgin moon," few generations together! The family of the traditions of fourteen generations never bothered about the needs and miseries which lay around like yesterday's flowers, not in their ceremonial joy of living together. The brothers, with all their internal fights and discord, fought together the common enemy to safeguard the prestige of the family. In times of danger, they put their heads together against the gushing current of a river in spate.

But this cyclone destroyed the joint family in the villages for a few thousand rupees. House repair loans were given at the rate of two-to-three thousand rupees per family. Therefore, families which had four-to-five survivors were separated from each other. All young men and women above eighteen claimed money for their separate houses. The son was separated from his old mother. The wife was separated from her husband for a mere two thousand; the garland of the joint family that beautified the Mother of Utkal broke into smithereens, mingling in the dust of self-interest and greed.

Hereafter, the new houses that would rise would not be around the big courtyard where the Odia women met in ritual festivities. The block-pattern houses would not come up again. People did not have that ability nor the love for the beam-touching closeness. The house loan money would raise a few weak, badly planned Indira Awas-like houses. For the coming generation, the joint family would only be grandma's tale, and the famed rural beauty would be only an imaginary painting.

Now the election cyclone was fast approaching, giving strange colors to the flood of relief and rehabilitation. People were saying that, while most of the voters were dead, let the election wave play out-but at least our leaders should set foot on this soil! Otherwise, after the cyclone, the leaders, instead of working in their constituencies, would have started running to the capital Bhubaneswar. Now those who would get tickets to contests would move in these villages with their entourage, decking their necks with marigold flowers imported from Kolkata markets, and would shed crocodile tears on the loss of life and property caused by the super cyclone.

They'd exploit the misfortune of the simple villagers. A few leaders had announced that they would go on hunger strike for a day (after a five-course meal in the night) as the central government had not yet declared the super cyclone as a national disaster. Some innocent, gullible villagers believed with sincerity this farce of democracy, and the idea of popular mandate. The cunning leaders thought, like the cat drinking milk with its eyes closed, that these innocent, rural folks could not see through their games.

These people were happy with the little they got, like getting a straw from the floods, and to exploit their simple faiths, they must act out the election farce with perfection. How could these people distinguish between genuine and false tears? Give them a taste of their tears. They would know all tears are salty, even glycerin tears-why worry then?

Relief materials and money have been pouring in from the center, other provinces, foreign countries, and voluntary organizations. There is no dearth of food, clothes, and money for the rehabilitation of the victims of the cyclone. Yet, the government asks for more. The catchword is give; give more food, clothes, and house-building materials. It's heard that the major issue in the election campaigning would be the implementation of a rehabilitation program of thousands of crores, received from different sources.

The leaders, bureaucrats, ministers, and engineers are

overactive in investing crores in aimless projects, only to grease their palms without trying to understand the ground realities. They create new problems in the name of solving problems for the homeless, destitute, cyclone-hit people. In the list of the dead, the actual dead are missing, whereas the livings find a place in the list and merrily collect the compensation money.

To enter the lists of the dead, the victims are compelled to bribe the officers from top to bottom. In certain cases, to get the compensation money for the dead, suits have been filed in the courts. Unable to prepare an authentic list of the dead, and failing to assess the loss of property, government simply prepares a hurried list and raises the compensation claim. Looting midway half of the money meant for rehabilitation, the officers somehow disburse money in a mad rush and beat their drums of success.

If that much money has been disbursed to the deserving, then how is it that so many people are still roofless under an empty sky? How is it that the victims don't get the benefits of the crores spent on rehabilitation? The work of the local volunteers in the international service organizations has become more fatal than the cyclone. The people are now beginning to understand that no government or nongovernment organization is selfless or motiveless. Many have left Erasama after making tall promises to the homeless poor. Only the citations of their praise fly like flags, here and there. It seems government has no control over the NGOs. Fine! Entering your house, the so-called philanthropists would eat away the whole plate of goodies, throw crumbs at you, and take away all the credit after cheating and looting you; and again, would claim to be gods for the poor and helpless? Has the owner of the house no control over the imposters?

In these days, everyone who visits Erasama converses in English. The villagers are thinking, Will the British rule again? Bikram Balabantaray understood that, for people exposed to the hot sun and cold nights, rice was more important than language. Bikram was thinking of a plan, a blueprint. He has been thinking and planning for many things in the past few days.

He knew that his plan was difficult to implement, but not

impossible. Bikram was not a man to give up his efforts to make the impossible possible. He who has encountered the enemy for months together at the Kargil front, he would never leave halfway any impossible task. Here, so many kinds of enemies are having their way. Throwing a handful of relief rice, they are out to suck away the vital energy of the people of this area. Therefore, this village soil is truly the operational arena for a real soldier.

Those who died fighting the sea and those who survived they never thought of the ifs, ands, and buts while fighting. Man has to fight the air for his survival, although air is life, has to fight water, although water is life, has to fight the soil, although it is his shelter, has to fight vegetation, although the vegetation sustains him. Thus, it is said, duty is blind, and often man has to fight against himself; has to fight out his own inferiority complex and baser instincts.

The fighting spirit is the natural instinct of all living creatures. There, the question of victory or defeat does not arise. Here, all houses have mingled with the slushy earth. Saline water has destroyed the fertility of the soil, and the vegetation has been wiped out. Family and friends are all gone. Those who have survived fighting, they have to fight the reverse currents ahead and live. Bikram is the fighting jawan of the Kargil war.

But the survivors of this holocaust are a hundred times more obstinate fighters than Bikram. The dead are martyrs. The cyclone-rain-flood-enduring soil is also the epitome of the fighting spirit. This soil would never surrender or retreat. But if man retreats, who would raise this earth?

It's easy to roll in sorrow and misery; not easy to rise from the dust, but not impossible. This man has made roads, blasting the Kargil Mountains, has made the impenetrable trek worthy. Why then, the men of this village would not rise again gathering the scattered shreds of this earth?

Bikram saw that the cyclone had not subsided; everyday, it breaks and blasts so many things in the heart and soul of man. But is the counting of the dead over yet? The dead tree foliates automatically. Is man worse than trees?

The wood burns; but, for that, fire is needed. When wood rubs against wood, fire is sparked. But here, all are dead wood, lost in their own sorrow. If they do not work together, how can fire rise? Sizzling, they would turn into ash. Someone must act as fire to rekindle these dead woods. To unite them emotionally, someone must come forward. If someone does not burn the fire to awaken them, these men cannot move a step forward. How can Bikram return to his own work field, leaving these people? Is this not the work field of Bikram?

The soldiers have rescued the victims from inaccessible places, burned the bodies, straightened the twisted electric poles, cleared the roads for the relief trucks to come in, and then returned to their own arena of work. Their duty was over. That was their instruction. But is Bikram's duty over by doing that much? Does this fulfill the destiny of these men? Should he also return after counting the bodies, cleaning the roads for the relief trucks to enter the villages, and, allowing the cynical exploiters to enact their farce, leave the helpless dependents to their fate?

Yes, he should. That was the order for all soldiers. What option was left for the disciplined and dutiful Bikram Balabantaray? Bikram is committed to the dream of reconstruction of these villages. But, for that, the discipline of the army job does not permit him to defy orders. That day, Bikram stood before his captain, Ajay Malhotra, with an application in his hand.

The captain was a judicious and large-hearted officer. He was as strict in observing rules and regulations as he was sympathetic to the personal problems of his subordinates. At times, he was so perturbed at the suffering of the people that Bikram felt he was not simply an officer in the army, rather was a social worker, a relative of the people of Erasama.

Without reading the application, he said, "You definitely think that you should stay here for a few more days. Good. I'll recommend grant of leave for you as a special case. The colonel is also pleased with your sincerity and hard work. You top the list of persons who are sincerely dutiful and possess service mentality in their work here. I know you would have worked with the same commitment, had this been some place other than your own village. You have shown your exemplary courage and patriotism. You are a jewel of our department. Your future in the army is bright. For how many days of leave you have applied? Fifteen days, a month?"

In a polite but firm voice, Bikram said, "I have, for the present, applied for extension of my leave. In fact, I have requested for voluntary retirement in view of the devastation of my village, and I hope my application would be considered as a special case. Your kind recommendation would be a real favor, Sir; you have seen the situation here."

The captain was more surprised than amazed. In a skeptical tone, he asked, "Have you applied for premature retirement? Have you thought over it carefully, or just applied in a fit of emotion? You know, in a short while, you may be promoted to the rank of an officer. What would you do, living in the village your entire life? Floods and cyclones are a matter of regular recurrence in Odisha, almost every year. And, for that, you would give up your job halfway?"

Bikram replied humbly, "One lifetime is not enough, sir. Here, the villages have to be built anew. Out of the deluge shall rise a new village. A new age will dawn. We have to begin everything from zero. The cyclone has destroyed only the houses, but pain and sorrow have broken the backbones of everyone. This cyclone was thousand times more devastating than the usual floods and cyclones every year. If all of us are not united and working together, this village cannot rise again, straightening its back."

"But you have no one of your own in this village. You can resettle these villages if you extend your leave for two months. That, I hope, is enough time to inspire the survivors here to rise on their feet. Thereafter, why should you stay here? Rather, you would gain much if you serve the country and retire at the proper time. I'm saying this for your good. You consider this, and raise your own family. Make a house in a city and give the right kind of education to your children so that they would be proper citizens. Why should you live all your life in this flood-cyclone prone area? Your application is not unfounded. That may be considered sympathetically. But if it is accepted, you may be deprived of many advantages. Think again calmly, and apply. Apply for extension of leave only."

The captain returned the application, but Bikram did not take it. With folded hands, he requested, "Sir, my dreams and my future depend on you. My heart breaks when I think that I have none of my own in this village. This soil is most dear to me. And this village is an integral part of my country. I want to give a new form and shape to my village. This village shall be the first village to rise from the debris of the deluge-a village of the Satyayug. There would not be any illiteracy, corruption, violence or lethargy here. All would be fighting men like the soldiers, all would love this soil, this country.

"This would be a flawless village of greater India, taking the Bangladeshis, Pakistanis, Hindus, and Muslims together. One day, this village would give birth to hundreds and thousands of secular and sacred villages. Inspired by the ideas of this village, all dividing lines separating man and earth would fade away. Why should there be any war thereafter?

"Perhaps this deluge occurred only to establish peace, friendship, and non-violence. Change is the aim of destruction. This is not the end of the world, but a glorious resolution."

Mesmerized was Captain Malhotra, for, although there was sentimentality in Bikram's emotional outburst, there was a ring of truth. No exaggeration, no self-propaganda, no political ambitions. In every word and sentence of his reverberated his authentic conviction.

The captain accepted his application and wrote his sympathetic recommendations. Shaking Bikram's hand, he said, "My best wishes for you. I'll help you in every way to the best of my capacity. I trust your representation would be accepted. But don't forget that the country may need your services in any emergency."

"I'll be ever ready to serve the country any time, sir-even after retirement, I'll live like a soldier. I am committed to my country; I have mentioned that in my representation. Depriving myself of the defense of my country to take responsibility of raising my village is not any less painful, sir. You alone can understand that clearly. If I can serve my country again, I shall consider myself fulfilled." Bikram's eyes moistened.

"I'll try to the best of my capacity within the limits of my power. May God help you," said the captain.

"I'll be beholden to you forever, sir!" Bikram's voice was choked. The captain took his leave, feeling morose.

TWENTY SIX

A head, the temple of Goddess Jagulai; behind, crematories of villages. A bone-weary Kartika sat down on the temple steps. A short distance away from the lowest step was a square tank. In the blue mirror of the tank water, the white lilies were gazing at their fair faces in the early bathing hour. Hadn't the lilies experienced the magnitude of the deluge? Did they not have any sorrow?

Taking holy dips in this water, many men used to offer palmfuls of water to the sun god and then went on a darshan of the goddess. In the same water, corpses floated, rotted, and mingled with the slushy water. Using the same slush, the lily stems are now raising their heads. The flowers have started blooming as before. The goddess would be worshipped with the offering of these flowers; in a few months, Bhalukuni, the goddess worshipped by virgin girls, would shine bright and beautiful with the same flowers during the festival.

But the same virgin girls would not be there-yet there is no change in the smiles of the lilies. The only difference is that the flowers fade out, new flowers bloom, the new faces of the flowers look like the old ones. They apply the salve of hope on the shores of sorrow. In these new lilies, the faces of the old ones are seen, the faces that glistened like the faces of the virgins.

The faces of the flowers have no identity distinguishing one from the other. Lucky! Man has an identifiable face; bad luck. Hence, wherefrom would the old faces come back again? Is my Renu really alive?

A one-room, earthen house is seen close to the west side road. The low, earthen walls seem to be held in the lap of a polythene cover. Kartika advances toward that house as if he has discovered the hidden wealth of the worlds. If jhoti is there on the walls, it's Renu's place; he had that irrational faith. But, going near the house, he's frustrated. The walls were not even polished ever, by even cow dung. Maybe this lone house was never there before.

Whose house is this?

A teenager was sitting in the small, dusty courtyard of the house. The thick plait of the luxuriant black hair of the young girl dispelled the image of the fresh lily from his mind. The simple guileless face of the girl refreshed his drooping spirits, more than jhoti on the walls. The unseeing eyes of her mother were, perhaps, focused on the distant horizon, beyond Kartika. For her, Kartika was empty space. She had assumed that the presence of Kartika had no prospects for her.

Kartika asked, "Have you received the compensation for your cyclone-damaged house? How much? Two thousand or three? Your house looks brand new.

"We have received nothing. To our misfortune, we came after the cyclone. We haven't suffered the cyclone here".

"Where were you before the cyclone?"

"Midinapur, my father-in-law's house. My father's house is here in village Kiada".

"Here you have the market of corpses. You develop world-weariness when you see those rotten bodies. You must have come to see your parents after the cyclone, but why did you stay here, and how did you build a makeshift house?"

"At Midinapur, we were daily wage earners and worked hard to survive. There, you don't get work every day. Here, plenty of relief was given after the cyclone. Maybe some got more and some less, but we could get something. It was said that a food for work program would start here. Moreover, my brother received a compensation of one-and-a-half lakh rupees for the death of our parents.

"We thought at least we'd get work and food and some share of the compensation money. But I never knew that my brother was so greedy and hardhearted. Didn't give us even hundred rupees. Rather, he said, 'What share for the daughter from the compensation money for the death of parents?' It seems married daughters have no rights, even on the soil of their parents' house. In this area, relief was not adequate. Now we survive on daily wages."

"This house of yours will be razed to the ground if a whirlwind blows for a minute. Where would you go with your children? It's better if you go back to Midinapur."

"If this house blows off in a whirlwind, it would be better for us. We'll get compensation for the broken house and even an Indira Awas. In this region, cyclone and flood are annual affairs. Where is a cyclone in Midinapur? For that reason, my husband asked us to live here. Again, it's my parental village. What's wrong with that?"

"Have you purchased this plot of land? This is government property."

Before Kartika finished asking, the mother of the teenager gave a derisive laugh, and said, "The houses you see here, who has purchased any land? Even my father had not purchased any land here. All these are illegally occupied. The leaders enlisted their names in the voter list and gave them slips. We lived here by living here. If you are a voter, then you felled the jungle and harvested the land. Knowing everything, the leaders looked the other way. Wherefrom have you come, that you do not know these things?

"I was born here on this soil. My father had come from Bangladesh and had harvested this land, ate and sold the produce, saved and lived here. His sons enjoyed their father's income. Yet, our father gave us in marriage in the house of laborers. Now my brother gained from the death of our parents. I was married off, hence."

Kartika retraced his steps in a hurry. He knew the sad consequence of such a land grab. Thousands of Bengalis were swept away, without any trace. Their children couldn't get the compensation for their death. The dead and the living were equally cheated. Rather, a few heartless people of this area said, "The Bengalis have been finished. That serves us well. Why should government pay any compensation? Are they of this village or this soil?"

O' how merciful and loving is man! Yet, how very selfish and cruel!

Here, the sorrow of the orphans is an unending tale. The uncles and relatives, greedy for the compensation money for the dead parents, shed crocodile tears, holding the orphans, crying, "O' my poor darling." But they use them as bonded slaves and enjoy free labor.

Bikram Balabantaray is planning to free these orphans from the clutches of their relatives and do something for their rehabilitation. Bikram is from a warrior family; not a soldier alone, he is also a poet, has read the scriptures and epics. He has knowledge and, above all, a conscience. This region now needs a leader like him. But he is in the armed forces. He has been honored with the bravery award for his services in the Kargil war, and he also been promoted.

In a few days, he would return to his workplace. This region would be really orphaned in his absence. If a tree dies, another can be planted, but if the soil dies, what can man do? Kartika's head started reeling.

Hereafter, in this region, would rise rows of Indira Awas houses. Could the ill-constructed Indra Awas shelters protect these unfortunate people from another cyclone? Instead, strong houses built with the compensation money for dead parents could save the survivors. But would the wounds of the heart ever heal with death compensation money? Kartika was unable to think of how he would build a concrete house with the compensation and sleep in it. Many other young men and women are tortured by the same thought. It's not easy to live a life in a house built with the blood-smeared brick and mortar of father, mother, and siblings. All are not heartless.

Providing a makeshift roof over the heads of homeless people and taking credit for it is like beguiling innocent children with the tuneless music of mechanical toys. Whereas, there too there is loot on the way, bribes, lies, dishonesty, heartlessness, and unlimited hypocrisy. Kartika thought of running away somewhere from this heartless environment. For whom and with what hope of happiness would he see these things here? If real life is so deceitful, so cruel and sorrowful, then Basu Rath's theater party is better. In an imaginary world, one may rather get a moment of joy and happiness, may forget the pain and horror of the past life. But even that much is not easy to get. It's not easy for man to live like a true human.

The village on the east side was named Ahiraj Bedi-the name is there, but the village is gone, men are gone. The sea has swept it all. There, however, is seen a one-roomed, temporary shelter. Mud walls covered with blue tarpaulin.

The girl's mother said, while removing stones from the rice, "It's no one's house. A group of orphans live there. A few forlorn women live there, posing as the mothers of the orphans. Mother or what? Eating a few morsels, they merely survive, mourning for their own children. Someone is blind, another mad, and some others are dumb or retarded. Has the government ever become fathers of children, or childless women mothered anyone? In that case, the earth would have been heaven.

But that unfortunate woman called Renu is a real mother. She bemoans that the sea dragged her child away from her shoulders, but she is kind and loving toward the ill-fated children. She doesn't cry, doesn't laugh, and doesn't speak. She moves like a dead person, but she cooks, feeds the children, sleeps with the children in her lap, wipes their tears and snot. Poor woman! They call it the house of love. What love?"

She made a face mockingly. Then, Banchu Uncle's daughter, Renu, is alive! But was there only one Renu in this area? Kartika ran on that uneven road with hope and fear undulating his mind.

If Renu was alive, Kartika would get back half of his lost world. The other half depended on Renu's wishes. Seeing him, Renu need not laugh; if she only cried, Kartika's hot, humid, hopeless world would swell and overflow.

The walls of the so-called house of love had never experienced the soft touch of love from any hand. So where was the question of the subtle jhoti on the walls? Like an abandoned cowshed, that earthen house was looking deformed. A few naked, half-naked children were strolling outside the house like stray dogs. Watching them with unseeing eyes, a young widow, looking like one who had lost her prime, was standing forlorn and lost.

Seeing her, heartbrokenKartika became emotional. What transformation had come over her! Driven out by her husband on a dowry dispute, she'd lived with her parents, wearing a big vermilion mark on her forehead, looking like the village deity. But now, devoid of the vermillion, the young widow looked decrepit. Had the heartless cyclone befriended forever her stone-hearted husband? There was no child in Renu's arms. The cyclone had taken away even her child, cutting off a piece of her liver. Fateless Renu, losing her child, husband, and father, was now a walking corpse.

But why was she here when Bipin and Baikuntha were alive? Of course, Bipin and Baikuntha did not have a roof over their heads. But they were males. They could sleep even on the river sand. Yes, Renu had done the right thing by coming over to this orphanage.

Hearing footsteps from behind, the widow turned and stared long at Kartika. Renu's face looked so wooden and stern, like that loveless house of orphans and destitute, that Kartika felt he was looking not at Renu, but her corpse.

Losing all his sense, Kartika clasped the naked hands of Renu and asked in a sobbing voice, "O' Renu, can you not polish the loveless walls of this orphanage with soil and draw jhoti on them? Is it not enough to have faith in God, that you have survived this killer cyclone? You may mourn the dead, but for that, there is no scriptural authority that you would be a corpse while being alive! That is sin. Your husband was cruel, yet you mourn for him. Although he has not left behind any pleasant memory for you, you would mourn his cruelty. Your mind and heart are made of such elements.

"All right. No problem with that, for that distinguishes man from animals. Now, tell me, Renu! Would you again wear bangles in your hands, wear the vermilion on your forehead; polish the mud walls with the soil? Would you wipe off the old sorrows from your heart? Would you draw again the feet of goddess Laxmi on dead walls? Would you draw the pitcher, peacocks, lotus with rice paste-tell me Renu, believe me-I can't see your destitute face when I'm alive.

"What more would I tell you, Renu, about my true feelings? Only for you, I said no to Padma. I dragged my feet and delayed confirmation in the case of Girima. Believe me, yes, believe me."

Renu replied straight, mercilessly, "Yes, I can draw jhoti on the dead walls, can wear vermilion on my plain forehead. I would do whatever you ask me to do, and I would put the entire compensation money for the death of my husband and son at your feet. But can you find my son? People have seen the dead body of my husband, but my son's body is not found anywhere. How can I believe that the apple of my eye is dead? I am blind, not seeing them. Where are my eyes to draw on the walls?" The streaming tears actually made her blind.

Kartika reassured her, "Dear Renu, try to see the world through my eyes. You are not alone in sorrow. My sorrow is not any less. If we join our sorrows, life would pass on its course."

Having lost all faith and trust in everybody, Renu said clearly, "When I entered my father's house with my son in my arms, at that time, none assured me as you have done. Had my father heard this, he would have died peacefully. You are not the only one brother Kartika. Many young men known and unknown are loitering around me to put vermilion on my forehead. Money is power, you know. But such a long life is ahead, and how much is one-and-a-half lakhs? There are such fortunate destitute here in this orphanage, who would get three-to-four lakhs. Go to them, Kartika."

"Fie! This cyclone has made you so heartless? You have never said such harsh things to anyone," Kartika said sulkily.

Renu retorted sullenly, "The women for whom no groom was available, for the sake of the death-compensation money, strings of men are pushing each other out. Seeing such drama every day, I now know the true colors of everyone. Finally, you came to put salt on my wounds?"

After such a long time, from the tear-blinded eyes of Renu, the embankment-breaching, saline tide gushed onto the tightly clasped hand of Kartika. Kartika released his grip from Renu's hand before he himself was blinded by sorrow, and he retraced his steps back to the void of his world.

But, turning back, he saw his empty world suddenly full. On a bald farmland were standing Bikram Balabantaray and Bhudan Das, waiting for him. Seeing them, Kartika burst into tears. He couldn't know whether in joy or sorrow. Kartika embraced the two friends, one by one, and wailed aloud.

Bhudan said, "Hey, you hero! Does grass grow on top of a hill? Standing on top of a mountain of sorrow, how is it that, still, tears flow from your eyes? Your eyes should have turned into stone, as ours!"

Suppressing his sobs, Kartika said haltingly, "From the top of the hill, stones do fall and turn into dust. My condition today is like that."

Bikram stroked the back of Kartika and said, "Hey, as a drama hero, you must have jumped over many an insurmountable peak of sorrow! Life is nothing but a play; who better than you here can be found who can jump over the mountains of sorrow like a real hero? Look at me; I'm a soldier. For me, this is a battlefield. I'm fighting. You are a hero. Whatever has happened was the climax scene of a play. After that reunion, try reconciliation and dreams of a new life, forgetting the past. Does anyone see a drama where there is no sorrow? Has anyone lived a life without pain?"

"Yes, you're speaking the truth. Hereafter, one has to only act; to act as alive after death," Kartika said. His eyes were no longer streaming tears. A resolve was born immediately in him and spread its branches.

Bikram shook hands with him and said, "Yes, you have to act, but only as a hero. We are all the side actors. Here there are many heroines, diverse goals, no chance of any rivalry between us. All of us are in the same boat. If the boat turns turtle, all of us would die, therefore, each one of us must hold an oar."

"But the navigator is one; He who stays unseen. He turns the boat, and He straightens," said Kartika.

"But the boat sinks if the hand does not grip the oar," said Bhudan.

Kartika said, "You have convinced me in many ways. What's to gain, pleading ignorant? Now, tell me, what shall we do?" Kartika walked ahead. Bikram and Bhudan followed. All headed toward an undamaged mosque that, from a distance, looked like an island in the sea.

Searching for her village, an unfortunate woman was walking on a pathless, strange world. Where would she go? The cyclone had reduced everything to nothing. How long she'd been walking, when the last morsel of food fed her belly, she had no memory of it. When she gained consciousness, she could know that the rest of her life must be lived alone. She would not get back the dear departed, nor the villages or landscape of the days gone by. She has no past, no future.

The clothes on her body are torn and disheveled. She is not aware of that; hunger, thirst, despair, and fatigue have overpowered shame, etiquette, and mental resolve. She has no hesitation to beg for a handful of food from anyone; no hesitation to lay the stiff, tired body on anyone's veranda to get back her breath.

There are no trees on the side of any road to take shelter under, to rest awhile; no house or veranda in any village to accept charity from hospitable strangers. No mid-village platform or altar anywhere. Not a drop of rice water, even in the once-rich households to offer the hungry. Where from would it come, when there was no rice in the house? No hearth, no utensils, no roof, nothing. Roots, tubers, creepers, the food of the poor during droughts, were all dead and gone. Not a drop of water to quench your thirst.

The lonely woman, searching for her village in this confounding world, had turned to stone in her own agony. She had lost everyone except herself. Had God saved her from the cyclone and a python only to suffer?

When her hand went numb in the strong, muscular arm of some warrior, she didn't know then that she was gliding, clinging on to the tail of a python. The python too was being swept off by the gushing current. If in panic she held on to a snake and was pulled into its encircled embrace, how is she guilty of anything?

That day, when she opened her eyes and discovered herself in the coiled grip of the python, she had given up all hope for life. The python was so weak that, when she freed herself from its grip, placing her foot on its body, it did not react, but she again fell into water. Floating, she'd held on to a thorn bush. Her palm skin had been peeled off and she'd fallen unconscious. When she'd come back to her senses, she could tell that she'd been standing the whole night, holding on to a bamboo bush.

At dawn, she still had no choice but to stand, for sitting would have meant drowning. The morning after the cyclone subsided was a Saturday. From dawn to dusk, the water level in the field was high, and she'd stood limp in that water. From a distance had been heard the panicky call of villagers. "Mother, aunt, brother, sister-come! Wherever you are, respond."

She didn't know that she was standing fully naked in the water. At the call of the people, she'd come to her senses, looked at herself. She had realized the futility of human life. Seeing hundreds of naked corpses, she had understood that the human body is a mere frame. The life-force makes its illusion on the body. When the call comes from above, the life-force deserts it in a moment; the body with which it had so much attachment for so long, it goes away, maybe to heaven. The body remains like a hell hole till it disintegrates into earth. Whereas, for this body, the entire drama of life! Food for the belly, clothes for the back, oil and turmeric, alta and vermilion, jewelery!

Actually, life is a vital fluid, the body a case, and another layer on the case are clothes. How unworthy is this body and more unworthy is the raiment? But why worthless? No, no, the dress is an aspect of culture. She is standing in water, covering her breasts with the thorny bamboo bushes, ashamed to go to the shore. Standing at the threshold of death, why so much shame for this fisherwoman? No shame this; this is prestige.

Had she died, she would have been floating, naked, and the survivors would have said, "Alas! Alas!"

But, escaping death, if she walks naked to the shore, people may say, "Alas! Poor girl," but they would despise her wordlessly. And she would die of shame. She could not walk in the village again with her head held high. Immersed in such thoughts, she did not give a call. Shivering out of cold, she did not ask for help, lest somebody should see her in that state.

When some people, seeing her from a distance, came to her in a raft, she shouted, "Don't come here, brothers, I have no clothes on me."

The raft stopped. All men are not inhuman. Someone threw a saree at her. Wrapping the saree on her body, she shouted, "Rescue me, brothers. My body is stiff. The cold has numbed my limbs."

People rescued her, warmed her body with fire, and brought her back to life. They gave her a handful of rice flakes and asked, "From which village are you, child? Who are your father and brother? If they are alive, good. Otherwise, go to the destitute shelters arranged by government."

Thereafter, she started moving in the uncharted path to search for her familiar world. Many unfortunate ones like her were moving in search of their place of birth. She lost herself among those. Placing a leaf plate in the free kitchen, she ate khichdi to her bellyful. She could recognize her dear Erasama market, although the face of the bazaar was totally changed. There, the relief work was going on. A variety of flags of the philanthropic donors were flying. No mourning was heard anywhere. Seeing the soldiers, she searched for a familiar face. Then, she thought, "it is good that the young man died fighting for the country and became a martyr, made Erasama proud. Had that daredevil soldier Bikram Balbantaray come to this village for the Dussehra festival, he would have faced the fury of the cyclone and would have gone into the mouth of the sea through the Jatadhari estuary. He may be an army hero, but before the cyclone, a mere mortal. He would have slept among the thousands of corpses here. Instead of calling him a martyr, people would have said, 'an unfortunate Erasamite.' God's decree is great."

She consoled herself. How many forms has death, and what meanings! There is a great deal of difference between dying fighting the cyclone and dying fighting the enemies of the country. Bikram had chosen the latter. Therefore, he was more fortunate than the thousand young men of this area, even in death. Her eyes filled with tears, thinking about the fortunate death of Bikram, in the midst of all her misfortunes. Did any one of these strings of soldiers know Bikram?

She thought of asking someone about Bikram, and then she thought "Once you know about his death, it's futile to know other things about him. Who recognizes whom in this chaos, who keeps information about others?". Therefore, she didn't search for anyone, didn't search for her lost poetry book, nor her own future. For whom the poems, for whom the dreams of future? Where the soil has become unknown, the earth faceless, there where everything becomes strange, she may be rid of sorrow and pain.

So thinking, she walked away from the din of the place that was once the hub of her life. Along the banks of Hansua River, on the seashore, instead of trying to search for the footprints of known and dear ones, she stared blankly at the empty horizon and walked straight on. Walking for a while, she stood at a lonely point of the seashore where the fate of the boats and rafts had shattered in the cyclone. Gathering the pieces of the boats, she felt that she was collecting the lost days and her lost father and brothers, who, like these broken pieces of boats, could never be joined together again. With folded hands, she prayed to the sea to return her fate and adolescence and to return her father, dearer than her own life.

TWENTY SEVEN

The sea returns everything; doesn't owe anything to anyone. The sea is a liberal giver. If you offer anything to the sea, it refuses to accept in a loud roar and throws back the gift on the shore. It takes in one hand, returns on the other. In childhood, she'd always loved this give-and-take game with the sea. When she threw a small thing into the sea, the sea used to throw it back on the wet sand of the shore.

One day, taking out a bunch of flowers from her bun, she'd thrown it to the sea and said lovingly, "O' sea! I have given you the flowers of love. You are now my husband! This flower is yours. If you return it, I'll be angry. I'll sulk. I'll never marry you. You have given us food, clothes, fate, and futures. This flower is a token of my gratitude. I'm a poor fisherwoman, what could I give you? You have your treasures of jewels. Moreover, you've given birth to goddess Laxmi, who is Annapurna, the goddess of plentitude, the giver of sustenance. What want do you have? You accept my flower, for my sake."

But no! Even her flowers were thrown back on the wet sand, mutilated. That day, she had cried a lot, thumping her feet on the wet sand. She'd thought it was arrogance on the part of the sea not to accept anything from others. Yet, she had loved the arrogant sea! One who is born in a coastal village, can she live without loving the sea only because the sea at times licks off the villages?

Some demented woman, with her hair disheveled, was sitting at a distance with her face down, wasting her tears on the wet sand. The seashore sand was wet with her own sorrow. Does it wait for anyone's tears to get wet? Drawing lines on the wet sand she was, as though computing her horoscope.

Not in soft murmur, but aloud for everyone to hear, she was saying,"O' Sea! I believe that you would certainly return my child and my husband! As you released me, release all my loved ones gracefully. Otherwise, I will not move from here. I will die without touching food or water in your name."

People were crying, "Alas!" and looking at the madwoman. They were talking amongst themselves that, after the cyclone, that woman had been sitting at that particular place and muttering those words endlessly.

Someone said, "Hey, you! Serving of food has already started at the free kitchen. People in hordes will take away everything. If you want to eat, come quick with us."

The madwoman replied with her face down, "You all go. I will go when my son comes. With whom shall I leave my child if I go?"

People went their own ways, wondering about the woman; for if the rice and dal were finished, no one would cook for them again.

At that time a cry, "Mother! Mother!" reverberated the shore, and a child came running. The demented woman did not raise her head. She was familiar with such orphan cries. That was not the cry of her child. Her child's cry was sweet like music.

Saying, "Mother, mother, my mother," the child came running, swelling the heart and eyes with uncontrollable tears, and threw its cold, soft body on her back.

The madwoman smelled the scent of the child's body, up to her heart's content, with her eyes closed. It was not necessary to recognize the child, opening her eyes. The same face, the same tears, saliva, the same sobs and the same smell, the same hunger in its belly, the same despair, and a chest full of orphan pain. It was the same desperate howl of, "Mother!"

Without opening her eyes, she pulled the child to her bosom, poured on its face warm, passionate kisses, andthrust her breast into its mouth, holding it tight on her bosom.O'the long-saved ambrosia from her breast flew onto its lips. The child suckled in the same manner, and drank like a calf free from its tether.

"Ah-ha! A mad woman! Who knows whose child that is? But she says it's hers!"

"Yes, she would pounce on someone else's husband and claim him to be her husband," someone said, not in jest, but with pity.

The madwoman did not care for that. Holding the child in her arms and kissing it madly, she walked along the sandy shore, maybe in search of her safe village, where there would be her home and hearth, neatly thatched roof, and on the roof would be rolling gourds and pumpkins and a pot full of watered rice, dry fish in a pitcher hanging from the roof, raw chili in the backyard. Oh! She was dying of hunger.

Her husband must be returning from the fish godown, tired and hungry. Who bothers about her own hunger? But in no direction could she see any trace of a village. Maybe the villages were pushed back by the sea. But the madwoman did not bother about that. When her child had been found, where would the village go?

A gush of breeze blew softly the unruly tufts from her face. Like the half-burned, oil less wick of a blown-out lamp, her body was half-singed. Her face was half bright and halfsooted like the copper lamp. The unforgettable beauty of her joy and sorrow mixed, and her half-bright face was seen by Kartika, who was searching for something absentmindedly in the sand-filled spaces.

In a pain-fraught, voice he called out, "Padma! Are you Padma? I have come back. I am your Kartika brother. I am also looking for my bosom friend, Bhagya, your husband. He is no more, dear Padma. He jumped into Jatadhari estuary, trying to save a madwoman, as witnessed by Baikuntha Tarai.

"The sea has wiped off the vermillion mark from the foreheads of many unfortunate women. You console yourself. I will be the father of your son. I will marry you. Do not distrust me, for I had refused to marry you the other day."

Kartika burst into tears. Kartika forgot his love, melted by compassion. Renu's face faded away from his eyes with the vapours of sympathy and compassion for Padma.

The madwoman stood, stunned. She looked at Kartika's face with baleful eyes. She said satirically, "You would marry me? For the few lakhs death compensation for my husband and father, perhaps, you have such fondness and concern for me? Who was dying to marry you then, and who is crying to marry you now? Fie! All around are lying the bodies of family and clan. Standing in the midst of a crematory, you are planning to wear the groom's crown only for my money? So inhuman?"

"No, no, Padma. Do not speak like that. I too would get the compensation money for the death of my parents. Why do I need so much money? Seeing your condition, I feel guilty. Your marriage was fixed with me. When I refused, you were married to Bhagyadhar. Had we married, the vermilion mark from your forehead would not have faded. Thinking of that only, I say these things. Is it a fault to have developed pity for you?"

"What did you say? Pity, compassion? You would marry me out of pity? Where were you so long with such a large heart? Out, out of my sight, else I will eat you up."

Clasping the child to her breast, the poor woman advanced her steps toward some unknown village. Kartika looked back. No, Padma is not worthy of pity. Kartika himself is an object for pity.

The child was crying bitterly. In that blank, quarterless void, another madwoman was running behind her in search of some certainty. She was shouting, "Padma, sister-in-law! Padma, sister-in-law," but Padma did not turn back, as if she was advancing toward her destination with a sacred resolve.

Let her walk. The road would definitely come to an end. If Padma found her village, Girima would definitely get Padma and the child in her arms. Another orphan was sobbing for its parents, looking at the bosom of the sea. Girima lifted the child to her arms without thinking about consequences, and she almost ran. Like water dousing fire, the child stopped crying and looked with bewildered eyes at the loving face of Girima. Girima kissed the saliva-and-tear-smeared face of the child again and again. She had never suffered birth pangs herself, but she was transformed into a mother at that moment.

The supercyclone had thrown children helter-skelter, emptying the laps of parents. Girima, by now, had gathered about ten to fifteen children from the fields and shores. She was determined to set up a village in a lonely place on the banks of a stream, under the bald shade of a few stumps of trees.Padma sister-in-law was at times mad, and at times a housewife. But as the number of orphans increased, she had no time to go mad.The two sisters-in-law were alive, had met, and had resolved to live together. That was not a small thing in the aftermath of the wild dance of the deluge.

Life would not go forward with relief rice and dal. Women, in particular, are never comfortable with donatedfood. How could they be? Is that living or housekeeping where there is no aroma of cooking, where there is no fragrance of rice boiling in a pot, no appetizing smell of baked fish, dry fish, or crab?

What is woman without a home? Is the human child a pup or a kitten? Does life ask for only rice, dal, and khichdi for the belly? How long can man live depending on the doled-out food from the free kitchen?

Therefore, that day, a determined Girima had brought from the relief center pots, pans, and also rice and dal to cook for the children. The relief officer was asking about the welfare of everyone. She had told him, "We will not eat free food anymore. We will work for our keep. We will set up our village. You give us work and give us food in return for our work."

The relief officer was glad. He gave assurances that, if people work on making roads, he would give food as wages. Girima was satisfied, and when she started walking back, she saw that a line of destitute women was following her. At their waists, a child each. Someone was holding her own child; someone was carrying an orphan. There was no doubt that the government sheds-or "homes of love"-would automatically waste away like abandoned cowsheds.

The whirlwind came every year, emptied the trees, blew off the thatched roofs, but it was never heard ever that groups of ghosts moved around freely after the whirlwind returned. But this blasted cyclone had reduced the villages to such a bad state that, after nightfall, clusters of ghosts and goblins were moving in groups. The survivors, in the midst of heaps of dead bodies, had already spent so many fearful days and nights.

The ghosts never frightened the survivors when they were hungry and in despair, having lost everything. But after everything settled down, the ghosts came out of the festered bodies and moved freely. Some people had sighted them. After nightfall, from the joints of the heaped up, broken trees, people heard the thwack of the axe on the trees.

At times, people heard the sound of bones breaking on the pyre. Wailings are heard and also the fearful calls of goblins. At times, the fire from burning pyres is also seen from quite a distance.

People say that the unpurged souls cremate themselves, rising from the rotten corpses. The government machinery, NGOs, religious institutions, and volunteers take the credit for counting the heads of dead men, yet thousands of cadavers continue to fester for months. Hence, what options do the ghosts have except to burn their own bodies? There, the people who have survived the terror of cyclone are not in a position to sleep peacefully because of the ghost menace. What can government do on this? The police or anyone else?

Those who cannot ward off thieves, they cannot ward off the ghosts. Besides, it's not the duty of the government or police to handcuff the ghosts. As there is no relief arrangement for the ghosts, some people have encountered the ghosts eating their own flesh, and some of them have kicked the bucket already after few vomits and loose motions. And some have gone mad or demented. Some young men and women, possessed by the ghosts, have started doing many a mischievous thing.

May be the ghosts are sick of eating relief food and possessing young persons, and they shout, "Give us mutton, chicken, fish heads, or else we will twist the heads of the living and eat them up."

The sanyasis and sannyasins have performed Yajnas for world peace, burning mounds and mounds of ghee. The banners of their sects were fluttering in the breeze. Elegantly dressed in their glad rags, the sanyasis and sannyasins appeared in the midst of their devoted followers to the accompaniment of cymbals and drums. Nonstop distribution of prasad was on. But there was no room for these unfortunate villagers. They must pay their respects from a distance and return to their fate. It is only for their peace and welfare the sanyasis have come from far-off places to perform expiatory sacrifices.

The villagers have not yet atoned for their sins. In their state of obsequies, if they came near the sacrificial fire, the Yajna would be polluted. The blessings of the sacrifice would not be achieved. The ghosts and gnomes would be more rabid and mischievous. Even the living might turn into ghosts and make this region a ghostly hell.

Therefore, the gullible, innocent survivors have bowed to the sacrificial fire from a distance. But where is the result? Who has been purified? The sanyasis and sannyasins have already left on their world tour after collecting the offerings of the people. But the ghosts are still unwilling to forsake their village soil.

Girima was praying, staring wide-eyed at the void from the ruined sacrificial cauldrons. "Give all the ghosts and goblins salvation, God. Don't torture them anymore. But before releasing my father's soul, confront me with his ghost at least once, so that I would finally believe that the man who was cut out to be immortal, that pious and godly Udhab Mangual, my father, is no more. Touts and cheats like Narku Routray, Tahali Mohanty, Dhadi Barik, and others of their ilk survived, but Kalki destroyed selectively good men like my father, Golmasta, Bhairab Uncle, Banchu Uncle, Gandhi Uncle, and Bharat Uncle! What justice of yours is this?"

People were saying that the indomitable ghost of Udhab Mangual was roaming on earth. Many had seen him. He moved in the dark and disappeared in the shades of broken trees, breaks tall trees with fearful cries and fells wood with rhythmic strokes. Fire is seen from that direction, other ghosts rise from the edges of the Bijuria river-then is heard the axe strokes.

Also heard in the croaking voice of Udhab Mangual, the rise and fall of horse dance songs. Girima believes that the ghost singing the undulating tunes of horse dance was none other than her father, Udhab Mangual. Humming the horse-dance song, her father rowed his boat like a man possessed, and was doing everything with the help of the young lads. But Girima was so unfortunate that the ghost of her father did not show up even once."All right, let him not show up, but let the ghost be well."

Girima, however, knew that even after death her father's ghost must be worrying about his children and grandchildren. Girima could visualize tears rolling down the ghost's cheeks, although Udhab Mangual had never showed his weakness while alive. Girima bowed down near the sacrificial cauldron and prayed.

"O' God, if you don't mean to release the soul of my father, at least don't give tears in his eyes. Let his ghost roam around his village, rivers, and sea freely. If not today, definitely tomorrow his ghost could meet with me." Girima knew, even as a ghost, her father would never harm anyone. He was now a merciful and loving ghost of this area. Men like her father, after being ghosts, did miracles for the good of the living.

A few sparks were still emanating from the embers in the abandoned sacrificial cauldron after the priests had left. They appeared like a flash of hope in the midst of despair. That spark was enough to find your way in the darkest core of a forest.

From the fields made saline by feeding on the flesh and blood of the dead villagers, Girima collected a few strands of straw and rolled them into a tight rope ball. Picking up a cinder from the extinguished cauldron, she put it on the ball of straw. She felt as though she had touched the sacred fire to the faces of the dead villagers.

That's it. No point anymore now mourning the dead. Giving charge of the orphans to sister-in-law Padma, she had come to collect some fire and firewood. After getting the fire, she felt like she'd gotten everything. In the flattened villages, even fire was invaluable. Shaking the torch of the straw ball, Girima turned homeward. Home! Yes, home! Where the hearth fire was lighted by a woman; that was home, that was housewarming.

Where pain and pleasure, tears and laughter rend the sky, that's a village. Where women cook rice and curry, there life flows, man survives. What worry then?

The deluge was not the end, rather a new beginning, thought Girima, while watching the rice cook. The children were waiting for their meals with leaves spread out in front of them. The women served rice and dal. The fragrance of a new life wafted from this hot food.

What to do, how to live? The people do not see any way out. Waiting for government aid, half of them had died by now, and the other half had no more tears to shed waiting for government help. To hell with the government!

The village near Ambiki Panchayat, about three kilometers toward the sea, has now a signboard. Upto two lakhs would be given for house construction under the food-for-work scheme. Girima, Padma, nor Renu saw when that signboard was hung. Otherwise, the women of this place would have cut their throats and drunk their blood. Such hypocrisy? Here there is no road, no food, and no work-nothing.

Molding mud, the women have made their shelters. Some NGO's have made roofs for them with polythene, gunny bags, and such stuff. The make-shift houses look like a village. Such villages have now come up in large numbers by the efforts of enthusiastic young men.

Girima has heard that, in place of the washed-away villages of Abhayapur and Lavanipur in the Ambiki Panchayat, a new world has been raised on the dead, salinated areas. Even brick houses too have come up here and there. But no one is able to say whether school buildings have been repaired or newly constructed. People think of only rice and dal when the day breaks. Who, except Girima, thinks about schools?

Girima moved her eyes from one end to the other. A dry swamp. There was no ridge in the middle, absolutely plain. No documents of ownership, everything had been swept off. No harvest, hence no fight over thine and mine. Good from all angles.

Girima and others are teaching the alphabets to the children, also the oral multiplication table. According to the age of the children and according to the capability of the teachers, the children are learning orally; no blackboard, no notebook, no chalk, no slate, nothing. Leave alone government initiative, even God does not bother about the forsaken folk.

In the food-for-work program, boats were being built on the banks of Saomlia River! Girima worked there. She was the daughter of Udhab Mangual. She has never built boats, but has heard and seen. She could know intuitively that the boat-builders who had come from the cities were working for the profit of the contractors, on the recommendation of the political leaders. The way they were working, the boats would sink. It might not even go that far. Before touching water, those may break.

The planks of wood were joined mindlessly. The boats would sink. In fact, the planks were cracking up, as they were unseasoned. The boats were lying like the unwanted crematory pitchers. The contractors had left after collecting their profits. The people were looking up to the sky expectantly.

Fishing is now possible in the river, but the boats are lying like a mockery. Girima thought, "Had that sprightly young man, Bikram Balabantaray, been alive today!". No, he would not have been her husband, but he would have been a great support to the survivors of this area. But why think about him? No choice but to go at it alone. Yet she would not allow the destitute women and children to go to the home of love, to be identified publicly as destitute.

Let the loo of despair blow over. When the monsoon would break, the minds cracked up by sorrow and despair like the gaping earth would again be moist. In the soft soil, hope would spread its birth cries. At that time, it would be a work of merit to get the widowed young women, Renu, Sarala, Prema, Jyotsna, Lavani, Kuanri, Sudasa, Kahri, Jhoti, Bhagabati, Nihari, Pahili, Koeli, Fatima, Noorjahan, Roshanara, Nagma, Sophia, and Mumtaz-married.

It's not a sin to get married again if the husband deserts or dies halfway through life; not even a deviation from tradition. In this area, second marriage was not new. But let the proper time come. For the leaves to spring up on the branches of broken trees, it does not take much time. But hope would definitely take a long time to germinate in shattered minds. Like getting butter from churning sour curds, man has not only the power, but the art of achieving happiness by churning sorrow. It's not reflective of man's resolute power; it's an art of living. Man is blessed with that art.

While cooking for a flock of children, she was reminded of her father. Since she rarely went to the kitchen, her mother used to grumble, "Let me see which governor's house you would go to that you would not cook rice and curry? Would you not dry the fish, and simply write songs, swaying in a swing? I'm telling you, only for this you would be kicked out of your in-law's house like that Renu, and return here. You'll not last a year there. Then you would understand. A woman, be she a teacher or a minister, would definitely go to the kitchen."

Girima had been rolling in laughter, and Udhab Mangual, taking her side, used to say, "Oh-ho! As if cooking is a more difficult task than making boats! My daughter is intelligent and literate. Let the marriage be finalized. She will enter the kitchen automatically. Cooking rice and curry, she will serve me first. Shewill cook tasty food like my mother at Bandar village. For me, the old Bela grandma was also an expert cook, and you too. Yet mother had a fine hand, entirely distinctive.

"Wait. When my daughter learns cooking, everybody

will inhale the aroma with joy. Do you understand? My daughter is the child of Mahanadi. In her hands, fish creolewill be most tasteful. I'm just waiting for the day when my daughter will cook fish creole, and I'll gulp gleefully a big bowl of hot rice. Why are you not taking it seriously? Let the engagement be over."

The engagement ceremony was over at Shendhakud, and the marriage was fixed; even then, Girima did not enter the kitchen. She told her mother, "If father gets the taste of my cooking now, he will never go to my in-law's house. If at all he goes once, he would never desire to go again. The first time he goes there, my in-laws would send me with him to return with post-marriage gifts for their entire family as part of dowry.

"They would say, 'Return after you learn cooking.' That's what I want. Leaving our house, our village, especially my father, I can't stay continuously in my in-law's house. When I come back for the post-marriage gifts, I will stay here for six months or one year with the plea of learning how to cook. Tell this to father."

Let it go. Now, there is no marriage or post-marriage return, father, mother, in-law's house, nothing. But Girima is cooking rice and curry. Making cakes and delicacies is different; cooking rice and curry is a natural thing that comes without training to women. Pressing the rice from the boiling pot, Girima senses whether the rice is ready. She filters the ricewhen the spiced juice boils. She puts the small fish in the kadai.

One day, Girima told everyone, "Till today, we have not cremated all these dead bodies. The souls inside the dead bodies are in torture. Howwould they accept our offerings? Let's go and burn the bodies by setting fire to the twigs and dried leaves. We'll bow down and say, 'Whoever is tortured in your festering bodies, we have cremated you all.' Then we'll wash our hair and take a dip. Then we will cook and serve food. This is our duty to our forefathers."

The sun was about to set. The fire rose into flames up to the sky. The women and children all bowed down. All went on their ways to do their work. Girima sat with her hand on her cheek, leaning against the wall. The night would end by the time the fire was extinguished. Then, the holy dip. She had no more tears in her eyes. When sorrow thickens, the tears too get frozen. Her eyes were dry like a summer swamp where the saplings of hope would never germinate again. Dreams too would not rekindle.

TWENTY EIGHT

Compassion too is a source of pain, makes man wallow in self-pity. Who would like to live on the mercy of others? Who likes to beg food from another to live? But there is no choice, after the cyclone, but to live depending on others' mercy, charity, and compassion.

Those who have now queued up for the relief packets, shouting, "Give, give," none of them were beggars, not even bribe-takers like many government servants. They'd once had everything. They'd toiled hard, basing their livelihood around paddy, betel leaves and fish, and were living happily for generations. The poor had their parents. Beggars never returned empty-handed from their doors, guests and strangers never returned unfed. Their homes were crowded with friends and relatives. The numerous festivals in Odia tradition were celebrated with pomp and show, with exchange of gifts year after year. They were all established people of an age-old tradition. True that the cyclone has made them homeless, but not rootless.

Today, when the same established people are queuing up for a morsel of food or a piece of cloth to cover their bodies, the relief distributors could not see how their injured pride was bleeding inside. In total indifference, they were getting photographed, offering a handful of rice or a piece of cloth to the affected people. They were getting their pictures published in newspapers. Pictures were also taken in the free kitchens. Now, these people did not need free food or clothes. They needed rehabilitation and work for food.

It was heard at first that the free kitchens would be closed within a fortnight. Now, government has declared that these free kitchens would run for one year. In that case, these young men would never work. They would become shirkers. They would feel that it was their right to get free food. People say that these were not kitchens for the cyclone-affected people, rather election propaganda centers. The chief minister was changed within a month of the cyclone. The election for the legislature was ahead.

The basmatiand other rice, blankets, and other essential stuff in the relief kit, worth ten thousand rupees each that had come from Texas, had been looted on the way before reaching the relief centers. Polythene worth lakhs of rupees simply disappeared. Marking that, people were rumoring that the present government would be kicked out within three months. Therefore, the good things that were coming as aid were actually meant for the political leaders. The foul-smelling rice, fungus affected flour, and torn clothes and blankets were the actual relief materials in the cyclone-affected rural areas.

Not the super-cyclone, but ravenous politics was now rising as the super calamity for the people. When the survivors, after the devastation, were lying exposed to the wrath of winter, foodless, shelter less, naked, instead of standing as protectors, these leaders were preparing for the next election. This relief work might help them in getting votes, and, with that in mind, all political parties were now competing with each other.

Udhab's ghost was watching everything, standing under the cover of the broken trees. He thought that the assembly elections had really saved the cyclone-affected people of this zone. Otherwise, these leaders in the remote villages of their constituencies would never have burned dead bodies. Now they were not hesitant to clean the filth from their own constituencies. They diverted the loaded relief trucks coming from other states to their own constituencies and personally supervised the relief work.

People think of them as charitable, selfless workers. Political clashes, here and there, have been reported because of the competition among them to divert relief trucks to their own areas. The dictum might is right is followed by the leaders. Those who have more power might divert more trucks and load the victims with more relief materials than they need. But there are still certain remote villages where no material has reached, no leaders have ever visited

Because of inequitable distribution of relief materials, the amity that had generated after the cyclone has now gone. The sympathy has petered out. Now, in the villages, there is more of jealousy and ill feeling.

The other day, some leader arrived at the Erasama block office. Around his neck, a garland of imported marigold flowers from Kolkata. People said he was an important minister. In a few days, the election dates would be announced, and hereafter, the national leaders too would make a beeline to these areas. The prime minister and other central leaders, including leaders of the opposition parties, would come to visit the debris of Erasama. Therefore, notice has been given to the relief officers to suspend relief work for a week and make arrangements for the welcome of the national leaders. For this, the environment must be clean. Therefore, it was more important to burn the dead bodies still rotting here than to distribute relief. Otherwise, what impressions would the national leaders carry back? Besides, how would their choppers land in the midst of rotten bodies?

When people came, hungry and fatigued, walking along pathless broken woods for relief to the Erasama block, they learnt that relief work had been stopped. Taking this opportunity, the opposition parties created trouble in the block office. They shouted, "Is there any more mindless work than cleaning the environment for the leaders at the cost of relief work?"

Some leaders squatted on the block veranda, on hunger strike, forcing the authorities to resume distribution of relief. The opposition did not let go of such opportunities in view of the impending election. As if they would have compensated the loss of people in a single day, if they'd been in power!

Bikram stood before the hunger strikers. Behind him was

an army of volunteers. They were now known as Abhay Force. In a firm voice, he said, "Stop this relief farce. Give work to the people. Give them boats and nets. Give them ploughs and pick-axes. People would work and eat. Stop these free kitchens. Give food for work. How long would these proud people live on charity?"

Bhudan ran toward the leaders. He snatched the garlands of marigold from their necks and threw them toward a bare tree standing in front of the office. When the police advanced toward him, he shouted, "Tell your chief minister to learn from this tree. The tree blossoms flowers for others, bears fruits for others, spreads its clan for the happiness of others. The tree doesn't wear the flowers as garlands. The time has come now to garland these trees. We must now be strong like the trees, with our own inner strength. We must elect leaders who live for others, like the trees. You go away from here. Enough drama has been enacted here. No more."

A few more garlands have, in the meantime, adorned the minister's neck. Biscuits were distributed to the children, who were shouting "Give, give," imitating the grown-ups. The minister was putting the garlands on the children, removing them from his own neck. Like the devotees fighting to snatch away frills of Lord Jagannath's tahia, the auspicious crown, the innocent, unfortunate villagers were tearing off flowers from the minister's garlands.

Bhudan Das shouted, "Who do you think you are? Do you think of yourself as the Lord of the Universe, Jagannath? Why should the garlands of your neck fall on the necks of our people? Because you think these people are dumb, you would dupe them? See, these people belong to this grand earth. No way inferior to you. By doing this, you are not insulting us. Rather, you are being insulted-is this your culture? Is this how you behave with others?"

By that time, photographs of the minister throwing garlands at the people were being taken. Sakula Mohanty snatched the camera away from one of the photographersand asked, "Why the pictures of the minister are taken? Has he done something great here? Where was he so long? He hasn't come here today to console the affected people. Instead, he has come to make a stage rehearsal before the Prime Minister's visit. And to tell the people that their government must be elected once again. After such a long time, his soul cried for the cyclone-hit people, is it? Go away, go away from here. Leave us to fight our fate by ourselves. We belong to Jagatsinghpur. We are not fated to live like rootless creepers."

By then, following Bikram's sign, the young lads of Abhaya Force had started removing the banners of all NGO's and religious organizations. Taking this opportunity, some antisocial political activists instigated the hungry mob to loot the relief godown. A few opposition party leaders, taking some old shoes from the heaped-up relief shoes, tried to put a garland of shoes on the minister's neck. The police had to resort to a bum-rush to maintain peace and order. The sensation-hungry newsmen, seeing the emerging chaotic situation, became active in collecting facts and taking pictures.

Bikram appealed to all with folded hands, "Brothers! I'm a soldier; discipline and sense of duty are in my marrow. As you cannot earn merit by treading on a sinful path, so no constructive work can be done by indiscipline and transgression of the rule of law. Respecting the constitution of the country is our sacred duty. The minister is a constitutional figure. Insulting him is insulting the constitution.

"Our respected minister must have understood by now that to exploit the poverty and suffering of the people for political gain is no more acceptable. A farce is now being enacted by hunger strikes, rallies, and writing poems and stories on the devastated people of this area. Thereby, not even an iota of our suffering is lessened. This area is now a museum of corpses and a zoo of the survivors. Relief must stop from today.

"From tomorrow, let there be food for constructive work. Let the people reconstruct their own villages. Let them reshape their lost lives. To live with honor is our human right. The relief tents must be dismantled today."

The people fell silent and slogans were raised. "Long live Bikram Balabantaray!"

The minister asked one of his henchmen, "Who is this fellow? People here treat him as a deity! It would be good to bring him to our party. The assembly seat of this area can be won by the influence of this man. For the election campaign, we want such an articulate young man."

One member of the minister's inner circle went to Bikram Balabntaray and respectfully asked, "Who are you, my boy? Which village were you born in? What's your name? What are you doing? Our chief minister wants to know. You're very fortunate."

Bikram replied in a calm voice, "Where is my village, house, or father, that would give you my identity?"

Bhudan said satirically, "You don't know who he is? Even this CM does not know? How could he know? This poor fellow could not become a martyr. Had he died, the CM would have known him, for he would have laid wreaths on his mortal remains, cameras would have clicked, and all would have seen. This unfortunate fellow, fighting bravely, was missing in the Kargil war. Because of his ill luck, hereturned to his village, and here he has staked his life to work for the survivors of his birthsoil. The government of India has honored him for his bravery. Why should the ministers recognize him? He is not a black marketer, industrialist, or millionaire. What's the point in knowing such people?"

The minister heard the sharp criticism of the protestors with a smiling face, as if a hermit unmoved by praise or blame.

One of his close men told the local leader, "These rural people appear to be quite politically conscious. They seem to have information about the country. Enlist this Kargil hero in our party. If necessary, instead of Tahali Mohanty, we would give a ticket to this young man. Put him in a car, and take him to Bhubaneswar. How much time does it take to pacify these people!"

"But this fellow is in the army. How can we take him in our party?" the local leader asked.

"Why should this young man go to face death again? Find out how many years are left in his army service. How much does he earn, and what monetary benefits is he likely to get from his service? If you pay more than that, see whether he would not follow us like the calf behind the cow!"

Another said, "This lad is saying everywhere that he would dedicate the rest of his life to the service of this village."

"In that case, he has already nursed political ambitions. Because of all sorts of mismanagement, people have lost faith in our government. Now our party is in danger. Search for such young men and take them into the party."

Narku Routray had been out of power for the last five years. This time, the ruling party has been badly mauled in the parliamentary elections. After the cyclone, as three CMs had been changed in the state, the administration was on the verge of collapse. It's not an unfounded apprehension that, in the ensuing assembly election, the ruling party would sink without a trace. Therefore, it was rumored that Tahali Mohanty and Narku Routray would not be given tickets in this area. If the party gives tickets, there is no need to change the party. But if their own party betrays them, they have already planned for a new independent party.

Narku Routray was thinking to enlist these dynamic young persons in their new party. At that time, the minister's confidante said, "Sir! It'll be better if we take a decision in the party office. You needn't worry about this area. This matter would not be difficult for me. I've become middle-aged, testing the pulse of these people."

The minister declared, "For one year, the relief arrangement will continue. The free kitchen also will run. The headcount of the dead also will continue. The longer the list of the dead, the better for us. More aid will come from the center, and the central government will declare this supercyclone a national calamity, under pressure. It would be good for us if there is not a single festered corpse in this area, polluting the atmosphere, before the prime minister visits.

"More than the survivors, these uncremated dead bodies beat the drum of the incompetence of our government. The people swept away by the high tide area somehow are returning after two or three months. They create more problems. Declaring them dead, some of their relatives have already taken compensation money by bribing officers for their death certificates. How is the government guilty of that? Hereafter, unless the dead are identified, restrictions on certificates shall be imposed. Government are not averse to giving compensation, but if the corruption, lies, and bribe-taking does not stop, government would take harsher steps than the super cyclone to check corruption."

"Victory be to the CM! Long live the CM!" The cries reverberated in the air-the hearty shouts of the camp followers. The minister's car turned toward Bhubaneswar from the block office. While the sycophants said that the area has been sanctified by the CM's visit, the people never bothered about that.

"This is not the time to count the heads of the dead. Hereafter, we have to count the heads of the living. Death may be man's destiny, but not the goal. The goal is life. Searching for life while holding death in the fist is man's destiny. Death is not a disease that, if you apply some salve, counting the heads of the dead, they would return from the land of Yama. There is no treatment for death and no compensation."

Bikram squatted on the veranda of the mosque to get back his breath, and spoke again. "Our near and dear ones died. We lengthened the list of the dead. Why should there be any praise for this, and what do we gain from that? Where the bribe money determines the compensation for death, aid for house building, allotment for Indira Awas, there, whether the dead are identified or not does not matter much. The deluge that happened here, had God himself come with a team of volunteers, He could not have identified all the dead, nor could he have cremated them all. So, forget about the dead. Let's start now to count the living, and then we may know that the reconstruction work has really started."

All were sitting on the veranda of the undamaged mosque. That shelter alone had opened its lap for the survivors, irrespective of caste, creed, or religion. Sitting there, a few survivors of the Ambiki Panchayat village, who could have been counted on fingertips, were discussing the balance sheet of the pain and misfortune of the people.

Of course, the Kali temple on the edge of the crematory was undamaged. But the liberalism and equality of the post-cyclone days were not there anymore. Kundala Panda's son, Panchuki, had started his prayer and worship rituals there. The lower caste people were forbidden to go to the temple, as before. As the cyclone-hit lower caste people had taken shelter in the temples, the temples had been desanctified; hence, a spiritual cleansing was going on in all temples, including the Kali temple.

Holding Yajnas and special sacrifices, the temples were restored to their original purity. But the mosque in Pakistanpara had no such caste discrimination. The platform around the banyan tree at the center of the village was cracked in widening circles and had gaping holes in it. The villagers, therefore, could not use it for their meetings. The first post-cyclone village meeting was held in the mosque courtyard.

In the midst of the handful of optimistic young men, Drona Sir was sitting like the dilapidated banyan tree. But, like grandfather Bhisma in the Mahabharat, he silently listened to everything, sleeping on the bed of arrows. He had no doubt that these youngmen had found their way. It might be difficult to reach the goal, but it was a good sign that they were on the right path.

Those who sit tight, folding their limbs, and never walk, thinking that the path is arduous, are useless. The super cyclone, for various reasons, had made many a young person fatalistic and fearful of work, but under the inspirational leadership of Bikram Balabantaray, many youngmen had tightened their belts to set their own houses in order. Sheikh Ghulam Mustafa had invited many stragglers to the mosque to give them shelter.

Bipin said, "What count should we take of the living? We, who are sitting here, are the only living beings around these ten to fifteen villages who are determined to fight our calamity. There is no hope for any survivors anywhere here. They would have come here by now, had they been alive. We must decide what we can do. How many Gandhis were born in our country? How many Ramas, Krishnas, Jesuses, Nanaks, Madhusudans were born in this world? You just wait and see. Under the guidance of Drona

Sir, we would march forward like the monkey force of Rama. You just wait and see how many people from other villages would join us to work for this area. If you have faith in God, don't distrust man. Does God do anything himself? He does things through man only. Don't you remember the Bhagabat lines? 'I do and get things done through you. You have no way without me.'"

Everyone chanted the lines.

"You see! As you automatically repeated these lines, the others too would join us spontaneously," said Bikram in a happy state of mind. "But we have to be patient."

"Then what's our plan for tomorrow?" asked Baikuntha.

"We would not speak the word "tomorrow" from this moment. Promise now. And whatever we do, we would do from today, from this moment," said Mantri Mallick.

Bikram smiled, a smile of approval. He said, "Mantri Mallick is our leader. Let our work begin from now. First, we'll move around the villages of Ambiki Panchayat and count the living heads, not the dead. We'll release our children and mothers and sisters from the shelter house of the government. We will set our own villages, build our houses, and settle ourselves. How long should we depend on the charity of others to survive?

"In our new village, the word destitute would be banned. I would apply to the relief commissioner, and all of you would sign on it. Yes, you would sign after reading it and understanding it fully. We are all educated here. We would teach the others who are illiterate. No one in our new village would remain illiterate or jobless. Everyone would be literate and self-reliant."

"Yes, all of us would sing. So far, the relief trucks have not come to our villages. We have already repaired the roads by our combined efforts. Now the trucks can come to our area. How long should we run to the block office for a handful of relief?"

Bikram stood in the middle of the gathering, and said, "You people, then, have understood like this? Are we going to live forever by stretching our hands before others? Hereafter, we would work and earn our keep; set up villages, set up schools and from tomorrow, no relief. We will apply to the relief commissioner to give us food for work. We all will go and gherao the free kitchens. We'll boycott the handing out of food.

"We'll see how our young men will sit, leaning against broken walls on empty stomachs, playing cards, mocking at the strength and energy given by God. When hunger burns their bellies, they all will work with us, eat with us, and join us in our rehabilitation program. If you people cooperate, nothing would be impossible."

At the selfsame time, piercing the darkness was heard as stated in Bhagabat, "By the power of duty, compassion, and service, what is impossible on earth?"

Startled, all of them stared into the darkness. No one was aware that, meanwhile, the moon had risen. A dark shadow appeared and suddenly vanished.

"Ghost! Ghost!" some people croaked in fear.

"Nonsense! Does the ghost read the Bhagabat? This is the voice of Udhab Uncle. Perhaps his spirit is watching our activities," said Bhudan.

"No, no, no ghost! Udhab Mangual's soul is keeping an eye on us. He is not a goblin of evil, but a soul of bliss. Therefore, he urges you to work like determined men."

"But where are the witch doctors? The cyclone has swallowed up all those who were here in this area. Only ghosts are here. We'll be the feed for the ghosts here."

While such conversation was going on, hysteric laughter was heard in the darkness around. The lantern was put out after a few flickers. Everyone howled in panic. Bikram lighted the lantern with matches and said, "Good that all witch doctors have been cleaned out from here. The shamans and witch doctors are more dangerous than the evil spirits. We will not search for the witch doctors, but for the people of knowledge and quality. It's now my responsibility to locate the ghosts. The direction from which comes the cracking sounds and the sound of felling trees, I'll go alone in that direction. The ghost cannot escape from me. I have come back fighting with the Pakistani ghosts, day and night, in one piece. Have faith in me."

Bipin said, "If we trust you, we would again float in mid-sea. You're a government man. Heroic soldier. You have been promoted, your salary has been hiked, and you have been awarded and honored. You'll go back to your place of service, closing down the relief centers, driving away the witch doctors, and instigating the ghosts. What worry or want do you have? You are not destitute like us. And who do you have here, so that you would stick to this village?"

Bikram looked with baleful eyes at Bipin. Even in the lantern light the reddish-brown glow of his eyes was visible. His voice was choked with pain and injured self-respect. He said, "What did you say? What want do I have? Again, who do I have in this village? What need do I have? The people of the village may not understand my wants and needs or who is dear to me, but I must explain to you that there is no difference between my dear ones and yours.

"You say I have no one of my own in this village! Therefore, I have no reason to stay here! Half of the men gathered here have none of their own in this village. Why haven't they left the village yet? Is there no other village in this world, where there is no drought, storm or cyclone? Okay, I have no bloodline in this village. But can you say that I have no relationship with this village and its soil? To tie me to this village, is not the soil enough? If man's ties with the birth soil is severed after the death of his family and bloodline, then there would not be anything called a village or a country. Listen to me, all of you!

"This village is mine. I have every right on this soil. All those who are alive now are my family. All are my people, my own. I am not going anywhere, leaving you now. Together, we will do the reconstruction and regeneration of this village. As I was ready to sacrifice my life to protect my country form the enemy, so I vow to dedicate my life to save this area from floods, cyclones, droughts, illiteracy, and superstition."

"What about your service? Rising from the level of a jawan, you are now elevated to a higher rank, and, like this, one day you will be an officer. Can you sacrifice such a good job, prestige, and self-respect for this village? You are a great son of our area, our pride and honor. How can we wish that you kick the job and live here with us unfortunate people and suffer all pain and torture? Do you think we are so selfish?" said Bipin.

Bikram's eyes were moist. Staring vacantly at the distant sky, he said, "For whom this salary? Who's there to enjoy it? If I rise to the rank of an officer, I don't have my parents, brother, or sisters to rejoice over my promotion. Friends, relations, my childhood friend, Bhagyadhar, and his father, brother, and sister." Bikram paused.

Bipin understood. Bhagyadhar's sister, referred to by Bikram, was not Charu or Taru or Marua. She was Girima. Sighing deeply, he said, "There is no one now in Udhab Mangual's family. Only Bhairab Uncle's daughter, Bhagyahdara's wife, Padma. But she is raving mad."

Bikram said, "Why then any attraction for the job? To tell you the truth, this army service was never a vocation for me; it was service for the country. It is not a big thing to kick the job, but how can I kick my service for the country? I have applied for voluntary retirement. Let's see what happens."

From the darkness around, loud clapping was heard. All shouted, "Ghost! Ghost!" In the next moment, joining the clapping of the ghost, all of them supported Bikram's resolve. All their fears and apprehension were gone. In the distant darkness was seen light, abright light-or was it fire?

Bikram said, "Let the morning come. We'll search for the living heads and be together."

"Okay. Let the night end. As long as the sun is there, can any night be endless?" Drona Sir said, raising his head. He was visualizing the future with his eyes closed.

Returning from the other world, wading through many an untrodden way, Saraladas Mandal had located his birth soil. The sand dune near the Ambiki fair was no more there. On the days of the regular fairs, no vendors gathered. Yet he could locate the soil where he had given the first birth cry, had grown up, and had his worldly life. The sea had carried him Lord knows where. Whether mercifully or mercilessly, he was thrown somewhere; that too he never could know.

After gaining consciousness, how he came, almost sleepwalking, to his birthplace, he couldn't understand. He heard lot of things about Utkalmani Mandal's great sacrifice, superhuman courage, and inimitable service to man-how Utkalmani rescued about fifty to sixty persons from the jaws of death, and how he himself was sucked into the mouth of Jatadhari estuary. He heard everything.

He also heard that his family and clan had all been killed by the cyclone; had mingled in the slush and mud of this soil. Utkalmani's wife, Mandodari, had survived the cyclone, but could not tolerate the loss of her husband and children. One day, she'd hung herself from the banyan tree, standing firm at the mid-village platform with the relief saree she had with her.

Bharat Mandal was born in undivided India. By a quirk of fate, he'd become a Bangladeshi; again, he became an Indian, leaving Bangladesh to live in Ambiki Panchayat. His children were born in this loving village. In the Odia primary school, they learned the alphabets, read the Madhusudan Rao grammar, and also read the Bhagabat of Jagannath Das, the Ramayan of Balaram Das and Sarala Das's Mahabharat-all in Odia. They spoke in Odia, sang Odia songs, and ate the rice cakes, watered rice, dalma, kanji, and other Odia cuisine. They also adopted the Odia cultural festivals. They accepted the Odias as their kith and kin. They voted in the elections, shared the joys and sorrows of Odisha, their brothers and relations mingled in this dust.

But after his brother Utkalamani's sacrifice also, is he counted as a Bangladeshi? The soul of Gopabandhu made him die for others, and, after all that, his brother has no dignity. Who is he searching for then, in this soil, being a Bangladeshi? Does he not have anyone here? Does he not have any special connection with this soil?

Sarala Das Mandal stood, absentminded. He was not recognizable because of his dirty, shabby clothes, and his beard, which had grown during the calamity. Someone asked him, "Hey! Who do you search for here? Why don't you go to the relief camp?"

"Who should I search for? I'm trying to find myself. Who am I? Where's my village? Which is my birth soil?" Sarala Das said in a choked voice.

"This fellow is stark mad. Many like this man have lost their minds after losing their near and dear ones," another commented. Sarala Das was not hurt by such comments about him. Because, in this comment, there was a streak of sympathy mixed with the derogatory words.

Standing on deserted ground, he asked a lone wayfarer, "I heard that many people from this village have been swept off into the sea. The majority of the victims are from this Panchayat. It's unfortunate."

"Who said that many people from this village have been swept off into the sea? You must have heard some rumors. Only two from this village have died in the cyclone," said the man.

"But I heard that, from these coastal villages, hundreds have gone into the sea," Sarala Das said in utter amazement.

"Oh-ho! You are perhaps speaking about those Bangladeshi refugees! They are all finished. How long would fate have tolerated them? They destroyed our forests, put us into danger-the sea has finished them all. Tit for tat. Why should they be our villagers?"

The wayfarer moved toward the riverbank. The strokes of sorrow in his heart made him realize that he was alone here. He had no village here. But where would he go? Where is his country? He advanced his steps in this hopeless world, aimlessly. Maybe beyond the horizon he might find his motherland and village. While walking, he came across many unburned bodies, half-burned skulls, and bones. It was not possible to distinguish whether those were Bangladeshi, Pakistani, or Odia bones.

At that moment, a shadow came thumping toward him, stood glaring before him. Sarala Das too stood up. Like getting the treasures of life, he said, "Mantri! You!"

Mantri recognized him by his voice. Embracing him, he said, "Brother Sarala Das, where were you so long? We thought you were no more. You could recognize me easily. I was the crematorydevil; my appearance, therefore, has not changed much.

But you look like the devil himself. Here, everyone looks like devil. Difficult to recognize. Well, you are now found. One more head, that too a head like that of Sarala Das's, will now enter our list. Today was auspicious. Bikram Balabantaray's fist is now stronger. Come now, let's go."

"In which list has my name been entered? Dead or alive? I have no country, no village; I'm a Bangladeshi refugee. Therefore, my name would not be entered in any list." He started weeping.

Embracing him, Mantri Mallick said, "See these skulls? Their bodies have already mingled in the earth. This was the Bengali village. Next to that was the Pakistani Pada. There too heaps of dead bodies mingled in this soil. It's true that one who leaves a country does not get a motherland again. But he gets soil. To whatever corner of the world he goes, the earth does not cast him aside. God has created this soil and earth; man creates what you call motherland. Because of that, the country divides people.

"There is no mine and thine on the earth. You'll get a new world here, never mind a motherland. We have vowed to create a new world. Bikram Balabantaray will explain everything to you. I can't go deep into matters. Come with me. He will tell you everything." Saraladas followed Mantri Mallick in search of a new world.

The battle of Kurukshetra is over. The bodies of family and clan are spread over the earth like seeds. The survivors, lying on the bed of arrows, feel that this kind of survival is worse than death.

Bikram stood, staring at the zodiac of the earth from the void of his reality. The sea had wiped out the boundaries and borders of all the villages of this area. Why? Was it only a moment's madness? Are the villages not his? Are these villages not the undivided India, including people from Pakistan and Bangladesh? No, no, this is the whole world. Maybe the super cyclone was a warning to the people, only to make the humans conscious of the wholeness of creation. See the void all around.

Borders separating village from village are not there. The trees marking the borders are not there. The seat of the gosain, the seat of the Sadhu, the village market and festival platform, the small earthen temples, the thatched roof of the school building-nothing is there. Everything is wiped out.

TWENTY NINE

Government could not clear the heaps of broken trees. Rather, it declared, "Clear away the broken trees." The wood thieves had a field day. They cut away not only the broken trees, but also the unbroken ones, and started their own woodworks and godowns, thereby earning millions. There is no one to question them as to why they felled the living, unbroken trees. And who cares if anyone asks? Chaos has reigned over an area that had a disciplined life of its own before.

Gazing at the horizon, Bikram said, "See! You have read in the books that the earth is round. Now you've seen it with your eyes. This is not our village; our world is the new world of Satyayug. We don't need a new sky or a new sun. We need new soil and new earth. Those who have lived here would die here and be born here again. Who are our parents? None.

"This soil is enriched by the flesh and blood of our parents, family members, and relations. This earth is our mother, the creator is our father. If we live like one family, one caste, we can withstand all calamities. Otherwise, we will be crushed under the weight of our own sorrow. There would not be a soul left to cremate us. What do you say? Shall we build a new world or simply dissipate?" Bikram expressed his own thoughts.

Saraladas Mandal said, "Yes, we need a new world, one that must be built by new soil and new elements. The clay of Hindus, Muslims, Bangladeshis, Odias, and Christians would raise our walls. From that soil would grow a new harvest. We are all with you. We only wish that we will not be deserted halfway."

"Where shall I go? If the call of the country comes, I have to go. But I'll come back again. I promise."

"I still believe that even grass would not grow here," said Bipin.

"Grass would not grow; let it be. But on this soil shall rise mighty trees. Only we have to control ourselves. Different people come and sympathize with us for their own ends. They do not allow our youth to rise from the bottomless pits of their own helplessness," said Akhtar Mian, Golmasta's nephew.

"Here we are all fishermen. We have caught fish, made prawn farms, have invited the sea to our homes, but now we are all floating in deep waters. Who would control the boat? When God's boat was sinking in the sea, it was the fisherman who controlled the boat. Being boatmen and fishermen, we cannot control ourselves?" Bikram said.

"Yes. We are the inheritors of the fisherman tradition. We'll dispel the deluge. We'll create our own God in the new world. We will worship one God, all of us! Agreed?"

The chorus of the answers resonated in the sky, "Agreed! Agreed!"

At that time, carrying two axes, came like the typhoon the father-son duo, Bharjan Mallick and Mantri Mallick. Bharjan said, "Who said you'll install God here? We don't need any god. Which god saved us? Rather, all deluges are caused by that plot maker. All these caste-culture divides are only for that God. Only for that God, Panchuki Panda today did not allow me to climb the temple steps. I had been there to tell him that, when I get the death compensation money, I'll give half of it to his son and daughter-in-law. Throwing my own two children, I saved his Debu, hence, I have a soft corner for him.

"Panchuki Panda said, 'Hey! Have you become a Brahmin because you saved my son from drowning? You low caste fellow, forgetting all duty and etiquette, you are rushing up the steps? Only because the people of the Kaliyuga did not respect caste and religion, the super cyclone hit the land and the sea rushed in! Do you wish to call in another deluge? Go, go-out you go. Stay within your limits.'"

Mantri Mallick said, "Come, let's destroy all temples in this area. We'll break even this mosque. Be he God or Allah, there would not be any building in the name of God here. We'll build houses for man. A few are playing with us in the name of God-doing business. These are the malefic of the society. They browbeat us and cheat us. It is better to declare ourselves as thieves and loot people. So much violence only because of these gods and deities. Let's kill all these Gods first-then other things."

Snatching the axe from Bharjan's hands, Bikram said, "Where did you get this invaluable thing? If you search around this entire area, axes and diggers are like dreams. The sea has dragged them all into its belly. Well, then. With this axe, we shall start our temple building-not for Gods, but for men. If we can give a roof over the heads exposed to rain and cold, that would be our temple. And-no temple or mosque-nothing shall be destroyed here. God shall not be killed. We would create a new God. Here, only building and creation-none shall utter the word destruction."

"We'll give birth to God!" someone shouted.

"Yes, from conscience, consciousness, that's our God. We have lost our consciousness due to calamity. We'll again give it a new birth from our own conscience, our own realizations. God is never communal or regional or destructive. God is universal, all-loving, and a creative energy. The deluge is also a creation of God. All deluges declare the end of Kaliyug and usher in the Satyayug. This is the intention behind all deluges," Drona Sir said.

"Who should we worship, then, in our new world?"

"The god within man. Service to man would be our divine worship."

From the distant darkness was heard the familiar lines from the Bhagabat, "One who sees all with equal temper, he has no friend or enemy."

"Who? Udhab Mangual? If you are alive, come show the path to these children. If you are dead, then take birth again, here. We need you," Drona Sir said.

Bharjan Mallick bowed at the darkness, and said, "Our gods are Udhab Mangual, Golmasta Mian, and Bharat Mandal, the Trinity-Brahma, Vishnu, Maheswar."

"In all bodies, sits Narayana. This is the endless, primal truth." In the darkness, the voice was heard, and then faded again into the darkness.

Drona Sir said, "Here, on this platform of this mosque, let a chapter each from the Bhagabat be recited every evening. Udhab Mangual's soul would rest in peace. This would be the head of the Satyayug village."

"Let chapters from the Quran be also read here," said Bikram.

"Yes, let's worship both on the same seat," said Bhudan. Wiping his tearful eyes, he again said, "Had father been alive, he would have been very happy."

Gandhis are born in the worlds of sorrow. They never live to enjoy happiness. Fighting for man's emancipation, they never care for their own ties; otherwise Gandhi Das wouldn't have died such a death, thought Bikram. In the dark sky, a lone star was smiling bright.

Bikram wished he had garlanded Mantri Mallick, baring all buds and flowers, had they been in bloom, for he had toiled hard in raising houses one by one. On the wasteland, to paint a flawless picture of a village, each was holding color and brush according to his ability. Bipin, Rafik, Baikuntha, Alwar, Akhtar, Kaibalya, Saraladas, Kartika, Bhudan, and Ranbir Maiti's son, Nirmal Maiti, who had just passed his studies in law from a Cuttack college and so many others had contributed their combined strength in the making of the village. Even some, like Bharjan Mallick, braving their declining years, had labored hard in building houses.

Even then, Bikram's joy was incomplete like the half moon. A few were toiling, while quite a few were celebrating. Even now, they eat from the relief camps and play cards sitting on their verandas-as if kings and Zamindars are enjoying the labor of their bond slaves. Not only the young lads, but also some aged men were trying to forget their sorrow in the joy of playing cards. Bikram went near them; they invited Bikram to play cards.

Bikram said, "If I play cards, I will win. But not on this broken veranda. When strong verandas come up in the new houses, all of us will sit and play. We'll pass the nights thumping cards. You too, come. This village belongs to all of us. None of us here have any land deed for the land, no ridges or fences. How shall we live if we do not forget mine and thine till we receive the documents of ownership?"

"Why? Where has the government gone? We have voted them to power. They should manage us in our troubled times," one replied nonchalantly, fixing his eyes on the cards.

Bikram was not irritated, only pained. The leaders of this area had kept these men like parasites. Their political game was to shoot, placing the guns on their shoulders. They would come around if the facts were properly explained to them. If the wild bulls were tamed, why couldn't the human beings be receptive?

Bikram sat near them and asked, "If someone hands over begging bowls to you, would you prefer to nurse your belly by begging?"

"Why should one beg? Don't we have any prestige or family aristocracy? Now we have been victims of a natural calamity. Therefore, we depend on relief materials and free food. Let government settle us properly. We will manage our houses," one of them said.

Bikram said, "I'm happy that you are prestige-conscious. In a natural calamity, it is the duty of the government to provide relief to the victims. But there is a time limit to provide relief, because if relief continues for long time, it has a psychological impact on the people. People bury their self-confidence and grow like parasites. That creates a more dangerous situation than the deluge. Everyone knows that the relief farce will not continue forever. One day, it has to end. They will go their ways, leaving us to our fate.

"By that time, we must have become so lazy and dependent that there would not be any choice for us but to move with begging bowls in our hands. For that reason, during the great Na'Anka famine in 1866, the British government stopped relief work within a definite time frame. Those people, at that time, were not as educated or conscious as we are today, but their sense of dignity was unshakable. They had named the free kitchenschattar and banished those who lived on the chattar food from their villages. They had to live a life of shame.

"Even in those days, the illiterate people working in the food-for-work scheme had helped in establishing the world-famous colleges like Ravenshaw College. And from that college emerged so many scholars and scientists. Why should we eat from the chattar for months together? Stretching our hands, accept old and new clothes? Depend on government instead of building our houses on our own?"

The lads kept the cards aside and listened to Bikram with interest. One of them asked, "Such a big college could be raised by the labor of people in the aftermath of the great famine? Why then can't we raise a hundred times bigger college than Ravenshaw College here? Why should our children remain half educated by not getting seats in Ravenshaw College?"

Bikram was delighted. Bikram said, "That's our aim. But, first of all, we must have a roof over our heads and clothes on our back; then only our roots will grow deeper, and we may start climbing up."

"But what do we have now? What did we ever have? Mud house, river, stream, sea, boat and land. Earn, and the pot boils for half the family. Every year there is drought, flood, and cyclone. When did this world give us scope for enjoyment, hey? Rather, despite being destitute by this super cyclone, we know what enjoyment is, for the last few days. Should the leaders only enjoy while we toil and turn into crabs? You see our enjoyment, but turn blind in the case of the leaders?" one said.

Bikram laughed, and, in a calm voice, he said, "The leaders do not toil any less, brother. Poor fellows, they never sleep in peace. When not in power, they are worried over acquiring it. And when in power, they are more worried, lest the chair should slip away. We can't understand their tension. We are, rather, happy and satisfied compared to them."

One butted in, saying, "You lecture better than the leaders, hey! Are you contesting in the next election?"

Bhudan spoke out. "It would be really good. We need a leader like him; selfless, patriotic, guileless, bold, honest."

"Enough, enough!" Bikram was ill at ease at Bhudan's compliments. By that time, all were eager to listen to Bikram, setting the card game aside. Finding the moment opportune, Bikram placed his hands on their shoulders, and, looking at them with loving eyes, said, "Dear brothers! Did we ever know what this world, this soil had arranged for us and what it would keep for us in future? Our forefathers have toiled hard to give us a culture, a civilization, a tradition, a system of faith, literature, music, and science. All those have not been swept away by the sea. The cyclone has not destroyed them all. The roots of human culture have pierced down the bottom of the sea to the other side of the earth. From one viewpoint, the cyclone has not destroyed anything at all. What appears to have been destroyed is a new pattern of life ahead.

"As the broken, flattened brass pots are made anew, exactly like that all these workers, volunteers, army men, and police made roads, straightened the bent electric poles for us. They rescued our people, and cooked and fed us for so many days. Are they our sharecroppers, and we the Zamindars? One would go on planting trees, and another would simply eat the fruits? What kind of arrangement is that?"

Bikram sensed that everyone was listening to him. With more enthusiasm, he said, "Whenever our forefathers earned fighting the water and wind, they saved and built. They left everything for us. See? How many known and unknown dead bodies we have walked on and crushed to rise up from the waters of the deluge to land on soil? They have not pressed us into the slush. Are we not grateful to them? Our gratitude to them is to complete what they have left unfinished. If the village were lost, their names too would be lost. Do we want that to happen? Would their souls rest in peace if we allow that to happen?"

Changing the mood of the conversation, Bikram said, "The assembly election is ahead. We must elect the right candidate."

"O' this was then an election campaign! Why didn't you say that in the beginning? Okay. We'll vote for you. You first see that our houses are built. Set up the villages. Get the ownership rights for us, and raise the fences and ridges. Only then may we till the land. Otherwise, what's the point in ploughing another's land?" an aged man said.

"Who forbids you from occupying your own land? We are now in difficult times. They say there is no rule in bad times. Therefore, forgetting the mine-thine ownership rights, we have to work hard. If we depend on government, we would be lying out here in cold and dew, and the salinated lands would remain fallow. What would you eat?" Bikram said.

A young man said, "It's obvious that you'll be a minister. Why don't you do things for us?"

Bikram replied, "I'm one among you, an accountable man. Who would make me a minister? Even without becoming ministers, we can set up our own village. This is my aim."

One thoughtless man said, "We'll try to get an election ticket for you. Or else you would contest as an independent candidate."

Bikram smiled and said, "I love freedom. Let's see when the time comes."

At that time, Mantri Mallick suddenly appeared from somewhere like a hurricane and said, "Don't you know brother Bikram? He fought in the Kargil war and brought victory for India. From whichever party he contests, victory is his. But the fact is that he has no party. He was not in politics from the beginning; he doesn't know the manipulative ways of the politicians. Therefore, poor chap, he would not last in political fights. He is a heroic martyr. Would he fight these rats?"

Someone laughed and said, "Hey, he is alive! Why are you calling him a martyr?"

Bhudan said, "Mantri is a wild fellow, but in his words, there is a subtle truth. Our Bikram has escaped by a hair's breadth from being martyred. But he is a martyr-like hero."

"In that case, no false yarn is necessary to fight elections! If we sing of his heroic tale, people would be influenced."

Bipin said, "If you have not been influenced by him, why should people be influenced by him? People know only note for vote. It is easy to buy votes. If you do not join us to form a party, where does the question of Bikram's election victory arise?"

All of them threw away the cards. Tying the towels around their waists, they said, "In our village, everyone would have a concrete house. Let brother Bikram promise that."

"Brick and mortar buildings would come up, but first of all we must have faith on the soil. From the soil comes bricks. Soil is the basic element of the brick. For a shelter overhead, we must first have an earthen house."

"Hey! If we raise our houses, our foster fathers would be annoyed. Different states have adopted different districts. In some areas, more than one foster father has begun the reconstruction work. But here, in our area, not a single foster father is seen. Let's go searching for a foster father, leaving this card game. Our area would be full of strong buildings," said a young man while chewing betel.

Mantri Mallick asked, "In this area, there is not even one betel farm left. How could you get the betel here?"

"Why? Do you think betel was available only in Ketaki's shop? Ketaki is no more, and so nobetel is available in this area? But does that mean we'll give up the habit? Have you given up rice since there is no paddy or rice in our homes? I asked for a betel from a babu. How does it affect others?"

Mantri Mallick gave a strong left-hander slap on the cheek of that lad, who was nursing a freshly growing moustache, and said, "Stretching your hand to strangers, you ate free food to save your life. You wore the used clothes of others to cover your shame. But why did you beg for a betel? Lazy bums like you go in search of foster fathers to have houses built for them. Are you not the youngest son of the Rout family? You people are fit for nothing, aberrations of time."

"Go away from here, wherever your eyes take you. Here, our sacred village would be built with the honest sweat of our brows. If any foster fathers come to our village, I'll break their heads."

Mantri Mallick's red eyes were roving like a disc. Bikram patted him and calmed him down. He said, "Is this the time to indulge in fights? You do your work. Leave what the others do or don't do to me. All these are children of this soil. By virtue of this soil, all of you would lend your head and heart in the sacred construction work. You just have patience. Have you ever seen fruit-bearing trees overnight?"

"Okay, you hypocritical gentlemen. Leave this place. This game is gone. These people would not allow us to play cards peacefully. Hey, we'll vote for whosoever we like. Mixing soil and water, we will raise houses for others, till other's lands, set up an ideal village, and, do you think, listening to your empty speeches, we'll vote for you? Hey, brother, you must be trained for electioneering if you wanted to be a leader. Hearing your dry words, who would vote for you, eh?" another said while shuffling cards. All of them again returned to the card game.

Bikram changed his direction, not his goal. The sun and moon change their course every day, but not the goal-light, warmth, and life! The wind changed course, but the goal was the same-life. The rains changed its direction, but the aim was the same-green vegetation! How beautiful is life! How desirable and how rare! Thousands had left halfway before running their course! The goal of those men had to be achieved by the rest of those who were alive.

Bikram is one of those who are alive. Why one? One behind another, like Bikram, the line of new men is long. Forsaking the card game, those laggards would one day join this line. The unruly streams of rainwater flowed from the highlands in different directions, but finally all mingled in the river. When a river flowed, she automatically grew wide. To live, one has to flow-this is the essence.

In a shop, a hoarding advertised, Super Cyclone, Super Discount. But who is there to buy even at discounted price? This too is politics. The party in power claims that by their presence, commodities have become cheaper for the benefit of the people. The opposition parties are campaigning singing cyclone-kirtan in the villages with music parties. The poets have composed varieties of kirtan, plays, and choric songs.

A group of Kirtan singers approached the new village risen from the deluge, dancing all the way. The candidate Narku Routray, with a garland of marigold flowers around his neck, is appealing for votes to the people with folded hands, a twisted smile around his lips.

The fearless brigade rushed toward the election campaign shouting, "Stop! Stop!" They blocked the procession. Bipin said, "Don't enter our village. This soil is sacred; sacred because, any MLA or minister has not yet stepped his feet here. No relief truck has come here. No saint or sadhu has performed any Yajna here. We have started the karma-yajna here. We are farmers, fishermen, and workers. We have no time to entangle ourselves in election campaigns."

"But it's your right to participate in the elections. Vote is your right. Why should you give up your rights?" Narku Routray asked.

Taking off the towel from his head and wiping off his sweat, Bhudan said, "What rights have been given to us, hey? You have ruled over the last five years. What right have you given anyone? The children of this area haven't got the right to study. When you were the education minister, you built building after building for yourself. Have you built a school? Go, go. We have some intelligence. Whoever we vote for is also our right. Is it your right to hoodwink us?"

The kirtan group moved away. No point in campaigning in the rotten village. Where a fool like Bikram is a leader, to expect votes is like netting in floodwaters. Narku Routray returned with his pride.

Some city service holders of the block office and political

analysts were discussing that Bikram Balabantaray was a hero, but a dullard. The reconstruction work was getting bogged down because of the frequent visit of the officers and political leaders. The officers had to serve the leaders and their henchmen, relegating the victims to the background.

Getting the information that Bikram's application for voluntary retirement had been accepted, a local leader of the ruling party had come to Bikram with a proposal. They took Bikram to the Jagatsinghpur dak-bungalow in a vehicle. Bikram went with enthusiasm. At least he would have a direct interview with the chief minister without interference of the sycophants. That was an opportunity for a free discussion. At least he would have the chance of presenting a factual picture of the loot going on in the area.

Before the Chief Minister, Bikram stood fearlessly with his head held high.

The Chief Minister said, "Please sit."

"This is not the time to sit, sir. I've come, wasting a day's work."

"What work do you have now? We've been informed that you've taken voluntary retirement from the army."

"Where is the retirement from serving the country, sir? I've resolved to serve the village. That too is service to the country-honorary," said Bikram.

The minister said, knitting his eyebrows, "Where is the village that you serve? All the villages of your area have been cleaned up. I was not in power during the super cyclone. I would have taken precautionary steps, had I been in power. At least so many people wouldn't have been killed. Let it go. Odisha is unfortunate!"

Bikram asked in wonder, "But now that you are in power? We have great expectations of you."

"If our party returns to power again, I'll be the CM and can expedite the settlement and rehabilitation work. I need your cooperation toward the realization of our goal. The people of your area have trust on you. You join our party. We'll make you a candidate from your area in the election. We have information that you'll win if you contest. If our party gets the majority, it would be possible to develop this state. Do you agree?"

"But sir, I'm busy in the reconstruction work of our area. When do I have time for politics?" said Bikram.

A henchman of the Chief Minister laughed aloud, and said, "What reconstruction work can you do, hey! What can you do without government help?"

"The birds have built nests on the broken trees. The ants have made holes in the salinated soil. From the fallen trees, new branches have started growing, new leaves are also growing. Which government has helped them? Likewise, the people of our area have built huts to escape the coming winter. You haven't seen those things."

"No need to see. A person with foresight need not go to ground zero to see everything. Those huts are like bird nests, it is clearly visible. In a gusty shower, those would be blown away. Don't you need concrete buildings? Don't you need cyclone shelters? Don't you need to put barricades around the seashores to save the villages? We have so many plans. Ramachandra bridged the sea! What's impossible for us? Only we have to be voted into power."

"Glad to hear that!" said Bikram.

"But without doing your duty if you are happy, the results would be short-lived. Therefore, follow the advice of our CM. You'll enjoy the outcomes," the henchman said.

"We'll give you a ticket for the assembly elections. All your expenses would be borne by us," said the CM.

"But why this unasked-for kindness on me, when there are so many experienced politicians in this area?"

"Because you have a bright image. Moreover, people know you here as a young poet. People don't read poetry, but they feel a sense of pride when they get a poet as minister or chief minister. Our CM is not a writer, but before this election, he has resolved to write poems and stories. If you try, what is impossible on earth?" The henchman was delighted by his self-praise.

The CM smilingly said, "We are going to bring out a newspaper and a literary magazine. You would find a place there. You can inspire people by your speeches, charm people by your poetry. Therefore, you have all qualifications to become a candidate."

Bikram said in a level tone, "Pardon me. I cannot accept this offer of a ticket to fight the elections, as I do not have the most essential qualification."

"What is that?"

"Sir, I've killed people to defend my country. But for that, I have been honored instead of being jailed. Therefore, I am not a jailbird. There is no criminal case against me. In short, I am not in the list of murderers or criminals. This is my disqualification. Therefore, I feel I'm not qualified to fight elections."

Saluting the Chief Minister in the army style, Bikram turned his face and came out. He had neither interest nor need to know the reaction of the CM.

"At what price could Bikram be purchased?" the henchman asked a local politician.

"He is not for sale. He has already taken a vow to spend his entire retirement compensation money on the new construction in his village area. The death compensation money of his parents too he will spend on his project. He will get fifteen acres of land free as an army man. He has planned to develop some welfare project on the land. Therefore, he has applied to the authorities to give him that land near his village," the local politician said.

"Would this young man finally become a yogi? He has no desire of his own! He is really disqualified to be a candidate. Such selfless men, while trying to purge the system, delay the process of development of the country. Who doesn't know this? It's good that the evil star has been evaded," said the CM.

Whether it's a Yajna or a cremation, the fire rises up. Like the soul leaving the body, the fire rises up and melts into nothingness, and then blows out. What remains is the burnt, and half-burnt wood, embers, like the burnt-out past, the ashes of what once was a body. But the remains of the past never go to waste. The embers of the past strengthen the foundations of culture and help the course of tradition. From the peaks of sorrow flows the stream of hope, of new life. Even after the deluge, if one man is alive, life does not stop.

So many pyres burned, so many Yajnas had the last pouring of ghee, and the fire melted in nothingness. But here, life did not appear to be flowing in.

The assembly elections were now over. The election promises burst like water bubbles. Those who hijacked relief trucks and over distributed the materials in their constituencies to win the elections were not seen again after their electoral victory. The relief trucks now were diverted toward the houses of their relatives and friends. The house-building aid, the compensation money for the death of relations, the Indira Awas, prawn farm repair, road-construction money, all was swallowed up by the void.

Instead, the henchmen of the victorious leaders exploited the voters, and after oiling their palms, were of no avail. Government received all the accolades by allowing other states to adopt some of the worsthit areas for rehabilitation. The state government had no compunction against begging for aid from home and abroad. Whatever aid came, nothing of it reached the helpless people of the coastal villages of Abhayapur and Chandanpur.

There were no free kitchens anymore, no victory feasts or celebrations. Even then, some lazy youth, surviving on tea and puffed rice, went on playing cards.

One day, while Mantri Mallick was searching for a matchbox to burn the card packs, a roar was raised, "Fire, Fire! Houses have caught fire. Come and help."

As people had run, seeing the gushing floodwaters from behind, so they ran seeing the rising flames ahead. Throwing away the cards, the lazy young men too jumped from the verandas and ran fast. These lads had such strength! Why then such dependence on others to set up their own houses in order? Bikram ran through the fields, overtaking others toward the burning houses. Which village was untouched by the sea that such flames were rising?

Bikram paused for breath when the fire was extinguished. The others paused too. When their breath returned Bikram laughed aloud and said, "Hey brothers! How foolish we all are! Where do we have houses here, that fire would catch them?"

All looked at the fire. Before them were a few mud and wattle shelters with polythene roofs. Yes, it may be called a hamlet. The destitute had made these makeshift shelters in a group with the hope that government would settle them in new houses one day. This is the picture in Erasama everywhere. Someone, perhaps in angered pain, had set fire to the large heap of broken branches and leaves. Butwhat was the gain? The fire was extinguishing, the smoke was smouldering. The face of the horizon was red.

When they were about to return, Bikram said, "Some people shouted 'Fire, come running,' and you ran, leaving your work and the card session? Why? Let him douse the fire whose house has caught fire. If he doesn't, his house, his village would be reduced to ashes. Why did you run like heroes to extinguish the fire? Would anyone have given you wages for that?"

A lad said, "Bah! What do you say? When a house burns in a village, all go to quench the fire. Even when a nearby village burns, people from eight-to-ten villages in that area come running to help fight the fire. Who then comes for caste, religion, or relation? This is the culture of our rural life. Does anyone bargain for money in such cases?"

"Why, what would government do? Why should we do anything when there is a fire-fighting department? The fire engines must be coming, getting the news."

"By the time fire engines arrived, the fire would have licked up the roof, walls, and everything. Waiting for the fire engine means provoking the fire. Do such things happen anywhere?" said another lad.

Bikram, ecstatic in joy, embraced one after another. He said, "You are the real power. The feelings that you have for the village and villagers would unite us in our efforts. New houses and villages would rise because of your resolve. Waiting for the fire engines to quench the fire is like waiting for government to reconstruct our villages."

"It's better to have no government than such a government. We're not waiting for the government. Let government know that the people of this area have some prestige."

"Bravo, bravo," said Mantri Mallick, clapping.

Bhudan said, "Brothers! Let's join our hands and set up our own villages. In this small world, we'll give birth to a large village where there would be no caste, religion, faith, small or big divide. The first village after the deluge-we were waiting for you till now. From tomorrow, our work yajna would start. We couldn't complete our village rehabilitation when there was one lazy or truant in our midst."

"Yes, yes, we are prepared to contribute our might like the squirrels in the construction of the Ram Setu."

"No, no, not squirrels. We are the monkey brigade; if not of Mahatma Gandhi's, at least of Ramachandra's," said Alwar Mian.

Bikram patted their backs and said, "You go now. Tomorrow evening, the village council will meet at the corridor of the mosque. Let me see here who set fire to these broken branches mindlessly. We need a lot of wood in future. We'll plant trees and use the broken trunks of trees lying here and there in our reconstruction works. The wood thieves have not yet come here. We are lucky."

Like a fruit-bearing jackfruit tree, Padma was sitting with a lot of children in her lap. At her breasts where attached two orphan babies. Her hair was open like the thick leaves of a jackfruit tree; the head was covered by her saree. From a distance, she looked like a jackfruit tree. From close quarters, she looked like a mother.

"A well-organized village has come up here! Mothers are here, children are here, a hearth too! What more do you want?", thought Bikram Balabantaray. Going near Padma, he asked, "Who set fire to the dry woods, and why? We thought that some houses were on fire."

Padma and Bikram did not recognize each other. Padma pointed her hand toward the fire. "She has done it. Ask her."

Crossing a row of houses, Bikram moved toward the fire. Someone was spurring the dry embers with a long tree branch. A well-formed young lass, wheatish complexion, a bun down the neck.

"What're you doing? Why did you set the fire?"

"According to traditional last rites, watering ancestral bones for their salvation." It was not easy to guess who she was from behind. The voice was morose, sweetish like the tune of a half-forgotten song, half familiar, half strange! The dry branch had almost burned up to the base, but she was not mindful of that.

"Hey, hey! Your hand will burn!" Bikram snatched away the burning branch from her hand. She turned and stared at Bikram's face. Bikram saw her. The fiery branch was like a torch in Bikram's hand.

Both were tongue-tied, words failing them. There was no language to voice this unbelievable game of the gods. A stunned ecstasy in both their eyes, in both their fists, the fallen moon from the skies! Up above in the sky, there was already another plate like moon. Who knew what the moment was! The forehead of the sky is never blank.

The full moon was a thread away.

THIRTY

When sorrow weighs heavy on the heart, the eyes lose sleep. Bikram knew that, but did not know that, when joy overflows the heart, the eyes don't blink. Sleep had never tortured him, even when his soldier's heart was overladen with pain. When his consciousness was stupefied at the sight of the debris of the deluge, even at that time he was able to sleep, unable to think ahead. But after the futile, painstaking search for Girima andher sudden appearance before him like a fire goddess, after so many agonizing days, he spent the sleepless night in shocked delight.

Everyone was lying down, exposed to the sun and cold nights. How could they have settled all surviving women, collecting them from different areas? If a woman lies at the foot of a tree, a village emerges. This was proven by the temporary shelters of mud and wattle due to the handiwork of Girima. Till now, Bikram had been unrelenting in his search for able-bodied men who could help him realize the reconstruction of a new village; as if women could only sit idle.

Bikram was pleasantly surprised at how Girima, in a few traumatic days, could mould Renu, Padma, Gulrukh, Nazma, Akalima, Bibi, Champi, and many a woman, old, young, and sickly, uniting them with her love and care. Mantri Mallick spoke the truth, even though he was never a family man. He used to say that men are willing to work in the sun and rain, but to cook and serve rice and curry, we need women. Women are such that they toil alike in sun and rain. They take care of the indoors as well as the outdoors while looking after home and hearth.

All's well now! The village would not be incomplete anymore. In the morning, all would go to search for the mothers and sisters who have survived. They would bring the children, clasping them to their hearts. Food would be cooked in large, open hearths; all would be served together at a time. The taste of the food cooked by the mothers and sisters would satisfy every palate; the sweet murmur of the children sitting in a row would be heard. The wounds of the heart would be less painful. The wounds would heal as the days rolled by.

Since his encounter with Girima, Bikram had been very quiet. What could he have done? He could have said, "You are alive, I'm alive, but besides us, none are alive in our families." Girima knew by now she was the lone survivor in her clan; she had none to take care of her. But is it true that she has none? All alone in the world? Why, there is Kartika, there is Bhudan. Baikuntha is also there, Bipin and Satrughana of Shendhakud might also be there! He also is present!

It's a gross lie to say that we are all alone, unrelated. Ah-ha! If Uncle Udhab had lived, he could have been not only Girima's, but also everybody's strength and inspiration. Let him not do anything, but just sit like Drona Master and chant the Bhagabat. The youth would have progressed a lot by now. Udhab Mangual was the epitome of the value system of our villages. Till now, the boats had not sailed. There was no one left who could build boats. The government-supplied boats made the fishermen hopeless because of inferior workmanship and lack of sea-worthiness.

Bikram was awake the whole night, dreaming and thinking. The morning would come with a new resolve. But, at midnight, Bikram felt as if someone called him, not by his name, but by tapping sounds. At midnight, only ghosts beckon you by sounds, but Bikram was not afraid. The earth did not appear desperate, but mysterious. What mystery?

Bikram walked forward to unravel the mystery under the

moonlit night. He had no fear, rather a strange excitement. A strange sensation to discover his inner being was making him restless. He could understand that the sensation making him restless was not worldly. He wanted to spread this sensation in every heart. This selfless, mystic sensation should go from body to body, soul to soul, and to the earth paled by sorrow and frustration. This was the sensation of creativity, born of dreams, that spreads to consciousness.

Bikram was chasing the direction of the tapping noise, but was distracted toward some unknown child's continuous wail. Adding rhythm to that cry of sorrow was seeping in that primordial tune of the lullaby, "Away, away from my baby you demented fellow, go and sleep in that field where the ragi is thick."

Whoever's was the voice, of Girima, Padma, Nazma, Aklima, Renu, or Champa, from whichever corner of the world, in whatever language, its heart-touching power was the same, the meaning was the same. My darling baby, my universe, my necklace, let not thorns pinch the toes of my rising moon, let him live for a million years. Sleep my dearest, my world, my wealth. What fear when I am with you?

Bikram could see his mother's moon-like face, and a sob rose in his resolute heart. Bikram broke down, fell on the sand, and cried for his mother. Gradually, he composed himself. He felt as if the unrelenting wail of the child was his. He felt that the earth itself was singing the lullaby. This earth, in which his and all mothers were mingled, leaving behind their children. When songs are heard from the heart of the earth, the human child has no way of backing away.

The moon set this side. Did the sun arise on the other? Bikram saw a group of mothers, with children in their arms, coming toward him with their bundles, in a single file. Leading the line was Girima, a child in her arms. Seeing Bikram, Girima said, "Before the sun gets hot, it is better to reach the village with the children. These weak children cannot tolerate the heat of the sun."

Bikram said, "Wherever you light the hearth and cook that

would be the border of our village. This place is prone to high tides. We'll put a barrage here for the tidal waves." Girima looked at the sea, wide-eyed. She thought, how arrogant is this solider! He hasn't seen the power of the sea. I have seen it. But she didn't say anything. Turning her back to the sea, she stepped forward.

All those standing were in deep sorrow. But did it mean that they would evade a drop of joy? When the mothers, aunts, and children gathered, it appeared as if nothing had happened, the devastations of the cyclone were only a rumor. The cyclone came and went away without shaking the faith of the humans. So many were alive, so many chirping children had survived. The cyclone had not wiped-out life completely.

Coming together after a long time, the living were tearfully excited. Women cried, the men wiped off the wanton tears. The feeding of children became a clamorous affair. Then they were all quiet.

The elders said, "The auspicious daughters and daughters-in-law of this village have offered ritualistic prayerfor all known and unknown people. For the salvation of the unredeemed souls, we would observe the obsequies for eleven days by giving up non-vegetarian food. The tenth day ceremony will be held, and on the riverside we all will tonsure our heads for all those who have died in the cyclone. On the eleventh day, there will be mass prayer and last rites observed for everyone. Then we'll start the reconstruction work in full flow." Everyone liked the idea. All resolved to eat once a day, simple, salt less, oil less food for ten days, as per tradition.

In the evening, rice and dal were cooked. All ate. Mantri Mallick said, "For ten days, food pots must be placed for the dead in the crematory. That is my responsibility."

Bharjan Mallick said, "When your father is alive, why should you go to the crematory at the dead of the night?" After many years, Mantri obeyed his father.

At midnight, Bharjan went to the crematory, searching for the banyan tree at whose foot the purgatory pots were normally placed. He kept the pot somewhere, not finding the tree in the darkness. The obsequies were over after eleven days, but Bharjan insisted that the rice pots for the dead should be given for a month. Then only would the souls attain salvation.

"Which priest told you all this?" Asked Bhudan.

Bharjan said, "Here, everyone is a priest. Sir has said that he who wishes well of another is a priest. But my wife has told me in my dreams that all will eat together and the rest of the food in the cooking pots will be offered to the dead for a month. This is our age-old tradition."

Mantri Mallick thought, "Well, whatever his wife said, father has followed that austerely. Maybe this will give peace to the agonized soul of my mother".

It was decided earlier that, after the obsequies were over, the brick kiln would be lit. Bikram threw a spanner, saying, "Let's all be restored to our social faith. We have flouted many a tradition just to save our lives. We have no caste or culture. We cannot begin our work till we are purged of our transgressions."

Hearing this, Bhudan lost his temper, "Why so much fuss over good work? We should have lighted the kiln today, taking the auspicious name of Lord Jagannath. You say you are a soldier, and the soldier does not believe in any caste or creed! You said that you'd bring some reforms in the village, after the Kargil war! Is this the reform? All of us agreed to build a village without considerations of caste and religion or language and faith. Then what's the meaning of rehabilitation into the caste? What values or principles we have transgressed, that our caste and religion have been defiled? Moreover, who here would join which caste or religion?"

Bikram said, "We have stretched our hands before others, accepted the gifts of others. We have lost our character by stealing relief materials. Instead of cremating the dead of our family and clan, we have got it done by others. We have allowed the charitable trusts of other states to clean our villages instead of doing it ourselves. Not only that, we have declared our own children orphans and have begged for the mercy of others. We've given false certificates to get compensation money. We have bribed officers to get house-building aid. To get some money, we have alienated our own parents. What more evidence shall I recount of our depravity? We haven't lost our caste alone; we've lost our character. The derogatory drums of our selfishness, lethargy, and the desire to usurp others' property are making news all over the world. True or false?"

All were stubbornly quiet. What answer could they give? Small or big, all had lost their character in some way or other. Therefore, it was agreed unanimously that all of them should rehabilitate themselves into their caste. But which caste? Such questions arose in everyone's mind.

Sarala Das Mandal said, "The majority caste of this area is fisherman."

"But the highest caste of this area is Brahmin," Panchuki's nephew, Dibakar, said.

"Then what about our community?" said Alwar Mian.

"All of us would stay here. Nobody needs to leave. The caste is the human caste. Are we not all humans?" said Bikram.

"Y-e-s, yes, we are all born humans."

"Is not man the best creation of God?"

"Y-e-s."

"Then we are of one caste. The best and also the majority."

"Y-e-s."

"Then tear away that sacred thread. Tear away that basil rosary from your necks."

"No, no, there lodges the Brahman!"

"Doesn't the Brahman live in the mind after the sacred thread is thrown away?"

"O' that is true. How can there be a Brahman without the Brahmin?"

"Brahman is in everyone. There is no universe without the Brahman. Why should the Brahmins alone have the sacred thread? We'll discard all orthodox customs which divides human beings."

"Yes, we'll discard casteism. These telltale signs of the tilak, rosary, saffron clothes, and topi-turban should be thrown away. Even without those things, God would remain in us."

"Allah too."

"His name is Ishwar and Allah, the same."

"He would give noble thoughts to everyone."

Voice mingles with voice, tune with tune.

"Ishwar, Allah is your name. Bless with wisdom everyone."

The brick kiln was lighted with fire. It was resolved that everyone would have a roof over his head before the onset of the monsoon.

Without seeds, the farmers of Erasama could not start sowing in the farming season. The sea had snatched away the seeds from the hands of the farmer; the saline waves had seeped into the soil. This year had passed, somehow, and they had survived. But they could not depend on the handouts forever. The cyclone relief was not a permanent arrangement. And by this day next year, there would not be any relief-why should there be? There was no hope for the next harvest. What to do?

The earth was not unkind, but had become infertile. The sea had not only snatched away the smile from the farmer's face, it had taken away food for five years. Why only five years? There was no hope that a blade of grass would ever grow here. The farmer was at his wit's end. The agricultural officers were not seen anywhere. The promise of supplying seeds, manure, and even ploughs had been a mere election gimmick. In this area, all were farmers and fishermen. If the land was not nourished at the right time, would the farmers depend on begging? And if everyone is a beggar, who would give alms?

There was no dearth of river and sea in this region, but ninety percent of the land was not irrigated, hence the farmers depended only on the mercy of the raingod.

Government has done nothing. The sea has wiped out the protective embankment near the sea. All the two-hundred-and-fifty kilometers of it. There is no chance of any government help forthcoming. Why then build houses, only to be sacrificed to the sea?

First the ring embankment must be built, and then the soil must be enriched.

"What's the use of building rows of houses? You die if you depend on government help, and if you don't, then also you die. Rather, it is better to live in tents on the roadside, and live as laborers. There won't be any fear of the sea, nor of starvation, death."

When Kartika said this, Bikram said, "Okay, let's stop the work here. Evening has come. What work can be done in the dark?"

"Where's darkness? Our women folk have lighted the hearths. Rice and curry will be cooked, and then dinner for all. This evening, the village council shall meet. If five minds come together, light will burst open ahead."

Work was in progress. In the zeal for work, the strain was bearable. Everyone was talking amongst themselves. Bikram said, "The new moon comes striking the hour, not merely to disintegrate, but to make the other fortnight bright and full. This is the perseverance of the moon, a Karmayoga. The crescent moon does not become full moon overnight. The deluge too is a karmayoga.

"The deluge that came was not the first, nor the last. The human tree shall rise, defying the deluge, shall spread its branches to the endless sky, shall adorn human culture by its leaves, flowers, and fruits, shall keep alive the human tradition. The experience of death of the past shall show the path to encounter future calamities. New villages will rise. New dreams shall come true.

"Gradually, the fear of death, the fear and tension of experiencing death again, will subside. Life is a stream. If rocks come its way, it would carry the rocks in its rhythmic flow. Finally, it leaves behind the rocks or crushes them to sand. This is Karmayoga. I fought for my country at Kargil. I have seen rivers flow crushing the ice, seen the rivers gaining speed by countering all hurdles and blockades. The future hurdles which you panic about now, think of them as rocks on the face of a mountain spring. If we flow fast, those rocks will be crushed to dust."

"Can we move fast on hungry stomachs? When the hungry tide rushes in through the open mouths of the estuary, these villages without embankment will be uprooted by the strong currents and flow fast in the same karmayoga back into the same sea. Yes or no? What do you say?" Kaibalya Mishra retorted.

It's the duty of the soldier to stay calm in the turbulent battlefields. That was the crowning essence of Bikram's personality. Life is the battlefield. If you are disturbed, you miss your target. Bikram readied himself again to speak in a calm voice. He said, "We are in a battlefield. Danger chases us from all sides; barriers, enmity, and roadblocks often make your own mind rebel against you. This crisis is more dangerous than the Kargil war because here we have jumped into the thick of battle without training or preparation. But we will be trained and experienced while fighting, like the human child learning to walk by trying. The soldier in the battlefield is not afraid of death, but of defeat or withdrawal. Shall we withdraw? Shall we beg on the roadside?"

"No, who wants that? But what about this government? Why did we cast our votes? For the leaders to raise their mansions?" one commented.

Mantri Mallick spat on the ground and said, "We have taken a vow not to take the name of the government. Shall we go back on our resolve?"

Bikram said, "I'm reminded of Japan today. Such a small country, but look at their resilience! Every year, they suffer from earthquakes and tsunamis. Towns and villages break and fall, but the Japanese never crack."

Trying to resolve the arguments, Bikram said, "Yes, we have nothing. No plough, no seeds, the soil is dead. Yes, I agree. I also accept that government has no presence, no concern for the people. Yet, listen to me carefully. I've seen the world more than you. I've fought in the war. I've learned from encounters with death. Would you please allow me to speak? I am not making a speech. What I'm going to speak is a blueprint of our dreams. Please listen to me about how we shall live."

"Okay."

"Standing shoulder to shoulder, we will till the soil, raise harvests, eat together, sharing the food. Together we will live, facing joy and sorrow. This is not a new idea in the coastal villages of Jagatsinghpur district. Rather, it is an old way of life here, a tradition. For generations, the tradition of cooperative farming has been prevalent in this region, transcending the barriers of faith, caste, gender, and status. To speak the truth, it's not a physical togetherness; it is a cooperative of souls. Here, no one is the king or Zamindar or subject. No one is a landlord, no one a sharecropper.

"Here, all are masters and all laborers. When labor, sweat, and dreams are poured on the soil, the soil wakes up to life. The harvest laughs in full glory. When the small self-interests merge and become a universal dream, cooperative farming realizes its goal. Even without ridges and fences, the ownership rights are never lost in the cooperative farm. The individual holdings are in memory, in the official records, but seen from a distance, the entire farm always looks like a vast, green carpet, dear to everyone. Whenever, in whichever corner the flowers bloom, the milk wells up, or the grain-laden saps emerge, or the ragi field turns brown, or the moong and black grams ripen, everyone feels proud and happy that it was theirs-our food for the year, our life.

"The distinction between his and mine disappears when they see the farm in full bloom. We feel like a large, joint family, enjoying the blessings of the earth. Voluntarily sharing each other's convenience, they have gained food and life hundred percent."

"Hundred percent! How?"

"Here, one does not sit idle while another toils. In cooperative farming, there are small and big holdings, but there is no distinction between small and big. If someone does not work, he is punished. He has to pay compensation for the loss of labor. In this kind of farming, the distinction of religion, caste, class, and economic status disappears. The Brahmin and the Dalit would till the land together, and together they would wet the soil with their sweat.

"In our vision of farming, democracy shall be the basic principle. No principle of opposition to mass interest or individual interest shall be entertained here. There may be some emphasis on ownership rights, but the focus would be on equitable labor. The basic rule is to contribute labor proportionate to age and energy. In our new agricultural policy, there would be no sharecropper or landlord."

"What would the landless do then? He would only toil and have no share in the harvest?" Bhudan asked.

"In our new world, the word landless would not be used. He who is landless, the landowners would give a share of their land to him. Everyone has a right on the earth; everyone has a right on the food grains produced here. Man is not born with ownership rights on this earth. He who is landless today, one day he had land of his own. He lost his land to the moneylender's deceitful machinations. The moneylender became the landlord.

"Their bellies swelled, wealth increased, and land widened. In our new world, there is no place for people who give their thumb impressions for money; no mercy for the lethargic parasites. The old and young shall work and eat and read; shall live like humans in a civilized world."

Someone queried, "Someone's land would have a bumper crop, someone's land would have meagre growth. Who would be responsible for that? While someone would produce only husk after hard toil, another would enjoy healthy grains. What justice is this?"

"We know who owns how much land, but who owns which plot is not recorded after the deluge. Therefore, whether bumper harvest or meagre growth, it would be divided proportionately; we have to share our good fortune and misfortune equally. That is our fate. There is no room for individual interest or rights. Yes, there is individual dream and individual effort."

"But the leaders forcibly occupy government land and become owners of larger shares in the cooperative farm. They don't toil, but collect their shares. Everyone knows this."

"Within the perimeters of our world, there would not be any illegally owned land. No leader would be a shareholder in our farm. We teach our leaders how to bite our hands by stretching them for their mercy. We play into their hands and ultimately get involved in litigations, police cases, and lawyers' guile, while the leaders sit cross-legged and enjoy the fruits of our labor. If disputes arise on our farms, we'll solve them. No one would ever climb up the steps of a court. Let's all take a vow."

"Why talk about cooperative farming here? Our problems are different," said Kaibalya Mishra.

"Whatever problems now arise over farming, the immediate solution to those is cooperative farming."

"How?"

"The people of this area are infamous as litigants, as the soil and brain in this region are fertile. But since the super cyclone has destroyed thousands of heads, there are no plaintiffs and defendants in matching proportion. And if there are plaintiffs and defendants, there are no witnesses. Therefore, all pending court cases have been solved by nature. We should therefore dispose of all court cases because evil minds are on the hunt for plaintiffs, defendants, and witnesses. Even amongst us, there are people who have court cases against them, and there are disputed lands. If we do not work together with singlemindedness, we may not rise for three generations."

"Now the ridges have been washed out. The fields are salinated; layers of sand have covered our farmland. We have no plough, no bullocks, no seeds, nothing. If together we do not till everyone's land, much of it would remain unploughed. Who would till the land of those old men and women who have lost their young sons, those daughters and daughters-in-law who have lost their parents, brothers, and husbands, and those who have been orphaned? Would those people die?

"No, forgetting 'his land, my land' considerations this year, we would bring under the plough all land in a cooperative scheme. We'll work for them without asking for wages. Let's eat and live, and when we grow in confidence, we may think of ridging or fencing individual holdings. The sea has washed away all documents, and the seniors are not there to tell us whose land is where. But does it mean that we would allow land to go waste?"

"Why does a man steal? Because one eats, and the other merely looks at him-is it not? If everyone gets his bellyful, why would one steal?"

Alwar Mian said, "Shoulder to shoulder, we'll till the land. But where are the seeds?"

Bharjan Mallick asked, "Without raising the embankment along the coast, why should we begin farming? For the sea to swallow it in a swig?"

Bikram said enthusiastically, "The embankment would be constructed, and seeds too would be arranged".

"How?"

Bikram said, "We'll teach government the right lessons. The International NGO and our government, together, are planning to follow the cyclone-resistant systems of Bangladesh in our cyclone-prone areas. In Bangladesh too the tsunami-resistant programs are not implemented. But they give advance warnings to the people so that they bury their valuables and go on to safe places. After the cyclones, they return to their villages and retrieve their valuables. All their lives, they dig holes and bury their fates."

"Bah! What a welfare state!" said Sarala Das Mandal.

Patting his back, Bikram said, "We'll not do that. We would implement the cyclone- resistant programs of Holland. If Holland could do it, why can't we?"

All looked eagerly at Bikram's face. At that time, Girima lighted a lantern and placed it in the middle, which meant that cooking was not yet finished. After food was cooked, the children would be served first, and then the others.

Bikram raised the wick for more light. Laughing, he said, "In our ungodly region, the lantern is the best. We can't depend on electricity. As such, our region was always in darkness. Now, after the cyclone, government has got a plea. Well, let it go. I will tell you about Holland. If you like it, we'll do accordingly. Holland is a country three meters below the sea level. There too cyclones come, but people do not leave their homes and rush out to high places."

"Then the matter is over. Are there still people in that country?" Dina Behera asked anxiously. Bikram observed the faces and saw the eagerness to know about strange countries and unknown people.

Bikram said, smiling, "Not ordinary people. Educated and very advanced people are there."

"The sea must be rushing in during cyclones!"

"Yes. Would the sea ever give up its nature? But it is beyond the sea to enter the villages and cities. There, the government have reassured the people by raising strong embankments all along the coastline."

"But our government is planning to have a marine drive from Digha to Gopalpur, instead of constructing an embankment here to protect our villages!"

"Because the marine drive means more expenditure, hence more kickbacks for the ministers and officers," said Bipin.

"Forget it. Instead of criticizing the others, let's think how we shall live."

"We'll fast onto death at the doors of government. We'll break our hunger strike only after getting written commitment for the construction of the embankment," said Dhadi Barik.

Bikram gave a derisive smile and said, "Yes, you'll get the promise in one day! Wherefrom would they get that kind of money? And even if they arrange it, by the time the plan is implemented, two or three cyclones might have blown over us, throwing us to the sea as offerings. Our headache would not be there, and government too would be worry-free."

"What shall we do then?" everyone asked in a chorus.

Patting Bipin's back, Bikram said, "Our Bipin is an engineer. He has estimated that if a thirty-to-forty foot high embankment for thirty kilometers on the coastline here could be raised, the people of the villages gathered here could be protected against the sea. Let's gather our own people and unite them to build the embankment with government-supplied materials. Government would know that people's power is stronger than government machinery. What do you say?"

"It's difficult to unite so many people."

At that time, Girima from behind said, "We mothers and sisters would move from village to village and appeal to the people to come together. I believe that people would join us. After experiencing such a calamity, who would depend on government instead of taking charge of their own protection? Why didn't I allow the children to stay in the shelter homes?"

The women raised their choric voice. "We would bring people together. Our people are not inefficient. The deity of this region is Mother Sarala. Our region hasn't lagged behind in restoring the dignity of women."

There was a shout of joy. The grown-up men said, "We too would join you in going from village to village. Would you not take us with you?"

Bikram said, "Don't think we'll have only an embankment or cooperative farm. The fifteen acres of land that I would get would be used for setting up schools, colleges, computer training centers, strategic planning centers, training institutes for advanced farming technology, and many more things. Development of agriculture is not enough. The farmer must also prosper. Our aim is not to make the rich fish dealers richer by our developed pisciculture. The fishermen too should be rich."

Bikram's aspirations embraced heaven, earth, and the netherworld.

"If out of hundred, five dreams are realized, we would feel that our aim has fructified. It does not matter what is achieved, more important is to see that our people grow in self-confidence and shake off their inefficiency and fear. Government would feed people perpetually-such things never happen in any country."

Although Bipin was not as optimistic as Bikram, he too rose above his despair.

"Now let's eat," declared Mantri Mallick.

Bikram said, "No appetite today."

"Dreams do not fill the belly. The belly is filled by rice and curry. The cruel reality smothers your dreams," Kartik said.

"True, this is not the time to dream. My dream and reality are to see that so many orphans eat, study, and become something in life. Come, the food is getting cold," Girima said.

"There is another life over and above rice and dal. For that, you have to dream. There is no man in the world who has not dreamed in sleep and wakefulness."

Bikram thought as much, but did not say anything.

Breaking Bikram's chain of thought, Bhudan said, "You haven't touched the food. What are you thinking?"

"Many things. Nothing in particular."

"But in those many things, there must be many people!"

"Yes..."

Padma, Girima, and Nazma served the second helping.

Bhudan asked, "Who? Whose thoughts made you forget rice and dal? I was famished."

"Me too, but the person's memory fills the belly."

Padma paused. Girima waited to listen.

"Who could this dream girl be of this hardened soldier!"

Sitting like a stone, Bikram said, "When I am reminded of Udhab Uncle, hunger and sorrow disappear. The body gets a lion's strength."

"I too remember father when I sit down to eat. He couldn't eat food served by me." Tears rolled down Girima's eyes.

Bikram said in a choked voice, "Udhab Uncle never made anyone cry. You cried over my words. Please, for my sake, wipe off your tears. There is so much to do ahead. For my sake tears are forbidden when we build things."

"Fie! O' fie! Why are you speaking like a woman? That too is forbidden here. Be a soldier-be strong," said Girima in mock disapproval.

Bikram stared at the lowered face of Girima attentively. His belly was overfull. He had never looked in the eye of any young woman. He couldn't know in that soft darkness whether colors flashed in the eyes of Girima. She moved away, serving dal.

Nudging Bikram, Bhudan quipped, "What were you seeing in my sister's face? As if you were not seeing, but drinking!"

Silencing him, Bikram said, "I was seeing a full village, a luxuriant paddy field of India, seeing a woman's compassionate motherly form."

Bikram would have continued, but, interrupting him, Bhudan said, "Bah! You are entirely unromantic. A lump of ice like the Himalaya. You'll remain forever a soldier-well, eat."

"On the Himalayas too there is vegetation, and streams

flow. Don't you know about the Ganga, the sacred river?" Bikram said, laughing.

"Ok. Stop lecturing. The rice is getting cold." Bikram ate.

Moving further, while serving dal on the leaf of Bharjan Mallick, Girima said, "Why did soldier Bikram remember my father sitting with food?"

"Because your father was not a mere father-he was a great navigator."

Girima's eyes became wet.

The birds, which had flown away deserting the village, had now returned, accepting their fate, to the wry, smiling, broken branches; had rebuilt their world of twigs and straw. The birds do not depend on government aid-never depended on anyone for a roof over their heads or food for their bellies. The birds, in this respect, are more intelligent than men, more advanced. The homeless humans suffered from cold and dew, depending on government; would have been lashed by the rains had they not united to fight for their own survival. Walls are now raised in no time with burnt bricks. The roof is to be laid. With the food-for-work program on, the roof too would be laid soon. Coconut branches were not available to use for temporary roofs-all are living now under polythene roofs over earthen huts.

One-roomed houses, a veranda and in a corner of the veranda, a small kitchen. That's enough. Where are the large families now? This cyclone has stumped everyone. Let it be. Like the leaves emerging from the broken branches, in due course, the families too would start growing. Small and healthy families would thrive and grow. All would be fed and clad. All must be able to read the Bhagabat of Jagannath Das, the Ramayana of Balaram Das, the Laxmi Puran, Sarala's Mahabharat, and the Chandi Puran. Over and above these, if they read Bhima Bhoi, Fakir Mohan, Radhanath and Gopinath Mohanty, better-why better, they ought to read.

At the head of the village, a library building is coming up. If Bikram gets his land allotted by the army, many schools, colleges, and other institutes would gradually come up. God willing, top-class institutions would grow in Erasama so that good students from Cuttack and Kolkata would come here to get trained for jobs and research. Why not?

At the entry point of the village was the house of Danakarna Mishra's son, Kaibalya. Adjacent to Kaibalya's house were the houses of Bharjan and Mantri Mallick. Next to their house was Alwar Mian's house and the houses of Kartika Majhi, Bipin, Baikuntha, Girima Behera, Padma Behera, Renu Dei, Moira Mandal, and ten or twelve children with them. The women folk had adopted a child each. The children had found love and home.

THIRTY ONE

Like the happy chirping of the birds that have returned to the lap of the village, the children, finding mother's laps, have resumed their childish pranks. Their stubborn naughtiness and childish tantrums are noticeably free and fearless now. Their noisiness and frolic sound like the sacred trumpeting of conch shells and fill the blank spaces of the mind. Like a bunch of assorted flowers, the stunned symmetrical faces of the children now look beautiful and fair.

Before the crow caws, the combined symphony of the children repeating a-b-c-d is heard. The choric chant of memorizing arithmetical tables wakes up the lazy sleepers as the sweet anthem of a morning rally of school children. Life has come back. The celebrations of life have started. Before sunrise, the mothers cook and feed the children, teach them their lessons, and go out to the villages to collect volunteers to work for the ring embankment, leaving the children in the charge of the older men and women. The dreams of the field heroes like Bikram and Bipin are going to be fulfilled by the love and cooperation of the women folk. If there is love, blessing and goodwill, behind the strong resolve of a leader, it is easy to conquer mountains.

The movement to collect seeds has already begun. The imported seeds supplied by government are one-crop varieties. That has a short longevity. It's a conspiracy of the bureaucrats to make the farmers permanently dependent on government. The farm eggs and seeds are great for one crop-then those are seedless, dead. The seeds used by our fourteen generations are not only eternal, but also ambrosial. Those seeds could be sown for generations and harvested. But, excepting a few rooted families, where are the seed-preserving people nowadays? But none have any objection to farm on advanced methods if they get quality seeds.

Thieves have looted the belongings of the dead and lost men. Taking out the gold and money, they have thrown behind the empty boxes. Moving through the farmland and fields, Mantri Mallick is searching in the boxes and bags-but where are the seeds? No trace of anything.

That day, a group was drying their sweat after the day's work, sitting on the breezy veranda of the mosque. Kartika Majhi said, "Everything is going on according to plan. But where is the plan for the real thing?"

"Real thing?"

"Yes-do you think finally we'll set up a monastery here? Would we all live like sanyasis and sannyasins here for the rest of our lives? A roof on four walls is not called a home. Is it not necessary to start the family to make the houses, homes?" Kartika said.

All were silent, including Bikram. Silence is the sign of agreement. "But now it is not easy to fix up matches for marriage. Let the broken minds get used to homely living", Bikram thought and said that openly.

"Yes-that's true. But what's wrong to unite in marriage those who have already become homely, finding an auspicious day?" said Bipin.

"Okay. Make a list. Let's decide first who would tie the permanent knot with whom, but not one-sided. The bride and groom must desire and love each other," Bipin said.

"Now, no one has a mind to love. If they like each other, it's enough", thought Bikram and said, "But no one should raise issues like caste and dowry."

"Who has the wealth for dowry? No one here has a caste or horoscope. And that's good," said Kaibalya Mishra.

"But some like Panchuki Mishra may find flaws," Bharjan quipped.

"We have already exiled him by denying fire and water. People like him are not a part of our new village. Why bother about him?"

"But this Dhadi Barik is like a squirrel, sometimes on our side, and sometimes on their side. He is like a chameleon, changing colors at convenience. But he is a guileless man, let him be here with us," Bhudan said.

"Well-that's for later. We've no time for those things now. Let housing and farming be our priority now," Bikram said.

Kartika said, "Then let's start with two marriages first. Blow a conch shell and clap. Nothing elaborate. No worry."

Bhudan looked at Kartika with interest.

"I'll marry Renu, the widowed sister of Baikuntha and Bipin. Initially, she had broken down in misery. But now, I hope she is willing. Ask her and find out," Kartika said without hesitation.

"Because of me, Bhagyadhar's wife became destitute. Had I not taken Bhagyadhar to the prawn farm that fateful night may be he would have survived. I've no objection to accept Padma as my wife. Ask her for her consent," said Bipin.

Bhudan looked deep into Bikram's eyes and asked, "Would there be only second marriages in this village? Would not the unmarried ones get married? Did you not write letters from the Kargil hills that you'll bring reforms when you return to the village?"

In a calm manner, Bikram said, "Where did that stop? That reform has started with Kartika and Bipin. Let the broken homes be joined first, then we'll think of new homes."

"Do the broken homes block the path of the new homes? Many boys and girls here have crossed the marriageable age. Is it not our responsibility? No one has parents or guardians. Nazma, Shabana, Alwar, Razzak, Hakim, Maina, Gelhi, Girima, Bhudan, Kaibalya."

Chopping the ongoing list, Bikram said, "I see then that we'll be busy in matchmaking. When you are trying to realize larger goals, such small social issues lose their priority. But I had heard that Udhab Uncle has made an engagement agreement for Girima. Similarly, there are many young men and women here for whom some promises were made. Let's proceed after ascertaining facts."

"Yes, without valid reasons, the engagement should not be dishonored," said Kaibalya.

By that time, lanterns were already lighted in the houses. The evening prayer of the children surrounding Drona Sir was on.

"O' Lord of the universe, master of my soul. O' primal parents, O' all knowing Lord. Your mercy be praised. There is no parallel to your ocean of mercy. Your mercy be praised."

Closing his eyes, Bikram joined the prayer. "Your mercy be praised."

In joy and sorrow, like the vermillion dot on the forehead of a married woman, the morning breaks with a scarlet mark on the horizon, and the night fades. Rain, storm, or wind never wipes off the vermillion dot on their forehead as symbol of their marital status.

Renu, Padma, and all other unfortunate women had wiped off their symbols of marital status themselves because to do that the hands of the family and clan were not there. But a few unfortunates had not done that, nor had they broken their bangles. They were waiting single-mindedly for the return of their husbands. When the dead bodies of their husbands were not seen, how could the women who had held the hands of their husbands, vowing before the sacred fire, accept their death, even months after the cyclone? Why should they accept widowhood on hearsay that others had seen the bodies of their husbands? If tomorrow the husband returned and saw the ghastly appearance of his wife, he would die, and while dying, would think," this woman perhaps was praying for my death, otherwise, without searching and waiting, why did she wipe off the vermillion dot from her forehead? And for whom?"

Of late, Renu and Padma too were wearing the vermillion mark to display their married status saying, "Without seeing the dead faces of our husbands, how could we erase them from our lives?"

The old and experienced women pitied them. "Alas! These helpless women have gone half mad, let them do what they like. Who would wipe off meaningless vermillion? This is not any less cruel act."

Bikram had not noticed that till now. How could he miss that? Maybe because for Bikram, the glory of a woman is not represented by the vermillion mark. For him, a woman was graceful in many ways. Which woman came to the world without grace, beauty, and virtue?

Better to finish off this mass marriage before the monsoons. Girima was so busy and tense with her group of children that, at the mention of marriage, she was fuming, as reported by Renu to her brother Bipin. But does it mean that she would remain a celibate spinster?

The moon dozed off. Bhudan returned, leaving his assigned work. Who else would probe Girima's mind? One that understood her was Udhab Uncle. He is now gone. From our villages, thousands died. Many austere and morally upright men could not escape.

Girima said, with tears in her eyes, "That the sea should have spared my father, as he was deeply religious and good, I cannot say. But no one could trace his dead body. By the time I reached the village, the Anandmargis and the army had already burned numerous bodies. The rest were rotted and had mingled with the earth. How would I think that my father's last rites have been observed? My whole family is gone. I'm the lone survivor. Is it not my duty to cremate my father observing all rituals? More than his death, what pains me is that I could not observe the obsequies and perform his last rites."

Girima had been the darling of her father. In the absence of her father, Bhudan thought it prudent to gauge her mind. Thinking like this, he reached the rear of the house, searching for Girima. In the last few days, Girima herself had prepared a plot of land for growing vegetables. She had herself dug out the land with an axe, and she had planted various things, getting seeds from the weekly market. She was taking as good care of the kitchen garden as she was of the children. Girima was not there. She was sitting with Bhagyadhar's widow Padma who had a dot of vermillion on her forehead, and looking like a village deity.

Bhudan asked point blank, "Bipin Tarei wants to marry you. A long life is ahead of you. Bipin is a good fellow. He is educated and Bhagyadhar's friend. What do you say?"

Padma said, "Some, goaded by greed for money, and some, out of pity, propose to marry me. Is a second marriage necessary?"

"No, not out of pity, but with love Bipin has proposed. He would take good care of you."

"And my children? Three children cling to me."

"The children would belong to both of you. Bipin has agreed to that. Bipin is the architect of our bridge, a crown jewel of our village. You are lucky."

"Let go-don't mock my fate. Who suffers my fate except me?" Padma said tearfully.

"Your fate would now return brighter. Mother Sarala is there for you."

"Okay-Let Mother's wish be fulfilled" said Padma.

Bhudan asked, "Where's Girima?"

"There. Since morning, she is weeping, sitting at the base of that bald coconut tree beyond her vegetable garden. She has not touched food or water."

"Why is she crying? What new tragedy has made her cry?" Bhudan was worried.

Padma said irritably, "How can anyone know if she does not speak? I'm tired of asking. She doesn't speak, goes on crying."

Bhudan ran up to Girima. Staring blankly at the empty field, Girima was sitting, leaning against the stump of a tree. The tears had dried up. Seeing Bhudan, she started crying again.

"What happened? Tell me Girima, what's wrong? Why do you cry? How could you think that you would alone absorb all your sorrow when we are here?" Bhudan sat near Girima, but she went on sobbing with her head hung down. Did not speak a word. Bhudan got irritated and said, "Udhab Uncle is not here, that he would stand stretching his palms, lest your golden tears should fall on the ground. Must we work or sit here, looking at the sobbing girls, waiting for them to speak?"

Even then, Girima did not break her sobbing silence. That morning, Drona Sir had sent a message through Dhadi Barik to Girima's future father-in-law.

"Girima is alive. Udhab Mangual performed the engagement on the holy mahaprasad. It must be honored. Girima's parents and brothers are dead, but her relation and village brothers are there. The marriage should be celebrated as scheduled. If they do not want to dishonor their mahaprasad pledge, they must come soon and fix up the date."

Drona Sir had dictated, and Bipin had written in his beautiful handwriting. Dhadi Barik was expected to return by evening with their reply. All were waiting. It was less problematic if eight-to-ten girls married at a time. With one feast, the ceremony would be over.

But why did Girima cry? What's the cause of her sorrow? Bhudan went and brought Bipin, Bikram, and other working brothers. Seeing so many men, Girima wiped off her tears. Looking at everyone with her tear-swollen eyes, she said, "I felt like crying, and I did. Is there any want of sorrow for crying? Why are so many people bothered about it? Would you not allow a person to cry in peace?"

Bikram stood tall and broad before Girima. In an accusing voice he said, "As you wish to cry in peace, all of us here wish to work in peace. If one of us cries, can we work in peace?"

Girima rose, dusting herself. She said, "A person cries all through life in different ways. The soul cries. All tears are not visible from outside. I cried not to stop work, but realizing that there is no point in working so hard. Okay? My sorrow is mine. I'll not cry anymore."

Girima sent everyone to their workplace. But Bikram stood like a block of wood before Girima. He thought Girima had turned into stone. Why did she melt? If Girima lost faith, who then would save these women and children?

All had left. Girima was sitting, looking at her garden with unseeing eyes. She was not aware that Bikram was standing, transfixed, by her side.

Bikram asked, "If you don't tell me how the stone broke into a stream, I'll not go to work. In our village, none can share the death of others, but definitely can share their sorrow. If you do not open up your heart, no work from tomorrow. Really, what's the value of so much labor if the tears don't dry up?"

Girima said sulkingly, "Others could not see, no matter. But that you don't see my pain is my greatest sorrow."

"Honestly, I am a novice to know the mind of a woman."

"Where everything is lost, who cares for a woman's heart? The most challenging meditation is to gauge the mind of the earth. What if the head gets a roof? Not a blade of grass is growing here! The seeds I got from the Erasama market germinated beautifully. I was waiting for the red leaves to break out. Today, I saw that those tender, awakening seeds were dead. Whoever had sown whatever seeds, all have similar fates. This earth is dead. If the earth dies, can man survive drinking the air? How would my children survive? I had great expectations. All my hopes are dead. Should I not cry?" Girima's eyes again welled up with tears about to burst out.

Bikram felt relieved. He had imagined Girima's sorrow so deep-rooted that none could ever redress it. But he saw that Girima's sorrow was his joy. If this woman has so much sorrow for the soil, then the soil could be desalinated-the soil could again yield ambrosial harvest-if not today, tomorrow. Bikram sat in Girima's garden, caressed the soil. Love softened his rugged voice.

He said, "Believe me. I'm the son of a soldier, a fighter during war, a farmer during peace. My parents and grandparents could read the pulse of the soil. I can too. This earth is now in a tranced sleep, sleeping over the layers of blood and bones of men. The deluge ends, man dies, but the earth lives on. When man's ambrosial hand holds a fistful of ash that turns into soil. Where man pours out his life that turns into the primordial home.

"The poison of the churned sea will lose its effect. The Mahanadi of nectar will flow in the furrows of this soil. The earth is now in a creative trance. This is not eternal sleep. It is divine sleep dreaming new creation. Not understanding this much, you wept and moaned for nothing!"

Girima stood, lost in herself, looking at the barren earth. She thought, "this whole world belongs to man. Golmasta, Majhi, Mohanty, Panda, Mandal-who doesn't have the right on this earth? Who can drive them away from this soil?"Fortified by their flesh and bones, rows of houses were coming up on this earth, and on this soil would laugh the golden harvests. Silently, she was grateful to the soldier for having restored her lost faith.

She said, "In the name of God I promise, no one will see my tears again. You go. I'm sorry I made you waste time."

Everyone's house was built. Only Drona Sir was homeless. He said, "Now I'm searching for the real house. What will I do with this unreal one? You all are young. May your houses be strong, may you live for million years. Leave me out of this. Today, on this veranda, tomorrow on another's; I must just live out a few days. You are giving me food twice a day. I've suffered the pain of thousand houses crashing down before my eyes. Now I enjoy watching the houses rising here in the new village."

"But you are the pivot of our hope. What's the use of our houses if you are homeless?" Bhudan said.

"During partition, so many people became homeless. To speak the truth, since then, the father of the nation, Mahatma Gandhi, became homeless. If my children get roofs over their heads, I'll have my home. I'll not suffer like Gandhi," Drona Sir said, while drinking his jaggery tea. "Get done with the auspicious work. Who knows when my call will come from my home!"

At that time, holding an umbrella over his head, Kelu Behera from Shendhakud village arrived. Dhadi Barik was leading the way. A mat was laid near Drona Sir. Kelu Behera sat on it. He was treated to some refreshment-jaggery tea with some biscuits. Without any ado, Kelu Behera straight came to the point.

"I had heard that every one of Udhab Mangual's family

was gone. I was broken down. But sir, by sending the message through Dhadi Barik, you have done a great favor. Otherwise, I would have been guilty of dishonoring the holy engagement. My daughter-in-law being alive, had I fixed my son's marriage elsewhere, I would have committed a great sin. God is great. He has saved me from a great sin. Let's then finalize the date of marriage. Now that Drona Sir is the guardian of all here, he would decide."

"There is no rule in a crisis. Do it any day in the name of the all-merciful Lord Jagannath."

"Let the good work be finalized soon. In the coming bright fortnight, I would find an auspicious day and take my daughter-in-law home. Why should my son come in a palanquin to this graveyard? And to whose house? How cruel is God?" said Kelu Behera.

By that time, men and women had gathered. Would Girima really marry and go to Shendakud? Everyone thought that she was lucky that, in her would-be father-in-law's house, all were hale and hearty, and they were willing to take Girima as their daughter-in-law.

Bhudan called Girima, and said, "Bow down to your father-in-law. You are your own guardian now. We have nothing to say. What do you say?"

Girima bowed down covering her head, and stood aside. Her head bowed down, she could not speak.

Padma, dressed as a newly married woman, came and stood before Kelu Behera, and she bowed down. Standing aside respectfully, she said, "Girima is my husband's younger sister. I know her mind. This village was her birthplace, now it is her workplace. It would be difficult for her to leave this village. If you permit her to come here once in a fortnight or a month, she would not dishonor the mahaprasad pledge."

"Okay. What daughter doesn't come to her father's house? And how far is it! If she has taken up work, let her complete it. And that too good work! Why should anyone say no?" Kelu Behera said.

"Bikram, what do you say? You were speaking about some reform!" asked Kartika. Bikram stood silent.

"Brother Kartika! Behera Uncle has come to take a destitute girl without any dowry. Moreover, not even a year has passed since the death of her father and brothers, and no obsequies have been performed. In the name of Jagannath, such a marriage in itself is a great reform. The people in our area are so large-hearted, I know now. Our region and even Odisha has been defamed as heartless and self-centered after the cyclone. But such angels are in our midst!" Bikram said in a voice of gratitude.

"May Sri Behera be blessed. A good-natured daughter-in-law like Girima would bring the virtues of Laxmi and Saraswati to his house. We can't give any other dowry than that. If Sri Behera agrees to that, why should we have any objection?" Drona Sir said.

"Had Udhab Mangual been alive, maybe the question of dowry would have arisen. Even his dead body was not seen. But his soul must be watching how his soul honored his pledge," Dhadi Barik said with joy.

Behera looked askance at the vermillion dot on the forehead of Padma and said, "I had heard that all the five sons of Mangual were dead; how then does his youngest daughter-in-law look newly married?"

No one replied to this question. Kelu Behera's face was darkening fast. It was obvious that he was worried. There was one son alive then to share the Mangual property! In a grave voice he said, "Had Udhab Mangual been alive, what dowry would he have poured in? He never settled the dowry issue till the end. He was a good man, I admit, but a great miser-close-fisted. Rather, after his death, his daughter would come to my house with a lot of money. We'll see later whether she will get the death-compensation money for her brothers. If you spend some money, anything is possible here-but she would get one-and a-half lakhs compensation money for her parents. Mangual would not have given more than that."

The air seemed suddenly suffocating. All faces became pale. Sweat was beading on all foreheads. All became silent.

Kelu Behera now arose and said, "I'll send word after consulting our astrologer about the date."

At that time, Girima stood up from a corner of the veranda with a child at her waist, her head covered with her saree. She stood at the foot of the steps. Without compromising her dignity, she said in a clear voice, "I have vowed on my parents that I'll not take their compensation money. I have donated that money toward the education and settlement of these orphan children. Therefore, I have no right on that money. My sister-in-law does not have any resources except to send me off in a new saree."

Kelu Behera's advancing steps paused. Holding the umbrella in his armpit, he looked at Girima. His eyes moved quickly over all faces each at a time, as if the deluge were a moment away!

In a roaring voice, fixing his eyes on Girima, he said, "Is there no government for these children? Are you such a donor like Karna? If I take such an outspoken girl as daughter-in-law, there would be a cyclone in my house. Good that this lass rebuffed me in the presence of so many people. No one would find fault with me if I refuse to take this girl home. Is she laying golden eggs that I'll take her to my house without anything? Let me tell this to all- no one should think of taking this foul-mouthed woman as daughter-in-law to his house. God has saved me from a disaster. O' what a calamity has been averted. There, a widowed woman, putting vermillion on her head, has become a guardian sister-in-law! Is this the culture of this house?"

Kelu Behera might have said something more, but when he raised a club, Mantri Mallick came running and screamed, "Leave this village, sealing your mouth! Otherwise, I'll break your head. We are lucky that our daughter has narrowly escaped the jaws of this shark."

Kelu Behera was not to be cowed down. He was a man of property. His son was in service. He'd never cared for these destitute. Threatening to lodge an FIR at the police station, he flew away like a typhoon along the fields, without turning back once.

Bhudan spoke aloud, "This fellow would die of his greed. Not much time is left for him."

"Let it go. Why should we think ill of others? God sees all. Enough that, thanks to God's grace, our misfortune has been averted. That's enough," said Drona Sir.

"God is kind," said Akhtar Mian.

Bikram watched Kelu Behera's route. Murky darkness was ahead. The sea waves were crashing on the shore not far away from the village. From the other side of the river, the same sound like cutting wood floated down.

Wood thief or ghost?

"Whatever be it, what fear of the shark living in the river? When you live in a crematory, you are not afraid of the ghosts," Bharjan Mallick said.

In sullen silence, Bikram was thinking of the way ahead. On whose strength shall he go, leaving such a big temple half-built? Who would complete it? Who would install the icon? He could not muster courage to tell them that he had to go.

When a child is born, the parents call an astrologer-priest for the naming ceremony of the newborn. But no one knew how to give a name to the newly built village. Therefore, a discussion had arisen about the name of the new village that had emerged like an island in the midst of a sea.

Let the debate stop-let the village have no name. But if there is no name, there would not be any address-how can the people of the world know about the village? This would not be an ordinary village. Such a village was the only one of its kind in the universe.

Kartika said, "Stop-before the child is born, no name is given. It's a bad omen. Let the auspicious house warming be over. Then the name of the village will occur to Bikram at the right moment. What's there in a name? The name of the village should be meaningful.

Everyone had a hearty discussion. Their hearts swelled as if all their problems were solved. Whatever be its name, the village was everyone's. The soil was everyone's. The rivers and gorges belonged to all. The whole world was theirs. Whoever lived on whichever side of the lines drawn, all were human brothers. The sky was father; mother, the earth; the trees, hills, and mountains, rivers, and birds were their relatives in the world family.

Before the evening lamps were out, the lamps of the sky brightened. All settled down for dinner. In the new-moon darkness, the night roared in deep silence. It was midnight by the time Bharjan Mallick reached the crematory with the food for the dead. Today, there was rice and dal, and also rice pudding. Bikram Balbantray was very fond of rice pudding. It was almost a feast tonight.

Between Hansua River and the sea, in a secluded place, Bharjan placed the pot of food for the dead.

Had Bharjan committed some indiscretion while serving food for the ghost? The direction from which the wood-cutting sound normally came, no sound was heard from that side. Bharjan advanced in that direction. The satisfaction that, if one ghost gets food, all ghosts are fed was no more in Bharjan's mind.

Another shadow stood before him, blocked his way, "Don't go there. Have you forgotten why Jagannath's image remained half done?"

"Who are you?"

"I too am a ghost. Man is a mad fellow. Do you think the ghosts eat as normal living beings? In the name of ghosts, how people are exploited and tortured here! You served rice and curry so long, without missing a day. You have done enough. Now it is no more required."

Bharjan thought, "Why should man be mad? This ghost is mad. The heartrending death that men died here, it is not strange that even the ghosts have gone mad."

He asked, "If the ghosts do not eat food offered to them, what about the ghost which ate this food every night? Is it not true? I have seen with my own eyes!"

"How do you know that the person who was eating that rice is a man or a ghost? So many hungry people are around. They don't like to beg for food. Therefore, it is not unusual that some of them ate the pinda served by you. All drama here is for the belly. But why are you coming here every night with food, and blame it on the ghosts? Do you think these ghosts have come from some foreign land? All are our relatives, members of our families. Once the ghosts assume a subtle form, they do not eat such food anymore-they get redeemed by smelling the love from the offered rice and dal."

"Hey you-are you man or ghost? You are so wise!"

"Do the ghosts cause inauspicious things or do injustice? You are utterly mistaken!"

Saying that, the shadow ran as though flying, and gradually became invisible.

Bharjan retraced his steps back in the opposite direction, as if someone called him and he followed, crossing some bridge to the seashore. He who was born in a coastal village and has grown old, for him the seashore is like the bathing place in the backyard. When Udhab Mangual had tied the boat, Bharjan had helped him by doing errands. Nights were spent on the seashore. Udhab Mangual often said, "What fear for the known sea?"

Bharjan sat on the sand. The intertwining sea and darkness had turned the sky into an inverted sea. No light from any fishing boat was seen from afar. In reality, there were no boats. How could light be seen?

For Bharjan, Udhab Mangual's words had scriptural authority. The fire of separation and loss flaming in his heart would have subsided, had Udhab Mangual been alive. He remembered lines from the Bhagabat to suit all occasions, moods, joys, sorrow, and mindsets. The lines always worked like balm on wounds.

The foaming sea was pushing Bharjan back in the darkness. The years Bharjan had worked with Udhab Mangual, he'd been a different human being. Udhab always thought that the sea was close to him, a part of his life.

He used to say, "This Sea is the womb of birth and death; the ecstatic tide is birth; the sad ebb dragging you to the unknown place is death. The ebb and tide of the waves is a game of the sea. Nothing really goes or comes. Everywhere, you have ebb and tide. In water and on earth too. Born from the sea, you mingle with the sea."

This earth, man, boatman, and also Udhab all came from and went to the sea. In the ocean of life, Udhab was a drop-no, no, half a drop, a half drop of the sweat of God is man. The other half makes up the tangible homes of horses, birds, and insects.

Bharjan could hear Udhab's voice in his mind, as though he was hiding somewhere here and reciting a couplet or two from the Bhagabat. As if not Udhab, it was the song of the roaring sea-this is the eternal song of the sea. The sea was nothing for him except death.

There were no shadows of the ghosts now, nor any sound that disturbed the nerves. But Bharjan would come with the rice pot because the midnight darkness covered up his agony on the soil of truth of the crematory. The long, melancholy roar of the sea pacified the trepidations of his heart, saying that all would go where everyone has gone-why bother about it?

The wind, as it were, sang in his ears, "As long as you are in this world, live with joy."

Pushing the darkness, Bharjan quelled his tears and sprinkled the seawater on his head. In this water had mingled all-all men and women of his family and his village. He too would mingle in this water. If not today, tomorrow! Why worry?

But the ghost did not eat the rice tonight; that worried him. Bharjan's mind was uneasy, although it was a mere ghost. What a polite ghost! Where did it go?

It is not easy to take leave of the sea, not possible to turn a deaf ear to the call of the Himalayas! The sea would strike its head on the shore. It would moan and roar while rushing at you with a loud laugh to take you in his lap. It would lose patience and break into the ebbing mode. But after returning with dignity, it would again be mad. Thus would go on the ebb and tide of his agony and ecstasy of sulking love, till he came back.

But when would he return? And would he return or not? In the life of a soldier, returning is uncertain. The victory torch of a wounded hero too may go out while returning. He cannot promise his return to anyone. Not even to the sea. The sea would sulk, but the call of duty from the Himalayas could not be ignored! It was the call of the motherland. The motherland was greater than the village.

So much tension and war on the wire fence of a geographical border, an artificial line in a map! So many deaths-unreasonable and irrational! Such a waste of life, youth, and dreams!

When you kill the men on the other side of the border, your patriotic mind is numb. The conscience too surrenders to the patriotism! Who loves to kill or die? Bikram thought that, if today, Alwar, Akhtar, and the Rafiks and Safiks who thought Hindu-Muslim to be brothers-went over to the other side of the heartless barbed wire fence, then this Bikram Balabantray might fire at their innocent hearts to earn a "Vir Chakra" medal from the President of India! Whereas, their forefathers had shed their blood to make this country free from British Raj! Whose country is this? Does it belong only to Bikram Balbantaray? Not Alwar Mian-not to the Akhtars, Rafiks, and Safiks?

Is there any want of agony in human fate, of unreasonable death and unwished-for ruin of the assiduously built personal world? Nature has its own fixture of calamities, one after another, like super cyclone, drought, flood, earthquake, volcanic eruptions, accidents, and epidemics-every moment a new death trap, as if life is only an accident-a wonder in the midst of mine fields! Why then so much of meticulous planning for mass destruction? Who gains-this country or that country?

But why is Bikram thinking like this. To what gain? The decision to launch wars does not depend on Bikram or Alwar. Bikram cannot control anything-corruption, war, or drought. But the right of self-control has not been snatched away from him. His heart is mortgaged to his patriotic responsibilities, not to emotional responses. Before the safety of the country, his self-preservation is meaningless.

All his other loves are less important before his love for the country. He can sacrifice, without any hesitation, all his emotional attachments, his love and fondness for people and things, for the country. There is no question of evading the call of the Himalayas for the safety of the country.

The sea is dear to him, Himalaya too. The Himalaya is born out of the sea. A country is born with villages coming together. Man has a blood relation, maybe a soul relation with the motherland. The sea would understand this. When he had everything and everyone of his own in his village, he was not so much pained at heart before to go to war, responding to the call of the nation as he is now. Today, he has none to tie him down to the village by love strings; yet, he is having unimaginable pain to leave the new village to do his duty for the country.

He had never imagined that his pain would be so very heartrending. Then, blood ties from his parents and family members, about seven or eight persons, pulled him. Today, everyone pulls him with the ties of a larger love-the soil, rivers, sea, hills, and gorges, vegetation, and even the ghosts and witches-all!

The lifeless brick walls, stones for the embankment, and the hearts of so many loving people now entangle him.

In a moment, the sun jumped out of the sea and asked, "Where are you going, forsaking your resolve?"

"At midday, if the clouds cover up the sky, it becomes dark. But does the day not move to its completion?"

"If you go away, who's there to fulfill your resolve, your dreams?"

"If the sun goes down, is there no moon in the sky? And the stars are no less bright!"

From under his feet, a red crab bit his little finger, and asked, "Are you not satiated, seeing so many deaths, that you are going to kill men again?"

"Not to kill men, but to try to stop war." Bikram took out the crab from under his foot carefully, lest its delicate leg should break. The crab tried vigorously to escape. With this crab too Bikram has a deep relation. He smiled and released it on the sand. The crab walked fast. Behind it was a procession of small, red crabs. These too were soldiers in a battlefield. Who lived in the world without struggle and fight? The struggle for existence of these creatures is in no way inferior to man's struggles. Germination too is a great fight, an embryonic revolution.

Bikram's mind was light. A bird asked, singing, "When will you return?"

"Every day."

"How?"

"Where am I going? I'm here. I'll be here, mortgaging my heart to the sea. I'm going. This is not going. This is living."

Taking a dip in the sea, he offered water to the rising sun. The disciplined line of the crabs he avoided by soft-jumping and moved village-ward. When a telegram comes to a village, everyone knows the content. Everyone knew that Bikram was to return to his base camp that very day. As long as a soldier is physically fit, he continues to be a soldier. What is retirement for a soldier? Man is an eternal soldier. Man's fight begins before birth-where does it end?

That was a spectacular morning. On the banks of river Hansua, crowds of people were jostling for space. Bikram's feet paused. Surrounding the Satyayug, the people were chirping in delight. The women were chanting. Getting a conch shell from somewhere, Mantri Mallick was blowing at it ceaselessly, till his eyes watered.

A boat was tied to the ghat. In the morning breeze, it was undulating, half in water, half on earth. As if in the flow of time, man is a boat, clinging on both to life and death. There was no owner, builder, or navigator-none. On the other side of the river, a skeletal frame of a man was sitting, holding his knees on his buried head, looking at the horizon in such a manner, as if he had reached a dispassionate point from which there was no return. As though he had no connection with whatever was happening on earth; an innocent, guileless, uncomprehending man; eyes and face lost to reality.

"The boat is stuck here to our ghat. Who could have gifted such a thing, except Viswakarma, the architect of heaven? This is the first Boat of Dharma, Satyayug. Udhab Uncle had given such a name to his boat. This boat has been built by the ghost of Udhab Uncle-or else, God," Mantri Mallick said.

"We'll row this in an auspicious moment," said Saraladas Mandal.

Bikram lifted up from the boat a bundle tied with old clothes, along with a broken part of a pitcher. Five small bundles were tied by an old saree into a larger bundle. Bikram had returned after his sacred bath. Holding the bundle, he walked ahead, followed by everyone. What's there in the bundle?

"Gold, silver, coins, rupees, cowrie?"

Maybe something unearthly was in this heavenly boat!

The bundle was opened in front of Drona Sir. Sir said, "The eternal seed-not the farm seed, seeds from an aristocratic home. Paddy, moong, black gram, ragi, horse gram; the five life-sustaining corns. Good times have dawned now. The reign of evil is over. These are not corn alone. In these seeds is present the Brahman! Our luck will turn now!"

Bikram tied the packet carefully, again. Sacred seed. Who should he hand this over to? Who would save this rare sacred wealth selflessly? To wake up the soil to fertility again, there is the creative energy of Brahma in these seeds. Today is his day-not to go away from this soil, but to come back to it. He looked at everyone. Everyone had the unwashed lethargy of the early morning on their bodies. Dull, hopeless faces.

Only Girima had taken a bath and offered water to the basil plant. Clad in a pitcher-bordered saree, she appeared. It was her daily habit. Her eyes were lustrous.

Bikram, fixing his eyes on the red hibiscus offered to Goddess Vrindavati, said to Girima, "You must keep this carefully till the planting day comes. This is not the eternal seed. This is eternal luck and love for life."

"Where from did you get this priceless wealth?" Girima stretched both her hands as if prompted by a divine sign. She received the bundle of the life-sustaining five-seeds. She could recognize the saree, which her mother had worn on her last night! She became tearful, but held the bundle carefully like holding a newborn babe.

With tears clouding her vision, she said to Drona Sir, "My

inner voice tells me that my father is alive-why doesn't he show up then? What wrong have I done to him?"

Drona Sir said in a noncommittal voice, "The tree knows when it would be a stump and die, and give way to light for the winking saplings under its shadow. At such times, even if you give new manure and sufficient water, the old tree never takes on life. If one tree stands immortal, don't you think the world would become a bald wasteland? Udhab Mangual was not a mere human; he was a selfless, divine soul. It's not strange for him to release the seeds and turn into a shadow at his own free will."

Whether Girima could understand the deeper meaning of Sir, she cross-examined, Bikram. "Why did you give me this?"

"I saw love in your eyes for the soil and seeds." Bikram re-crossed her. "Why did you receive them from me?"

"I saw faith in your eyes for this soil. These seeds would never go waste," Girima said delightedly.

Drona sir said, "The primordial boat, soil, and seeds are part of the celestial cycle. The cyclone will come and go, but life will continue its flow. This is life's principle."

"Let us now search for my father," said Girima.

Sir said, "The seminal thing is to search. Has anyone lived in this world without searching for things? You saw these seeds together and searched in the farmland. Now the boat will be released into the sea and you will search for him in the waves of the sea-he will be available in some form or other. I have already found him."

"Where?"

"He is standing among you. I see him."

Everyone looked around, searched, and bowed down to the seed packet pressed to Girima's bosom.

"Now let everything be auspicious," said Drona Sir, and he folded his hands at the unseen, divine Brahman!

Mantri Mallick reminded, "The auspicious moment will pass now. You'll miss the bus, Bikram!"

"Don't say that."

Bikram started to hurry. Padma placed the rice cake with jiggery in front of Bikram, as an offering for his quick and safe return. Renu brought condensed curd. Salbeg's wife, Aklima, brought fish fry, and said "Eat this, it is auspicious at the time of leaving home."

Mothers, aunts, and sisters served their love. How much shall he eat?

Eating hurriedly, drinking water in large swigs, and washing his mouth, Bikram bowed to Drona Sir. Nazma, bringing moist vermilion from the Basil deity, made a mark on Bikram's forehead.

Holding the umbrella, Mantri Mallick said, "Come soon. Otherwise, you'll miss the bus."

"You evil-mouthed-" Bikram came under the umbrella. A few drops of rain started to fall.

After walking a few steps, Bikram paused, turned back, and took an eyeful of his dream village. Leaning against the basil platform like a garland of affection, the women folk were staring at his path. Holding the five-seed packet, like the locket of a necklace of flowers, was standing Girima, watching him advance. Three children, joining their hands around Girima's waist, with heads craning, were looking at him. Their intertwined hands looked like a flowery belt around her slim waist. Girima looked like the mother earth.

All of a sudden, Bikram turned back. The umbrella was in Mantri's hand. A beam of sunlight like divine blessing played on Bikram's face.

"Why did you break this auspicious journey? Did you forget something?" asked Aklima Bibi anxiously.

"No, I didn't forget. I remembered."

"What great thing was it that you turned back?" asked Drona Sir.

"No, I did not retrace my steps. I stopped to complete the couplet. When poetry flashes, you can't stop it."

"What poetry?" Bhudan asked eagerly. Girima's face brightened.

Bikram uttered like he was making a pronouncement, "The name of the first village on earth is Basumatipur - means, mother Earth."

THE END

About the Author

Pratibha Ray was born in a remote village, Alabol of Odisha state, India in 1944. She studied in the oldest and most prestigious Ravenshaw College, now a University in Odisha. Later she worked as a Professor in the same college and was awarded the 'Gem of Ravanshaw" by the University. After a long and rewarding teaching career, she was elevated to the constitutional post of member, Odisha Public Service Commission. Her doctoral research was on "Intellectual Achievement and Responsibility of slum children" and Post Doctoral research on the Criminal propensity of the most primitive Bonda Tribe of Odisha .Subsequently, she has written a voluminous novel 'Aadibhumi', based on the Bonda tribe, translated into English as 'Primal land'(Orient Black Swan). As a writer she has always been drawn to themes of the oppressed and down trodden people of the society. She is the author of 22 novels and 26 story collections, 10 travelogues, poetry collections, essay collections and an autobiography. The most acclaimed fictional work of the author was 'Yajnaseni' for which she received Bhartiya Jnanpith Trust's Moorti Devi award in 1991. She is the first and only woman writer till date to receive this coveted award. This novel has gone into its 106th edition which is unique in Odisha and rare in India. Apart from various National awards, she is the winner of prestigious national awards like Sahitya Akademi. She is the winner of the coveted Bharatiya Jnanpith 2011, the highest award of India for literature. She is a household name in Odisha and most parts of India due to her translated works. Her creations revolve around various subjects such as racial constraints, mythology, history, social issues and the perennial struggle against violence and terrorism.

"LOVE AND LET LIVE" is her motto.
"GIVE ME YOUR HEART, I WILL GIVE YOU GOD" is her mantra.
"Basudheiva Kutumbakam" is her philosophy.
"My country is my paradise" is the voice of her soul.

About the Translator

Prafulla Kumar Mohanty is a celebrated literary critic, creative writer and bilingual poet. He is the recipient of Central Sahitya Academy Award for literature and has translated into English the stories of Odia Sarala Mahabharata, the first regional epic of India. He has also translated many Odia books into English. Formerly professor in English and the Principal of Ravenshaw College, he now lives in Bhubaneswar.

BLACK EAGLE BOOKS

www.blackeaglebooks.org
info@blackeaglebooks.org

Black Eagle Books, an independent publisher, was founded as
a nonprofit organization in April, 2019. It is our mission to
connect and engage the Indian diaspora and the world at large
with the best of works of world literature published on a
collaborative platform, with special emphasis on
foregrounding Contemporary Classics and New Writing.